About the a

Although Lucas has worked as a journalistic writer in Spain, an artist in Cumbria, and a grumpy and grime-covered engineer in the industrial heartland of Yorkshire, he is best found wandering hilltops, swimming rivers or nibbling upon wood sorrel as he forages for mushrooms through the hedgerows, forests and wild spaces of leafy olde England. A bard at heart and one whose writings are inspired by and honour this ancestral and ancient tradition; a tradition that seeks not just to entertain, but to foster a communion with nature, a love for life and the drinking deeply from its well of timeless wisdom.

THE WHISPERING PEARLS

For David and Cyndi,

Bless you both and may you
enjoy the journey!

Lucas iii

_L_

LUCAS DAVEY

THE WHISPERING PEARLS

Vanguard Press

VANGUARD PAPERBACK

© Copyright 2022
Lucas Davey

A CIP catalogue record for this title is
available from the British Library.

ISBN 978 1 80016 286 0

Vanguard Press is an imprint of
Pegasus Elliot MacKenzie Publishers Ltd.
www.pegasuspublishers.com

First Published in 2022

Vanguard Press
Sheraton House Castle Park
Cambridge England

Printed & Bound in Great Britain

Dedication

For my children, and this beautiful Earth we live on.

Acknowledgements

The author would like to thank all the precious souls who helped support and shape this novel. He would also like to express gratitude for the people and places that offered him and his writing both sanctuary and inspiration:

Rebecca Davey
Fiona Macphee
Charlotte Holloway
Vladimir Megre
My parents and all those ancestors who lived their lives with courage and grace.
The villagers and villages of Vinayo and Piedrasecha, Leon, Spain.
The Nahmanides Institute, Girona, Spain.
The Order of Bards, Ovates and Druids.
The villagers and village of Staithes, East Yorkshire.
The coast and wild spaces of St Bees and Cumbria.

PROLOGUE

'Why has it turned so cold?' the child asked, almost in a whisper lest the sound of his voice break the stillness.

'It is the Earth my child. She has begun to make ready.'

'I sense her sorrow. Why does she weep so?'

'She has seen what must come to pass. She has foreseen the darkness and the torment. She has heard the cries of the children as they... curse our names.' The mother's voice trailed off and she looked across at the rainclouds gathering above the granite cliffs.

'So they have chosen,' said the child with a breaking heart. 'But a sun will die! The garden will burn! How will such sorrow be endured?'

The mother looked down at him tenderly.

'A sun can be reborn. A garden replanted. Don't ever forget this.'

The child looked across to what appeared to be the last refuge of sunlight at the crest of a great rock as it climbed out of the ocean and rose upwards towards the growing ceiling of heavy cloud above it.

'Will they still help us?'

'Those that can, will.'

'And the others, what will happen to them?'

'They will fall into darkness and suffer our same fate. That is the price of their aid.'

'Then tell them to stay!' the child cried with a look of anguish on his face.

'It is not our decision but theirs. They come of their own free will. They love us as their own. The Eledh will not abandon us to face this alone.'

The child's eyes filled with tears of compassion. The evening sun had long since sunk past the distant horizon but, in spite of the rain which began to fall, the light on the cliffs remained as bright and golden as before. Through his tears he could just make out the bright forms of the tall Eledh standing high above them, the ethereal tips of their wings rising like lotus petals beneath the falling rain.

'How will I find you?' he asked. The mother remained silent. 'Tell me how I find you!' The mother turned to him and wiped the tears from his adoring, ageless eyes. The child seemed so delicate, fragile like a feather, yet within him she could sense all the energies of creation so gracefully condensed into his small, perfect frame. Looking at him sometimes was like looking into the living ocean.

'I wish I knew,' she whispered. 'I fear we have already forgotten so much.' The child shook his head, but the imploring look in his mother's eyes silenced his protest. The child sighed and moved closer into her body and rested his head on her chest. As always, he felt her love wrapping around him, warming him like the summer sun. As she held him, the air surrounding them began to glow with an iridescent light. Together in silence, like two stars shining against the darkening sky, they stood: two perfect souls, woven together as one.

From the crest of the rock, a long mournful sound rose above the bitter wind whipping off the waves and a dark, winged shape appeared to stumble, then, letting out a heart-wrenching cry into the evening sky, toppled slowly over the edge. Like a dying sun, the winged creature tumbled and rolled through the air before plunging like a stone into the black waves below.

'It has started!' the child gasped and fell to his knees.

'Oh, not yet!' cried the mother to the heavens. 'Please not yet! I am not ready to let him go!'

The child groaned and doubled over in agony. Already a dark shadow was gathering around him. The mother tried to lift the child's grimacing face to hers, but it was like trying to lift a cold stone with a flame and her hands could get no purchase. As the shadow darkened about him, she could see his spine and legs beginning to buckle as if under some terrible weight. 'Help us!' the mother screamed upwards towards the Eledh but the light at the crest of the rock had died completely and the rock was shrouded in darkness.

'Ama!' the child cried. Desperately the mother tried to take him in her arms but it was as if he were already a thousand miles away.

'I love you, my child. My Mabon,' she replied weakly but his eyes had grown dull and she watched as the last light of recognition in them flickered and died…

'Ama…'

CHAPTER 1

'Come sit by my fire boy. You look tired and cold.' Kai was indeed cold and his armour had started to weigh intolerably upon his young shoulders, but the unexpected sight of a fire meant he must have strayed a lot closer to the encampment than he realised.

'Thank you. Your offer is tempting but I must return to the battle. My Lord is displeased with me enough already.'

'A battle you say? And yet I see more mud than blood upon you. Did you not engage with the enemy?' Kai tried to see past the flames to see who was interrogating him but each time he tried to steal a look the flames jumped as if caught by the breeze and blocked his view.

'I did engage... the enemy, but...' Kai let his words falter as he remembered his only encounter during the whole night had been against a youth so lacking in years and bearing a cuirass so ill-fitting the slight frame that he had appeared more like a child at play in borrowed armour than a genuine Moronan warrior.

'But...? Was it because the enemy was just a boy like yourself and you could no more bring yourself to strike at him than he at you, is this not so?'

'How do you know of this?' demanded Kai, his disquiet growing, for he had hoped none had borne witness to his cowardly act. The voice laughed.

'It is not my place to condemn nor commend your conduct. Only you can do that. Come. Sit and warm yourself a while. This night has dragged on for long enough. Rest here until the light of daybreak can guide you back to the path you have lost. Already I see the dawn beckoning over the horizon.' Seeing a faint line of molten bronze creeping up on the horizon Kai resigned himself to wait out what little remained of the night and sat down as near to the blazing fire as the heat would allow. As he rubbed life back into fingers and toes, numb with cold, he again tried to steal a glance to see who it was addressing him in so familiar a manner, but as before the flames seemed to catch on the breeze and flared up to bar his view.

'Forgive me for asking my young friend, but as you wandered the night lost and alone a vision presented itself to you, did it not? Tell me, why did the vision cause you to weep so?' The comments so caught Kai by surprise the young warrior leapt to his feet and, rounding the fire angrily, sought to confront the speaker for none but his lord dared speak of his affliction so openly… and yet, when Kai reached the opposite side, he found nothing but shadows dancing beneath the night's sky.

'Where are you? Stop hiding like a thief!'

'A thief I may be but what makes you think I am hiding? I am here beside you where I have always been.' Hearing the stranger confess to being a thief Kai thought wise to draw his sword and began circling around slowly with his back to the fire, scouring the darkness for signs of any hostile or sudden movement.

'I am first aide to the High Lord, commander of the armies of the Furud,' said Kai trying his best to hide the tremor of fear in his voice. 'I command that you show yourself to me!'

'Well, if the High Lord's servant commands it then show myself I must.' Kai looked in all directions, expecting at any moment for the thief to leap out upon him, but no one appeared.

'Stop playing games and step into the light so I can see you!'

'But how can I step into the light when I *am* the light? It is you who must step into the light lost child.' The speaker's last words were punctuated by an unbearable heat that Kai could feel burning upon his back. With a growing sense of foreboding Kai turned around, but never in his wildest imaginings did he expect to see that which next greeted his incredulous gaze, for there in place of the roaring camp fire rose a horned being of light and flame that was as terrifying to look upon as it was beautiful to behold.

'Are you… the th… thief?' Kai stammered, barely able to get the words out.

'A thief come for you I may be… or are you a thief come to steal me?' As the fiery being spoke the words like a riddle it stretched wide its wings which blazed with such brilliance Kai had to throw his arms across his eyes for fear of going blind.

'And wh-what do you mean by that?' Kai asked, dreading the answer.

'What do I mean?' it laughed, the words leaving its mouth in crackles of flames. 'Oh, soon you will know young witchblood... or should I call you bullblood?' Kai had heard more than enough and set off running into the darkness as fast as his numb toes could bear. On he ran into the night, not stopping until the sounds of laughter had been left far behind and the crest of a rust-red sun had broken the horizon. Indeed, it was not until he heard a familiar angry bark of "Worm!" being called from the brow of a hilly rise just above him that his desperate flight came skidding to a halt.

'I'm here my Lord,' Kai replied breathlessly. 'Wait there. I'm coming straight up.' When Kai reached the top of the rise a small party of steel-clad warriors emerged from the shadows. Their leader, a tall and imposing man whose hair seemed streaked as much with blood as with silver, bore down upon Kai as though he would drive him back down the hill he had just climbed.

'Wretch! Where have you been?' Kai dropped his eyes as he always did when his lord's fury turned against him.

'My apologies my Lord. I encountered some... difficulties.'

'Difficulties! Perhaps you believe that because you empty my piss pot you are somehow exempt from my wrath?'

'No, my Lord.'

'Then where have you been? Why have you taken so long?'

'I...' Kai began, not knowing where to begin. 'I... ran into... wolves.' Kai had no idea why he had suddenly felt so compelled to lie.

'*Wolves!*' the warlord spluttered.

'Yes,' Kai replied trying and failing to deliver his reply with anything like the gravity such a comment needed to render it anything but ridiculous. 'Very... big wolves. Like this...' To make matters worse Kai proceeded to hold his hand above his head as if to demonstrate their impressively unnatural size but caught such a look brewing upon the warlord's battle-scarred features that he immediately returned the hand quickly to his side. 'I found your sword,' he added hoping by drawing the warlord's attention to the long and cumbersome object still strapped to his back he might redirect the conversation away from his failings, though, of late, his "failings" seemed to be the only topic worthy of conversation. 'I trust the battle still swings in our favour?'

'*Swings in our favour!* The battle is *ended*, you worthless muck! Thanks to you I had to kill a dozen Moronans with my bare hands!'

'A deed worthy of a bard's song, my Lord, I'm sure.'

'A song and twenty lashes, you can be sure of that also!' Kai flinched at the thought. 'Enough lying boy. I know what you have been doing. I can see it in your eyes. I know the visions bring forth tears. Tell me what you know. Tell me what you saw!' Kai dropped his head, letting his dark hair fall across his face like the bars on a prison window.

'There is little to tell,' he began hesitantly, '… only something… stirs. A great change perhaps, though I know not how nor in what form it will come, but I feel it is upon us already.'

'Then speak! Describe what you saw!' Kai sighed. He knew what he had to tell would do little to ease the punishment that awaited him, but duty bound him to speak, nonetheless. Resigned to a flogging, Kai closed his eyes and began to recall his vision.

'I saw a lone rock standing upon a war-ravaged plain. Upon this rock was the nest of a great bird; a bird whose wings were plumed with feathers as keen as the sharpest blade and whose cry rang louder than the roar of a hundred-thousand men. Though both rock and nest were blackened and burnt from the fires that raged across the earth below, inside the nest a clutch of eggs remained. I watched as one of the eggs, warmed by the flames, began to hatch, but from this egg came forth not a bird, but a serpent hungry and fierce as sin itself.'

'What did the serpent do?'

'It…'

'It what?'

'It… devoured both eggs and bird, tearing at the bird's flesh until its feathers rained from the rock like ash.' Kai lifted his gaze to show he had nothing more to tell.

'Did you see anything of my triumph? Anything of the bull?' Kai shook his head.

'Bah! Serpents and birds! You'd better not be hiding anything important from me boy. You know what I'll do if you are. I am displeased enough with you already.' Kai bowed his head and remained silent. He knew if the warlord discovered he was keeping secret his encounter with the horned being of flame he would risk a punishment far worse than twenty lashes, yet every time he considered disclosing what he'd witnessed he found he had neither the desire nor the ability to recount even the slightest detail of the event.

'Well?' said the warlord noticing Kai fidgeting with discomfort. 'Is there something more you want to tell me?' Kai shook his head.

'So be it,' the warlord said turning away. 'Then you can bring my shield. We will speak more of this later. We have a witch to burn.' Less than impressed the warlord now intended for them to confront and burn a witch, Kai dutifully retrieved the shield that weighed almost as much as Kai himself and followed the old warrior and his men into the thick scrub and woodland that covered the rise. Soon the trees dropped away to their right leaving bare an old pilgrim trail worn from the hard stone of the hillside. The trail lay half-hidden amidst course thickets of gorse and waist-length grasses. Armies of ants criss-crossed the naked stone, endlessly foraging for scraps or victims to drag back to their innumerable nests. Further down the half-stripped corpses of their enemy began appearing on either side of the trail, their armour torn from their young backs like husks from ripe grain.

Following this grisly corridor, the group continued their descent until they reached the colossal ruins of the city walls which coiled tightly about the town as it sank down the hillside. All around, torn and splintered as if from some titanic struggle, great scales of stone lay, their scored facades serving as dull mirrors to the breaking dawn. Passing these the party entered a buckled gateway set in the wall's thick foundations and reappeared amidst a tangle of narrow cobbled streets on the other side. As they picked their way through the bodies of the slain, the corridors of stone appeared to lean in as they rose up on either side. Sometimes they closed above them, sealing them into dark, damp passageways that ran like petrified arteries through the town's broken heart. The distant drumming of a solitary blacksmith's hammer beat out a slow irregular rhythm, echoed only by the dull thud of their footsteps. Gradually the drumming faded until their path opened out into a large square dominated by an austere looking temple which squatted at the top of a wide flight of steps. Here a second group of Furud warriors, their steel armour and lion helmets glinting against the cold, grey backdrop, were dragging two girls, both of whom were wailing hopelessly as they clung futilely to the last shreds of their torn garments. Behind them, set above the entrance, the carved head of a bull watched the degenerate proceedings in silence.

'Halfwits,' Kai muttered louder than he intended. Hearing him the warlord snorted derisively but once beside the nearest of the assailants he promptly kicked the warrior to one side. Indignant, the warrior spun around in fury, his sword half-drawn, but realising it was Lord Rasalas who had kicked him leapt away from the girl as if she were a writhing snake.

'My Lord, I… I did not see you approaching. I was um…'

'I can see what you were doing. Perhaps attending to the fallen might have crossed your mind before you decided to start siring more bastard, witchbloods. Don't you think we have enough of those already?' Kai felt the warlord's words like a thorn.

'Of course. Forgive us,' said the warrior. 'We shall attend to them straight away.'

'Wait,' the warlord said, 'bring the girls inside. I have a better use for them.'

The interior of the temple, if anything, was even more austere than the exterior, with its single vaulted ceiling soaring upwards, supported in each corner by wide buttresses devoid of any ornament or decoration. Near the centre of the ceiling, a hazy light descended from a round window until it fell upon the curling horns of a gigantic bull which had been forged to look as if it were dragging itself by its forelegs out of the ground, its head and neck arched upwards as it bellowed silently towards the heavens. From its open mouth, a deep pit of glowing embers burned steadily, filling the atmosphere with a hot, scented smoke that rose in two thick plumes from the bull's nostrils.

'Where is my son with Lybesstre? Tell Magor I want that spell-casting hag here now!'

One of the warriors nodded and disappeared into a small vestibule nearby. After a short wait a second warrior almost as young as Kai, though with a face that bore nearly as many scars as his father's, returned leading a beautiful woman dressed in a simple cream robe who looked

20

anything but how Kai imagined a "spell-casting hag" would look. The woman's hazel-gold eyes framed by her long auburn hair betrayed a sharp intelligence and wisdom that contrasted with the youthfulness of her face. Though chained by the neck and hands, she still managed to walk with poise and grace. Even when Magor flung her at his father's feet she retained a look of calmness and control. 'Where is it?' demanded Rasalas. Magor looked at his father in surprise.

'My Lord,' he enquired guardedly, 'surely this is the bull you seek?'

'Where is it?' Rasalas repeated ignoring his son's interruption. The witch priestess continued to watch the old warrior in silence.

'Fetch firewood!' he barked. Quickly a large pile of wood was collected and deposited on the floor in front of him. 'Did you honestly think I came all this way to throw away the lives of a thousand men for this worthless lump of bronze? There are a hundred cities nearer my homeland which would have provided far easier and richer pickings than those of Tor Morona, yet still, you think you can play games with me. You know what I seek Lybesstre. You know the Furud do not visit such distant shores lightly.' Still seeing no reaction from her Rasalas pushed one of the young girls they had brought with them towards his warriors.

'Hang her by her ankles over the bull's mouth!' Soon the warriors had the terrified girl suspended above the bull's open mouth like a fly from a web. Lybesstre looked on in alarm but still refused to speak.

'Lybesstre, I know you are no worshipper of hollow idols. I know what power you and your witch horde protect. Where is it? Where is the bull's horn? Where is the Horn of Aatxe?'

Lybesstre looked away from Rasalas and, half closing her eyes, spoke as if she were speaking to someone standing right beside her.

'Why call such a one as this? Why call one so violent, one so consumed by his own darkness?'

'Who are you talking to?' demanded Rasalas trying to follow her gaze but seeing nothing but empty space. Lybesstre frowned momentarily as if confused then her eyes flicked across to Kai before returning her gaze to the old warrior.

'You say you know what power I protect. You know nothing Rasalas. Are you so vain to believe you could have taken this city if the ones I serve had not allowed you to do so? Are you really so foolish as to think you can simply take the gifts of the Eledh by force? This city was lost long before you came. It was lost the moment it turned its teeth on the innocents it was built to protect. You have no idea what you seek.'

'Lower her in,' said the old warrior unimpressed. 'I want her screams to be heard twenty leagues from here.'

'Please!' cried Lybesstre but it was to no avail for the girl's screams of fear soon turned to screams of agony as she was lowered into the bull's smoking maw.

'Enough!' Lybesstre begged, the tears visible upon her face. 'No more. I will do as you wish. I will take you to the horn.' Rasalas looked up to see hot flames licking about the bull's face and the metal around its mouth and nostrils begin to glow an angry red. 'I have said I will take you to the horn of Aatxe! What more do you want?'

'I want you to swear an oath even you cannot break. Swear yourself into my service. Guide me to the lost gifts of the Eledh and I might consider sparing what remains of your temple harlots.'

'I swear on all I hold sacred. Just, please, let the killing end!' Rasalas paused a moment as if weighing up the truthfulness of her words then walked over to place a large, gauntleted fist about the woman's neck.

'Then show me the *real* bull,' he said through bared teeth. Lybesstre nodded but as Rasalas turned away from her Kai could have sworn he caught a smile play out upon the witch's lips.

'If the rope still holds lift what's left of her out,' the warlord instructed his warriors but Kai had already anticipated the command and was hauling on the burning rope as if his life depended on it.

'Damn you boy! Did I instruct *you* to lift her out?' Kai detected the threat in the warlord's voice and quickly surrendered the rope to the hapless warrior propelled rudely in his direction. Rasalas shook his head as if in despair.

'Bring torches boy. The rest keep feeding the flames. I want the fires hot for when we return.'

Kai dashed off to carry out the warlord's wishes, pulling burning torches for himself, Rasalas and Magor, and would have returned with them immediately had he not caught sight of the girl being lowered to the floor beside him. There were no signs of burning upon her body anywhere.

22

'Well?' enquired the warlord impatiently.

'Here my Lord,' he said realising he was still gawping at the girl who was now staring back at Kai with an expression of equal curiosity.

Once the torches had been handed around, Lybesstre led the group to a darkened stairwell near the front of the temple. This they soon discovered wound its way down into a vast crypt that ran back under the full length of the temple floor. In the flickering light Kai could just make out row after row of alcoves containing temple witches sat in silent meditation. He brought his torch close to the face of one of them and gasped. Desiccated strips of pale-yellow skin hung across the bared grinning teeth of a corpse. All around the corpse, and even on its lap, a collection of small urns had been placed.

'These are the mummified bodies of my foremothers,' responded Lybesstre to Kai's startled reaction. 'Even in the afterlife they sit and watch over the cremated remains of the beloved daughters who served under them.'

'Revolting,' said Magor grimacing as he observed the yellowing skin on the corpse's ancient face.

'Sarsvata passed from this life over nine hundred years ago,' replied Lybesstre quietly as if recalling the name of a recently deceased friend.

'I still see no bull,' said Rasalas impatiently.

'This way,' she replied and guided them to an alcove at the end of the crypt. At the back of the alcove was a wooden panel that opened to reveal a concealed, though not entirely hidden, passageway behind it. Rasalas glared at Magor.

'Who was meant to have searched down here?'

'I'll find out my Lord and deal with them myself,' the warrior said with a show of innocence. Kai said nothing but let slip a look as if he knew Magor himself were to blame. When Rasalas' back was turned Magor leant across and whispered angrily, 'Careful where you cast your eyes witchblood,' then patted the pommel of his sword. Knowing Magor's threats were not to be taken lightly Kai quickly averted his eyes and turned to follow Lybesstre.

Beyond the alcove, another long and winding flight of stairs led them up and out into blinding sunlight. When his eyes had adjusted to the glare Kai could not help but stare in open-mouthed wonder. A beautiful garden enclosed by ancient walls spread out before them. From every gully and crack of the walls, wild sprays of pink and lavender flowers cascaded down to lemon and pineapple-scented carpets of chamomile and thyme. The air was alive with the hum of bees, whose hives seemed to be everywhere, whilst twittering birds dashed excitedly back and forth through the rich foliage and colourful blossoms, their mouths crammed with feathers and moss to line their nests. In the centre of the garden, a vine laden with grapes yet to ripen climbed over a small temple. Above the door, as with the main temple, the head of a bull had been carved, but this time the bull's horns held a golden sun. Lybesstre raised her face and hands to the sky as if in prayer.

'The House of Aatxe — the sacred heart of our city.' As she finished her prayer and lowered her hands Kai could have sworn the air around them had become charged with energy.

Strangely subdued the group followed Lybesstre into the temple. Inside the building was again devoid of any decoration or ornament but, unlike the sprawling gloom of the great temple they had just passed through, this was bright, airy and cheerful. Beneath their feet blossom petals had been scattered across a simple floor of packed earth. To one side they could see an old, wooden spinning wheel, whilst in the centre, a circle of stones surrounded a large, deep font filled not with water but with a fine golden sand. Part-buried in the sand a jewel-encrusted hilt sparkled alluringly in the warm sunlight which entered from a ring of delicate rose-tinted windows set high in the smooth, curved walls. Rasalas' eyes burned hungrily when he spied the hilt.

'There he is!' he growled and, removing his gauntlets, placed himself over the font.

'Wait! You cannot simply take the Horn of Aatxe like a piece of fruit snatched from a peddler's basket! Aatxe must first deem you to be worthy.'

'And if Aatxe does not? What then?'

'Then you risk condemning your soul to a cycle of unimaginable darkness.' Rasalas looked at her with contempt.

'You waste your time Lybesstre. Your folktale and superstition won't deter me. My soul is long beyond saving.'

'My Lord,' said Kai unable to remain quiet any longer, 'what if there is some truth in what she says? These are not men and beasts of flesh and bone she speaks of, but of ancient gods and curses!'

'Silence! I'll not be fooled by this witch queen's cunning. The heart of a viper hides beneath that pretty breast. She hungers for that which she cannot have. She knows she hasn't the strength to take the horn herself. This is why she hides it from those who do.'

'Watch your pride Rasalas. There is much you would do well to learn about me and why for so long the Eledh have kept the sacred horn hidden. The horn's whereabouts were kept secret not to protect it from the likes of you, but to protect those, like you, foolish enough to covet Aatxe's power. It is they the Eledh wish to protect. Neither Aatxe nor any of the Eledh has any need to fear the likes of you.'

'Don't test my patience Lybesstre any more than you already have. If I didn't have such need of your insolent tongue, I would cut it out here and now.' Rasalas turned away from the woman and, ignoring her warnings, defiantly grasped the horn with both hands. Almost immediately the sand began to glow and a sweat broke out on Rasalas' brow. Besides the font, the spinning wheel began to turn as if being worked by unseen hands.

'What's the matter?' asked Magor. Rasalas' face contorted into a grimace of agony.

'Help me!' he screamed. Magor and Kai ran over and tried to pull the warlord free, but to no avail. Turning their attention to the font, they both pushed furiously at it, trying to tip it over, but it resisted all their efforts. The golden sand glowed like molten metal. Magor drew his sword and, seizing Lybesstre by her robe, held the point to her windpipe.

'What sorcery is this? Release him or by the gods, I'll skewer your neck to the floor!'

'I cannot. His pain is of his own doing. It is merely a mirror for the harm his own black pride has done to his soul. Be patient, the initiate must be assessed and sealed to the contract before he can be released. If you try to release him now, you will kill him for sure.'

'Then you'll die first!' Seeing Magor's bloody intent Kai suddenly found himself catching hold of Magor's sword arm, though great knew he the consequences of appearing to side with the warlord's enemies.

'Unhand me, boy!' Magor cried as he tried to tear his arm free, but Kai held the arm firm, even somehow forcing the sword from Magor's fist so it clattered to the floor. 'Traitorous dog! Is this how you show your loyalty?' Magor spat and tore at Kai with his other arm but in spite of his superior strength and years, Kai somehow seemed equal to the warrior's every move and refused to let go. No matter how much Magor twisted and fought he seemed incapable of breaking Kai's grip. Suddenly, Magor's hand flashed down to his side. Kai's face instantly tightened and he looked down. Protruding from his thigh was the hilt of a small dagger. Seizing the advantage Magor hurled Kai to the ground and sent a vicious kick into his head. Kai reeled from the blow and dropped dazed to the floor. Magor turned to Lybesstre. Strangely she had made no attempt to flee but met his enraged gaze calmly.

'You'll pay dearly for this!' he said and reached for his sword but before his hand could even touch the hilt a wheel of blinding light spun out from the font repelling the warrior with such force that he smashed into the wall of the temple and crumpled senseless to the floor.

***

When Kai had recovered his senses, he sat up and gasped. A sea of glass stretched away from him on all sides. Neither the temple, Magor nor Rasalas were anywhere to be seen. Instead, in the centre of the stone circle where the font had stood, a huge and muscular bull paced back and forth snorting and pawing at the ground angrily. The bull's glossy coat gleamed at first red like flame then turned black like polished obsidian beneath the light of a billion stars which wheeled dizzyingly through an infinite void above him. At first, Kai was afraid, but as he realised the bull's attention lay not on himself but elsewhere, he began to find its display of beauty and raw power strangely enthralling. It was as if the magnificent creature were duelling with an invisible foe. Lybesstre knelt nearby, her eyes closed as if in meditation, her lips moving as if in prayer. As the mysterious words of her prayer reached Kai's ears an all-too-familiar figure of ethereal light and flame began to manifest between himself and the bull. Kai instantly recognised the figure as the very same horned being he had encountered during the night, yet it was this most

26

unexpected of allies that seemed to be drawing the bull's furious attention away from both himself and Lybesstre. Stranger still, the graceful way the flaming figure weaved and slipped effortlessly out of the bull's path every time it charged reminded Kai more of a dance than a conflict or duel. He could even hear its unearthly voice lifting as though in song above Lybesstre's own. Gradually the bull's fury abated and, with a heaving chest, it came to a stop. Kai watched spellbound as the figure approached the bull and pressed the creature's broad snout into its glowing chest. Seeing the creature so distracted, Kai quietly began to draw his sword, but the instant the tip of the blade cleared the scabbard their mysterious ally let out a great laugh then vanished, leaving Kai staring straight into the bull's fierce gaze. Kai's heart leapt in his chest. Gripped with fear he lifted himself onto his feet and retreated backwards as best he could, but the pain in his thigh and the wheeling motion of the stars reflected in the mirror-like surface beneath his feet sent his head spinning and he clattered clumsily back onto the hard floor. The bull, its nostrils flaring dangerously, began to pace towards him. The pain in Kai's leg was excruciating. He tore the dagger from his thigh and tried lifting himself up once more, but blood started pouring from the wound. Dizzy and weak, all Kai could do was lift himself to his knees and begin to crawl away as the bull continued advancing menacingly.

What was he doing? Even if he could run there was nowhere to escape to. Kai stopped his retreat. If this was to be his end then at least he would face it with what little courage remained, however futile that might be. With a huge effort, Kai raised himself to his feet and, fighting an overwhelming desire to flee, turned to face the bull. The bull, sensing Kai's defiance, stopped to paw at the ground as if relishing the challenge then, with a deafening roar, dropped its head and charged. Kai barely had time to cry out as the bull exploded into light and thundered into him, sending a stabbing, searing pain straight into his heart…

CHAPTER 2

Kai sucked in a lungful of air as if it were the last breath he would ever take… or was it his first? He lifted a hand to his heart expecting to find nothing but a charred, bloody tear, but the flesh seemed perfectly intact. Even the few fine chest hairs that failed so miserably to cover his boyish skin showed no signs of burning. He was most definitely still alive… but how…? Or why? On the other side of the temple, Magor leant shakily against the temple wall rubbing his eyes. Nearby Rasalas crawled across the dirt floor, raking thick fingers through the sand and debris of the shattered font until the sparkling hilt and full, curved length of the gleaming horn emerged like a snake from a dune. Spying it the warlord snatched the horn to his breast then, grasping a handful of blossom, from the temple floor, cast the blossom into the air. As petals, like pink confetti, rained to earth the old warrior let out a bestial cry.

'When you have finished shouting, you might want to have someone tend to your servant's wound.' Rasalas looked across to find Lybesstre winding a bandage about Kai's wounded leg.

'What happened to him?' the warlord demanded.

'Why don't you ask your son?' Kai let out a weak yelp of pain as the witch priestess exerted pressure on the wound.

'Magor?' Rasalas' jubilant mood was already starting to fade.

'He tried to betray you,' Magor replied curtly. 'I thought servants were trained to protect their Lord. Instead of protecting you, he tried attacking me. He got what he deserved!' The warlord's face blackened.

'I suggest you choose your words very carefully Magor. He may be a marrowless sap, but that is still *my* servant lying there, not some slave whore serving the ranks!'

'You've always said his mother was a whore. Perhaps we should consider changing his role?'

'Enough!' Rasalas cut Magor's insolence with a sharp blow across his face. 'Now tell me what happened.'

'Kai didn't attack Magor,' interrupted Lybesstre coldly. 'He tried to stop him from killing me. That is all.'

'And is that such a bad thing? The witch simply watched as you burned. I thought you were dying.' Rasalas glared at both of them, not knowing what to believe.

'Why does the boy writhe there so? The wound seems small.' Kai felt himself being shoved rudely by the warlord's foot. 'Get up worm!' Desperate to comply with his lord's wishes Kai tried to stand, but it was as though the strength had been drained from his body and he fell back to the ground.

'You must let him rest,' appealed Lybesstre. 'Something… unexpected is happening to him. Something remarkable… or dreadful. Time will tell.'

'What do you mean woman?'

'It appears the spirit of the relic now resides… within Kai.' Rasalas' eyes darted back to Kai as the significance of Lybesstre's words sank in. Suddenly his eyes flashed with anger.

'That traitorous runt! Now I understand what he was hiding from me. Now I understand why he could not look me in the eye. He saw this coming and coveted my power for himself. How naïve of me to think I could tame the likes of him. I should have left him where I found him. Well, he shall pay a heavy price for his betrayal!'

'Your servant bears no guilt Rasalas. There is no betrayal here, no stolen opportunity. The Aatxe's horn still retains the same power it did before.'

'You had better pray it does. I'm not one for sharing power with witchbloods priestess.'

'I do not pretend to know what Aatxe has in store but I do know that Kai did not ask for this consciously. There is no way he could understand any of what has occurred here. In fact, such was the force with which Aatxe's spirit entered him I'd be surprised if he remembers anything at all.'

'So the boy has none of the horn's power you say?'

'None. Kai is merely playing host to a lost and desperate soul.' The warlord paused a moment then let out a guffaw.

'So the boy has been possessed by a cow! Ha! I should have known bringing him along would prove more trouble than it was worth.'

A sudden noise and movement caught their attention. All three looked down to see Kai again trying to rise, though this time his eyes were glazed over and his body trembled as if entering a fit.

'Quickly,' said Lybesstre, 'I sense Aatxe's spirit stirring. This might play in your favour Rasalas. If you wish to learn the location of the lost gifts of the Eledh then let me speak with the boy before the spirit withdraws.' Rasalas hesitated then nodded. Lybesstre eased Kai back down onto the temple floor and placed her slender fingers on either side of his head.

'Try not to move. You must try to speak with us, Kai. Tell us what Aatxe is showing you?' Kai's lips moved but his words were inaudible. 'You must try harder. I cannot hear you. Tell me what you can see.'

'A city of gold,' he said faintly. Rasalas' eyes lit up and he too leant closer so he could hear more clearly. 'A city of gold buried beneath a desert. The desert is bathed in the light of a rising sun.'

'Go on,' said the witch priestess. 'I am listening.'

'I am following the sun. The desert gives way to a land of deep gorges. One is so deep that the light of day never reaches the bottom.'

'Go down. You must enter the gorge. What can you see?'

'It is like night down here. Wait, something is approaching from the far end.'

'What is it?'

'A storm. A storm of sand.'

Kai's body tensed.

'There are serpents. I have never seen their kind before. Their skin burns red like flame. They are rising out of the ground. They are everywhere!'

'Relax,' said Lybesstre. 'They cannot harm you. What are they doing?'

'They are feeding. They are feeding on the corpses of men. Their bodies litter the floor. I think they are warriors but their torsos are so crushed I cannot tell.'

'Try to describe to me what they are wearing?'

'It is difficult to see. Wait. There is a golden shield. It bears an emblem.'

'What is the emblem?'

'It is a lion. A lion slain by its own claw. The storm is almost upon me. I want to leave.'

'Stay. You must stay and tell us more. You cannot be harmed.' Kai's breathing quickened.

'I can hear the wind shrieking. No, it is not the wind. It is something else. Please, I want to leave!'

'Stay! You must stay and tell me more. I need to be sure.'

'There is something in the storm. Great shadows. Oh, Gods! What creatures are these? Oh, Gods!' Kai's body arched and his eyes rolled into the back of his head. Quickly Lybesstre placed both hands on his chest and began to utter words under her breath. Slowly Kai's body began to relax and his breathing steadied.

'We must find your servant a bed safe from vengeful eyes. He will need my help and much rest if he is to fully recover. It will not be safe to stay in the city for much longer. Already the neighbouring cities are mustering their armies to recapture Tor Morona. We should leave as soon as possible.'

'Oh, I'll find a bed for him,' said Rasalas. 'Have no fear of that. But we are not leaving for the ships yet, not until you have told me all you know of this golden city and whatever those monstrous creatures were that Kai described.'

'There is not much time. The neighbouring cities will already have word of your blasphemy. You will see how your offences rouse a nation to fury.'

'Then more the fool they,' Rasalas sneered. 'I will hear what you know, witch, but not now. First, we shall feast upon this victory. Magor, have my servants set a table for us.'

'Where?' asked Magor.

'In the great temple of course. We shall dine before their gods.'

'Very well my Lord. Shall I have them slay the lambs we brought?'

'No. My appetite is whetted for something more... substantial.'

'Like what then?'

'Like... a bull!'

A great table was brought and weighed down with every delight the servants could forage or force from the city's frightened residents, but none caught the eye like the roast beast, with curling horns dripping with stolen temple honey, at the table's centre. Chuckling with delight, Rasalas drew his sword to carve thick slices from the bull's hindquarters.

'A little longer over the fire?' suggested Magor eyeing the pool of blood collecting at the bottom of his plate.

'Nonsense!' uttered Rasalas. 'Drink your wine and eat. Another cup of this Moronan vinegar and you won't taste a thing!' The table roared with laughter.

'Now where is our storyteller? Lybesstre! Where is that devious crone?'

'I am here my Lord,' said a quiet voice. All eyes turned to look at the auburn-haired woman still knelt watching over Kai who had been placed on a berth nearby.

'Time for your tale, I think. Tell us about this golden city!' Lybesstre leant down to whisper something in Kai's ear then rose to join the warriors at the table.

'Very well,' she said sitting in a chair vacated for her. 'I will tell you of the legend of Amon Pur — that is if any of you are sober enough to listen.'

'Just tell us what you know.'

Lybesstre closed her eyes and waited until a hush had filled the lofty temple chamber then began to speak in a voice like scented musk.

'Four thousand years have elapsed, four thousand almost to the day when Amon Pur and his legions set out to find the gardens of gold, the mythical land of the Horim. After two decades of crushing and brutally suppressing his enemies, Amon Pur believed himself invincible and immortal. Claiming to be a descendent of the gods, he set about filling his domains with monuments and lavish temples to immortalise his name and deeds. Yet, so enamoured with plunder and bloodshed and with no more enemies to fight, he soon tired of sitting in his luxurious palaces listening to the tiresome concerns of concubines too heavy with child to catch his roving eye and turned his gaze to distant shores. Often had he heard the whispers of a land richer and more wondrous than any man could imagine; a land where veins of the purest gold ran like broad streams through the green pastures and gentle woodlands of the peaceful Horim. And so, the seed of longing was sown and continued to fester and grow until Amon Pur could think or dream of nothing else. Unable to bear it any longer Amon Pur mustered an army of ten thousand of his strongest warriors and set sail in search of the lands of a legend.

'Yet the price of his ardour was great. With just one legion of men remaining did Amon Pur finally set eyes upon his heart's desire: the gardens of gold. Skipping and dancing like children did the men of Amon Pur enter that land. Yet what foreboding they felt when first catching sight of the mighty Horim. As giants are to locusts so appeared the Horim to the warriors of Amon Pur. "How are we to defeat such monsters?" asked the men of their leader. Disgusted by their cowardice Amon Pur took up a lance, and in a rage, hurled it at the nearest Horim. With deadly accuracy, the lance pierced an eye of the creature who roared in pain and, knowing nothing of the violent ways of men, ran in mortal fear of those vicious creatures. And thus did the legion of Amon Pur begin to murder and hound and drive the gentle Horim before them until there was no refuge for the few that survived but in the remotest and darkest places of that land. With the Horim gone, Amon Pur ordered that slaves be brought, and the trees and pastures were laid waste and the gold ripped from the earth until great scars filled the land. Once more did Amon Pur wish to immortalise his deeds and glorify his name and so ordered a great city to be built — a city of gold. Yet with the trees gone and the land growing ever more barren, his dreams of a new empire quickly withered and died. Still, Amon Pur and his ageing warriors remained in their golden city until the last of the rivers had run dry and nothing remained but desert and sun. As he sat upon his golden throne, a rumour reached the ears of Amon Pur; whisperings that the Horim lived on; that they had escaped with a treasure of such power and enchantment that it enabled them to live in caverns beneath the desert without food or sun.

'Again, desire consumed the thoughts of Amon Pur and tore at his soul and for one last time, the legion was summoned for battle. With hearts afire and shields emblazoned with gold, they marched into the desert to seek out the last of those mighty fallen creatures.

'For forty days and nights they crossed parched lands and desert until, at sundown of the last day, they came across a land filled with deep gorges. At the foot of the deepest gorge, the soldiers of Amon Pur found the foul-smelling openings of huge caverns and knew they had discovered the secret refuge of the last of the Horim. With shouts and drumming of shields, the legion of Amon Pur marched along the gorge hoping to flush the timid giants out of their holes. Little did they anticipate the horror they were about to unleash. Heavy had the years of darkness and fear weighed upon the Horim. Insufferable had been their exile and incarceration. Tormented and twisted beyond recognition the once gentle creatures came shrieking dementedly out of their caverns and bore down upon the warriors. Such was their fury and might that a cloud of dust arose like a storm before them and concealed their coming until they were fully upon the stricken men. No more would the legion of Amon Pur walk the sun-drenched streets of their golden city. With their passing, the winds blew in and the legion and their golden city were lost under dust and sand. Some say the Horim, desiring never to be disturbed again, buried and sealed the entrances to their caverns and returned to the depths to sleep and await death. Some say they lie there still, deep beneath the layers of rock and sand of the desert.'

The warlord's eyes sparkled as he listened to Lybesstre's story. 'Now there's a horde worth dying for!' he said.

'Perhaps you intend on taking your horde with you in the afterlife?'

'Save your preaching for your flock Lybesstre,' said Rasalas. 'Just tell us if you can guide us to this city and gorge or not.'

'With Kai's sight, maybe I can. Though I have sworn only to help you find the lost treasures of the Eledh, not fill your ships' coffers with gold. However, the message was clear. To find the gorge where the lost legion of Amon Pur fell, we must first find the buried city and follow the rising sun for forty days. What you do with whatever else you find is your business.'

'Where is this land that we must journey to? Does it still have a name?'

'Our journey takes us far across the southern seas to Kugarra, to the lands of the Uati, the Reed Dwellers.'

'Then let us make haste. The sooner we set sail the sooner we can begin our search.'

'And leave so ill-prepared?' Lybesstre said.

'What's to prepare? We have stores and men aplenty. The ships are ready. What more do we need?'

'Men skilled at tunnelling into the earth.'

'What for? We have shovels! The men can dig.'

'This is no beach we seek. Deep will be the layers of earth and sand burying the caverns of the Horim. Four thousand years of shifting desert is a long time. Much of the sands and dust blown in by the desert winds will be compacted and hard. If haste is what you desire then you had better find men used to tunnelling through rock and earth.'

'Then I will send orders to Caronte. He will know where to find such men. Magor, go to the ships and haul that scoundrel of a sea captain out of the taverns. Have him ready his crew immediately. I have a use for him and his black ship.'

'What orders shall I give him?'

'Tell him I need miners.'

'Is that all?'

'That is all. Oh, and take that worthless little scrub with you. The gods and the sea air can decide his fate.'

'But I told you I will need his gift of sight if we are to be sure of finding the Eledh's gifts,' insisted Lybesstre. 'If you do not place him in my care, he will have little or no chance of recovering. There are no physicians among your ships with the skills needed to restore him to health. He is too weak. Send him away and you risk losing the way to finding the gifts forever.'

'Very well. Take the witch as well Magor. Watch her carefully though. She is more dangerous than a nest of harpies. Make sure she keeps the boy alive. If she tries anything throw her overboard. We shall await you in the Southern Straights.'

CHAPTER 3

Blue lay there, eyes closed, listening to the swirling rush of the wind and sea outside, trying to decide where the sound of one began and the other ended. The strong wind caused the roof tiles above her head to clatter as though a bull were impatiently pacing back and forth waiting for her to rise. She opened her eyes and stretched a small hand upward towards the sloping wooden panels lining the underside of the attic roof. They were near enough for her to be able to press an open palm against them. She did this every morning. She liked the low wooden ceiling with its beams. She liked how it made her feel she was in the belly of a ship. Blue closed her eyes again and imagined the slow roll of a warm sea…

…The rude clatter of tiles once again broke her sleep. With a sigh, Blue threw back the covers and, though not tall for her years, had to stoop to avoid hitting her head on the low attic ceiling as she shivered her way over to a solitary window. Heavy condensation coated the small, windowpanes and a cold draught leaked in where the old wooden frame had rotted and crumbled away in one corner. Running the back of a thin, grimy finger down one of the wet panes of glass she peered out at the dimly illuminated cliffs rising on the other side of the cove. A greasy brown cliff crake turned to eye her insolently from a nest wedged between the chimneys of an adjacent cottage. How long had it been sitting there waiting for its mate to reappear? Blue could only hope the chicks were still alive.

Blue looked past the nest towards the black mass of mine workings rising ominously above the muddled horizon of the small fishing town of Stod. If it weren't for the mine the view might almost have been considered pleasant. Still shivering she turned away and reached for a pair of worn and filthy drawstring trousers and an equally filthy tunic which had a large leather pocket crudely sewn onto the front. The trousers were too long and the tunic swamped Blue's wiry frame, so she carefully rolled up the trouser legs and tied a strip of leather around her middle to hold the tunic in as best she could. Blue then reached under the pile of mirounga skins she used as a bed and pulled out a small pocket knife bound in a beautiful walnut and brass casing. It was probably the only thing old Eofor had ever given her. For that matter, it was probably the only thing anyone had ever given her. Stuffing the knife into the front pocket of her tunic, Blue slipped through a narrow opening out onto an equally narrow staircase.

She scampered down the stairs and paused briefly on the landing to listen at a closed bedroom door. The room was unusually quiet. Normally Blue would be greeted on her way to the lavatory by thunderous snores and coughing. She thought about knocking but decided against it. Old Eofor would no doubt be blind drunk as usual and no amount of knocking could ever rouse him. Perhaps he's finally gone and choked on his bottle thought Blue mischievously and headed to the lavatory.

The "lavatory" was tiny, squeezed into what once must have been little more than a storage cupboard. It was connected to the rest of the cottage by a tiny passageway that Blue could only walk down if she twisted slightly at the hips to avoid her shoulders from scraping against the walls. Inside a bedpan, a large jug of water and washbasin were all it contained. Hanging on the wall above the washbasin a faded charcoal drawing depicted a scene of the old docks as they once had been before the mirounga and fish stocks began to disappear. Grim-faced fishermen, their backs to the harbour wall, sat looking out to the horizon, their stony expressions concealing their concern for the boats still to make it safely into harbour. Blue lifted the water jug from under the washbasin and emptied half its contents into the basin. Above it was a mottled and cracked looking glass. She leant closer. She looked terrible. Chafes, scratches, bruises and dirt seemed to cover every part of her body; the copper tinge to her fair hair lost beneath a film of grey grime while tired black rings circled her large pale, grey-blue eyes. How long had she been here? She suddenly felt very lost and alone.

It seemed like forever since old Eofor had dragged Blue from the crab-infested mud of the harbour. Numb with cold, half-dead from exhaustion and spewing up brine was how Blue had arrived in this remote fishing town on the northern coast of a godforsaken and forgotten part of the world. Since she was unable to remember who she was or where she had come from, the old man gave her a name and offered to take her in. She often wondered why he'd done it. Perhaps he'd been unable to face seeing another poor sod dragged off to work in the mines. At first, things had been okay, pleasant even, but when the fishing stocks started to disappear, the old man had no choice but to sell the cottage to the mine and send Blue to work. That had really hurt him. He'd even tried going to the mine himself, but when he begged them to take him on instead of Blue, they'd just laughed at him. When he became belligerent, they threatened to put them both in with the penitents if he didn't go away. It wasn't long after when old Eofor finally gave up for good. He sold his boat for a pittance, hung up his boots and, bottle in hand, simply waited for the decay to set in.

Blue looked away from the looking glass and towards the landing. She was growing uneasy at the lack of noise coming from the old man's door. She really ought to go check he was all right. Blue dried her hands and hurried back to the old man's bedroom door.

'Eofor?' she called through the door. Again, there was no sound. Blue lifted the latch and opened the door enough so she could peer into the room. The stench of vomit and liquor enveloped her. 'Oh, Gods!' she cried and ran into the room. Inside an old man, still wearing a wet oilskin, sat slouched against the leg of a worm-eaten wooden stool. The old man's lifeless head was flung backwards and a trickle of blood and vomit ran down his chin onto his oilskin. In one hand he still held an empty bottle of sack, though it smelt like he had mixed it with something stronger, and in his other, he had hold of a muddy boot which he had managed to remove just before falling unconscious. The bittersweet odours of rot, liquor and the sea filled the room.

'Oh, what have you done!' said Blue helplessly as tears ran down her face. A strange combination of grief and frustration washed over her. She tenderly stroked the old man's hair then shoved his head away in despair. His lifeless body rolled over and his forehead hit the stone hearth with a sickening thud. 'Oh sorry. I'm so sorry Eofor,' she said frantically trying to reposition the body. That was when she saw the caked blood running down the back of the old man's head and neck. She quickly removed the oilskin and lifted his filthy shirt. A horrified gasp escaped from her lips. Eofor's body was covered in shallow lacerations and hideous yellowing bruises. She slumped down beside him, wrapped her arms around her knees, and sobbed. Perhaps the rumours that the black ship had returned were true? And if the black ship was back, then so too were the loathsome herders.

Eofor had only spoken to Blue once of the black ship and he'd been so drunk at the time that Blue could hardly be bothered to listen.

'Its sails, are made from the shkin of dead men,' she remembered the old man slurring at her whilst waving a trembling finger for dramatic effect. She'd laughed at him and told him to shut up. Of course, others in the town also loved to spin incredible tales of the black ship and those that sailed it. Some of the townsfolk would love to huddle in groups on street corners talking in hushed tones as they swapped fearful tales of the demonic slave ship manned by giants, monsters, or cannibals, or whatever else their excited imagination could cook up. Others of course were slightly less impressionable and talked instead of the ship being just another pirate trader manned by thuggish fortune hunters. Both sides seemed to agree, however, that whenever the ship appeared on the horizon those known as herders would be sent ashore to sniff out the few unfortunates still to be found staggering through the streets after the inns had locked their doors. Whether or not they were demons, monsters or just men, what was certain was that whenever the black ship appeared people quickly began to disappear.

What if Eofor *had* run into the herders? Blue looked down again at the pitiful sight of the old man. Perhaps he'd put up too much of a struggle? Perhaps the herders had simply beaten and tortured him for their own amusement? What the hell did they want with an old man like him anyway? He was just about as useless a drunk as there had ever been. Suddenly the hopelessness of her situation hit her like a rock. What on earth was she going to do? She knew what would happen when the mine bosses found out her guardian had died; she would be interned with the penitents. The bosses had already begun to grow tired of Eofor's perpetual excuses for his late payments. With Blue being alone and little prospect of the rent now ever getting paid, they would have no hesitation in interning her... and that didn't even bear thinking about. Penitents were the most wretched and pitiful of all the mine's vast, wretched and pitiful workforce. Ever since the discovery of the mysterious whispering pearls, the penitents had been treated like prisoners and worked like slaves. Some said their work didn't even involve extracting the pearls but getting rid of them, either by destroying them or carrying them into the deepest chambers of the mine to be buried forever. This secretive work would always be carried out under the strict supervision of the most feared of all the northern races: the black-eyed Speris. Forbidden from any outward displays of emotion and isolated from the rest of the miners, like pale wraiths the penitents could occasionally be seen drifting silently through distant passageways under the constant watch of the Speris. One could only guess at what horrors they endured in those dark, lonely chambers.

That decided it. Blue had no option but to cover up the old man's death — at least for as long as she could until she could work out a way of getting away from the town. She leapt up and began shoving and dragging the old man's body over to a grubby reed mattress that lay on the floor of the room. With a final heave, Blue pulled the body onto the bed and dropped the old man's grey head onto an equally grubby mirounga skin which had been rolled up to make a pillow. The girl then tugged the sack bottle out from the old man's stiff fingers. 'That's ten bits bloody wasted,' said Blue throwing the bottle angrily to one side. Blue reached into his pockets to see if there was any money still left to salvage. She pulled out two small coins and a piece of smoked fish probably intended to be part of their dinner. That wouldn't even last her until the next day let alone until she received her paltry few coins at the end of the week. She'd just have to live off what crabs and dog whelks she could forage from the bay until she picked up her next wage. At least the old man couldn't blow what little she earned on liquor any more. Again, the stench of vomit hit her. What would she do with the body? It wouldn't be long before the stink of a dead body started attracting unwanted attention to the cottage. Perhaps she could burn it in stages in the hearth. The thought of burning the old man's body disgusted her, but the fear of being interned with the penitents was even greater. Blue looked out of the window towards the harbour. Many of the cottage windows were still dark so she still had time to collect whatever driftwood had washed up in the night before the miners began the weary

40

hike to the cage. It wouldn't be long though before the first cage began its slow descent into the depths of the earth. She'd have to hurry.

Outside the air, as ever, carried the thick scent of the alum fire heaps which still smouldered at the base of the cliffs. Standing in the shadow of the cottage, Blue took a couple of seconds to compose herself then headed as casually as she could down the narrow streets and winding stairways towards the quayside.

When she arrived, the tide was unusually high and the waves crashed over the huge boulders of the old sea defences as if they didn't exist. If anything, they made the sea more furious as it found itself suddenly confined within such insultingly inappropriate space that it spat infinite quantities of muddy foam over anything coming within five yards of the harbour wall. Blue walked to the end of the wharf, wiping spray from her face and clothing and stopped in front of a heap of broken spiny pots. Behind her, a piece of yellowed parchment had been nailed to a noticeboard informing the fishermen of new regulations governing the landing sizes of mirounga, fish and shellfish. They needn't have bothered, she thought. Apart from Eofor the only other remaining fisherman in the town had turned to smuggling to earn a living. The rest had either left or gone to work in the mines.

No one knew for sure why the mirounga and the fish had disappeared, but most knew that both the hunting and the catches started getting poor soon after the discovery of the first whispering pearls. Rumour had it that the miner who found the first whispering pearl had been so captivated by its beauty that he had tried to keep it for himself. It was also common knowledge that the same miner was later found wandering terrified to the point of insanity amidst the labyrinth of pitch-black tunnels. Stranger still, although many of the fishing towns and villages along this stretch of coast had their folktales and legends of ghosts and apparitions, ever since the mine had closed off the eastern face so the Speris and penitents could search for the deadly pearls, hardly a person remained who didn't claim to have seen a phantom or ghoul of some description or other. Even Blue had seen the one they called the grey girl standing at the top of the cliffs. Blue had even been able to make out the wet leaves clinging to her naked skin and the forlorn expression on the girl's young face as she clasped her hands to her chest, perhaps waiting in vain for sight of a ship or soul that would never return. Blue could have sworn the apparition had turned to look at her just before she faded like sea mist.

A shiver ran down Blue's spine. She looked up towards the cliffs half expecting to see the figure of the girl standing in the pale light of the dawn, but, to her relief, no one was there. A crash and boom near to where she was standing brought her attention back to the jetty as the churning waters of the sea rushed over the end of the landing stage. Bundles of driftwood and torn netting were flung onto it as if teasing her to go down and collect them before the waves swept them back again. Blue knew better than to risk collecting driftwood when the sea was in this mood. The same month Eofor had dragged her from the sea, a fisherman had washed up dead not far from where she was standing. When they examined the body, they found black seaweed encrusted under his cracked and broken fingernails. The poor soul had fought his way all the way back to shore only to find that once there he was unable to pull himself to safety. How many times must he have hauled himself out of the water, cursing his tormentor, as he clawed his way back up the rocks only to be torn off again by the ferocity of the breakers? *It's no good,* she thought, somewhat relieved that the wild weather had foiled her repugnant plan. Perhaps she could find a more dignified way to hide the body?

Another wave punched into the harbour wall and showered her with spray. She shook the dirty seawater off her as best she could and decided to set off to the mine before she got another soaking. The last thing she wanted was to have to walk along the cliff tops in this wind with sodden clothing.

Walking along the harbour, Blue approached the derelict smoke houses on Kipper Corner. To the right of these the river appeared to be flowing backwards as tidal waters surged into it from the sea. The chains and ropes holding the few small boats moored there were straining to almost breaking point. Blue crossed the bridge and followed the steep path until she stood at a point overlooking the entire town and harbour. Across the bay, she could just make out her attic window peeking out above the jumble of tiled rooftops. Seeing it reminded her of poor old Eofor's battered body. Shaking with anger she turned her gaze to the faint grey line of the horizon to see if she could spot the black ship. There was nothing — just an expanse of fizzing white breakers.

'Mornin' Blue.' Blue almost leapt off the cliff in fright. 'Steady now girl, tha'll probably not want to go for a swim just yet. Bit of a chill in the air.' Blue turned and awkwardly returned the big, beaming smiles on the faces of Algar Gladwyne and his son, Ælfweard, as they appeared over the rise of the cliff top. 'How's old Eofor?' Algar said with a wink. The colour drained from Blue's face, though she quickly realised that the wink undoubtedly referred to Eofor's usually drunken state.

'Oh, s-same as ever,' she stammered as she fought to recover her composure. Algar and Ælfweard were nearly always the first of the miners to arrive at the mine and, unlike the rest of the town's population who hated everything to do with that sweating, smoking hellhole were probably the only people in the entire community who actually managed to greet each day with a smile on their faces. Ælf, though slightly younger than Blue, was already quite tall for a miner, the majority of whom tended to be short and stocky and beamed with an impossible aura of indestructibility. No matter how hard or unpleasant the job was, and Ælf's father seemed to delight in testing his son's endurance and abilities to the limit, Ælf seemed to sail through it all and come out at the end even stronger and, to the mine bosses' annoyance, cheekier and more rebellious than ever before. Ælf, like Blue, was what the miners called a "shaft rat". The shaft rats at the mine were probably the scruffiest and most unruly bunch of children ever to walk the earth, yet for all their coarseness and mischief, they all shared an unspoken bond, the sort of bond that can only come about through the shared experience of extreme hardship.

'Saw that damned black ship t'other day' said Algar as they walked along together towards the mine. In places, the cliff road appeared to have had great bites taken out of it where the alum workings had been. On some nights strong winds could fan the oil-rich fire heaps of alum into raging infernos that could be seen from leagues out at sea. Some of the heaps were still smouldering and wisps of steam and smoke whipped over the top of the cliffs giving the path leading to the mine a hellish quality. 'Bad omen. Bad omen indeed,' he continued. Blue noted the smile had gone from Algar's face. *So it was true*, she thought. Poor

Eofor. If only she could summon a monstrous creature from the ocean depths to drag that stinking ship to its grave!

The mine itself was situated where the land started flattening out into farmland a hundred feet or so below the highest point of immense cliffs. The few grim buildings and chimneys on the surface gave little clue to the sheer vastness and depth of the mine lying far beneath the surface. Some of the underground tunnels, particularly those that reached the location of the whispering pearls, were said to go out under the very seabed itself. Of course, since the discovery of those perilous pearls only the penitents and the cloaked figures of the Speris still got to travel into those remote parts of the mine. This, so the Speris informed them, was to protect the town's residents from the pearls and their dangerous, even deadly, influences.

As expected, the three of them were among the first of the miners to reach the southern cage doors. On one side four juvenile pit hogs strained in visible discomfort as they toiled to shift the great iron-bound oak beams of the winch which was used to raise and lower the cage. Every so often one would squeal in pain and fright as the crack of a heavy whip bit into its flesh from the muscled handler standing over them. As the miners started filling the chamber Blue almost wished the handlers would whip the hogs a little harder. She desperately wanted to avoid conversation with any of the miners. Above all, she wanted to avoid any unnecessary encounters with the bosses. Gods how she hoped Eofor had paid for their lodgings this month. The lift cage seemed to be taking an interminably long time to arrive. Suddenly Blue's heart began to race. At the back of the chamber, one of the mine bosses had walked in and appeared to be scouring the chamber with his eyes as if he were looking for someone. The fact his eyes seemed to stop whenever he caught sight of a shaft rat only made her fears worse and she tried desperately to conceal herself behind Algar's broad back. Peeking out from behind the miner Blue noticed the boss had entered with two other men. One of the men had a full and angry red face, though she couldn't be sure whether its colour was from the man's ill-humour or from drink. The other man, though much younger, was taller, burlier and appeared to be wearing some kind of scaled armour which every now and then would catch the light of the oil lamps from under his heavy shirt. The man was clearly a warrior of some sort. In the presence of these two mysterious strangers, Blue noted with unease, the usually bullying and belligerent mine boss seemed uncharacteristically cowed and almost painfully courteous.

Before Blue could observe the men any longer the tell-tale grating sound of the lift cage arriving caused a sudden press of bodies at the cage doors. Ælf instinctively put an arm out to protect her and steered Blue into the back corner of the cage. Blue waited anxiously as the cage filled up, then, as the last miners shuffled in, to her relief the cage doors slid closed and with a loud cracking of the whip and squeals from the pit hogs they began their long descent deep into the earth.

Blue made a final inspection of the wall of sombre faces in the cage in case the boss and his strange guests had somehow slipped in unnoticed. Only when Blue had convinced herself that they definitely weren't there was she able to relax enough to be able to turn her back on the occupants and let her gaze rest lazily on the moving wall of the shaft. The upward motion of the wall combined with the rushing sound of the air being forced down the shaft from the great wheeling blades of the fan far above them was quite soothing and she quickly found herself settling into a trancelike state. Indeed, the sound of the air rushing by appeared to take on a strange resonating quality as if it were echoing deep within her mind. Suddenly, Blue felt a lurching sensation in her gut. Was the lift cage falling? She gripped at the bars of the cage and looked quickly at the faces around her but they remained as expressionless as at the start of their descent. What was wrong with her? Her heart was pounding in her chest. She closed her eyes and tried to control her breathing, hoping that by blocking out the falling motion of the cage she might be able to calm herself down. What the bloody hell was wrong with her? The noise of air being driven down the lift shaft started to be drowned out by an even greater rushing sound in her head as an overwhelming sensation of disorientation gripped her. She fought the temptation to throw herself to the floor of the cage and gripped onto the cage wall even tighter.

'Is thee all right Blue?' came a kindly voice and she felt a hand placed on her shoulder. Almost immediately the awful sensation subsided. It was Ælfweard. 'Is thee feeling ill? Tha looks worse than a mouldy turnip.'

'No. No, I'm fine. Thanks,' said Blue quickly recovering her composure enough to glower back at the shaft rat for his unflattering comment. 'Forgot to have any breakfast this morning. Must be hungrier than I thought.'

Ælf reached over and deftly undid the leather bag hanging from his father's shoulder and, without Algar noticing in the slightest, pulled out a hunk of bread and cheese which he quickly shoved into Blue's hand.

'Here. Take this,' he whispered. 'Fat old bugger eats too much anyway.' Smelling the bread and cheese made Blue realise just how hungry she was so, with a guilty look in Algar's direction, started cramming the food into her mouth as though she hadn't seen food for a week. 'That's right,' said Ælf with a wink. 'Get that down thee.' When Blue had finished eating, the shaft rat took a flask of water from his belt and insisted Blue drink some of that as well, only turning his back to face the cage doors once he was satisfied the colour had returned to her cheeks.

The rest of the descent seemed to take an eternity before the cage finally entered the familiar pillow of sticky, hot air that told Blue they were arriving at the lower end of the shaft. The miners too sensed it and started readying themselves for the day's work. Instructions were called out and tools were checked before the cage finally came to a shuddering halt. Blue searched through the mass of moving bodies for the familiar tattooed arms and shock of black hair of her hammer, Caelin. She hadn't noticed him in the cage but he was a short man and she might have missed him. No. He'd missed the first cage. Damn it! That was so unlike him. Blue knew shaft rats were forbidden to enter the mining areas without their hammer, but she was so frightened of encountering the bosses that she decided she would just have to chance a beating and wait for him at the test shaft alone.

Looking for the right moment, Blue slipped alongside the back leg of one of the pit hogs as it followed submissively behind its handler, who strutted ahead of it like a cockerel leading an ox. Blue had never walked so close to a pit hog before and glanced nervously at the powerful muscles rippling under the thick leathery skin of the tree-trunk sized legs as they thudded down heavily beside her. She knew what she was doing was stupid. One sudden sideways movement and she would be crushed into the tunnel wall without the pit hog or handler even realising she'd ever been there. This particular hog was clearly a veteran of the mine and the thick wiry hairs that usually covered its body had been completely scorched from the backs of its legs. Its hide too was a mass of pitted scars from the years of cruel whippings it had endured. To her surprise, Blue felt tears of pity come to her eyes as she looked at the poor, miserable thing. How could so powerful a creature be so oblivious to its own strength? A hundred handlers couldn't have stopped it had it a mind to leave that horrible place. Sadly, Blue knew that rebellious pit hogs were almost as rare as whispering pearls.

All of a sudden Blue found herself with an irresistible urge to reach out and touch the animal. Whatever possessed her to do what she did next, she would never truly comprehend. Perhaps she wanted to try to give comfort to the poor creature? Perhaps she merely needed to touch a living being whose suffering was greater than her own? Whatever her reason, no sooner had Blue's hand stroked down the flank of the animal than the creature squealed in fright and reared sideways, slamming Blue towards the tunnel wall. In that split second Blue managed to curse her incredible stupidity and awaited the bone-crunching impact… but it never came. Instead, Blue found herself hurtling through the air and then falling, sliding, and rolling until, with a painful thump that knocked all the air out of her lungs, she landed in an untidy heap… in total blackness.

One of the first things Blue had learnt when she began working in the mine was that there were two types of darkness. What most people referred to as darkness was not really darkness at all. It was merely low light that if you waited and strained your eyes hard enough you would eventually see at least the dim outlines of the immediate world around you. In absolute darkness, like the total blackness in which Blue now found herself, all those familiar shapes and references to the daytime world have gone. There were no shadows. There was nothing to distract Blue from her total isolation except the sound of her own breathing. After a while such blackness ceases to be empty space; it takes on substance; it acquires weight.

Blue reached out with her hand and with outstretched fingers felt nothing but the wall of emptiness in front of her. She wasn't surprised some people became hysterical in the dark. It wouldn't be hard to imagine spectral hands reaching out and grasping her fingers… or were they? Blue snatched her hand back quickly and nervously rubbed her fingers. *Stupid girl*, she thought. It was just her imagination. Perhaps if she waited for her eyes to adjust, she might be able to make out the distant glow from the tunnel she had been flung from? She waited. She waited some more. Nothing. Even the faint squeals and yells from the pit hog and its handler had faded and were now completely gone. She could see nothing. She could hear nothing. She daren't even shout out for surely that would bring her straight to the attention of the bosses. She was alone… and growing very afraid.

Blue didn't know how long she'd been fumbling about in the pitch blackness before her eyes again began playing tricks on her. It was as if at times the blackness wasn't empty at all but churned with formless shapes that floated into the periphery of her vision, only to fade like a dying flame the second she tried to focus her eyes upon them. At times the air surrounding her seemed to take on a faint blue or sometimes even golden hue which would almost immediately fade to black the second she shifted her weight or breathed a little too heavily. It reminded her of a nervous wild animal driven by curiosity to investigate a strange new creature, but the slightest movement or sound would send it scurrying for safety.

She was just beginning to lose some of her fear and almost get used to the experience when, almost inaudibly, a faint sound began. She strained her ears to try to catch where the noise was coming from but struggled to identify any specific direction for its source. It was as if it was coming from the very earth itself. Steadily the noise continued to grow stronger until it felt like a storm was raging through her skull. Blue threw her hands to her head and rocked herself back and forth. What the hell was happening? First in the lift cage and now here. Was she ill? Was she going insane? Suddenly a feeling of terror gripped her as from out of the darkness a spectral grey hand emerged and clasped itself about one of her own. As it did, a dreadful sense of being slowly uprooted from the earth overcame her, like a child torn from its womb. Blue screamed but as fast as it had appeared the hand withdrew leaving something gripped in her hand that flickered with a faint golden light through the gaps in her fingers. She opened her fingers and gasped.

Hard, cold and beautiful beyond description, Blue looked in stunned silence at the perfectly formed whispering pearl gleaming in her open palm.

For a while, time ceased to matter. In fact, nothing mattered to Blue; just delicate swirls of shimmering fire. Blue could only stare in disbelief and wonder at what she had been given. Tilting it one way and then another she watched spellbound at the play of light coming from the pearl's surface. No, not just the surface, there was a depth to it too. It was as if the light and beauty in the pearl responded to her gaze; as if it was reaching out to be held and admired. And yet it wasn't just a physical beauty that she saw. She could feel it too. She could feel it coming from within the pearl and pulsating outwards. She could feel it pulsating through the earth; through the rock around her; through the air she breathed; she could feel it pulsating through her very body and soul.

Strangest of all was her sudden knowledge of and connection to her surroundings. Blue knew she was in a natural fissure between many layers of rock. She also knew instinctively which way she would need to climb to get back to the mine tunnel. Stranger still, she even had a sense of the ancient life of each of the layers of rock and crystal minerals around her. She could sense that the rock upon which she sat had once formed at the bottom of a warm sea. Blue found she could even close her eyes and see and feel the passage of time in the rock, feel how the sun slowly baked and evaporated the sea, first into steamy lagoons and then slowly, turning to desert. She saw strange creatures stubbornly wallowing in the last of the evaporating waters, biting and fighting over their ever-diminishing territories. Then the skies cooled and the forests appeared. Great trees, soaring higher and broader than anything she could imagine as life, colour and sound burst all around. And then a hush descended—as if all life held its breath to listen to just one, tiny noise. A single soft step at the forest's edge. The step of a human child.

A noise brought Blue back to her surroundings; it was the distinctive sound of men's voices. She had better get back.

Blue slipped the whispering pearl into the pocket on the front of her tunic and felt her way back up and along the fissure until she could see the pale glow of the mine tunnel ahead of her. The sound of voices in the tunnel caused her to stop a few feet from the mouth of the fissure. A man

49

was talking angrily with at least one other just a few feet from the opening in the rock. She crept slowly to the edge and carefully peered out. Her heart almost leapt into her mouth. There stood the mine boss with the two mysterious visitors. Blue darted her head back into the shadows of the fissure and was about to scramble back down into the sanctuary of the blackness from where she had just escaped when curiosity got the better of her. Striving to hear above the pounding of her heart she leant forward as far as she dared and listened.

'It's no blasted business of yours why I need so many of your miners anyway! All I want to know is when will I get the three half-decent shaft rats you promised me? So far you've only given me one!' Blue guessed the voice belonged to the red-faced man.

'You'll have them both soon I promise,' answered the mine boss. 'The lad's father will be going out soon. The second the boy's alone they'll have him. The girl's proving to be more of a problem. We can't find her. If you're in a hurry why not take some of the penitents instead? You could take as many as you like.'

'Don't treat me like a fool.' The man hissed. 'Do you really think I want the Speris breathing down my neck? Besides, you know damned well the penitents are nothing but skin and bone. Have you forgotten what the Speris are like? They'd never survive the crossing. No. I want the ones we agreed on.'

'Just make sure your herders don't get carried away with the boy's father. I can't afford to risk losing both the boy *and* the father. They're the best two we got. Just so you know Caronte, I don't like your methods.'

'I don't pay you to like them,' the voice snarled. 'Of course, if you have a problem, you could always take the boy's place yourself. A good man like you would always be welcome on my little ship.'

'No Captain,' said the mine boss quickly, 'of course there's no problem. You can have your miners. Just please finish your business quickly and leave.'

'If you could actually find the damned girl then maybe we would leave!'

'I assure you, Captain, we are looking everywhere. We've searched the mine from top to bottom. She isn't here. She probably panicked after finding what your herders did to the old man. You needn't worry though, she won't stay hidden for long.'

'She had better turn up soon or I swear it'll be you who finds yourself chained in the hold of my ship! Come on, let's go. We're wasting our time down here.'

Blue listened in horror as the men departed. The two strangers had definitely come from the black ship. She could also now be certain it had been the ship's herders who had killed poor old Eofor. Poor, helpless old Eofor. What had he ever done to deserve such an end? Eofor wasn't capable of hurting anyone. Well, except himself of course, but why hurt an old man? Was it because of her? She was probably the most experienced of the shaft rats but she was also famous for being outspoken, mischievous and, when she'd had enough of working, downright lazy. The mine bosses had probably talked up her worth just to be rid of her. But who was the boy? Suddenly Blue knew exactly who it was they had been talking about. It was Ælfweard. The boy they were talking about just had to be him. He was by far the best of the shaft rats. Algar and Ælf's strength and speed at digging the test tunnels was almost legendary. Oh Gods, how was she going to get out of the mine and warn Algar and his son? If only she could get to the lift cages without being spotted. She waited until the noise from the men's footsteps had faded before summoning the courage to peer out into the tunnel again. It was empty.

Blue slid out of the entrance to the fissure and began to edge as quietly as she could along the wall of the tunnel, trying to keep as much in the shadows as possible. Occasionally the light of a lantern would catch the crystals in the rock and send a shower of tiny stars skimming across the surface of the tunnel wall. Despite its entrancing effect, Blue felt horribly exposed and vulnerable whenever she had to pass through these unwelcome patches of light. Nevertheless, she was starting to grow equally concerned at the number of lanterns she had passed that weren't lit. A closer inspection of the next lantern confirmed her worst suspicions. The well of oil under it had burnt itself out. She checked the next. The same. This, and the all-pervading silence, could mean only one thing. The shifts had all finished. The last of the miners had gone home. She was alone.

How could she have been stuck down the fissure for so long without realising it? It didn't make any sense. More importantly how on earth was she ever going to get out? If she waited until morning for the first shifts to begin it would be too late. Ælf and the other shaft rat would already have been taken aboard that accursed ship and who knows what the herders would have done with Algar? Panic gripped Blue and she started to run towards the chamber of the lift cage. As expected, the chamber was as empty as the tunnel and the cage had gone. If Captain Caronte and his men were the last to leave the mine then the hog handlers at the surface would have also left—and even if they were still there who was to say that Caronte and his men weren't still loitering at the surface? What should she do? Should she risk being caught and handing Ælf and herself to Captain Caronte, or should she wait and risk losing any chance of warning Ælf or getting out of the mine until the morning? No, she'd have to risk it. She was Ælf and Algar's only hope... and time was running out.

Blue placed her hands as high up on the leather binding around the end of the rope as she could and tugged with all her might. At first, she thought the rope wasn't going to budge, then, slowly, it began to drop down steadily before suddenly lifting up again. Timing her momentum perfectly Blue began to spring up and down on the rope. Surely the bell would now be ringing loudly on the surface. Yet the heavy chains of the cage failed to move. Blue tried again, this time pulling the rope harder and longer. It was no good. If the hog handlers had still been there, they would have heard her by now and would have sent the cage down. It was pointless continuing. There was only one other option left open to Blue: the cage at the eastern face.

Blue had almost blocked this option from her mind altogether, so reluctant was she to enter the deepest area of the mine now controlled by the Speris. At least she could console herself with the thought that if they were still there, she had the advantage that they wouldn't know who she was. Perhaps she could convince them that she had got lost and had managed to miss the last cage? Better still, she might even find the cage unattended and could slip out of the mine unnoticed? It had been a long time since Blue had visited the eastern face of the mine and she hoped she could still find her way there. Even if she couldn't there were no other options left open to her. She had to try.

Half running, half stumbling Blue made her way through the maze of tunnels and chambers as best she could. At times she found herself plunged into total darkness and had to feel and scrape her way along the tunnel walls. At one point she even had to wade waist deep through icy waters that were so salty they burned the skin of her legs raw. Thankfully, besides the flooding, the route had changed little and Blue soon began to hear the faint clamour of activity in the distance. Good, she thought, if work was still going on in that part of the mine, then they would have to still be operating the cage. All she had to do now was to try to get into the cage without getting noticed.

By following the sounds of activity, heat and the growing stench of burning oil, Blue finally arrived at the eastern face. Nothing, however, had prepared her for the hellish scene that unfolded before her eyes. Pale silhouettes of what once must have been men, women and children, their will and spirit completely broken, staggered and crawled under crippling loads across a vast underground cavern. From smoky black tunnels that peppered the cavern walls Blue could hear the sharp clang of iron striking rock and the tormented squeals of pit hogs… Blue shuddered. There were human screams as well.

On the far side, a huge iron crusher slammed down every few minutes sending shards of rock and dust flying into the air. The rubble and dust that remained was then frantically shovelled and swept into baskets and dragged away by emaciated figures across to a huge furnace that belched great gobs of fire and molten rock into the atmosphere every time a load of crushed rock was thrown into it. On one occasion, as if totally out of keeping with the scene, an almost hypnotically beautiful cloud of pearly golden flame rose from the furnace like a phoenix taking wing. Blue instantly knew what was happening. They were destroying the whispering pearls. What chilled her the most about what she saw was that, although the miserable workers' visible terror of the robed Speris standing over them could almost be smelt in the stifling smoky air, the Speris did nothing to earn such fearful obedience. Not a whipping, beating nor even harsh word was given.

Not far below from where she was hiding, Blue noticed a worker who had been slowly wheeling one of the fire wagons towards one of the tunnels collapse to the floor. On his face was a look of total defeat. Noticing the lack of movement from the wagon one of the Speris silently approached the man. The Speris reached where the man lay and, placing a hand almost tenderly on the back of the man's thin neck, seemed to whisper in the man's ear. The man just shook his head and started to weep uncontrollably. By now another Speris had noticed the worker and also moved quietly to the man's side. This Speris also placed a comforting hand on the man, this time on his shaking shoulder. The two Speris briefly shared a look and then, with a flash of steel so fast Blue almost missed it, the first Speris sank a needle-like blade into the man's body. At first, seeing the man's body immediately go relaxed, Blue thought the worker had died instantly. But then an inhuman and horrific scream began to emit from his motionless lips. His eyes too, wide open in sheer terror, still moved wildly in their sockets even though the rest of his body remained perfectly still, as if paralysed. As silently as they had arrived the Speris lifted the man onto a nearby wooden cart and gently wheeled him out of the cavernous chamber. It was then that Blue noticed there were more of the same wooden carts positioned strategically around the cavern. She felt an intense nausea overcome her and retched violently. Recovering momentarily, she looked up, petrified the noise of her retching had drawn attention to herself. None of the Speris appeared to have noticed.

Taking a step backwards, Blue was about to turn and take flight from that repugnant place when an ice-cold, iron-like grip closed around her arm. She shrieked in fright and looked straight up into the large, black eyes of a Speris.

'Um, please. I... I'm so sorry. I seem to have got lost. I was wondering if I might use your lift cage to get back to the surface?' The Speris gave her a silky smile and nodded as if sympathising with her plight, but his icy hand remained vice-like around her arm.

'Really, this is just a silly mistake,' she said finding herself being guided painfully down onto the mine floor and towards the hot furnaces until they stood before a Speris dressed in robes of a much finer cloth. Where the robes parted above his chest Blue could make out the top of a circle of white flames surrounding a black disc, yet rather than being tattooed onto his skin like the tattoos of her hammer, Caelin, the white flames on this Speris' skin flickered and burned as if alive. Blue had heard of the deadly Atoshai who bore the black sun on their chests, but only one of them bore a black sun with living flames. Few had ever seen him and even fewer returned to tell the tale. Those that did return brought with them chilling tales of witchcraft and sacrifice.

The Speris holding Blue bowed his head low. Blue did the same but the grip tightened on her arm until she was forced into a kneeling position.

'Please, your… Righteousness,' she said with her head bowed almost to the floor, 'I work in the ash mines at the western face and foolishly let myself get left behind. All I want to do is get back to the surface and go home. My poor old mother must be sick with worry by now. You see I am all she has in this world.' Blue marvelled at her ability to lie after all she had witnessed. The Atoshai Master watched her quietly, as if giving her words careful consideration, then pointed with a long, pale finger to an area behind them. Her heart lifted. Perhaps he was directing her towards the lift cage? She turned her head and felt her body go cold. Directly behind them lay the unmanned fire wagon where she had witnessed the worker collapse. Blue fought the temptation to beg for mercy. She'd learnt enough about the Speris to know that any open displays of emotional weakness or sentimentality were abhorrent to them. She wanted to scream her frustration but knew if there was any hope left for herself or Ælf she would have to maintain a semblance of control.

The Atoshai Master watched with his hands folded across his chest as Blue was taken to the fire wagon, but when she and the other Speris reached it, the Master suddenly spun about on his heels and hurried to the lift cage as if the devil itself were in pursuit.

Blue glanced back to watch the lift cage depart without her and felt the tears of anguish and desperation welling up inside. Whatever had she done to deserve so cruel a fate? As hard as she struggled to choke back the tears that were fighting to break free, she couldn't help but allow a small whimper to escape from her lips. Suddenly the Speris' face contorted into a furious snarl and Blue found her face ground painfully into the floor. The force of the Speris' hand pressing down on her skull caused the abrasive rock to cut into her mouth and gums. She could feel herself shaking with fear.

'Please,' she said as steadily as she could through bleeding teeth and lips. 'Thank you. Thank you for this blessing a-and opportunity for salvation.' The hand on the back of her head relaxed and she was pulled off the ground and set back on her feet. Blue was hardly a stranger to hardship, but already she could feel her will crumbling.

Blue was still trembling when the Speris tied her left wrist to the back of the fire wagon and indicated the direction she was to follow. They were heading out into the remotest area of the mine — the area that lay under the very seabed itself.

Pushing the clumsy fire wagon along the uneven surface of the tunnel was a backbreaking task. At one point, unable to continue without a rest, Blue collapsed to her knees. This time the Speris didn't pull her up but knelt down beside her, placing a soft hand on the back of her neck. His face was so close to hers she could hear the breath whistling between his gritted teeth. Through his velvet touch, Blue could almost feel the needle-like blade sinking into her flesh. Finding a reserve of strength, she barely knew she had, Blue heaved herself back onto shaking legs and, grasping the hot handles of the wagon, began to drive one foot after the other. Before long each step was agony and sweat poured from every pore in her body. She could feel her strength fading fast and wondered how much longer she could go on? If only she could rest for a moment but she dared not stop, not even for a second, for the vision of what had happened to the wagon's previous owner kept haunting her every step.

Just when Blue thought she'd finally reached the limits of her endurance she felt the Speris' long fingers pulling her to a stop. They had arrived at the rock face.

Untying her wrist from the wagon, the Speris directed her to sit to one side. Suspecting this as part of some sick sort of game, Blue flopped warily against the wall and tried to take in her surroundings. In front of her was one of the oldest pit hogs she'd ever seen. Its dry, wrinkled hide was so cracked and scarred that it looked more like the bark of the wind-toppled oak that clung to life on the crown of the hill above Stod; a tree that had survived half a millennium of lashings by bitter coastal gales bearing salt spray, and mine grit. By the pit hog's side stood a desolate assembly of ashen-faced penitents who watched the two new arrivals with a depressing and morose air. Blue watched as the Speris eagerly primed the fire wagon for use and wondered why she'd been allowed this moment of respite. The last thing she expected from a Speris was charity. It was then Blue saw the feral look in the Speris' eyes and the tremble of excitement on his moist, thin lips. She shifted uncomfortably against the wall. She didn't like it. There was something distinctly perverse and unsettling in the Speris' behaviour.

An impatient glare from the Speris sent the penitents dashing about like frightened mice to ready the pit hog for work. Blue watched them nervously as they struggled to pull, cajole and, after a hog driver's heavy whip was produced, finally whip the pit hog into position. She looked across at the entrance to the tunnel leading back to the furnace chamber. What was she to do? She could try making a run for the cage, after all the Speris seemed completely absorbed in what he was doing. Carefully she tried standing up, but her legs still felt like jelly. She cursed. She would never be able to outrun the Speris in such a state.

With a sweep of his hand, the Speris sent the penitents scattering in all directions to get out of the way and edged the fire wagon closer. Just as the pit hog began to sense the growing intensity of heat, behind it an eruption of flames burst from the mouth of the fire wagon and enveloped the rear half of the creature in burning oil. The huge beast squealed in agony and threw itself at the rock face in terror.

'You're too close,' shouted Blue alarmed that he was going to roast the hog alive. The Speris gave a twitching half smile and, instead of pulling the wagon back, moved it even closer. A second blast of fire shot from its mouth. This time the poor creature found itself completely enveloped in searing flames. Now out of its wits in pain and terror, the pit hog tripled its efforts to flee and began heaving great sods of rocky debris and dust into the chamber behind it.

In spite of the rain of deadly hail, the penitents dashed back and forth in front of the wagon to clear a path. With the way clear the penitents scurried for the safety of the walls but just as the last of them was about to leap out of the way, a heap of rock came flying back and sent the man crashing to the floor. Raising a rapturous smile to the heavens, the Speris lifted his arms over the fallen man as if administering a blessing. Then, as if to punctuate his action, sent another massive burst of fire shooting from the wagon's mouth. This time not only was the pit hog enveloped in flames, but also the penitent who shrieked as a spasm of agony gripped him on the floor. The air around Blue filled with the stench of burning flesh.

'Stop!' screamed Blue. 'You're insane! Please stop!' Again, the Speris ignored her and, as if heartened by the screams of the penitent, swiftly readied the fire wagon for another blast. 'Do something!' Blue pleaded desperately with the others. They were too petrified to move and could only stare in open-mouthed horror as their companion lay writhing on the floor.

Unable to sit by and do nothing any longer, Blue launched herself at the Speris, her fists flailing wildly at his body and face. Barely flinching, the Speris swatted the small girl off him, shoving her away so hard that she crashed painfully onto the floor. Ignoring the pain, Blue leapt once more to her feet and threw herself at him with all her might, yet again the Speris shrugged off her attack and effortlessly flung her to the floor.

With a mouth filled with blood and dirt, Blue realised she still had the small knife Eofor had given her. She reached into her pocket and grasped the cold, hard handle, pulling it out to brandish it in front of her. This time she succeeded in getting the Speris' attention. Letting go of the fire wagon the Speris stepped back and fixed her hand with his black gaze. He looked terrified yet she hadn't even had time to open the blade. Blue looked down at her hand. It was completely wrapped in flames which were rapidly travelling up the length of her arm. Yet these were not the smoky, dull orange flames of the oil, but bright, vivid flames of gold laced with every colour and hue imaginable, all of which now swirled about her arm and shoulder as if caressing her flesh. Blue immediately realised her mistake. She hadn't pulled out the knife. She had pulled out the whispering pearl.

Feeling strangely at ease Blue watched as the beautiful flames continued to travel up the full length of her arm and then begin to spread across her shoulder and chest. As they reached her heart the fire intensified, quickly enveloping her entire body until she stood there burning like the dawn star.

Blue looked around at the astonished faces staring at her. How beautiful they looked. She felt a remarkable serenity descend upon her like a soft blanket. Walking over, Blue reached across and pulled the lever to shut the fire wagon down. She then walked calmly past the now petrified Speris and clambered over the piles of rubble to stand alongside the pit hog which had fallen quivering to the floor of its newly excavated tunnel. She knew exactly what had to be done. Stretching up, Blue placed a flaming hand on the scorched and blistered hide of the traumatised creature. The flames instantly began to spread out from her hand and soon covered the entire creature in the same golden light that surrounded Blue. Only this time, as the fiery light engulfed it once more, the mammoth creature did not squeal or panic or throw itself in desperation at the layers of rock in front of it. Instead, it stopped shuddering, sucked in a huge breath of air, and lifted itself onto its charred and bleeding legs. The creature then did something that no pit hog had done before: it began to burrow upwards.

Blue turned and smiled sweetly at the Speris and the penitents. 'I have to go now,' she said as if all that had just occurred had been the most natural thing in the world. 'You can come too if you want.' At first none of the penitents moved, then, one after the other a small group formed beside her. Those that remained dropped gratefully to the floor and fell into a peaceful state almost as if they were readying themselves for a long sleep.

'Well, goodbye,' Blue said and, indicating for the remaining penitents to follow, turned and headed back up the narrow tunnel. The Speris, still in a state of shock, made no attempt to stop her. Instead, he began to watch the slowly disappearing pit hog with an ever-increasing look of concern as if there was something he ought to remember but couldn't quite recollect what it was. Suddenly panic registered across his face and he gestured wildly for the remaining penitents to go after the creature. None of them moved. Instead, one after the other each of the penitents looked up at the glorious clouds of debris and rubble coming tumbling out of the newly dug shaft and smiled. They already knew where the pit hog was headed. It was headed towards the bed of the sea.

When Blue reached the lift cage, she looked around her. A considerably larger group of penitents than the original few who had left the mine tunnel now gathered before her. All were looking at the girl expectantly. Still glowing like the dawn, Blue walked over to two Speris who were standing nearby. Their black eyes widened and their thin lips pulled back from their white teeth in terror as the flaming girl approached them.

'I have need of your robes,' Blue said with a sympathetic look. The two Speris, without question or hesitation, removed their robes and almost threw them at her, then stood gawping at Blue with fear-stricken expressions on their faces. They were clearly oblivious to the fact that they were still half naked. If it hadn't been for the long needle-like daggers strapped across their chests the penitents watching might even have been tempted to burst out laughing. Blue thanked them then returned to the group with the robes. 'Put these on,' she instructed the two tallest members of the group. 'You must take the others to the surface. When you arrive, look at and speak to no one. Leave the mine by the north road and continue until you reach the fifth village. Only once you are in sight of the threshing barn there should you remove and hide these robes. The people of this village will help you. Do not wait for me. I have a different path to follow. Go now.' The two men nodded and put on their disguises, then began guiding the rest of the penitents into the cage. Once all were safely in, Blue tugged on the rope to alert the handler at the surface to begin raising the cage. The noise of grinding and clanking metal filled the chamber and both cage and penitents lifted into the air.

Blue wasn't sure at what point it began dawning on her where she was and how she had got to the cage. What she did know was that if she didn't get out of the mine immediately not only would Ælf and the other shaft rats have absolutely no chance of escaping the herders, if indeed it wasn't already too late, but she was going to drown. She looked at the cold, round pearl in her hand. It had become quite dull and lifeless. She put it into her tunic pocket and looked around. Where were all the Speris? She had a vague recollection of most of them fleeing the chamber shortly after the penitents had left, but a dull cracking sound quickly brought Blue's mind back to her immediate predicament. Yanking hard on the rope, Blue set the lift once more into motion. In the distance, the muted roar of rushing water could be heard coming from the depths of the mine.

Blue knew the sound could mean only one thing. The seabed had been breached.

It seemed an eternity before the lift cage appeared. Already the sea had started pouring across the chamber floor, threatening to rise up and engulf her at any point, but instead of greeting the lift's appearance with a huge sense of relief, Blue watched it descend from the ceiling with a sense of foreboding. Inside, the chilling outline of three robed Speris could clearly be made out. Furthermore, the flicker of white flames beneath one of the Speris' robes left Blue in no doubt that the Atoshai Master was amongst them. Blue knew she would have to think quickly. She looked back down towards the tunnels that led to the western face, but the fast-rising water had cut them off completely. It looked like the only way she was going to get out alive was at the mercy of the Speris… but Speris never showed mercy. What was she to do? It was then that Blue had an idea. Many times, had Blue witnessed miners being rushed to the surface with injuries, but it was always preceded by three sharp tugs on a second bell rope to signal a miner had been hurt. She doubted the Speris were aware of the emergency signal, but the hog driver operating the winch would know it for sure. She just prayed the emergency bell rope was still working. Knowing her timing would have to be perfect, Blue waited until the very last moment before giving three sharp tugs on the rope. It worked! The cage slowed and came to a stop just inches short of touching the ground and, more importantly, just before the cage dropped clear of the frame preventing the doors to be swung open. Before the Speris could figure out what was happening, Blue leapt onto the frame and just managed to scramble onto the cage roof before it began to return to the surface. Beneath her she could hear the sound of three cold blades being drawn.

A thud sounded beneath her. She looked down in time to see a stiletto blade being pulled free of the wooden panelling only millimetres from her foot. Grabbing onto the lift chain Blue hoisted herself clear of the roof just in time before two more blades came biting through the wood where she had just been standing. She looked up. The light from the surface appeared as little more than a star-sized speck above her. Below, the unmistakable surge of water could be heard rapidly getting louder. Surely the waters couldn't reach them this high? Whether they could or not, Blue knew she had to climb. If she were to have any chance of getting out of the mine alive, she was going to have to put as much distance between herself and the murderous Speris as possible. Link by link, throwing one hand over the other, Blue began to pull herself upwards. The grease on the chain and the occasional shudder hardly made the climb easy, but Blue soon managed to put a clear gap between herself and the cage. From below she could hear strange mutterings rising up the lift shaft, the words hovering about her ears like night moths. She could feel herself wanting to let go, wanting to surrender to the dictating pull of darkness rising beneath her, but just as Blue felt her fingers begin to loosen their grip, the light of the whispering pearl flared up and washed over her like a shock of cold water on a fevered brow. Blue gasped and hugged herself to the chain. How close had she come to falling? With renewed vigour, Blue began to climb with a greater urgency, desperately trying not to think how close she had come to death as she fought to block out the dark mutterings beneath her.

Suddenly sounds of panic from the cage below replaced the dark, mesmeric chant of the Speris. Almost too afraid to look, Blue ventured a glance down only to see the waters had reached the bottom of the cage and were being forced up the lift shaft faster than the cage was rising.

With a massive effort, Blue began hauling herself up the juddering chain as fast as her tired limbs would allow. Below her the sounds of panic grew... and then silence. Blue didn't need to look down to know what had happened. She could feel the cold spray of saltwater already licking at the backs of her bare ankles.

'Just keep climbing,' she said gritting her teeth, trying to think only of the point of light above her. Passing one hand over the other and only daring to look up, Blue managed just to keep pace with the rising water, but her limbs were tired and she could feel her pace slowing.

'Keep pushing,' she urged herself, but just when she thought she might make it, a surge of seawater rushed over her, the force and cold of which almost tore her hands from the chain. With lungs burning, somehow Blue held on until a faint glow illuminated the murky space around her and she felt herself being lifted clear of the water's freezing embrace. She gasped, gratefully filling her lungs with air, and looked down. Seawater was spewing out of the mouth of the shaft and was spreading across the surface chamber's floor. Flabbergasted, the hog driver hit the release lever for the squealing pit hogs and fled the chamber with them thundering behind him.

Not wasting a moment longer, Blue leapt for all she was worth and landed with a splash just clear of the shaft mouth. Barely managing to keep her head above the swirling waters, she let the powerful current carry her out of the chamber and into the welcome light of the setting sun. With barely enough strength to drag herself clear of the muddy lake forming beyond the mine's entrance, Blue managed to half-swim, half-crawl her way onto dry land. There, exhausted and shivering with cold, Blue lay gasping for air like a beached herring. Every part of her body and limbs burned from the climb, but she knew she couldn't lay there for long. She still had to warn Ælf.

Deliberately avoiding the path, Blue clambered and slid her tired body down the least steep section of cliff she could find, searching amongst the cottages below for the mottled frames of Algar's cottage windows. She knew it would be too risky approaching the cottage from the front, for she was certain Caronte's men, or worse, could be watching, but she might be able to sneak in by way of Algar's kitchen. She soon found it, nestled amongst the older houses at the lower end of the harbour. She knew them so well she could even name each one: Mizpah, Shangri-la, Blue Jacket, Venus, Singing Waters, Alma... Old Eofor had once told her they had all been named after their owners' boats.

Pausing briefly, Blue checked no one was loitering in the street opposite. Seeing nothing, she descended to the rear of the cottage and peered in through the window. She could see the sooty copper pot Algar always used to brew cups of sweet tea was still bubbling away on the black iron stove. Reassured, Blue gently tugged the window open, wincing as rusty hinges protested being disturbed. She leant in, expecting the smell of fragrant tea, but instead an unfamiliar, inhuman stench hit her nostrils. Instantly Blue knew something was wrong but before she could react, large hands seized hold of her and tore her violently through the opening into the room. She squirmed and tried to scream as sharp claws punctured into the skin of her arm and neck, but before she could utter a sound a leather pouch was pressed against her mouth. An acrid odour filled her nostrils and mouth bringing tears to her eyes. Desperately she tried to shake herself free of the cloying scent, but whatever had hold of her was far too strong and kept the bag pressed tightly to her face. She felt so tired. So, so tired. Why was she struggling? She couldn't quite remember. She just wanted to sleep. Blue felt her eyes closing.

'Ooh look,' said a rough voice. 'A little mouse for Basax's dinner!' The sound of harsh, guttural laughter faded into silence as she sank into a deep slumber.

CHAPTER 4

Blue felt pain… or was it just a memory of pain? She tried to locate the source with her hand but could barely lift it off the wooden boards beneath her. She could hear laboured breathing nearby but was unable to turn her head to see who or what it was. Even her eyelids kept falling shut before she was able to make sense of the blurry shadows in front of her. Was this a room or a cage? Was that water on the floor… or blood? Questions formed in her mind but refused to linger for more than an instant, slipping away into unreachable depths before she could offer any attempt at an answer. Strange forms and figures would slide from her dreams into consciousness and back into dream… or was she conscious? And then there was the boy. There was always the boy. His searching eyes, his voice calling out to her, never letting her rest, never letting her sleep. What did he want? Why wouldn't he let her sleep? And then the fever would return, and the other dreams would come again. The strange, strange dreams: the charging bull; the lions being swallowed by the storm; the eagle feeding its brood; the child with the face like the sun… which grew brighter… and brighter…

'That's it. Hold the lantern close to her face. Let's see her eyes.' Blue felt her eyelids prised open and light flooded in. She tried throwing her head to one side to escape the painful glare but she was so numb she couldn't move a muscle. She couldn't even shut her eyes as whoever had hold of her eyelids wasn't letting go.

'Well, there's life in there all right but it's not gonna be enough. She's been out nearly four days already. She ain't gonna last. Seen 'em like this a hunerd times. They 'as too much of that grass and they can't wakes up.' The man let go of Blue's eyelids and lowered his voice to a whisper. 'Caronte's letting the herders up later tonight. They's done with waiting. The ones who can't wakes up they's taking.'

'Tonight! That'll only leave one shaft rat. That Magor ain't gonna be happy.'

'Ain't my fault. He can go complain to the bleedin herders if he dares. It's them that's to blame, not me.'

'What they gonna do with 'em both?'

'What do you think? The herders says they throws 'em overboard, but really they eats 'em. They eats all the ones that dun't wakes up. They's already 'ad one of the miners, but they prefers the little'uns. It's part of the deal they 'as with Caronte. Keeps 'em quiet. They eats and they goes to sleep see. If their bellies are full, they can sleep for days. Keeps 'em out of the way of the crew. Caronte don't like 'em mixing topside too much anyway. Always causing trouble they is. They leaves them bags of kamph grass on too long deliberately to be sure of getting a few good meals. Caronte dun't care, so long as he gets his gold when we gets to land.'

'What you done with the one who woke up?'

'Gave him a hiding and shoved him in the slave hold with the others. Little runt. Thought he could give me trouble he did. See how he likes our luxury lodgings. That oughta settle him. He'll think twice before he tries anything again. If he does, I'll shove him in the well with Magor's pet. I'd 'ave thrown him overboard but I'll not cross that witch. Got the captain wrapped round her little finger she 'as. Been keeping her greedy little eye on the young'uns. Reckon she wants 'em for herself. Already told the captain to give her the girl when she wakes up. What for I daren't ask. Probably gonna stick her in her pot. Makes me blood run cold she does. Well, the girl ain't waking up by the looks of things and there ain't nothing I can do about it.'

'So what do we do?'

'We'll take this one down to the herders. As good as dead anyway. They'll find the body when they wakes up. The more meals they gets now, the longer they takes to come up. Might give the other a chance to come round.'

What! What were they talking about? They couldn't take her! She was still alive! They'd just seen she was still alive! Blue strained every part of her body that still had any feeling left. She had to move. She had to show them she could move! She heard a chain being unlocked near her feet. She tried to shout for help, but the only sound she could make was a faint groan.

'Right, take the feet, I'll get the head.' Blue screamed, but again only a weak noise issued from her lips. She fought with every ounce of strength… and moved her head. She could move her head! Again, she strained every muscle she could and managed to tilt her head to one side—just enough to be able to see the men out of the corner of her eye. Why did they have their backs to her? What were they doing? Then she realised. They weren't taking her at all—they were taking the other shaft rat.

Blue watched helplessly as the limp body of the boy was lifted by the two men and carried past coils of thick rope, rigging and sailcloth. She was clearly in a ship's storage of some kind. The door closed leaving Blue no more than a thin line of pale light by which to see. The air was thick with the smell of tar and old rope.

Blue had known the boy they'd taken to the herders. His name was Gyd. His father had been killed in a rock fall only months earlier. Not long after the accident the mother's moods had become increasingly erratic and she had started to become, as many in the village described it, "careless of her charge". In fact, Gyd's behaviour had become so unmanageable there had been talk of him being taken away from her altogether and interned with the penitents. Before his father had died, like the rest of them, Gyd had hated the mine. But after his death he couldn't stand it. The only way he could cope with going back in was by going a little crazy, picking fights with anyone, no matter how much bigger than him they were. Blue and the rest of his friends all knew what the real problem was. He was terrified. The shaft rats and his hammer did all they could to calm him down. They'd even cover for him, hiding their scrapes, bites and bruises, but it wasn't long before his antics had started to attract the attention of the bosses. From that point on it was only a matter of time before he was taken away. The bosses must have conned Caronte into taking him. If Gyd wasn't eaten by the herders it wouldn't be long before they found out he was nothing but trouble anyway.

Blue gritted her teeth… and felt her hands clench into fists. Yes! That was it. She could feel the adrenaline from her frustration and anger begin to return the feeling to her limbs. Those sons of bitches! There was no way she was going to just lie there and wait to be eaten. She had to do something! Blue furiously clenched and unclenched her hands, mustering her strength, fighting to get her blood and adrenaline flowing. It was working! She could feel a tingling in her arms as well now. She tried to lift them… and managed it! But she was still dismally weak and could only hold them up for a second. Exhausted, Blue let them flop back onto the floorboards. They felt so heavy. She tried again but this time barely managed to lift them at all. A third attempt and they barely moved. It was no good. She had to rest. Perhaps if she just closed her eyes and waited for her strength to return, she could try again. Oh, but she was so tired. She let her heavy eyelids fall shut. Just a quick rest, she thought.

'Wake up!' Blue opened her eyes in fright and for a moment could have sworn she saw two dim eyes peering at her from the shadows. She blinked. There was nothing there. She must have imagined it. It didn't matter. She had to rest. Blue closed her eyes again. 'Please wake up!' Blue opened her eyes. This time there was no mistaking it. A pair of tired, grey eyes blinking at her from the shadows. Whoever they belonged to, began to edge closer until the faint outline of a face could be seen. That face. She knew that face! She could have sworn it was the boy from her dreams: the worn expression, the sad lines of his young cheekbones and jaw, all told the tale of a life much too hard for one so young. Was he a cabin boy? He didn't look like one. What was he doing here then? How could she even see him in this darkness? There was no light other than the thin line coming from the crack under the door. Perhaps it was a ghoul like the grey girl she had seen on the jetty? Yes, there was definitely an unusual quality to the light illuminating him. Yet Blue didn't feel afraid. His breathing was erratic though and his brow furrowed as if whatever he was doing was taking an immense amount of effort and concentration. He reached across and placed a dirty hand on her chest. She noticed the nails were cracked and the fingers bleeding. 'I will give you what strength I can, though my own is fading. It won't be long now before the rains come again.' Blue had no idea what rains he was talking about but straight away felt a strange current of energy begin spreading from his hands across her chest and body, lifting the heavy drowsiness from her head and limbs. 'Find your friend,' he said. 'They'll be waking soon. I have to go now.' As he spoke Blue noticed him becoming dimmer before her eyes. Even before he had finished the sentence all she could see were his tired, grey eyes framed against the darkness.

'Who are you?' she asked but the eyes faded completely into the shadows. 'Wait! Don't go. How can I find Gyd?' Blue heard nothing but the creak of ship's timbers.

Perhaps this was just another vivid dream like all the others. Why should she even trust her tired eyes and ears anyway? Blue tried to move her limbs. This time they moved freely and easily. She sat up. Maybe she hadn't been dreaming and the boy had been real? Suddenly Blue noticed the centre of her chest where the boy had placed his hand was glowing faintly. Of course! Blue reached into the leather pocket on the front of her tunic and pulled out the strange pearl she had found in the mine. It was still in her pocket! How could they not have found it? Even the small pocket knife was still there. Well, the knife might come in useful later on but right now she had to find out where the men had taken Gyd. Blue gently held the whispering pearl in her hand and watched as the swirling patterns of fiery light came alive beneath her gaze. Very quickly the strange rushing noise she had first heard in the lift cage once more began to fill her head. This time, though, Blue experienced no feelings of terror or panic—just a delicious warmth and calm that spread from the whispering pearl to her heart and outwards. Blue could feel the vivid flames beginning to spread beyond and dissolve the confines of her body, continuing outwards from her heart like golden wings until they reached the very margins of her being, filling her with the sensation that she was able to expand beyond the limits of the very ship itself. She sighed blissfully. It was as if a tourniquet had been removed from her soul. Blue closed her eyes and allowed herself to drift out into the vast, endless pulse of living water that surrounded the ship. The experience sent shivers of delight running up and down her spine. How easy it would be for her to let go, to keep drifting away on that vast, flowing, pulsating current of life and forget all about the ship and her worries. But she couldn't. She had to find Gyd. In an act of pure will, Blue wrenched her consciousness back to the ship. She shuddered. How repulsive the energy on board now felt. Even the ship's timbers dripped with oppression, fear and death; as if the wood itself had absorbed the pain and heartache of all those who had ever suffered and died aboard that monstrous, floating hulk.

Blue had to remain calm. She could feel her revulsion and fear starting to block her senses. Even the whispering pearl's flames seemed subdued and melancholy. Taking a few deep breaths, Blue managed to settle herself and the pearl once more flared up. So long as she remained calm Blue found that by focussing and projecting her consciousness outwards, she was able to make sense of the foul and muddled sprawl of the ship. Slowly at first, then with more and more confidence, Blue began sensing her way through the gloomy caverns of mildewing wood, picking her way through every cabin, stairwell, storeroom and hold. After a while it was almost as if she were standing right there beside the sailors as they lounged in their canvas hammocks scratching at their ever-present lice. She could even smell the foetid air of unwashed bodies and the heady scent of the oakum and tar used to caulk the wooden decking of the floor.

It wasn't long, however, before a terrified commotion drew her attention to the upper part of the ship. She'd found the slave hold. The miners were all enclosed under grated hatchways between the upper decks of the ship. In places the space was so low that some were even forced to sit between each other's legs and were packed so tightly together that there was little possibility of their ever lying down or changing position. Hunched over, spitting threats and curses, a ferocious looking sailor prowled amongst them brandishing a whip which he seemed to delight in cracking above their heads merely to observe the ripples of panic it sent through their dejected ranks. It tore at Blue's heart to see such proud and strong men brought so low. Yet, finding no sign of Gyd or the herders, Blue knew she had to keep looking.

Finally, Blue came to the lower decks of the ship. Most of this area appeared to be reserved for storage, but towards the stern of the ship she found a hold filled with an almost impenetrable fog. It wasn't so much a physical fog, though the air in that part of the ship was certainly thicker and more rancid than anywhere else she had sensed, but a confused and dark fog of bitterness, malevolence and death. At last, she'd found the sleeping herders. Not all was malevolent though. In one corner, as if tucked away, a small patch of lighter, brighter energy could be felt. It had to be Gyd.

Gyd was alive. She could sense the life within him. She could feel his heart beating slowly in his chest and the shallow rise and fall of his lungs. But she could also sense the strength in him fading fast. She knew he wouldn't last much longer. Focussing her mind, Blue gently pushed her energy out towards him. Gyd's heart fluttered. Blue tried again, this time pushing even harder. The boy's heart fluttered again then settled into a slightly faster rhythm. She could feel his strength returning. Perhaps she could revive him there and then? Surely that would be the best solution. That way she could wake him without even having to risk leaving the storage room and he could find his own way out of there. Encouraged by her plan Blue pushed her energy out towards him again, but this time nothing happened. She tried again. Again nothing. It was as if something was getting in her way, like a cushion of energy blocking her. Maybe the whispering pearl had stopped working? Or what if a herder had woken and somehow was blocking her? No. The energy certainly didn't feel in any way malevolent and the whispering pearl, if anything, was glowing more strongly than ever. She tried one last time, pushing with all her might, but again her intentions to revive the boy were gently, but firmly rebuffed. Well, if she couldn't revive him from where she was, she would just have to go down there and get him out of there herself and get him out soon before any of the herders awoke to find shaft rat on their breakfast menu.

Standing up on shaky legs, Blue wobbled her way over to the door and opened it slightly. Normally the pitching of the ship wouldn't have troubled her in the slightest, having spent so many hours on old Eofor's worm-riddled boat, but in Blue's weakened state it was as much as she could do to stop herself being thrown to the deck at every wave. Hearing nothing Blue crept out into the gloomy passageway and, doing her best to match her movements to the motion of the sea, headed in what she hoped was the direction of the hatch leading to the hold. In spite of her shaky legs, it didn't take Blue long to find it. Grasping the iron ring of the hatchway door, Blue heaved it open to see a long, narrow ladder descending down into the bowels of the ship. This had better not be a trap, she prayed, and began climbing down.

At the bottom, Blue held up the whispering pearl for light and looked around. Before she'd been forced to work in the mine Blue had been in the holds of a number of ships, yet none came even close to the breadth, length and depth of this one. Even the huge holds of the four-mast cargo barques that occasionally moored up in the cove could have fitted twice over into this one. From the cathedral-like rafters above, laden cargo nets creaked and swayed rhythmically to the ocean swell whilst below mountainous stacks of equipment, supplies and the spoils of war filled the rest of the hold like the poorly planned backstreets of some overpopulated town.

Suddenly a hissing breath exploded behind her. Instinctively throwing her arms up for protection, Blue spun around and braced herself in anticipation of the rough, clawed hands of the herders. Again, another hissing breath burst in front of her... and yet she remained untouched. Blue lowered her arms and looked for the source of the noise. For a moment she didn't know what to make of what she was seeing. At first it appeared to be a misshapen wall. Even stranger, its surface seemed to be moving and blinking at her. Another hissing breath burst in front of Blue and a strange, knobbly head disappeared into a hole in the wall. Blue peered closer and realised it wasn't a wall at all, but stacks of turtle-like creatures which had been placed upside down, one atop the other. Like the turtles Blue had occasionally seen being sold in the fish markets at Port Stroenshal, a port just south of Stod, the creatures had armoured shells and beaklike mouths, but instead of flippers they had short, fat, stumpy legs. Their heads too were different, with small, lumpy ridges protruding from the tops of their green, patterned skulls. Most of them were still alive and poked their heads out of their shells to watch Blue silently. Every now and again, whenever Blue made a slight movement, one would let out an eerie, hissing breath and its head would shoot back into its shell with a pop. Quickly recovering from her shock, Blue reluctantly turned her back on those unfortunate creatures and, to a chorus of hissing pops, carefully made her way across the mountain of stores until she stood facing a door at the rear of the hold.

Blue hesitated. She was certain there were no herders on the other side of the door, but it didn't make opening it any easier for she could sense them close by. Trying her hardest not to make a noise, Blue opened the door. Immediately a putrid cloud escaped through the gap causing her to gag and choke. Inside, foul miasmas rose up through the same wide grates she had seen fitted into the decks of the slave hold. It was obvious the room wasn't being used for storage. Instead, around the edges of the grates, seething heaps of maggots and cockroaches burrowed greedily through fermenting piles of bones, spittle and dung. Judging by the decomposing stalactites of filth hanging from the rungs of the ladder, the herders used the hatch above not just as a convenient place to be rid of any leftovers from their revolting meals, but also as a toilet.

Blue moved to the foot of the ladder and, holding the glowing whispering pearl tightly in both hands, concentrated on the deck above to see if she could detect any movement. There was none. The herders had to be asleep. Blue struggled not to shrink back in fear as one by one she picked up on the deep, rattling snores in their broad, muscular chests. Once she was certain they were all sleeping she quietly tucked the whispering pearl back into her pocket and, grimacing with disgust, did her best to climb the ladder without touching the worst of the caked-on filth.

At the top of the ladder, Blue lifted the hatch and instantly regretted it. If she had thought the stench below had been bad, the festering odour which now engulfed her was even worse. It was the same stench Blue had smelt just before being captured in Ælf's house—only this time it was far more pungent. She knew what the smell was now: the rank, stale breath of herders combined with the foetid stench of death. She covered her mouth and peered into the room. Close above her an oversized hammock with a loudly snoring occupant rocked steadily back and forth. Alongside the hammock, almost within arm's reach, the dim outline of an unconscious figure lay on the floorboards. It had to be Gyd. Blue closed her eyes and with the whispering pearl's help reached out with her energy until she could feel the slow beat of the boy's heart. She pushed a little harder, but instead of reviving him, the same pillow of energy she had sensed before formed between herself and the shaft rat, blocking any chance of waking him. What was causing it? Or who? There certainly seemed to be none other than herself awake in the room. Perhaps it was her fear of the herders that was causing it to manifest? Blue frowned. There was no way she was going to allow nerves to stop her when she was this close to rescuing her friend.

Doing her best to ignore the stench and close proximity of the herder above, Blue tried harder, willing the light of the pearl to push through the wall of energy stopping her. This time the pearl flared up and soft flames trailed from her hands and across the floor, but before they could reach Gyd, again the strange pillow of energy began to push them back. This time Blue wasn't giving in. Summoning all her concentration and willpower, Blue urged the flames on, driving them against the cushion of energy until, little by little, the resistance began to give. Buoyed by her success Blue persisted, pushing as hard as she could until, finally, she felt the energy give then evaporate altogether. Immediately the boy's heartbeat and breathing began to speed up. She had done it! A little more and he would soon be awake.

From above Blue heard the herder in the hammock roll over and a hand flopped dangerously close to her head. She froze as a cold finger brushed against her ear. Shifting her head, a hair's breadth at a time, Blue managed to remove her ear from its touch. She looked up. Instead of the large, clawed hand and hairy, heavily muscled arm of a herder, Blue gazed in shock at a tattoo of an octopus entwined uncompromisingly about a mermaid. There was no mistaking a tattoo like that. It was the tattoo of Caelin, her hammer! The way the arm was resting languidly over the edge and the loud snores which could be heard coming from the miner suggested Caelin hadn't a care in the world. How could that be? Did he have any idea what danger he was in? She couldn't believe it! How did he end up sleeping in the same room as the vile herders? Perhaps he was their captive? No, even from Blue's limited vantage point she could see no attempt had been made to shackle or restrain him. Surely, he hadn't betrayed her and the other miners by collaborating with Caronte? No, Blue couldn't accept that either. For all of Caelin's impatience and short temper, particularly when it came to dealing with Blue, he was at heart an honest man. Perhaps he was simply struggling to shake off the effects of the herders' kamph grass and awaited the same ghastly fate as Gyd. Yes, that must be it. This she hadn't anticipated. Now she would have to wake up both of them. At least the constant fidgeting and scratching coming from the hammock — in spite of the snoring — suggested Caelin wasn't far from waking up himself. Perhaps, if she woke him first, he could help her carry the still sleeping Gyd down the ladder to the relative safety of the main hold before she woke him up completely. Caelin was a silent man by nature and would be far less likely to cry out when woken than the jumpy and unpredictable Gyd. Yes, Caelin being there might just work to Blue's advantage.

Still, something felt very wrong. The oppressive atmosphere in the dim room troubled her deeply. It made her chest so tight with fear she could hardly draw the foul air into her lungs. Clutching the whispering pearl in her hand, Blue climbed out from the hatch and peered in at the sleeping miner… and immediately wished she hadn't. Throwing a hand over her mouth to muffle her scream, Blue looked down at the short, stubby spines protruding over the crown of the broad, bald head of what could only be a large and very ugly herder. Clenched in its hairy grip was the bloody arm of Caelin. It had been torn from the miner's body with such force that part of the shoulder and chest muscle were still attached. No doubt the herder had dozed off before finishing his meal.

Blue quickly smothered the light of the glowing pearl with her hands and held her breath. All she could hope for was that the herders were sleeping too deeply to have heard her half-stifled scream. She could hear her heart pounding like a drum. The room was horribly quiet. Only the hammocks made any noise, creaking like the slow pendulum of a clock. After what seemed an eternity, one by one the snoring from the other hammocks resumed—all, that is, except the herder holding Caelin's arm. Why wasn't he snoring like the others? Blue waited a little longer. At least the fidgeting and scratching had stopped. He had to be asleep. Blue inched away from the hammock and stopped. The herder remained quiet and still. Blue took a bigger step away. Still the herder gave no indication it had woken up. Blue let out a quiet sigh of relief and turned away.

'Leaving so soon little mouse?' A large, hairy hand closed around her mouth. Her heart lurched then sank. She knew there was no point in struggling. 'Basax could smell you in his sleep little mouse. Now, why don't you show Basax that pretty little stone you've been playing with?' The hand tightened around her mouth until she thought her jaw was going to crack from the pressure. Terrified, Blue opened her palm and allowed the beautiful light of the glowing whispering pearl to spill out into the room. The herder gasped and snatched the pearl from the girl's hand like a greedy child. Almost forgetting about Blue altogether, the herder gawped at the whispering pearl in wonder, and just like Blue had done in the mine, started turning it first one way and then the other, utterly mesmerised by its beauty. Suddenly, as if abruptly waking from a dream, the herder shook its head and stuffed the pearl into a pouch at its waist.

'Basax in no mood for sharing,' it growled and threw Blue across its broad shoulders then, scooping up Gyd in similar fashion, it leapt down the open hatch with the two shaft rats slung one atop the other like sacks of potatoes.

Blue's wits were so battered by the time the herder came to a final stop that she had no idea where they were nor how long they'd taken to get wherever it was. She couldn't even tell if they had climbed or descended the countless flights of stairs and ladders used by the herder to avoid detection. In fact, Blue's wits were so battered that it took her another good half an hour to realise the herder had lost any interest in either one of them, and was now squatting atop a large bundle of spear shafts like one of the many stoop-necked gulls that rested on the ship's yardarm whenever the weather turned ugly. In its hand gold and rainbow flames danced teasingly before its wide eyes and gawping mouth. Gyd lay beside her groaning softly to himself as he struggled to shake off the effects of the kamph grass. It didn't even seem to care that an open crate bristling with cruel looking barbed swords lay within their easy reach. Blue stretched out her hand and ran a finger over the sharkskin binding of one of the swords' grips. The herder didn't even look up.

'Gyd!' she whispered as loudly as she dared. 'Are you awake?'

'Aye. But I wish I weren't,' he groaned. 'What's that smell?' Blue put a finger to her lips and nodded towards the herder. Gyd followed her gaze and laid eyes on the frightening creature for the first time. The colour instantly drained from his face.

'Stay calm,' Blue hissed. 'He's in a world of his own. If we go now, he won't notice a thing. Believe me I know how distracting that thing is. If we stay quiet, we'll make it out of here, I promise.'

Gyd remained staring wide-eyed at the herder. The creature's dull green eyes were starting to mist over and a trail of saliva hung from its fang-like filed teeth.

'What is that thing he's looking at? It... it's beautiful.'

'It's a long story. I'll tell you later. First let's just get out of here. Do you think you can stand?' Gyd didn't answer. Instead, he was looking around at their surroundings with a confused look on his face. Suddenly, the full realisation of where they were, sank in.

'Aye, Blue,' he said, 'I'll stand all right.' Gyd pushed himself up onto his shaky legs and, with a face like a storm, grasped hold of one of the sharkskin handles.

'Gyd don't!' Blue cried out realising his intent but Gyd was already lunging at the herder.

'Murdering bastard!' he shouted as the blade sank into the thick hide of the herder's shoulder, causing the creature to yowl in pain and the whispering pearl to leap out of its paw. Spitting fury, the wounded creature spun around and swiped Gyd to the floor, lacerating his cheek with its long claws. The shaft rat struggled unsuccessfully to rise, flapping the sword weakly in the herder's direction, but Basax was already leaping after the fiery pearl as it skittered across the wooden floor. Blue snatched a second sword out of the barrel and moved to stand over Gyd protectively, waving the sword in front of her dangerously.

'What are you going to do little mouse?' the herder said with a sneer as it slipped the recovered whispering pearl into its pouch. "Basax not in mood to play."

'Let us go,' Blue said trying to sound threatening but instead sounding more like she was begging for mercy.

'Oh, Basax too hungry to do that,' replied the herder and repositioned its huge bulk to block the door.

'Come any closer and thee'll pay dear!' gasped Gyd clutching a bloody hand to his face. Without warning, the herder suddenly let out a ferocious snarl and sprang at Blue, sending the sword spinning out of her hand. Before Blue knew what had happened, she felt her feet kicking helplessly in the air and the herder's hand clenched firmly around her throat. Beneath her, Gyd struggled desperately for breath as the herder's foot pressed down on his chest. Blue clawed at the fingers choking her but the herder's murderous grip only got tighter. Lights flickered at the corner of her eyes and her lungs felt ready to burst. Suddenly Blue heard a door being thrown open and the sounds of people entering.

'Let them go!' The voice was distinctly female.

'Do as you're told, Basax!' ordered a second voice. Blue felt the grip around her throat lessen.

'These mine!' snarled the herder, turning on the intruders.

'Not yours, herder, *mine*! This is *my* ship and everything on it is *mine* until I say otherwise! You had better not forget that.'

'You forgetting deal Caronte?'

'Don't you worry Basax. You'll get your meat. In fact, I've just had my men deliver a fresh one. If you hurry there might be some left.'

'There'd better be,' Basax growled and glared hungrily at Blue and Gyd as he backed out the door. Blue shivered.

'Oh, and Basax,' called Caronte after him, 'I'll not mention to the others that you tried to have this little picnic on your own.'

'Thank you, Captain,' said the woman when all were sure the herder was gone. 'Thank you and thank the gods we found them in time. I would have been loath to have lost the only serving girl on the entire ship.'

'You're welcome, my dear. Filthy creatures. If only I could find a more civilised way to secure their services. I just hope the girl lives up to your expectations. Of course, if she displeases you in any way, you may take your pick of servants from any of the other slaves. No doubt Basax would be delighted to see her again.'

'I'm sure that won't be necessary,' said the woman flashing the captain a captivating smile. Reaching over, she took his hand lightly in hers. 'Really Captain, you are a true gentleman. I don't know how I would cope with that beastly Magor without your constant protection and kindness.'

'My dear, so long as I am captain of this ship you are my honoured guest. Anything you need, anything at all, is yours for the asking.' Blue noticed the captain blushed like a bashful child every time the beautiful woman batted her large, hazel-gold eyes at him.

'Perhaps if you would also be so kind as to see to the boy's wounds for me. If the girl doesn't shape up then perhaps the boy will be able to serve me.'

'Of course, my dear.' Caronte gestured to two sailors hovering in the doorway. 'Get a quart of vinegar from the stores and clean his wounds… and tell the quartermaster to give the boy something decent to eat.'

'Now, with your leave, Captain, I think I would like to retire to my chamber. I trust the girl's sleeping arrangements are taken care of?'

'Everything is exactly as you requested it. A cage has been installed in your quarters where the slave can sleep. I must urge you, though, to be most wary. She proved quite a handful to capture. A most resourceful creature, if you don't mind me saying. Take a firm hand to her often and keep her under lock and key whenever you have no need of her.'

'Thank you, Captain. I shall take no risks.'

'Are you absolutely sure you would not like me to post a guard outside your door?'

'Quite sure, Captain. I know of ways to guarantee the girl's obedience.'

'My dear, I do not doubt you in the slightest.'

Seeing how hopelessly and unquestioningly Caronte ceded to the woman's every whim and fancy meant Blue didn't have any doubts either. There was something utterly compelling about this stunningly beautiful woman, yet the edginess of the sailors who hovered at Caronte's shoulders was also painfully apparent. Blue was convinced that the woman had to be the witch she had overheard the sailors talking about. Whenever the woman cast a glance in their direction, they would hurriedly drop their eyes as if fearing her glance would freeze them on the spot. One sailor even started to tremble and perspire when Caronte's order to place shackles on Blue forced the poor man to kneel within a finger's breadth of the woman's sweeping robes. Once Blue's shackles were secured, Caronte took the key from the sailor and presented it to the lady with a grotesque bow and flourish as if he were presenting her with a diamond ring. The woman appeared delighted with her "gift" and coquettishly hung it about her neck.

'Accompany the Lady to her chamber,' ordered the captain, his face awash with contentment at her acceptance of his absurd gift. The sailor flinched as if the captain had lashed him with a whip. 'My Lady I bid you a fond goodnight.'

'Goodnight my dear Captain.'

***

The woman's chamber was situated in the upper rear section of the boat in quarters of such opulence that Blue could hardly believe they belonged to the same ship. In the soft light of burnished lanterns fantastical creatures and exotic scenes from distant lands, exquisitely carved directly into the woodwork of the ship, drifted past Blue's gaze. Blue had almost forgotten where she was until a scene of chained and naked captives being whipped and thrown overboard quickly brought her back to her senses. Next to this scene, the woman unlocked a door and stood to one side to let Blue and the sailor enter before her. The sailor held back, squirming under her impatient gaze like a stoat in a snare.

'Hurry up!' she said impatiently. Blue could feel the man's hand trembling on her back as he ushered her into the room before him.

Inside, Blue was relieved to find there was no large pot at all. Instead, the warm light of a pale evening sky drifted through broad, gilt-framed windows overlooking the endless blue of the ocean beyond. Beneath them a large bed covered in plump, scarlet cushions sat beside an elegant desk and fitted dresser. Upon this desk scrolls of paper with strange inscriptions lay beside a wide, steaming bowl of food and a small crystal carafe of wine sparkled invitingly. Just as Blue began to feel her apprehension start to lift, the woman walked across to open what looked to be a cupboard for storage set neatly into the wooden panelling of the cabin wall. As it opened, Blue set eyes upon the cold metal bars of a cage. Her cage.

'Put her in then leave us,' the woman instructed and busied herself drawing heavy embroidered curtains across each of the windows. The sailor, desperate to be gone anyway, threw Blue into the cage and, without awaiting further instruction, fled the room.

Whether it was from exhaustion, or whether it was from the relentless and unforgiving spate of cruel misfortune that had befallen Blue, the sight of the cold bars of the cage in which she was now penned like an animal was too much for her to take. Drawing her knees and arms up as close to her shivering body as her chains would allow, Blue surrendered to all the misery and heartache that had been building ever since she found poor old Eofor lying dead on his bedroom floor. Sorrow welled up inside her chest then gushed forth as a river of tears which poured down her face and onto her grazed and dirty hands. Blue buried her grief-stricken face trying to disguise the sound of her crying but she knew the witch could hear her. Between sobs, the girl could hear the soft pace of the witch's feet on the wooden floor. A key turned in the lock and the cage door swung open. The witch reached in and pulled one of

Blue's hands away from her face. Blue looked up defiantly though she knew she had no fight left in her.

'Forgive me,' the witch said tenderly and continued to hold Blue's hand.

'Wha... What?' Blue stammered. Was that a tear running down the witch's face?

'Forgive me. If the captain or any of his crew suspected that I intend to help you then we would both be undone. We have to maintain appearances at all costs.'

'Appearances?' The witch's words sounded so unreal. Could this woman who so clearly filled the sailors' hearts with dread actually be someone in whom Blue could trust?

'You *must* trust me.' The woman answered as if reading Blue's thoughts. 'If only I had succeeded in stopping you from waking your friend, I could have got to you sooner.'

Blue's eyes hardened and she snatched back her hand.

'You mean that was you who was trying to stop me saving Gyd!'

'I wasn't trying to stop you. I was trying to help you save him. Did you not for once think of the danger you were getting yourself into marching straight into a nest of herders? You nearly got yourself and your friend killed. I knew Basax had caught hold of your scent and was waking up. If only you could have waited a little longer, I'd have got there myself. Did you not realise I was trying to stop you from waking the boy to help you?'

'I... I didn't realise?'

'Of course. For one who seems to know so much you really have an awful lot to learn—particularly when it comes to identifying friend from foe! You made me look an absolute fool in front of that idiot captain. It's hard enough to keep up this ridiculous act without you throwing me to the floor in mid-conversation. I had to pretend I had fainted. It cost me valuable time and nearly both of your lives!'

'I threw you to the floor?'

'You really don't have a clue of what you are capable of do you?' the woman's voice and eyes softened again. 'Blue is your name, isn't it?' Blue nodded wondering how she knew. 'My name is Lybesstre. I am here to help you. It seems certain... "gifts" are awakening within you, though why, I have yet fully to understand. Whatever the cause, without my guidance, Blue, many of them will be wasted like seeds scattered in the wind. We cannot afford for that to happen. I need you to trust me, Blue.'

'I'm not capable of anything,' Blue confessed realising Lybesstre mistakenly believed the mysterious properties of the whispering pearl were somehow Blue's own. 'I don't know anything. I have no… gifts. None of it is me… It's all the… it's… it doesn't matter now anyway. It's gone. Basax has got it.' Blue pulled away from Lybesstre's touch.

'What's gone?' said Lybesstre suddenly listening intently. 'What does Basax have?'

Blue didn't know why but in the little time she had spent in Lybesstre's company her fear and distrust of the woman were already starting to melt away. In fact, she couldn't help but like her. In spite of Lybesstre's obviously terrifying effect on the superstitious sailors, to Blue she had such a pleasant feel about her that all of Blue's thoughts of her being a witch had all but vanished completely. Even as Lybesstre's eyes peered intently into hers Blue still felt there was a genuine warmth, even love, coming from deep within them. She so wanted to trust her.

'Basax has got the whispering pearl!' she blurted out. Lybesstre's eyes widened in amazement and a smile appeared on her lips. Suddenly, she threw her head back and let out a peal of laughter that, far from seeming to ridicule or lay scorn upon Blue, washed over the girl like musical bells.

'I'm sorry for laughing,' Lybesstre said wiping away a tear, 'but now at least I understand how a High Wycce of the House of Aatxe was shaken off like a raindrop by a fourteen-year-old novice girl.'

'I told you it wasn't me,' Blue said frowning in embarrassment.

'Oh, you sweet, innocent child,' Lybesstre said and, taking Blue by complete surprise, she placed a kiss on the girl's forehead. 'You really don't know what you have found do you?'

'No, I… Well, I guess it's a cursed stone of some sort. I know it makes you ill. At least that's what everyone says in the mines.'

'Makes you ill! Oh, my sweet girl, it's the whispering pearl that has made you well! It's the whispering pearl that has made you whole again! It is a divine gift and blessing beyond my wildest hopes.'

'A blessing? If they are such a blessing then how come the Speris are destroying them? How come the fish and mirounga started disappearing soon after they started finding them? How come the whispering pearl destroyed the mine and now sits in the pouch of possibly the most loathsome creature I have ever laid eyes upon? And what are these Eledh anyway?'

'Stop! Stop!' said Lybesstre. 'Too many questions at once! Sit down; let me take those shackles off and I will try to answer what I can in words that you will understand. Just don't try to understand everything at once. There are forces at play here that even I can barely begin to comprehend.'

Blue sat down and Lybesstre unlocked the shackles, allowing them to fall off with a heavy clunk onto the floor. She reached over and poured a small glass of wine then muttered softly over the glass, causing a soft burst of vapour to leave the glass. 'Drink this. I would have preferred water but unfortunately beer and wine are all you can get hold of on this dreadful ship.'

Lybesstre sat down beside Blue as the girl, too hungry and thirsty to care what she was drinking, gulped down greedily all the witch gave her.

'I think we ought to start at the beginning,' Lybesstre said once she had made sure Blue was comfortable. 'At least as near the beginning as knowledge will allow for there is much yet to be revealed. Firstly, the Eledh were once well known to the elder races. They were beings of incomprehensible power and wisdom who came to us from the heart of creation millions of years ago. When they first arrived, they were able to walk, laugh and live alongside the firstborn sons and daughters of the Earth, yet whether they came to guide us or to learn from us I cannot say for mighty and proud were the humans that walked the Earth in those days. Either way, they gladly shared their knowledge and gifts with the sons and daughters of the Earth and bright like a star was the light that radiated from this planet during those blessed years. Yet, although the Eledh's love for mankind was immense, and whose knowledge and wisdom were almost without equal, for whatever reason they were unable to prevent mankind from beginning a slide into a darkness from which we could not escape. What caused the fall is not certain; some say a sun fell from the heavens, and with its falling, an indescribable sorrow descended upon the Earth whilst others believe the darkness was already here, lying in wait for the humans to arrive, plotting our downfall and sowing the seeds of jealousy amongst the other races.'

'What do you believe happened?'

'Me? I'm not really sure. Perhaps neither is correct. Perhaps both. Perhaps it was we who gave birth to the darkness within our own hearts. Whatever the reason, the Eledh soon realised they would no longer be able to reach humanity without their becoming drawn into the abyss themselves. Many saw no option but to leave, hoping for brighter days when they could return and once more walk on the sun-warmed soil beside the beloved children of the Earth, but there were those who could not bear to be parted from us and did all they could to follow, such was their love for their mortal companions. Few in number were they who succeeded in making the shift into the realm of shadows, yet when they got here, they quickly realised the Earth children had lost all memory of their celestial friends. Of course, the Eledh did all they could to help the humans recall even just a fraction of the glory that they once were, but, with breaking hearts, eventually they had to concede defeat and resign themselves to watching helplessly as those they loved descended into a hell.

'And so it was that the last of the Eledh, knowing they were lost to the eyes of Heaven, could do nothing but wait like fading shards of moonlight, praying for the day when we would awaken to hear their whisper and resurrect their memory, to resurrect their gifts, the whispering pearls being just one of them. As for the Speris and, indeed, many of the lost races of the Earth, they have since become so trapped in a nightmare of their own making that anything that forces them to step out of the emotional coma in which for so long, they have tried to hide quite frankly terrifies them. They are desperate to bury the truth from themselves. They are desperate not to look in the mirror and see how hideous they have become. Blue, you must understand the whispering pearls have no real power or magic of their own, at least as far as I am aware, but I do know they can reveal much of what has been kept hidden from you and much of what you have forgotten over the many lifetimes you have spent on this Earth. For most, due to the wicked lives they have led, this is a torturous process that will drive them to the very edge of insanity. But for a precious few, the whispering pearls can help unlock a depth of divine knowledge and power we can scarce imagine. The Speris know this and will stop at nothing to destroy them all for they realise the whispering pearls hold the blueprints for what the Earth and all who live upon her were meant to become before we fell from grace into darkness.'

'And what was that?'

'To be reborn. To be reborn not just as children of the Earth, but of the Sun!'

'But if these Eledh and whispering pearls are so wonderful, what about all the fish and mirounga that disappeared? The whispering pearls killed them all. My old Eofor lost everything because of them!'

'You must know Blue, though it chills my blood to say it, not all the Eledh that succeeded in coming to the Earth are wonderful. Amongst those who tried to follow us were some who fell prey to the darkness and became monstrous and terrifying indeed. They still lurk in the darkest corners of this Earth preying on the fearful and the weak. I pray that you never have to face one of them. As for the mirounga and fish that disappeared, if the Speris had not poured all the filth and waste from the mine into the ocean they might yet have survived. They suffocated the vegetation of the spawning grounds; that is why the fish and mirounga disappeared—not because of some imagined evil of the whispering pearls. And as for your destruction of the mine, do you really think that was such a bad thing? That mine had become a hive of cruelty and abuse, whose dark energy affected and harmed every living thing around it for hundreds, maybe thousands of miles. The Eledh understood this and guided you to destroy the mine for the good of all.'

'What about Gyd? Gyd was dying! It was the whispering pearl that healed him, not me!'

'You are wrong Blue. It *was* you. It was *always* you. The whispering pearl has simply helped you reawaken those gifts you carried within you, gifts you were always meant to use and impart to others.'

'But the whispering pearl is with Basax now.'

'Yes, that is an unforeseen turn I have to admit. It is a shame that Kai is in no state to speak with us. Perhaps there is something he has foreseen of which I am unaware.'

'Kai? Who is he?'

'Kai? He is known as a witchblood. A servant to Lord Rasalas, commander of the armies of the Furud. Rasalas is the one responsible for your enslavement. Once considered a noble man he has since become a power-crazed lunatic who suspects his servant to be both coward and a traitor. Kai is neither, yet Rasalas has him incarcerated in the bowels of this ship because he fears Kai might be tempted to try and usurp his new god-given powers. The gods have given Rasalas no power. They would never grant power to one such as he. A little healing from me and his vanity did the rest. The ancient relic Rasalas has taken possession of holds no more power than that of a colourful trinket. It never did. The power came from an ancient and mighty guardian known as the Aatxe. This great spirit now resides in his servant, Kai, along with all its power. Rasalas knows nothing of this but I do not know for how long I can maintain his delusion. What I do know is that the moment he suspects he has been deceived, we are all as good as dead. As for Kai, Rasalas has seen to it that his chances of survival be as slim as possible and has ordered Magor, Rasalas' son, to lock him in the deepest well of the ship. No normal person could ever survive such a crossing down there, yet he has not banked on the strength of Kai's spirit. I suspect this is why the Aátxe chose him. Nevertheless, Kai is very weak right now and I fear without our help he may not last the journey. We must also find a way to help the rest of the slaves. Caronte always captures more than he needs knowing that many fall sick and die during the crossing. We *must* strive our utmost to prevent this. We must find ways to get food and water to them without anybody realising. Caronte dotes on me such that he would never allow me to spend time down there. This task must fall upon your shoulders, Blue. If we can maintain the illusion that you are my personal slave then I am sure I could volunteer you for work in the slave hold whenever you displease me—which I fear needs to be often if we are to keep your friends alive. The conditions in that hold are terrible and the work will be far from pleasant, but it is perhaps the only chance we will have to help them. Would you be willing to do that Blue?'

Blue couldn't help thinking of her friend Ælf crushed together with the other miners in that sweltering heat and stench.

'Of course I will,' she vowed.

'I knew you would,' said Lybesstre tenderly. 'Now let us eat and get some rest. Our journey is going to be long and whatever strength we can preserve will give all a better chance for survival.'

CHAPTER 5

The "slops" were the worst. Not for the disgusting continual sight of
emptied bowels. Not for the nauseating stench; not even for the wriggling
maggots and other unspeakable parasites that plagued the poor miners,
sailors and soldiers of that accursed ship. No, the slops were the worst
because the large, iron-bound, filthy buckets that Blue seemed to forever
be hauling out of the slave holds and sailors' quarters quite literally
weighed a ton. Never in her wildest dreams, or nightmares, could Blue
have imagined that so much could come out of human beings, nor that it
could weigh so much. But she, and she alone, had to haul out and empty
each and every one of them — and not just for the slaves, but for every
single living being on that ship — animals included. Sometimes her back
and arms were in such agony that she didn't even care if the contents
spilled over the rim and showered her from head to toe in a lumpy soup.
She didn't even care about the relentless cruel comments and mockery
that she had to endure from the sailors. At least her revolting appearance
and smell ensured that not even the boldest and most immorally vile of
the sailors — and there were many of those — would ever entertain even
the slightest or most remotely lustful thought towards her. Who in their
right mind would want to have their wicked way with a living, breathing
pile of dung? As Lybesstre always made sure Blue always wore an
excrement-smeared cap over her long hair, she wasn't even sure that the
sailors realised she was a girl at all. In truth she wasn't even sure whether
the sailors actually realised she was a human being—rather some foul
progeny of the herders. After all, what human being could have
withstood what she had to endure for so long without wilting like a spring
flower in a swamp?

But she did withstand. And she did endure. She endured every foul
bucket, every aching pain, every taunt, every curse, every kick, every last
drop of filth… because if she hadn't endured, many, perhaps even most
of her friends, would certainly have died. The miners didn't see Blue as

revolting, they saw her as an angel of salvation. She was *their* angel; an angel come to lift their weary spirits and fill their hearts with hope like a bright star which penetrates a lingering winter fog. How many times she magically produced out from under her besmeared apron an edible root, a flask of ale, a hunk of bread, or cheese, or pickled fish no one could possibly have counted, but somehow, by some incredible miraculous means, Blue ensured that every man and boy chained and bullied and beaten in that sweltering den of cruelty received just enough to stay alive and to stay healthy — at least healthy enough to survive that hellish and interminable crossing.

In fact, Lybesstre and Blue's ruse was so convincing that not even the whip-happy, bullying scum-of-a-sailor who delighted in tormenting and watching over every precious moment of the slaves' miserable lives bothered after the first couple of days to pay any attention to Blue whatsoever. It was as if Blue had become invisible to him. The same could be said of the ship's quartermaster, who, amazingly, ceased raising so much as an eyebrow whenever Blue made a pretence of mopping the stores or removing his piss bucket. This was wonderful for Blue's clandestine smuggling activities as there were times when she had an almost free reign in those areas of the ship so vital to all of their survival. Of course, Blue suspected that Lybesstre had much to do with her apparent "invisibility". Blue could almost imagine hearing her strange mutterings and incantations whenever she was near those sensitive areas of the ship. However, Blue played her part well and worked hard at blending in with life aboard the *Nefari*, and though she was loath to admit it, she became quite a remarkable actress. Many times, sailors were seen fleeing in terror from the passageways leading to Lybesstre's quarters as the tyrannical witch would drag a kicking and screaming Blue to her cabin to receive yet another ferocious thrashing. The fact that the "thrashing" often ended up with the two of them collapsing onto Lybesstre's bed in fits of laughter actually enhanced Lybesstre's terrifying reputation amongst the ship's already highly fearful and superstitious population. Many were convinced that the witch priestess was, indeed, possessed by a devil for, so the ship's rampant gossip went, every time she thrashed her miserable charge, blood-curdling shrieks of uncontrollable delight could be heard issuing from her cabin. The morning after such beatings, Blue always added to the effect brilliantly by hunching over as if a rib or arm was causing her terrible pain, or at other times she might feign a horrific limp, dragging a foot pathetically behind her. The sailors who witnessed her like this tutted under their breath and, muttering a prayer to whatever god or devil they believed was protecting them from Blue's demonic mistress, usually hurried on past, saving their taunts for when her terrible injuries had somehow miraculously healed.

Sadly, to Blue's great consternation, not everybody she would have liked to have avoided remained out of her way. At first, Blue thought nothing of it. Blue's days had always been long and she had often found herself working late into the night. It was at night especially when every nook and bleak corner of that dark ship seemed to hide a shadow or silhouette that flickered and moved in the weak flames of the deck lanterns. During those early nights, an oft-petrified Blue had imagined that there was a ghoul or beast awaiting her at almost every turn, but she soon got used to the strange effects of the lanterns and the unsettling groans and creaks of the ship and learnt to quieten her fantastical imaginings so she could get on with her work. But on that particular night she couldn't help but feel there was something unnatural and unnerving about the shadow waiting at the end of the passageway. 'Oh, it's just your imagination again,' Blue said chastising herself for such cowardly thoughts. But the uneasy feeling just would not go away. The problem was the shadow barred the one and only way to the well hatch—and it was the well hatch that offered the only route down into the sloshing pool of festering water above which Kai's cage was suspended. Blue knew that the only thing keeping Kai alive was a thin thread of life—and Blue was that thread. Over the previous week, the wound in Kai's leg had been getting worse. So too had the fevers and he was rarely strong enough or conscious enough to eat whatever meagre offering Blue managed to smuggle to him from the quartermaster's stores. Nevertheless, Blue's persistent visits and her insistence that he eat and drink as much as he could of whatever she brought him was just enough to keep him going. However, his recent downward turn in health had meant he had hardly eaten or drunk anything all week and Blue had started to get very worried.

As luck would have it, earlier that day a small turn of fortune had given her cause for hope. As was her custom to do whenever she could, she had been loitering opportunistically near the quartermaster's store when a freak wave had dislodged and spilled the contents of one of the quartermaster's most guarded prizes: a barrel of apples reserved for the exclusive consumption of the captain. Without thinking, Blue had darted across, and before the quartermaster had even realised she was there, she had already stuffed two handfuls into her apron and dashed back out of the door. They were just what Kai needed. From her days in the fishing village, she knew exactly the signs of the disease they called "sailor's scourge". Often, she had sat at the quayside watching foreign merchant ships offload their sick and dying before heading back out to sea with their stores and supplies replenished. The yellowing of Kai's face and eyes, his bleeding teeth, his lethargy and weak limbs: they all told Blue that not only was he suffering from the leg wound, but he was also suffering from the scourge. Eofor had always shaken his head and cursed when he saw the pitiful state some of the sailors would arrive in. "Blasted incompetent captains!" he would say and curse some more. "Fresh wittles, Blue. Fresh wittles. That is all thee needs. A carrot or apple or two every now and then and they'd all be fit as fiddles." Blue never forgot. The trouble was that the only fresh food she could get hold of in plentiful supply were the sugar beets stored near the animal pens. The miners didn't mind these—any change from the stale tack and hard biscuits that were sporadically thrown at them was a blessing. But Kai was clearly beginning to struggle to chew and digest those hard roots— and even when he did manage a bite or two, they seemed to stick in his throat and, more often than not, provoke a violent explosion of coughing that threatened to finish him off long before the scourge did.

The shadow moved… or was it the flickering light of the lantern? 'Damn it Blue, pull yourself together!' She took a few paces forward and paused again. 'You can come out of there,' she called out tentatively to see if she could provoke whatever it was into either revealing itself or leaving—if, of course, there was anything to reveal or leave in the first place. Nothing stirred… but the shadow remained. Wait a minute, she thought, how stupid of her to forget. Near the start of their crossing this little-used corridor had been full of empty crates and musty heaps of old sackcloth. Obviously, some of the sailors had returned to using it for temporary storage. The shadow she could see sticking out from around the edge of the corner was probably nothing more than that: a pile of old sacks. Blue laughed at her stupidity and hurried ahead. She turned the corner and laughed again as her suspicions were confirmed: the shadow had indeed been nothing more than a heap of filthy sackcloth.

'What you want?' growled the sackcloth. Blue almost leapt out of her skin with fright. The sackcloth lifted its head. 'Go away!' it growled again, though the exertion of raising its head seemed to drain it of the last of its strength and its gaunt, bald head dropped back onto the floor. It was a herder. At least the broad skeletal frame upon which folds of dry skin and withered flesh now hung vaguely resembled a herder. Yet its near toothless gums and hollow, frightened eyes, far from inspiring terror, actually moved Blue to pity.

'What happened to you? Are you sick?'

'I'm dying. You killed me," it replied in an enigmatic, matter-of-fact way and continued to lie in a miserable heap on the floor.

'I... I don't understand,' Blue replied. 'What have I done? I've never even met you before.' The herder began to make a sickening shallow barking sound. At first Blue thought it was entering its final death throes until she realised that it was in fact weeping.

'Take it,' it said finally and opening an emaciated fist allowed something hard to roll across the floor towards Blue. As Blue reached down to pick it up, the space around her and the herder suddenly filled with a luminous, golden light. It was the whispering pearl!

'How did you get this?' Blue gasped as she swiftly recovered the dazzling pearl from the floor. 'Did you steal it from Basax?' The creature remained silent and Blue realised it had either fallen asleep or fallen unconscious.

Greatly relieved to have recovered the whispering pearl but with no desire or intention of ever helping a herder, even one as feeble and pitiful as this, Blue stepped around the mass of bone and began to climb down the hatch into the well. She was just about to close the hatch behind her when a sudden twinge of guilt caused her to pause. Impulsively she reached into her apron and pulled out one of the apples.

'I doubt very much you deserve this for all the wicked and terrible things you've surely done, but in case you do ever wake up, you might want to eat something that doesn't involve cruelty or murder,' and so saying, she tossed the apple at the pitiful, sack-like heap.

When Blue reached Kai's cage, she quickly realised he fared little better than the herder. His fever had still not broken and the shortness of his breathing alarmed her greatly. She feared if she didn't get him to eat soon, he would struggle to last the week. Perhaps if Caronte hadn't been so desperate to keep Lybesstre from entering any area of the ship that threatened to expose his grotesque and ridiculous pretence of being a suave and sophisticated gentleman, then Kai might have pulled through the fever. Lybesstre had almost persuaded Caronte to move Kai to more sanitary conditions so she could care for him, but when Magor found out their plans he threatened bloody mutiny. Fortunately, Magor's hatred for Kai did not run deep enough to risk incurring the wrath of Lord Rasalas by letting him die and so, after being sufficiently amused at Lybesstre's compromise to let the excrement-covered slop slave look after Kai, he had agreed that Blue be allowed to take him his paltry daily ration of hard tack and beer.

Reaching across from the ladder Blue waited for the roll of the ship to swing the cage nearer, then deftly hooked a small wooden bowl out through the bars of the cage. Into this she crushed some dry tack and then added chewed apple and watery beer to make a pulpy porridge. 'Kai,' she hissed returning the bowl the same way she had got it. 'Kai!' she said more loudly. Kai groaned feverishly but made no effort to eat anything. 'You can groan all you like but today, whether you like it or not, you're eating!' Done with speaking Blue pulled out the whispering pearl. She closed her eyes and let the now familiar flames of the pearl travel up her arm and engulf her in its delightful radiance. Sighing blissfully, she turned her focus to Kai, but the flames, instead of travelling out towards the cage as she intended, began to rise upwards.

'Where are you going?' she demanded but the flames appeared to have a mind of their own. Blue concentrated harder but the flames still failed to respond to her will. She closed her eyes tight and concentrated again on Kai. Suddenly, to her relief, she felt a thrill of energy as the flames surrounded and penetrated the weak and sickly body, momentarily flooding it with light… but there was something not quite right. It was then that Blue realised what was happening. It wasn't Kai's body she was healing; it was the herder's.

'Ugh!' Blue shuddered and dropped the whispering pearl into the two feet of foul water sloshing beneath her. She felt nauseous. How could the whispering pearl have favoured that disgusting creature over Kai? Yet, in spite of receiving no help from the whispering pearl at all, Kai was now weakly sitting upright and was dutifully slurping Blue's porridge out of the bowl.

'You… you're awake!' Blue said surprised.

'This is good,' he replied and scraped the last globules of porridge into his mouth. 'Do you have any more?'

'I can make you some if you wish—though I had to chew the apple myself.' Kai stopped chewing to scrutinise Blue's stain-covered apron and excrement-smeared cap and, in spite of his starved appearance, looked about to spit the last mouthful back into the bowl.

'Don't you dare!' snapped Blue realising what he was about to do. 'If you knew what I had to go through to get you these apples!' Kai's eyes lit up.

'Apples.' he said hungrily. 'Do you have any more?'

'Here!' she snapped and thrust two more apples through the bars of the cage. 'As you're feeling much better, I've got more important things to be getting on with.'

'I can see,' Kai replied eyeing Blue's filthy clothing again.

'Next time you can go and get your own flipping dinner!' Kai dropped his eyes and mumbled an apology but, in spite of this, Blue could still see the laughter shaking his body. Furious, she clambered down the ladder to fish out the whispering pearl, but in her desire to express her rage by stamping upon every rung of the ladder, she somehow managed to miss her footing and landed, plop, into the slimy, cold water below. This last action was simply too much for Kai, who gripped his sides and roared with laughter and didn't stop roaring until long after Blue had recovered the whispering pearl and stormed back up the ladder. Blue slammed the hatch in indignation, forgetting completely that the herder was still lying on the floor next to it and promptly tripped over the poor, dying creature, spilling the last of her precious store of stolen apples across the floor beside it. The herder groaned, but before it could completely wake up and take revenge for its rude awakening, Blue had dashed back up the corridor, leaving the apples where they lay.

The next day, once Lybesstre had managed to calm her young charge's fury down, Blue returned to the well, but instead of apples all she had been able to get hold of were sugar beets stolen straight out of the oryx feeding troughs. For some reason she had decided to stuff a couple of extra beets into her apron and thought nothing of it until, once again, found herself eye to eye with the herder. The herder appeared to have settled into that remote corner of the ship as if that were the only refuge where he could die undisturbed. Yet far from dying Blue found him to be in much better health and was eyeing Blue hungrily as she approached.

'I need to get past. Please don't eat me,' she pleaded fearfully.

'Apples,' was all it said and eyed Blue's apron greedily. Blue realised all the apples she had dropped had disappeared.

'I haven't got any more,' she said hurrying past nervously, praying as she did that the herder would allow her to enter the hatch. It did and Blue was able to make her way tensely down the ladder only to find Kai sitting waiting for his breakfast almost as expectantly as the herder.

'What's up with you?' he said seeing Blue looking unusually fretful as she worked quickly to turn Kai's hard tack into a porridge.

'Nothing,' she said delivering his meal rather frostily as she remembered his objectionable behaviour of the day before.

'What, no apples?' asked Kai prodding the porridge with a disappointed expression.

'No, no bloody apples!' snapped Blue and, throwing a couple of sugar beets through the bars, stormed back up the ladder. Upon her return, she found the herder squatting on his haunches facing the hatch in anticipation of Blue's re-emergence.

'More!' he said again and rocked back and forth on his haunches like a dog begging for food.

'Here,' she said coldly and threw the remaining sugar beets onto the floor in front of him. 'It's all I could find.' Like a cat the herder pounced onto the thick roots and, despite his lack of teeth, began ripping great chunks off with his hard gums. Regardless of the herder's apparent disinterest in turning Blue into his next meal, she couldn't help but imagine what other abominations that mouth must have ripped into and was grateful once the ripping and crunching sounds had been left far behind.

The next few days all followed the same pattern. Every day Blue would find the herder waiting on its haunches, ready for its next meal. Rarely would it speak to her, and even when it did it would utter little more than the odd monosyllabic grunt. The meals were hardly anything to get excited about and yet Blue noticed it getting stronger by the day— and not only did it appear to get stronger, but it ceased to resemble a herder at all. Firstly, its sloping shoulders and bent back appeared to be getting straighter, whilst soft dark hair also began to grow over the short spiny bones which ran up its back and over the crown of its bald skull. Even its teeth began to grow back, and not as the ghastly serrated fangs which the herders made such good use of to tear chunks of flesh off their victims, but these were white and broad and made the creature's face almost handsome to look at. In fact, it became so utterly altered in appearance from how Blue had first perceived it, that she decided that the creature couldn't be a herder at all. She even felt guilty for having been so callous and unsympathetic towards it during their first meetings—after all, it had somehow managed to get her whispering pearl back. Consequently, Blue decided that she was indebted to the creature and began doubling her efforts to spoil it at every opportunity. The creature, noticing the significant improvement to its meals, seemed more than ever to look forward to Blue's arrival. Nevertheless, Blue never felt inclined to speak of the creature to anyone, not even to Lybesstre, who had enough to deal with continually fending off the increasingly frantic, though painfully incompetent, advances of the love-struck Captain, than worrying about yet another hapless victim of that ship.

In the meantime, activity aboard the *Nefari* was starting to reach fever pitch. The Furud fleet had now completely reassembled and there was talk of their soon arriving at the Delta of the Great It-Eru, the river which led to the lands of the Uati. Already the waters of the ocean had changed from a deep blue to a cloudy green. Certainly, the rapid increase in temperature, which turned the bowels of the ship where Blue forever seemed to spend her time into a sweaty oven, also suggested they were getting closer to much more exotic climes. Even the captain, to Lybesstre's great relief, finally found himself too occupied to continually pester her and she was able to give Blue whatever help she could in obtaining food for Kai and the utterly dejected miners.

Finally, and Blue had thought the day would never arrive, she awoke to the soft sound of waves breaking on a sandy shore. She leapt out of bed and threw open the curtains of the cabin to find an endless sun-bathed landscape of golden sand greeting her eyes.

'We've arrived!' she said giddily and leapt back across the bed to wake up Lybesstre.

'Yes Blue, I know, we arrived last night, only you were so exhausted I thought I'd better let you sleep.'

'You mean you didn't tell me!'

'As I said, you getting a good sleep was more important than any misplaced excitement at our arrival.' Blue frowned and wondered why Lybesstre was so unenthusiastic. 'Don't confuse my caution for lack of enthusiasm,' said the priestess again somehow managing to read Blue's thoughts. 'Of course I too am relieved that this part of our journey is nearly over, but don't forget why we have been brought here, Blue. Whatever discomfort and exhaustion we have suffered on this ship may be nothing compared to the dangers and hardships we may yet have to face.'

In spite of Lybesstre's cautionary words they still failed to dampen Blue's spirits. For as far back as she could remember the furthest she had ever travelled away from home was to the old and dirty Port Stroenshal just south of Stod. This endless world of golden sand framed by a perfect azure sky was just too tantalising for her and she couldn't help but look forward to the moment they reached the mouth of the Delta and began to head inland.

'Here,' Lybesstre said more softly, finding Blue's unrestrained enthusiasm slightly infectious. 'You might like to try these. Some of the sailors went ashore this morning and brought them back with them. In my homelands they are considered quite a delicacy, though they grow in abundance along this part of the coast.' Lybesstre placed a small handful of dark red fruits into Blue's hands.

'What are they?' she asked wondering in mouth-watering anticipation what their sticky, aromatic flesh might taste like.

'They are called "bennu", the fruit of the sun bird. Try some, then you can take the rest to Kai and the weakest of the miners. They will help greatly in restoring their strength.'

Blue lifted the fruits slowly, and wanting to savour every moment, took a small bite out of one of them.

'They're delicious!' she exclaimed and began cramming the remaining fruits into her eager mouth.

'Be careful with the stones!' Lybesstre laughed. Blue ignored her and gulped down flesh and stone alike. When she had finished the handful, she looked around greedily for more. On Lybesstre's desk she spied a large bowl filled to the brim and was about to grab another handful when Lybesstre, still laughing, barred her way. 'Slow down!' she said smiling, 'They get quite sickly if you try to eat too many. Besides, we must make sure there are plenty for Kai and the miners.' This sobering reminder of the miners' plight was all Blue needed to halt her charge towards the bowl of fruit and she dropped her face in shame. 'Don't feel guilty Blue,' said Lybesstre gently. 'This terrible journey has been as hard for you as for they. You deserve so much more than a few bennu for all you have done. Please, eat as much as you like. I am sure I can convince that captain to give us more bennu than any of us can stand to eat.' Blue looked at Lybesstre gratefully but resolved that she would eat no more until she had taken as many as she could to the miners first.

Nevertheless, in no time Lybesstre had shown herself to be true to her word and soon an entire barrel of bennu sat beside the desk, filling the cabin with its exotic and deliciously sweet scent. In fact, Lybesstre continued to procure so much bennu from the extremely busy and distracted captain that Blue found by the end of the week she had slipped so much of it to Kai and the miners that they had actually started to look forward to their rations of dry tack. At least all had tired of it except the creature who Blue had mistaken as a herder. The perpetually ravenous creature never tired of the welcome change in his diet and wolfed down as much of the sickly, sticky fruit Blue could get hold of—which, thanks to Lybesstre's efforts, was no small amount. By the time the *Nefari* finally reached the mouth of the Delta Blue noted with great satisfaction that Kai, the miners, and especially the creature, all positively glowed with good health.

CHAPTER 6

The towns along the banks of the Delta — if "towns" is what you could call them — were far from how Blue imagined them, yet she watched enthralled as this sun-baked world of lazy silhouettes drifted past the cabin window. Sleepy, tanned faces peeked out from dusty doorways to watch the black hulks of the Furud glide upriver. How fragile their lives appeared to Blue. All that seemed to stand between them and the relentless march of the desert was a thin belt of green that ran along either side of the slow-moving waters. Even the river itself seemed less than welcoming as the broad, scaly backs of large lizard-like creatures surreptitiously sank under the brown waters whenever the ships sailed too close. Yet the further they travelled upriver, the smaller and sparser became the towns, until the crumbling walls of mud-brick and sandstone were replaced with thick beds of reeds that started to encroach upon the navigable channels of the river. Soon it was clear the ships would have to weigh anchor and begin to unload.

'What are those small hive-shaped nests I keep seeing in the reed beds?' Blue asked Lybesstre as she followed the column of humanity pouring off the ships into the encampment the soldiers were setting up along the banks of the river. Lybesstre smiled enigmatically.

'They are the homes of the Uati,' she whispered in Blue's ear making clear that Blue was to make no mention of it in front of any of the others.

'The Uati are birds!' Blue whispered back in surprise. 'I thought the villagers we've been seeing were the Uati.' Lybesstre laughed.

'That's what most people think. The Uati were here long before the arrival of any humans, but the Uati are neither bird nor human.'

'Are they not? Then what are they? Rodents?'

'Keep watching the "nests" and you may see one,' was all she said.

Whilst all that morning Blue kept one eye on the reed-beds, she also scoured the lines of men for any sign of the creature that had given her the whispering pearl back. Just before disembarking, she had taken the creature and Kai one last meal, but upon arriving at the hatch she had discovered the creature to have vanished. She was almost certain he was some sort of stowaway or escaped slave and, after all the efforts she had gone to restore him to life, she couldn't help but feel concern that he might have been caught and punished. Suddenly a loud crack of a whip and a shriek of pain caused Blue to fear the worst. Pushing past Lybesstre, she ran in the direction of the sound. Not far ahead a crowd of Furud warriors and sailors had gathered to jeer at the poor soul who was being flogged. It had to be her creature. Already she could see Caronte's fat legs pacing back and forth in front of the stricken victim.

'Not only do you seem incapable of keeping inventory, but you can't even keep roll call properly! Now where is he?'

'I dun't know!' wailed the voice. 'I only knows he was missing today when we started to unload. The rest of them herders has been asleep for four weeks. How could I have known?'

'Give him five for misplacing the stores, five for losing the herder and another ten for lying.' The man howled as the punishment was eagerly delivered. 'Now where is Basax?'

Blue knew she ought to be feeling a certain degree of guilt upon witnessing the poor quartermaster's plight, who no doubt was being punished for all the food Blue had appropriated on behalf of the miners, but when Caronte pronounced it was *Basax* who was missing, the full realisation of what had happened hit Blue like lead from a slingshot. The creature she had brought back from the dead *was* Basax. Blue felt the blood drain from her face and legs. How could she have helped bring back to life the very creature that not only had murdered and eaten Caelin her hammer, but had also threatened to murder and eat Gyd and herself? Surely there was only one reason Basax would have escaped and one reason alone: to exact some terrible revenge on Blue. The only way she could explain her not recognising the herder's familiar snarl and cruel features was that somehow the effects of the whispering pearl had made him so ill and caused him to lose so much weight that he had become unrecognisable. That must be why he had been so willing to give the whispering pearl back to her. Basax must have known the whispering pearl was making him ill.

A hand suddenly reached through the crowd and yanked Blue away from the heckling men. It was Lybesstre. At first Blue thought the priestess had slipped back into her role of Blue's ruthless and cruel witch mistress for the sake of the nearby sailors, but when the arm that Lybesstre had hold of actually began to burn with *real* pain, Blue realised the priestess' anger was not just an act.

'Is there something you haven't been telling me?' said the priestess turning on Blue furiously once they had reached a quiet spot away from the tents. It was the first time Blue had ever actually seen the priestess genuinely angry. Blue nodded sheepishly. She knew there was no point in lying.

'Is it to do with the disappearance of Basax?' Blue nodded again and felt tears coming to her eyes.

'Blue, tell me what you have done!' Blue could hold her tears back no longer.

'I had no idea it was him,' she sobbed. 'And when I fed him the apples, and then later the sugar beet, he started to look so different from a herder that I thought he was something else completely—a stowaway perhaps. I didn't tell anyone, because I was afraid they'd hurt him.'

'Hurt him! Hurt Basax! What were you thinking? Do you have any idea how much danger you have put yourself in?' Blue shook her head and hung her head in disgrace. 'Wait a minute. You said something about feeding him apples and sugar beet?'

'Yes.'

'And you actually meant to say, "apples and sugar beet"?'

'Yes? Well, there was also some bennu. Quite a lot actually.'

'Apples, sugar beet *and* bennu!' Blue looked at the priestess in confusion, wondering why she kept repeating the same words back to her.

'Oh, think girl! Herders eat meat and nothing else! In fact, herders only eat meat they have killed by their own hands. What are you talking about feeding him things like sugar beets and fruit? And as for bennu, any herder would have thrown up no sooner than look at them.'

'Well, he didn't throw up. In fact, after he gave me back the whispering pearl, that's all I could get him to eat. I couldn't get enough for him. He ate like an oryx.'

'Can it be possible?' the priestess said shaking her head in disbelief. 'You swear you are telling me the truth?' Blue nodded vigorously. 'And you say he gave the whispering pearl back to you?' Again, Blue nodded and produced the whispering pearl as evidence she was speaking the truth. Lybesstre continued to shake her head but the faintest flicker of a smile began to creep onto her face. 'I wonder... the whispering pearl? Can it be possible?'

Later that morning Blue had her first encounter with Lord Rasalas. Even by Furud standards she could see he was a large and intimidating man, powerful and tall in his steel armour who, with his silver-streaked hair and smouldering eyes, seemed to command the attention of those around him like a cobra cast into a crowd. Blue knew instantly it was an attention not based on respect, but fear. It was obvious from the way he was screaming at Caronte, who cowered apologetically on his knees before him, that the warlord had also found out about the shortfall in supplies. Caronte, for his part, kept trying to squirm his way out of trouble by repeatedly trying to shift the blame onto his quartermaster.

'And just how do you propose I am supposed to feed them all?' As Rasalas screamed the question he pointed the black, curling horn he was holding at the mass of rosy-cheeked miners chained together in the centre of the camp. 'And what have you been feeding them? They look healthier than my damned warriors!'

'I swear they have only been given the same rations I always give to slaves.'

'Then how in hell and damnation do you explain all the food that has gone missing? I'm starting to think you've either spent the entire crossing drunk, *again*, or you have lost your mind completely!'

'My lord, it was that witch you sent with us,' interrupted Magor nodding coldly at Lybesstre who stood nearby, 'He's done nothing during the voyage but follow her around like a lapdog. She's the one that's infected his mind, not the drink.'

'Well, Lybesstre, whether this is true or not, if you cannot conjure up enough supplies to feed them all and replace the ones this fat idiot has misplaced, then I'm putting half of them to the sword... and I'll put half your crew to the sword too so help me Gods!' Rasalas walked over to one of Caronte's sailors standing furtively nearby to enjoy the humiliation of his captain, but the sailor's enjoyment was soon cut short as Rasalas buried the horn in the sailor's gut. 'Laugh at this,' the old warrior said as he lifted the dying man off his feet until the man's blood ran down the horn's hilt and splashed onto the ground. 'That's just a taste of what I'll do if you don't sort this out,' he warned.

'But how are we to find supplies here?' Caronte wailed as the sailor dropped dead at Rasalas' feet. 'There is nothing but reed beds and desert? Nothing lives this far upriver. The river toads are poisonous and my men can find no fish larger than the size of a minnow!'

'That is not my concern. You have two days—or you leave here with half a crew.' Rasalas wiped the blood from the horn and glared at the assembled crowd as if daring anyone else to catch his eye. All dropped their gaze. 'Two days!' he warned and stormed back to his tent.

'What are we going to do?' Blue asked when she and Lybesstre were alone. Lybesstre shook her head and looked deathly pale.

'I wish I knew,' she replied.

'Don't say that!' Blue cried. 'How can you say that after all we've been through for them?'

'I'm sorry, Blue. Caronte is a lecherous old fool who can easily be bent to my will, but Rasalas is an altogether different prospect. Nothing I nor anyone can say will change his murderous intent.'

'What about bennu? Can't we collect enough bennu to save them?'

'We're too far inland. The warriors have already collected all that could be found, and that wasn't much. You've seen how close the desert grows to the banks of the river. Very little grows this far upriver. The only thing that will save our friends now is a miracle.'

'That's not good enough! I won't allow it! I won't stand around and wait for them to die!' Blue ran out of the tent.

'Blue wait!' Blue ignored the priestess and in despair ran as fast she could towards the reed beds, not stopping until the noises of the encampment were left far behind. Only when she found herself on a tiny island far from the river's edge did she stop to lie down and cry herself to sleep.

Evening was approaching by the time Blue awoke. Opening her eyes, the girl sat up to witness two yellow eyes like glossy beads blinking straight back at her from the round opening of a hive-shaped nest. The nest was just like the ones she had spent most of the day watching, with reeds neatly plaited together much like the triple-ended weave used by nimble-fingered Stod women to make whelk baskets. The yellow beads blinked at her twice more then moved closer to the mouth of the nest to reveal a leathery, almost human face with long, backwards-pointing ears that seemed as versatile as any limb, for whilst it observed Blue it managed to curl one ear forwards to scratch the tip of its nose before curling the ear back around the side of its head.

'So that's what you look like!' Blue remarked causing the creature to pop its head back into the nest. 'It's all right,' she said as softly as she could, 'I'm not going to hurt you.' After a few moments the small face reappeared and blinked quizzically at her. In its mouth it appeared to be crunching thoughtfully into the hard shell of a large beetle as it watched its visitor. 'You wouldn't just happen to have enough food in there to feed a few hundred men, would you?' The tiny creature blinked at her a moment longer, then, deciding she posed no threat, dived out of the hole and with a crisp plop disappeared into the water. Seconds later it reappeared with a long, cream-coloured tuber gripped between its shiny white teeth. This it dropped in front of Blue before diving back into the water to fetch a second, much fatter tuber also gripped between his teeth. Blue nudged her own tuber suspiciously whilst the little creature settled on the ground a few feet away from her and began scrunching eagerly into his meal.

'You can eat these?' Blue asked. The tiny creature seemed to smile and continued to enjoy his dinner. Blue picked the tuber up and sniffed it. It didn't have a very appetising smell—in fact, it reminded her a little of the stagnant, damp smell the mirounga skins used to have before they were fully cured and dried. Nevertheless, watching the pleasure the Uati was clearly deriving from devouring his own tuber made Blue start to think that perhaps she ought to at least try it. With a less-than-enthusiastic sniff and wipe on her tunic sleeve Blue lifted the tuber to her mouth and bit a corner off of one end. It was better than she expected. In fact, it was much better. It had a strangely crunchy, nutty consistency and a clean, starchy flavour that was actually very pleasant. Before Blue realised it, she had eaten the entire tuber. The tiny Uati, who in spite of his size had managed to finish his own much larger tuber in about half the time it took

Blue to eat hers, was sitting watching her with a look of satisfaction. Suddenly, Blue realised the significance of her discovery. Reaching into the water she pulled up a mass of vegetation. It was full of white tubers! She reached across to the other side and produced the same density of tubers with the slightest of pulls. She leapt up, thanking the strange creature as she did, and with a soggy armful of vegetation gripped tightly to her chest waded as fast as she could back through the reeds in the direction of the encampment.

'Lybesstre!' she cried upon reaching the tent. Lybesstre came running out, her face drained from worry.

'Where have you been? If Rasalas knew you'd gone missing he would have fed you to the herders as soon as find you!'

'Look!' Blue said triumphantly. 'They are everywhere! They grow under the reed beds. All you have to do is pull them up.' Lybesstre, like Blue had done, eyed the dripping tubers suspiciously. 'Watch,' Blue said and bit a chunk off one of them. 'They're quite tasty! One of the Uati showed me how to get them.'

'How could I have been so stupid!' said Lybesstre lifting a hand to her brow. 'How could I have forgotten the bread of the It-Eru? Quick,' she said slipping sandals on to her bare feet, 'we must hurry and take these to Caronte. We'll still need his cooperation as I doubt Rasalas will be in the mood to lend us any warriors or miners to help harvest the roots.' Together they hurried back onto the *Nefari* where Caronte had taken refuge from Rasalas' fury and, on finding him sulking in his cabin, showed him the mass of roots.

'Look! Food!' Blue cried triumphantly. 'Limitless food! There's enough to feed the entire army!' Caronte looked at Blue and the roots and scowled.

'Silence slave!' Lybesstre snapped with mock indignation as she reverted back into her role as Blue's mistress. 'My dear captain,' she said with syrupy sweetness. 'I felt so terrible to hear that man speak to you so poorly after the wonderful way you have looked after us all so I sent my slave here to see what food she could find amongst the reed beds. What the girl says is true. For centuries these roots were eaten in place of bread. With the help of your men, we could gather more than enough to replenish our supplies and stop any unnecessary and foolish waste of life—lives you worked so hard and selflessly to preserve. You *will* help us won't you my darling captain?' When the priestess spoke the word "darling", sweat visibly appeared on the captain's brow and he returned Lybesstre's calculated look of girlish vulnerability with a look of hopeless infatuation.

'My dear Lybesstre,' he declared gallantly placing his hands on his wobbling chest. 'Your words have lifted a heavy heart. By my life or the life of my men you shall have your supplies!'

Over the course of the evening Blue witnessed a heap of tubers the size of a small mountain, appear in the centre of the camp where they were quickly preserved in brine and stored in barrels. Just as Blue was starting to feel things were going well, two rough looking sailors emerged from the reed beds not far from the island where Blue had been hidden. They were hooting and hollering and very quickly an unruly crowd of leering warriors and sailors had gathered around them. Blue strained to see what the commotion was about but couldn't see past the mass of bodies blocking her view. Suddenly one of the sailors dashed off to the ship and returned with a small cage into which a wriggling, tiny brown figure was unceremoniously dumped. Blue watched the proceedings with a sinking heart. They had captured the Uati.

From a nearby large tent a hot and irritable looking Rasalas emerged and demanded to know why he was being disturbed so late. The crowd parted to reveal their captive. Rasalas, at first disbelieving what he was seeing, moved closer, then, his eyes opening wide with glee, roared with laughter and ordered the men to set its cage down next to Kai whose own cage had been transferred from the ship and placed near the oryx pens like a prized wild animal.

'Another freak for the collection!' he roared. 'Somebody, fetch a flute. I want to see if it can dance.' Almost immediately a small bone flute was produced and one of the sailors began playing a jig. The Uati sat calmly and watched the flute player with the same quizzical expression it had used to examine Blue. Rasalas drew his sword and tried prodding the diminutive captive with the point.

'Come on little monkey, dance!' The audience guffawed. Ducking hastily under the blade the Uati stood up. Thinking the little prisoner was about to perform, the crowd began to cheer and clap in time with the flute—but the Uati didn't dance. Instead, the small creature closed its eyes, took a long, deep breath… and began to sing.

What gave that song such unsettling charm and power to silence every warrior, every sailor, every slave Blue couldn't begin to comprehend, but even the horses and beasts of burden ceased their complaining and settled peacefully onto the hot, baked earth as if they were listening to its song as avidly as the men. In the pocket of her tunic Blue could feel the whispering pearl humming as if with pleasure. For how long they all sat there listening to the Uati sing no one was really able to say, but by the time the last man had drifted peacefully back to his tent, a thick veil of stars filled the night's sky.

Seeing the last warrior dawdle dreamily back to his tent was the moment Blue had been waiting for. She hurried over to the cage to see if she could find some way of unlocking or breaking open the door and releasing their little saviour back into the reeds.

'Why does he watch me when he sings?' asked Kai still awake and staring at his tiny neighbour with a dreamy fascination. 'What is he? He's hardly taken his eyes off me all evening.'

'He is one of the Uati.' said a woman's voice behind them. It was Lybesstre. 'He is an ancient survivor from an age when the Earth was still innocent and beautiful.'

'But he keeps staring at me every time he sings. What does he want?'

'He wants you to learn his song.'

'Learn his song! Why?'

'Because he hears the call of Aatxe. Aatxe's immense power resides within you and it is this power he wishes for you to unlock and master. Listen to the Uati and learn from him. His allowing himself to be captured is a blessing not to be taken lightly.'

'He *allowed* himself to be captured?'

'Of course. The Uati choose when they wish to be seen and by whom. He let the sailors capture him so he could be closer to you, Kai. It was the only way he could teach you.'

'What can he possibly teach me about power? He's shorter than my forearm!'

'Suspend your judgement. The reasons behind the lessons he brings to you will become evident with time. For now, it would be wise of you to observe everything he does closely. If it is his wish for you to learn his song then you must strive to do so.'

Kai frowned and stared dubiously at the priestess and at the Uati who peered back happily at Kai through the bars of his cage as if his captivity were a marvellous joke. Blue also looked doubtfully at the small creature.

'You too, Blue. You too have much yet to learn. You still neglect to use the your most precious gift.'

'What gift? You mean the whispering pearl?'

'No, not the whispering pearl. Your gift of healing Blue.'

'But I... I don't know how to heal.'

'Nonsense. Healing comes as naturally to you as breathing.'

'It does?'

'Blue, how do you think the miners survived the crossing in that crowded and filthy hold without any disease or ailment of any kind? When have you ever heard of such a thing?'

'Well, I...? It is strange for sure—but I figured you were doing something to help them.'

'Not I,' said Lybesstre.

'Then it must have been the extra food we gave them.'

'That helped, but it was not nearly enough for what they needed.'

'Surely you're not suggesting it was all because of me?'

'I am.'

'That's ridiculous!'

'Is it? Tell me, how did you feel when you walked amongst your friends and saw them penned and beaten like animals?'

'How did I feel? Well, how do you think I felt? I felt frustration and anger. I felt pity. I felt a desire to help them.'

'A desire backed with incredible determination and love. Blue, your desires, your feelings, they carry great healing power. In fact, they carry such power that the very universe shifts its alignment to accommodate those feelings. Blue, your walking amongst the miners on that ship was like spring water falling on parched earth. If you had abandoned them sickness would have spread amongst them like fire through tinder. It was your presence and your love that kept it at bay. If only you were aware of the energy and protective power you unleash with such feelings. It was feelings such as these that drew the whispering pearl to you—and now the whispering pearl has helped awaken your power. All that remains is for you to consciously begin to use it.'

'Use it on who?'

'On Kai for a start. It's high time you healed his leg. His spine and shoulders could do with a little straightening too. He has a terrible posture.'

Blue looked down at the dirty clothes half concealing the ugly wound and weakened muscles on Kai's leg and wondered if Lybesstre wasn't going mad.

'I know what you are thinking Blue. You look at his affliction and tell yourself it is beyond anyone's ability to heal, but you are wrong. *You* have that ability Blue and much more. You have always had the ability to do things that many would consider miraculous. You must stop letting your doubts sap your strength like an ague. Now that Kai has fallen foul of Rasalas' favour he will need your help more than ever if he is to survive the gruelling march across the desert that awaits us. Blue, he needs your help.' Blue nodded and sighed.

'Very well. I suppose I can try. What is it you want me to do?'

'I want you to learn how to channel the lifeblood of the Earth. Beneath our feet a force of unimaginable power courses through the Earth much like our own blood courses through our veins. You must learn to tap into this or risk using up your own reserves of energy. It is essential that you get this right.'

'Why? What will happen if I don't?'

'It could prove fatal.'

'Fatal! You didn't tell me this was going to be dangerous!'

'Then I suggest you try to silence that incessant chatter in your mind and concentrate.' Blue had not been aware that her mind had been filled with chatter, but now that Lybesstre made mention of it she did notice that her head was full of a constant stream of rather repetitive and meaningless thoughts.

'Okay, I'll give it a go,' she said and knelt down beside Kai's cage. 'What do I do?'

'Place a hand on each of Kai's feet then bring your attention down into the Earth.' Blue nodded and did her best to silence the frivolous chatter filling her head, though the state of Kai's grubby feet did little to help her concentrate.

'What am I looking for?'

'You are searching for a vein of the Earth's energy. When you find the vein be careful how much energy you allow to flow back through you. What might seem like a small flow of energy to you will feel like a force of incredible power to the one you are healing. If you allow too much too quickly you could end up causing more harm than good.'

Lybesstre's warning did little to boost Blue's confidence and she found herself fumbling in her tunic pocket for the whispering pearl.

'Leave the whispering pearl,' Lybesstre insisted.

'But...'

'Trust me Blue. You need to learn to do this without the whispering pearl. The whispering pearl has already served its purpose. It is time for you now to let your gifts unfold.' Blue returned the whispering pearl to the pouch in her tunic and gingerly reached through the bars to take hold of Kai's feet again. 'I suggest you search more towards the river. The flow of energy is always strongest under naturally flowing water.' Blue did as she was asked and tried to feel her way down to a point under the slow flowing waters of the It-Eru.

'It's not working,' said Blue after finding it impossible to think of anything other than Kai's mucky feet and how she wished he'd washed them first.

'Try again. This time call upon the Eledh to help you. They will hear you.' Blue closed her eyes and tried again, this time heeding the priestess' advice by silently calling on the Eledh to help her. As she did so she noticed the Uati had begun once more to sing. Calmed by the creature's sweet and soothing voice, Blue found her concentration being drawn as if by unseen hands down into the Earth to a point far beneath the river. At first, she sensed little more than endless layers of sand and rock, but then Blue started to sense something else; something akin to flowing water. For a moment Blue thought it might, indeed, be little more than an underground river, but as she drew closer, she realised it wasn't water at all but a powerful flow of energy that followed the course of the river above. Exhilarated, albeit a little overwhelmed at the force of energy she had discovered, Blue pushed herself into its flow. '

The rush of energy that shot upwards through the earth and out through her hands into Kai was ferocious. Kai yelped in fright and pain as his bones and flesh crackled and sparked. Blue realised instantly it was too much but found stemming the flow of energy was a lot harder than tapping into it. As best she could Blue blocked out the heart-wrenching cries of pain from Kai and with a great effort somehow managed to slow the surging energy. Meanwhile Kai gritted his teeth as tears of pain poured down his cheeks.

'Please stop,' he begged feeling he was being burnt alive. Kai didn't have to plead for long for Blue too was struggling to cope with the incredible energies being unleashed through her. Unable to stand any more, Blue threw her hands off and fell with a cry backwards into Lybesstre, who caught her in her arms like a mother might a child.

The energy subsided. The Uati continued to sing... and the camp remained still.

'Well done,' Lybesstre said with a look of satisfaction as she affectionately stroked Blue's hair. 'A little heavy-handed but with practice I'm sure you'll get better.'

'I'm sorry Kai,' began Blue, her voice filling with remorse as she looked at the limp figure lying on the floor of the cage. 'I didn't mean to...'

'He's fine,' said Lybesstre. 'In fact, he's never been better. Look, even his scars have disappeared.' Lybesstre's mention of his childhood scars disappearing was just enough to rouse Kai from his final death throes and inspect his wounded leg and body. To his astonishment there was no trace of any wound at all. He sat up. No pain! In a flurry of touching, squeezing and prodding he examined the rest of his body. There was no sign of injury or scarring anywhere! Even the weakened muscles of his injured leg looked to have filled out. If his cage would have allowed him Kai would have leapt for joy!

'Who would have believed it!' he said with a voice laced with emotion as he continued to run his hands disbelievingly over his healed leg, though none were more surprised at the outcome than Blue.

'He's... well. He's so...' Blue struggled to find the words.

'Healed?' said Lybesstre helpfully. 'Or was "handsome" the word you were looking for?' Blue dropped her eyes with embarrassment.

Smiling, the witch priestess turned to Kai. 'I suggest you feign a slight limp for a while. We don't need you drawing unwanted attention to yourself. Come Blue. We should leave. The Uati cannot sing all night long and when he stops the camp guards will soon remember what they were supposed to be doing. Tomorrow is likely to be a very long day for all of us and we will need to get as much rest as we can.'

As Blue turned to follow Lybesstre for some reason she found herself unable to hold Kai's lingering gaze. It wasn't that Blue was averse to being thanked by the young servant — for she assumed his gaze was one of gratitude and nothing else — it was the fact that something had changed in the way Kai looked at her, as if not just the flesh of his body had knitted itself back into place, but his eyes appeared to have burst into life like the eyes of a stillborn child brought back from the dead. The change in him had both unnerved and thrilled her at the same time and she couldn't begin to say why. Of course it had been a very long day and she was no doubt allowing her tired mind to play tricks on her imagination, but as she reached the tent and began to make ready for bed, the pleasant voice of a second singer rose above the voice of the Uati and floated out across the sleeping encampment into the starlit desert... The singer was Kai.

CHAPTER 7

It wasn't the sharp claws digging into the flesh of her legs, the hot skin beneath her face, or even the fact that she suddenly found herself hanging upside down that first woke Blue. What woke her seconds before the rough hands seized her and hauled her out of the tent was the unbearable stench—the unbearable stench of herders. With legs in the air and head bobbing up and down like a cork in a storm, Blue heard Lybesstre's frantic cries calling her name above the waking sounds of the encampment, but the sounds were growing very faint very fast and it wasn't long before they had faded altogether. Still the herders kept running. Blue had never seen a herder run, and even though she was absolutely terrified and convinced she was going to die, a small part of her had to admit being impressed with the impossible speeds with which the two herders tore across the floor of the desert. From her unfortunate vantage point Blue witnessed wide gullies and large boulders that the finest horse would have struggled to clear being leapt effortlessly without the herders even seeming to break their stride. On and on the desert flew past until the heat of the morning sun began to beat mercilessly down upon Blue and her captors' backs. Finally, as they reached the shade of a small rocky outcrop, the herders stopped and, panting heavily, dumped Blue onto the burning desert floor. Both of them looked around nervously.

'Him still there?' asked the herder who had been carrying Blue.

'No, we lost him.'

'You sure?' Both the herders sniffed the air.

'Can't smell him. Told you we lost him.'

'What was *him* doin out here?'

'Don't know but Garoa not like it. Him look like Jentilak now. Not natural. Not good.'

'Quick, we best eat girl now and get back before thems notices we not there.'

'You sure that her?' the other herder asked.

'It's her all right. Here, smell.' Blue felt herself lifted by the scruff of the neck and shoved close to the broad nose of the other herder. He sniffed her face and hair deeply.

'Yeah, that her. The shaft rat that took our meal. You thought Garoa and Ler forget you steal our food, did you? No one steal food from herders. Thought you leavin without giving Garoa and Ler the brekfust you took? Well, you very wrong.' Blue realised the "brekfust" they were referring to must have been Gyd.

'Get off me!' she yelled, kicking out at the herder as it reached over to grab hold of her hair.

Suddenly a heavy blow took the wind out of her and she felt a mass of muscle and bone crushing down upon her. 'Get off me!' she screamed again and tried to fight the creature off, kicking, scratching and biting at the herder's heavy torso. The herder lifted off her looking strangely groggy, but just as it was regaining its senses a second blow sent it reeling to one side. Although the low sun was shining straight into Blue's eyes, she could see enough to make out the shape of a third herder, yet this one, rather than join in the other two's feast, appeared set on robbing them of their prize—no doubt to eat her all by itself. Spitting blood, her kidnapper turned and snarled, but instead of launching himself at the new attacker, he began to back away.

'Traitor!' it spat.

'Jentilak scum!' snarled its companion who also seemed hurt and unwilling to carry on the fight. The two herders continued to back off until they felt sure they had put enough distance between themselves and their assailant, then together they turned and took off across the desert. Blue shielded her eyes from the blinding desert sun as the large silhouette loomed closer.

'Here,' it said offering her a large, hairy paw. Blue shook her head and shuffled backwards. The herder moved out of the line of the sun and knelt down. 'Here,' it said again holding out its hand. This time Blue could see its face clearly. The broad, white teeth and thick head of hair, the smell of bennu upon its breath... It was the creature from the ship; the creature Blue now knew to be Basax. Blue's head screamed at her to run, but her heart seemed to be telling her a different story. If Basax had wanted to take some gruesome revenge on her he would hardly be offering her his hand. She looked at the herder again. He certainly no longer had the look of that vile creature who had intended to eat both her and Gyd aboard Caronte's black ship. More importantly he no longer had the feel of that herder either—and no matter how afraid of Basax she was, Blue had to accept the undeniable truth that the very same herder had just saved her life.

Trusting heart over head, Blue took the creature's hand and allowed it to help her up, but no sooner was she upright than she found herself having to cling desperately to the herder's thick neck as he swung her onto his back and set off running across the desert.

'Where... are... you... taking... me?' she asked between the herder's long strides.

'Away from here,' was all Basax replied and continued to put as much distance as he could between themselves and the encampment.

***

How Basax could keep going in that blazing heat without stopping to rest Blue couldn't begin to fathom. Only once did he stop to tip over a boulder a team of horses would have struggled to move to reveal the muddy trickle of a spring beneath, and when he had drunk his fill, he threw Blue again onto his back and set off racing across the desert. Blue noted sourly that he hadn't even asked her if she might need a drink. It wasn't until nightfall that Basax finally afforded them both a rest. Quickly digging down into the dry bed of a narrow channel he again managed to excavate a muddy pool of water.

'Wait for mud to settle, then drink.' Blue waited for as long as her thirst could bear then slurped down the muddy water as fast as she could as if she had been drinking from the purest well. Basax sniffed the night air and peered out intently into the darkness. 'We stay until the kabechet sing—then we leave.'

'Kabechet?' asked Blue with muddy water dripping from her chin.

'Desert snake. Now sleep.' Blue wished she hadn't asked but was so exhausted that not even her fear of snakes could prevent her eyelids from drooping and her quickly falling into an exhausted and deep sleep.

'Eat.' Blue opened her eyes blearily. It was still night but Blue noted the chill air was filled with the sound of high-pitched chirrups. 'Eat. Breakfast.' Basax shoved something small into her hand. She grimaced as she realised it had wings. Nevertheless, she was starving so obediently crunched into whatever it was. The taste was disgusting, like runny, rotten eggs. With a supreme effort Blue swallowed it down not knowing when the next meal might come.

'Are you not eating?' she asked picking a slimy wing from one of her teeth.

'No. Basax not like snehem. Disgusting. Basax prefer fruit.' With a loud guffaw Basax produced a large handful of elongated fruits, the half of which he threw to Blue.

'Very funny!' Blue said and bit hurriedly into one of the fruits as much from hunger as to get rid of the awful taste of the snehem. 'Ouch!' she yelled as short prickly spines jabbed into the roof of her mouth.

'Take skin off first,' Basax said and guffawed even louder. Blue scowled and attempted to peel off the prickly skins without causing herself too much pain.

'Ouch!' she yelped again as a spine stabbed into her finger. Basax chuckled deeply and took the fruits back off her. Producing a razor-sharp claw from his finger he effortlessly sliced the skins open. In seconds all the skins had been removed and the peeled fruit handed back to Blue. Blue thanked him begrudgingly and bit into one. The fruit was full of small seeds and tasted a little old and fermented, but after eating them a pleasant fizzing sensation in her stomach soon spread to the rest of her limbs and she began to feel revived. Besides, anything was better than the "snehem" Basax had tricked her into eating. Suddenly the tiny chirrups that filled the air fell silent. Basax leapt onto his haunches and sniffed the air.

'We leave now,' he said and, scooping the girl up in his powerful arms, bounded out into the night.

CHAPTER 8

The morning of their departure was frenzied. Kai awoke to having the elation he felt at finding his injury and scars still healed dashed completely when he heard Blue was missing. Rasalas was furious; not because he cared in the slightest for Blue's welfare, but because he feared her apparent escape would incite others to attempt to do the same. He bluntly refused to hear of any suggestion that she had been kidnapped, and when confronted by a frantic Lybesstre, his response was to have her bound and thrown amongst the rest of the slaves until the "scheming witch" learnt to speak when instructed. In the meantime, Kai noticed the two herders skulking back into camp and feared the worst.

'You two come here!' Rasalas ordered spotting Garoa and Ler trying to slip unnoticed between the tents.

'Yes, my Lord,' they replied inclining their large, bald heads in his direction.

'Where are the rest of those curs? Go fetch them. I want you to bring me the head of that brat who has escaped. What you do with the rest of the body is your own business.' The creatures bowed and barely able to contain their glee, raced off to find the remaining herders. As the herders poured out of the ship and charged off into the desert, Kai began kicking the door of his cage in frustration.

'Contain your anger,' warned Lybesstre moving as close to Kai's cage as she could. Kai could see the priestess was as worried as he but could also tell she was doing her utmost to present a calm exterior. 'Provoking Rasalas further is not going to help Blue.'

'What help is there for Blue now?' said Kai. 'I know it was those two scum herders who took her. I could see it in their eyes.'

'So could I. But did you not also notice that one of them was carrying a wound to the side of its head and neither one bore the look of having eaten a recent kill? I think something disturbed them before they got the chance to finish what they had started. She might still be alive. You have to help me find her.'

'How am I supposed to find her? I'm locked in a cage!'

'Use your sight.'

'My sight? But it doesn't work like that. It just sort of happens. I don't really have any control over it.'

'Then it's time you learnt to control it.'

'Even if I could, what's the point? Rasalas has set the rest of the pack after her. If she's still alive she'll not be for long.'

'Please. Just help me find where she is.'

'Very well,' he said. 'For what it's worth I'll try, but the herders could have carried her anywhere. She could be miles away by now.'

'Distance is not important. Try to remember all you can about her; how she looked, how she spoke, how you felt when you were with her. It will help you make a connection. I will help you as best I can.' Kai looked unconvinced but closed his eyes anyway, trying to remember everything he could about Blue: her clothing, her voice, her smell... Kai screwed his face up as he remembered the excrement-covered cap and slop bucket.

'Perhaps a more recent memory would serve better,' suggested the priestess with a frown. Kai shook his head clear of the unpleasant image and tried to remember how Blue had dressed around the encampment. It wasn't all that different, only the cap and dirty apron had gone and, thankfully, with them the awful smell. Still, it was no good, he just couldn't get a sense of where she was.

'Don't give up,' said Lybesstre. 'Dig deeper. What other memories of her do you have? Use everything you can.'

Kai cast his mind back to those first days on the *Nefari*. They were all so blurred, so feverish. He remembered the apples and her falling into the water as she recovered the whispering pearl. He remembered visions too; visions of a great bird and a black rock that rose out of the ground like the hand of a fallen god reaching to the heavens... suddenly an image flashed in his mind.

'I can see her!' he gasped. 'She's alive!'

'Where is she?' said Lybesstre heartened by his words.

'She's in the desert... but she's not alone.'

'Who is with her?' Kai's eyes fell.

'What's the matter?' Lybesstre asked seeing his concern.

'She's been taken… by a herder.' Bitter disappointment showed on Kai's face.

'Are you sure?'

Kai nodded and sat staring despondently at the ground. Next to him the Uati sat with his eyes closed tight, though far from sharing Kai's pessimistic mood, the Uati looked as cheery as ever.

'What's he got to be so happy about?' Kai said scowling. Lybesstre looked across to see the small creature begin to chuckle. All of a sudden, a thought dawned on the priestess.

'How was the herder carrying her? Was he carrying her by the feet with the rest of her body slung over his shoulder like a sack?'

'No,' said Kai wondering what difference it made. 'She was holding on to his neck like this.' Kai demonstrated how he had seen Blue clinging to the herder's neck much like a child might ride the back of its parent. Lybesstre's eyes lit up and a smile played across her lips.

'Am I missing something?' Kai asked, bewildered at both their reactions.

'You most certainly are!' Lybesstre said laughing. 'I think we can stop worrying now. Blue is in safe hands.'

'Safe hands! How can she be in safe hands if she has been captured by a herder?'

'That is no mere herder. That is Basax, the strongest and most fearsome herder I have ever known. Only… he hasn't captured her. He's rescued her!'

'Rescued! How do you work that out?'

'Ever since Basax took possession of the whispering pearl and began to be nursed back to health by Blue, he started an irreversible process of transformation. Not only did he stop looking like a herder, he stopped behaving and thinking like a herder too. In fact, he's becoming more like a Jentilak!' Kai looked at the witch priestess as if she had gone mad. Seeing his dumbfounded expression, Lybesstre began to explain. 'The real name of the herders is "Atzerri". In their native tongue it means "Exile". Thousands of years ago, after the Horim disappeared, a terrible drought and famine spread to all the corners of the Kugarran continent.'

Lybesstre pointed at the desert all around them. 'We are still seeing its devastating effects today. The Jentilak, against all the odds, persevered against the endless drought and managed to scrape out a life for themselves, but those early days were very hard—so hard that a band of younger Jentilak began to grow impatient and tired of the constant toil and struggle and, convincing themselves they were acting from a noble desire to help their people, they secretly began to hire their services out to any northern merchant who could afford to pay them. Sadly, it wasn't long before the greed and decadence of the northern races began to poison the young Jentilaks' bodies and minds and, imperceptibly at first, they began to grow sick and change from within. After a time, they had become so unruly and destructive that their own people were left with no choice but to expel them. From that day forth they adopted the name "Atzerri" but in time became known only as "Herders". With no homeland and no dignity, they lost all self-esteem and quickly fell prey to warlords and slave-traders who prized their incredible speed, athleticism and strength. Over the centuries, their increasing willingness to indulge in every cruelty and vice has weighed heavily upon them and they have become changed beyond recognition. The Jentilak have always been spoken of as a noble and beautiful race to the few who have met them, so you can imagine just how far the Atzerri have fallen.'

'But how could they have changed so much? How could they have grown so foul?'

'They began to eat flesh.'

'Flesh!'

'No Jentilak would ever consider killing a living creature let alone cause it unnecessary suffering before eating it. They understand for the Jentilak not just the tormented flesh would be absorbed into the body, but the tormented spirit of the creature too. Over time, it wreaked havoc on the sensitive Atzerris' bodies, minds and souls.'

Loud shouting and a flurry of activity interrupted their discussion. Behind them the miners were being dragged to their feet.

'Get him out,' Rasalas shouted pointing across at Kai. 'Chain him at the rear of the slaves. When we get there, he is to dig like the rest of them.' The warriors did as Rasalas instructed and attached a collar and chain to his neck.

'Wait,' Rasalas said grabbing hold of the Uati's cage. 'Every time he drops it, he gets ten lashes.' The Furud warriors nodded and passed the cage to Kai who tried to hide his relief that at least it would be he who would be responsible for the Uati's transportation and not one of the warlord's warriors. 'The witch comes with me,' Rasalas said glowering at Lybesstre. 'I want her at the front of the column. It's time for her to prove her worth and lead the way… and she had better know where we are going or I'll cut her into such small pieces even that tiny freak will be able to eat her.'

Kai watched the beautiful priestess disappearing into the curtain of dust rising from the thundering hooves of a hundred great oryx, who bayed in protest under their heavy packs of tents, weapons and supplies. Finally, like a long serpent slowly unwinding its coils, the army moved off until the links of Kai's chain pulled taught and he felt himself dragged out into the searing desert heat.

CHAPTER 9

The sunsets were the most beautiful time in the desert. Blue hadn't imagined the sky could take on so many hues and colours. When she'd lived in the gloomy fishing town, it was rare to see the sky any other colour than drizzly grey. Further south, locals even gave a name to the colour found so frequently in the skies above her home town, referring to any rainy grey colour as "Stod grey". On the fleeting occasions there was any colour it would usually peek shyly over the horizon then discreetly slide back to whatever warmer parts of the world it had risen from. Here, in the desert, colour was a shameless flirt, exhibiting itself in every sensual hue and vibrancy. But for all its beauty, Blue knew it was the sign to start getting ready to leave. For the past ten days, she and Basax had travelled mostly by night. The desert nights were noisy affairs and the temperatures usually dropped so low that it was almost impossible to sleep anyway. So, instead they reverted to travelling by night and sleeping during the heat of day. So far Basax had always managed to find them shelter from the sun and just enough water to drink, not that Blue appeared to have much need for shade for her pale northern skin seemed to have become strangely immune to the sun's burning rays, never betraying so much as a hint of that ugly, angry red that so plagued the complexions of those Stod sailors reckless enough to venture too far south. Blue was also proving pretty resilient to the dry conditions, no doubt thanks to the long hours she'd spent in the oven-like tunnels of the mines, but the lack of food was starting to pose a problem. It wasn't so much that there wasn't any food, for Basax could hear or smell any moving creature from over a mile away, the problem was that Basax now categorically refused to eat any living thing no matter how small or insignificant.

'But you ate my hammer you stupid pit hog!' Blue exclaimed, exasperated that she couldn't even get him to take a bite out of the tiny lizard she had succeeded, at great physical expense, in capturing. Basax pouted like an infant.

'That was old Basax. That not who Basax is now.'

'But you're going to starve! *We're* going to starve!'

'Basax find fruit.'

'Where? We're in the middle of a desert! For how much longer do you think you're going to be able to find fruit?'

'Basax find fruit,' he insisted and continued to pout. Blue looked down at the tiny lizard pinned between her fingers. It was very pretty for a lizard, with its big, dark eyes and little pink feet.

'Damn it!' said Blue letting the lizard slip out of her fingers. 'Now your stupidity is starting to affect me!' What could she do? She knew that venting her frustration like this on the big herder was wrong, for without Basax she would have been dead long ago. Nevertheless, for all his speed and strength, she knew it was getting harder to find enough food for them both, and without food they were growing weaker by the day—and every day that Basax grew weaker was a day that their pursuers, who certainly didn't have any qualms about eating the living creatures of the desert, would recover a little of the lost ground between them.

***

The next three days gave Blue even more cause for concern. The desert had noticeably begun changing. The sky during the day seemed strangely gloomier and the nights were starting to become deathly quiet. Even the scant pockets of thorny vegetation that they'd been relying on for food seemed to be getting smaller and more sporadic. It was as if what little desert life remained was starting to abandon that desolate place for good. Blue was painfully aware that Basax was finding worryingly little to eat and, although he wouldn't admit it, she knew the distances they were covering every day were also decreasing. The few spiny fruits and bennu he did manage to find were simply not enough. Blue did what she could to ration her own share, but she knew what little she had stored in her pouch wouldn't last long if the patches of thorny scrub ran out altogether. Of course she did all she could to help Basax counter the fatigue and hunger, slyly giving him healing whenever she had an opportunity, but the healing too was getting weaker for not only did there seem to be less life above the surface, it was as if the land was ominously dying beneath as well.

'I don't like it. Something's not right here. How much longer until we get out of this awful place?'

'Don't know,' Basax replied with a shrug. 'Basax lost.'

'You're lost! What do you mean you're lost? I thought you knew where we were going!'

'Basax did. But now Basax don't.'

'How can you one minute know and then not know?'

'Too hungry. Too tired. Nose and ears not work so good when hungry and tired. Must rest.'

Only then did Blue realise just how serious their predicament was. Up to that point, the one thing Blue could always rely on was that Basax knew exactly where they were headed. It was that reassurance that helped Blue deal with the heat and the hunger and the thirst, but knowing that Basax's indestructible sense of smell and acute hearing was starting to fail brought Blue's fear and fatigue crushingly home.

'Do you think there is a chance the herders will have lost our trail?' she asked hopefully as Basax flopped onto the hard ground.

'No. Too easy to follow? Blue stink too much.'

'*I* stink! That's rich coming from a herder! Perhaps you ought to turn that fat nose of yours onto yourself once in a while.' Basax stood up with a hurt expression on his face. It had never occurred to him that he might smell bad. He looked down at his hairy chest and arms and, lowering his nose to his armpit, sniffed deeply. After a minute of sniffing and inspecting other areas of his body he lifted his head and announced with a triumphant smile:

'No. Blue stink worse!' Blue kicked a rock angrily in his direction and turned to sit crossly with her back to him.

'Anyway,' she said, 'who cares if we smell. At this rate the desert will kill us before the herders do. This is a bad place to be lost.' Basax shrugged again and sat back down.

'Good place, bad place. All the same to Basax. Basax not scared of dying. No herder afraid to die.'

'Is there anything herders are afraid of?'

Basax went quiet as he pondered her question.

'Espiritua,' he said finally and shuddered.

'Espiritua?'

'Spirits. All herders afraid of spirits. No herder ever go near them.'

'Spirits!' Blue said laughing. 'How can you not be afraid of dying but be afraid of those that have?' Basax shuddered again.

'Quiet. Basax not talk about it.'

Blue watched the herder with a bemused expression. He seemed so invincible, yet here he was quivering like a frightened pup at the mere mention of ghosts. Shame the herders hadn't known about all the ghoulish apparitions that had been witnessed around Stod. Perhaps Blue and the miners would still be there digging away in the depths of the mine if they had. Thinking about the mine brought back images of the Speris with their black eyes and false smiles and long, needle-like blades under soft, grey cloaks. Maybe being stuck in the desert with Basax wasn't quite so terrible after all.

'Come on,' she said pulling the big herder to his feet. 'I can't stand sitting here knowing what's out there looking for us. Try to get a scent of something. It won't be long before the sun is up. At least let's try to keep going until then.' Grumbling he stood up and sniffed the air. Suddenly he caught a familiar scent drifting on the desert breeze and growled.

'We must leave!' he said and quickly swung Blue up onto his back.

'Steady on!' cried Blue, struggling to grasp hold of his thick neck, as he hurtled into the gloom. 'Why such a hurry?'

'Herders!' he grunted and increased his speed.

**

By the time a weak sun had risen above the horizon Basax and Blue had managed to cover an almost impossible distance, but she could see that the effort was costing him dearly.

'Can't go on,' he croaked. 'Must rest.' Blue looked around. A sickly grey pall now hung permanently above the empty landscape.

'You could have chosen a nicer place to stop,' she complained, 'We're horribly exposed.' Blue looked up at the sky. Only a few days earlier stopping anywhere without somewhere to shelter from the blazing heat of the desert sun would have been unthinkable, but lately even the sun seemed to retreat from that miserable place.

'I don't understand it. There's never a cloud in the sky. Why is it so dismal all the time?'

Basax didn't answer. He'd fallen into an exhausted sleep. Blue stood up. She just wished there was something more she could do. Always having to be carried by Basax made her feel so useless. Should she try to heal him again? Probably not. What was the point? The last time she had tried healing him the veins of energy running under that part of the desert had been so weak that she could hardly feel them at all. Then a thought occurred to her. Perhaps she should be the one to guide him for a change. She could use the whispering pearl to find a way out of the desert. After all, hadn't she been able to find Gyd on the ship? The only problem was she had no idea how vast an area she would have to search before she found anything. A desert was hardly the same as a ship. But she had to try. Blue sat down and pulled the whispering pearl out of her tunic. Even after all this time its beauty still never failed to astonish her. She closed her eyes and shivered with delight as she clutched it to her chest, thrilling as its flames enveloped her, dissolving the boundaries of her body until she and the barren expanse surrounding her felt as one. Taking a deep breath to calm herself, Blue shifted her focus to the broad, empty stretch of desert they had just crossed to see if she could find any sign of the herders who pursued them… It didn't take her long. Bounding across the parched sand, maybe less than half a day behind them, the foul energy of a large group of herders was unmistakeable. Quickly she turned her attention to the opposite direction. Sweeping her gaze from left to right Blue scoured the landscape for any sign of a way out of the desert, but all she could sense were open stretches of the same lifeless rock and sand.

'Come on Blue,' she urged herself, 'find us a way out of here.' As she spoke, a familiar energy, like soft wings, wrapped around her shoulders and she felt her gaze drawn to the east. At first the landscape didn't look any different, but then, appearing at the limits of her senses, she got a faint impression of shadows; tall shadows that rose out of the floor of the desert— shadows that reminded her very much of trees. Just as Blue was about to return the whispering pearl to her tunic and tell Basax the exciting news she sensed a pull again as if there was something more she was meant to see; something lurking at the heart of the shadows. She strained to see what it was but her excitement at finding the edge of a forest had already broken her concentration and the vision faded.

'Get up!' she urged Basax. 'I know which way we have to go! There are trees to the east! The herders are getting closer so there is no time to rest.' Basax looked at the anxious and excited girl blearily as he struggled to wake himself and take in everything Blue was telling him. He didn't feel in much shape to walk, let alone run, but seeing the whispering pearl flickering in her palm and hearing the urgency in her voice, he realised she was being sincere. With a weary growl, Basax got stiffly to his feet and, more from habit than anything else, lifted Blue onto his back as he loped out into the grey morning light.

It was early afternoon when Blue's "forest" began appearing out of the gloom.

'What is this?' asked Basax looking ahead in dismay. 'Those not trees. Basax not understand.' Blue couldn't understand it either. She was certain the Eledh had guided them to that place, but instead of finding the edge of a green, living forest, they found a desolate and dead world of broken and petrified trunks that couldn't have known life for many thousands of years.

'What's happened to them?' asked Blue running a hand along the cold, hard bark of one of the trunks. 'They've all turned to stone.'

'This place very old. Basax not like it. We leave now.'

'And go where? Are you forgetting how many of your old friends are chasing us?'

'Old friends better than espiritua. Basax not go any further. Bad place. Very bad.'

'Don't be stupid.' Blue snorted. 'You're imagining things. There *are* no espiritua!' Despite Blue's reassurances, she couldn't help but feel that maybe Basax was right. Maybe there was something sinister lurking amidst the dead trunks. 'I don't get it,' she said. 'Why would the Eledh guide us here? There has to be a reason.'

'No reason. You make mistake. We go now.'

'I didn't make a mistake!' Blue said adamantly. 'The Eledh wanted us to come here. They wanted us to find this place. We can't just walk away because you're scared.' Basax didn't look scared, he looked terrified. Seeing him like this gave Blue an idea: if a herder as fearless as Basax was terrified of entering the dead forest, then maybe the other herders wouldn't want to enter it either.

'Basax, do you think the other herders would follow us through here?'

'No. Only crazy herder enter here. Espiritua everywhere.'

'Then what are we waiting for? You're the craziest herder of all.' Laughing, Blue stepped into the trees. 'See, no espiritua.'

Basax cowered at the edge.

'Oh, come on you big sissy. Nothing here will harm you. Aren't you tired of all this running? This is the only way we'll ever lose them.' Basax swallowed and looked behind him then back at the petrified trees but made no move to follow. 'Please Basax,' she said, walking up to him and placing his large paw in hers. 'You know I wouldn't survive a day in this desert without you. Don't throw this chance away after all you've done to save me.'

Whether it was the comfort of Blue's small hand clutching his own or the girl's flattering reminder that he was the craziest herder of all, Basax forced himself to take a pace forward.

'That's it,' said Blue encouraging him to take a second and then a third step. Basax looked about him as if expecting the shadows to jump out and devour him at any moment. Although at first, they progressed at little more than a snail's pace, Blue somehow coaxed Basax into keeping going until the edge of the desert could no longer be seen. 'See, there's nothing here but old, dead trees. Nothing to be afraid of.'

They hadn't been walking long when the sound of deep-throated growls at the edge of the forest alerted them to the arrival of the herders. Blue looked at Basax in alarm.

'Shall we run?'

'No. They not enter here. They too afraid.'

'Are you sure? How can you tell?'

'That's why they growl. Herder make no noise when hunting.' Blue let out a sigh of relief. So the Eledh *had* been guiding them after all. Now she was certain all they had to do to get out of the desert was to keep going through that fossilised wilderness.

These trees must have been huge, Blue mused, looking at the girth of the stone trunks they passed. *I've never seen tree trunks so large.*

'Trees from forests of the old days. Trees much bigger then. Tree spirits bigger too,' he said and darted a nervous look at the splintered trunk of one of the trees they were passing.

'Trees don't have spirits,' Blue said sniggering.

'All trees have spirit. Espiritua of old trees very powerful. Basax feel them. They trapped here. Not good to trap spirits of old forests. Makes them angry. Not good. Not good.' Basax's warning made Blue shiver... or was it getting colder?

'You feel it's getting colder?' Blue asked rubbing the goosebumps on her arms. Basax sniffed the air and nodded.

'Getting colder... and darker.' Basax was right. Ever since they had entered the petrified forest not only had the temperature been dropping, but also the light had been growing dimmer as if the sun's light and heat was unable, or unwilling, to penetrate the air which hung around the trees like a widow's shroud.

'This place is starting to depress me,' Blue admitted after they had walked at least another league through the gloom. 'It feels horrible, like it wants to suck the joy out of everything. This grey mist doesn't help. I can't seem to get warm.'

'Espiritua,' said Basax as if that explained everything. Blue frowned. The herder's obsession with tree spirits was starting to grow tiresome. 'We stop soon,' said the herder, hearing Blue's stomach growling. 'We find somewhere to rest and eat.'

'Eat what? I've only got three bennu left and so far, we haven't found any water. There's no sign of it.' Suddenly Basax stopped and again sniffed the air.

'Herders?' Blue asked apprehensively.

'No,' said the herder lifting Blue onto his back as he set off at a run. 'Water!'

***

At first Blue thought they were approaching a wide stretch of tall black cliffs, but as the herder's long strides brought them closer Blue realised — though she struggled to believe what she was seeing — that the cliff was in fact a fallen tree so immense that thick mists clung to its upper side. From here, rivulets of moisture ran down the trunk and collected in murky pools beneath. Like the other trees of the forest, the fallen tree looked to be completely petrified and where huge fragments of stone bark had fractured and fallen away, exposed areas of fossilised wood flowed in crystalline patterns that gleamed compellingly in the dim light. Even Basax had to stop and stare in wonder at the sight.

'Ankura!' he exclaimed in disbelief.

'Ankura? You know this place?'

'Basax know myths. Basax know many myths about great trees. Ankura was greatest tree of all. Ankura destroyed after great darkness come. All great trees destroyed after great darkness.'

'How do you know all this? I thought herders were stupid.'

'Herder people very old. Have long memories... but many stupid also,' he admitted as an afterthought.

'Do you think the water is drinkable?' But Basax had already answered her question by taking great gulping slurps from the nearest of the pools. Blue needed little encouragement to follow his example and ran over to dip her parched lips into the crystal-clear waters. The water was cool but as she drank it, she felt a strange sense of melancholy creeping up on her.

'Why does nothing grow here?' she said once her thirst was completely quenched. 'Surely something should grow?'

'Espiritua,' Basax said as always. Blue looked around her. All that sprouted from the dusty grey earth were pale stones that poked out of the surface like sun-bleached bone. Blue was starting to think there might be some truth in Basax's obsession with the espiritua. 'Come,' said Basax. 'Soon be night. Need to find shelter.'

Blue followed the herder until they came to a mass of tangled stone roots at the base end of the tree. Some of the roots reached so high that they disappeared completely into the grey clouds above. Even the most slender of the trees' roots were thicker than the girth of the largest of the petrified trees they had passed. Seeing the tree fallen like this filled Blue with an indescribable sadness that just wouldn't go away. She felt like the witness of a terrible and ancient crime, a tragedy the effects of which still hadn't dissipated. Basax too seemed downhearted and instead of charging off as usual to find shelter for both of them, dragged himself along behind Blue as if he'd lost all interest.

'What about over there?' said Blue in a subdued voice as she pointed to an area where two huge roots had entwined together to form a cavernous space beneath. Basax didn't even reply but simply flopped to the ground on the other side of the cavern and ploughed little furrows into the dirt with the long claws of his feet. Blue quickly found a dry area near the entrance and, like Basax, dropped onto the hard floor without even bothering to try to make the spot more comfortable. She was tired and miserable and really didn't care where she slept. She couldn't even be bothered to eat any of her three remaining bennu. What was the point anyway? They would probably only find more endless desert on the other side of the tree. Basax lay down with his back turned to her. Like her, he seemed to have lost all interest in food. Strange, Blue thought, Basax never went to sleep before her.

Blue wasn't quite ready for sleep so lay staring dejectedly at the bleak landscape beyond the opening of the cavern. Deep down, she knew there was something not quite right in the increasingly miserable state of mind she was descending into, but no matter how hard she tried to shake off the effects of the depression, one dismal thought seemed to lead to the next and she soon had no recourse but to surrender to the pull of a terrible melancholia. The cave was getting quite dark now as nightfall set in, so, with a heavy sigh, Blue turned her back on the depressing world outside and closed her eyes. Maybe a good rest was all she needed? On the other side of the cave, she could hear Basax muttering and growling whilst he slept. He sounded like he was having a nightmare—not that she cared any more. Who'd asked him to rescue her anyway? Gods! How she hated this place.

Blue awoke to a dull throbbing sensation near her heart. She ignored it and tried to get back to sleep. There it was again; a subtle, dull pulse over her chest.

'Stop it!' she groaned, but the dull beat continued. 'Let me sleep!' she said more loudly and as if to reinforce her point, hit her tunic pocket. The beating pulse grew stronger. Blue tried to block it out from her mind, but it was making it impossible for her to settle. 'That's it. I've had enough!' Blue pulled out the whispering pearl and hurled it across to Basax's side of the cave. The shimmering pearl narrowly missed the herder's head and skittered into a recess behind where the herder lay. As it stopped, flames began strangely to pulsate around it, sending a long shadow dancing across the recess walls. Or was it a shadow? Blue felt her chest tighten and her breath quicken. The shadow unfurled into two ragged, deathly black wings.

Even as that creature of shadow stepped from the darkness into the light of the whispering pearl, the darkness it emerged from seemed to cling to its black, leathery skin like molten pitch. Its ravenous mouth and skeletal face seemed forever twisted into an eternal grimace of torment and agony as sharp thorns and briars punctured every inch of the creature's body, growing through its flesh and skin as if the gods of nature themselves had wrought a terrible vengeance upon it. Behind it, thorny briars scraped and scratched across the cave floor like the train of a profane wedding gown. Its sunken, dead eyes, like poisoned chalices, seemed to stare at the whispering pearl with an insatiable hunger. Most horrifying of all were the splintered bones of its ribcage which gaped open to reveal a black, empty hole as if the creature's heart had been torn from its chest. Bent and silent it shuffled slowly past the sleeping herder and stooped over the gleaming whispering pearl. A lean, black hand stretched out from under one wing and a long, thin finger uncurled to touch the pulsating flames. As it touched them, the creature yanked back its hand in pain as if it had been scalded. Lifting its head in despair, the creature closed its eyes and let out a slow and agonising moan.

Nothing Blue had ever experienced came close to the terror of that moment, but far worse than the feelings of terror stirring within her, was the sense of the creature's complete and utter desolation. Paralysed as much with grief as with fear, Blue could do nothing but watch the terrifying apparition shuffle slowly towards her, dragging its mass of thorns ever closer until she could feel its cold, rank breath against her cheek and its ragged wings rasping against her clothes and skin as they wrapped about her, imprisoning her in a tomblike embrace. Held in the darkness, Blue began to feel herself being steadily drawn downwards, down into the depths beneath the tree roots, down into depths of hopelessness and despair she could scarce imagine existed. There, in that tragic place, Blue could feel all the lost spirits of that once great forest gathering together, gathering to share with her their unyielding misery, to share their hatred for all those who had condemned them to such an existence. Blue felt herself drowning, drowning in the same misery, in the same hatred and bitter regret. Yet, as she did, from somewhere deep within her, came the slenderest thread of compassion. It was little more than a sliver of light, but to Blue it was like a golden rope that steadily drew her upwards through the roots and back to the chamber. She opened her eyes... and knew what she had to do.

'I know what you are,' Blue said to the shadowy creature, who recoiled in fright at hearing the girl's voice, then hissed at the darkness, as if fearful some unwanted intruder were trying to steal Blue away from it. 'You can hiss all you want but you know you cannot keep me here. I know what you are. You were once the guardian and soul of this forest, weren't you?'

Hearing her words, the creature shrank back in fright and began to look at Blue with a mixture of dread and fascination.

'Basax wake up,' Blue said stepping across to pick up the whispering pearl and then leaning down to gently shake the herder's muscled shoulder. 'Wake up Basax. I'm going to need your help.' The herder's eyes twitched and fluttered open. 'Don't be afraid,' she said keeping her hand on his shoulder. 'There is something we must do.' It was then that the herder spotted the nightmarish creature watching them from Blue's side of the cavern.

'Aingeru Erori!' he gasped and, growling in fear, leapt to the back of the cavern ready to defend himself. The creature seemed to grow in stature and, spreading its wings, hissed menacingly at him.

'Basax calm down! Try to control your fear. It will only feed its suffering.' The herder nodded as if comprehending what Blue was trying to say but continued to hug as close to the back wall as he could get. 'I need you to go outside and dig down as far as you can at the base of the thickest of these two roots. Don't stop until you get through the hard crust to the darker earth beneath. No matter what you sense around you, just keep digging. I will follow you out. Move gently as I don't want to frighten the poor thing any more than it already is.'

'You not want to frighten *that*!' Basax said incredulously.

'Just do as I ask,' Blue said trying to keep both the herder and the tormented creature as calm as possible. 'Remember, it's not here to harm us, so long as we control our fear.'

Basax grunted and began to edge his way around the inside wall of the cave, keeping as far away from the terrifying spectre as possible. Once he was near the opening, he leapt outside and hurried as fast as he could to carry out Blue's request. Only when Blue could hear the sound of Basax's sharp claws scraping against the hard earth did she stand up and, keeping a careful eye on the shadowy creature, followed him outside. The creature, its fascination growing, followed close behind.

Making full use of his powerful arms and claws, Basax took little time to excavate a deep hole down through the hard, desert crust to the darker, softer earth beneath.

'That should be enough,' Blue said when he had dug to a depth of about two metres. She climbed down beside him.

'What we doing?' Basax asked looking up nervously at the winged silhouette which had appeared at the lip of the hole above. Blue placed both her hands on the root and closed her eyes as if she were feeling for something.

'The tree. It's still alive.'

'Still alive? Not possible!' declared Basax. 'Tree been dead for thousands of years!'

'No, it's not dead. At least not quite. I was nearly lost to the same darkness that claimed this poor spirit and so many others from this forest, but as I returned, I sensed a single grain of living wood still running up the heart of this root. It was like a faint sliver of light. I know it can be saved.'

'How can it be saved?'

'It must be reconnected to the lifeblood that once sustained it, to a vein of the Earth's divine energy. It's the only way to heal this place and free these ancient spirits from their torment. There are so many trapped here. It breaks my heart to think of what must have happened. We have to try to help them.'

Taking the whispering pearl from her pocket, Blue carefully positioned it on the black earth beneath her and placed her palms against the stony surface of the root. As she muttered a prayer, the whispering pearl's vibrant flames began to flicker and rise about her feet and ankles. Above them, attracted by the light, strange and terrible shadowy forms began to amass around the root and opening of the pit. The demonic creature continued to crouch at the lip of the hole, watching them and the whispering pearl like a hungry vulture.

'If this not work we in big trouble. Many, many espiritua.'

'Shush. I must concentrate. I need to find a vein of energy. There has to be life somewhere in this desert.' Blue furrowed her brow in concentration and focussed on the soil beneath her. Further and further, she reached down, through layer after layer of rock and earth, but it was all to no avail for the only vein she could find was so faint and so far down, she knew that, with the whispering pearl alone, she would never be able to bridge the gap between it and the fragile thread of life still trickling through the root of the tree.

'Hurry,' urged an increasingly distraught Basax. 'Espiritua growing hungry.' Blue looked up. The terrible shadowy forms above them appeared not only to be growing in number, but she could sense their hunger and dark energy growing too and with it so too were returning the feelings of desolation and despair that had almost overwhelmed Blue and claimed her for their own. Feeling the darkness building, the creature hissed in anticipation. Blue knew there was only one thing left she could do.

'I'm going to use my own energy,' she declared with a determined look.

'You doing what?' asked Basax with a look of concern.

'I'm going to use my own energy. I have to. It's the only way to save it. I'm going to have to do what Lybesstre warned me never to attempt.'

'That sound stupid.'

'What other choice do I have? I've felt their suffering, their torment. I cannot turn my back on them. There are so many trapped here. I could never live with myself if I didn't try to help them somehow.'

'What if you die?'

'I don't care. I won't abandon them here like this. If we don't help who else will?' Basax cast another worried look up towards the ghastly winged figure rocking back and forth on spidery legs at the lip of the hole above them then turned to face the root of the tree. 'Just try to keep them away from me for as long as you can. Here, hold the whispering pearl. Its flames should be enough to keep them at bay until I've finished. They seem to fear its light as much as they are attracted by it.' Basax happily accepted the whispering pearl and waved it at the hellish horde above them. Many of the spirits, including the black winged creature, hissed at his feeble gesture of defiance, but far too few for Basax's liking stepped back from the hole's edge. Sensing their numbers growing, Blue did her best to calm herself then placed her hands on the root, willing her energy to enter, but the surface remained hard and resistant, almost repelling her touch. 'Come on,' she said, 'let me in. Whatever it is we did to you, please forgive us.' This time she could feel the hard energy of the stone beginning to yield, softening to her touch until Blue found the flames from her hand could pass straight through the ancient stone of the bark. 'Thank you,' she said and, drawing as much air into her lungs as she could, poured herself, life and soul into the tree.

When Blue collapsed at the foot of the tree root, Basax was far from happy. Not only could he not rouse her from the unconscious state into which she had fallen, but much of the fire from the whispering pearl faded the moment she collapsed and lay flickering weakly in the palm of his big hand. The frail light of the dawn was still far off, but not far off enough to prevent Basax from being able to see the shadowy outline of the devilish creature slide quietly into the pit beside them. Like a guard dog, Basax stepped protectively across the body of Blue and snarled a warning, but this only seemed to encourage the demon. An atmosphere of expectancy seemed to be building in the air above. 'Get away!' the herder warned, but his fear was visibly growing, and his threats only seemed to feed the vision of terror standing before him. He could feel the air in the pit had turned icy cold.

'Blue please wake up,' he whimpered nudging the girl's small frame with his foot. Blue remained motionless on the ground. The air had grown so cold that each frightened breath left the herder's mouth in a

137

burst of white vapour. The ghastly creature was so close now Basax could smell the death upon its lifeless breath. Spreading its ragged wings about them, Basax watched helplessly as both he and Blue were enshrouded in an impenetrable darkness. From the ghastly hole in the demon's bony chest, Basax could feel a dreadful pull. Instinctively the herder snarled in defiance and delivered a ferocious swipe that would have ripped the head off any man, but his claws simply passed through the creature as if he had lashed out at a shadow. Yet, when the demon's own black fingers seized the herder's throat, Basax knew he was in the icy grip of death. Writhing and struggling with all his strength, Basax did all he could to break free of the choking hold, but nothing he tried could shake off the freezing fingers clenched about his throat. Dangerously close to suffocation, Basax gripped the whispering pearl in his hand, willing its flames to burst to life again, but no flames came forth. Instead, the whispering pearl continued to pulse and throb like a beating heart. As the strength ebbed from the herder's powerful body there was only one last thing Basax could think to do... he rammed the whispering pearl deep into the gaping cavity of the creature's chest.

The creature let the herder go and reached into the wound as if intending to remove the pearl, but flames, too hot for the creature's liking, began to lick at the opening and caused the creature to retract its hand sharply. Looking about desperately, it staggered to the pit wall and tried climbing spider-like out of the pit until a violent convulsion suddenly seized its body, throwing it writhing back onto the pit floor. Seeing the creature fall, Basax snatched Blue's unconscious body up in his arms and cradled her protectively as flames burst forth from the creature's chest. Soon flames had filled the pit and were spreading amongst the diabolic ranks of forest spirits congregated around its mouth. The air filled with a chorus of inhuman shrieks as their incorporeal forms burst into flame, some blazing so brightly that Basax had to shield his eyes with his hand. Through the gaps in his fingers, the herder could barely bring himself to watch as the demonic creature continued to writhe and scream before him.

Suddenly, in an eruption of colour and light, flames exploded upwards from the demonic creature's chest, bathing the area in showers of stars which streaked back down towards the earth like a hail of comets.

As the stars fell to the ground, Basax noticed some still hung in the air, hovering and flitting about as if they had a life of their own. Indeed, many even appeared to have tiny wings, some like the leaves of a tree whilst others resembling the petals of a flower. Two such stars even landed in the herder's hair. Thinking himself about to catch fire, Basax held Blue in one arm and patted furiously at the spot with his free hand, unaware that the small flames had already darted around to the back of his head and had vanished into the thick mane of hair at the nape of the herder's neck.

Believing the fire to be extinguished, Basax returned his attention to the demonic creature, expecting to find little but the charred shell of its exploded corpse. Yet far from finding a corpse, the creature's body seemed to be undergoing an extraordinary transformation. First, the darkness of its leathery skin and wings fell away from its body like the soot from a blacksmith's hammer. Next, the emaciated contours and lines of its face and body began to soften and fill out like a desert flower after rain. Even the thorns and briars that had punctured every inch of the creature's skin and wings began crumbling into dust as the ugly perforations and tears began to knit and heal as if they had never existed. The creature's wings, no longer ragged and torn, had a fiery, amorphous sheen that reminded Basax of the surface of the whispering pearl. Most striking of all were the creature's eyes, no longer lifeless, sunken hollows, but bright and beautiful like star-filled pools. It was in that moment that Basax realised that he was no longer in the presence of a devil or demon... he was in the presence of something divine.

'Basajaun, beti egongocera uda berricua,' said the angelic being staring into the herder's eyes with such a penetrating and loving look of gratitude that Basax caught himself blushing with embarrassment. Having addressed the herder in his own ancient tongue, the being then uttered a word that shocked the herder to his core. 'Ama Galdua,' it said and placing something in Blue's hand, leant forward to place a kiss on the unconscious girl's forehead. Not only had the being called Basax by his full name, a name Basax had spent a lifetime trying to forget, but it seemed to be conferring upon Blue a title so old and so sacred that not even the most sacrilegious and disrespectful of herders would have dared

make mention of it. Laughing at Basax's shock and discomfort, the being bowed a second time and disappeared into the root of the tree.

Too stunned to know what to think, the herder could only stare dumbly at the place where the being had kissed Blue, for there, in the centre of her forehead a point of golden light with filaments of emerald fire remained burning softly under her skin whilst beneath her tunic, even through the clothing, he could see her heart glowed like a small sun.

'Did you see that?' said Blue having woken the moment she'd felt the kiss upon her brow. 'Did you see?' she said again excitedly. 'It was one of the fallen Eledh! Do you know what this means?'

Basax blinked and tried to say something intelligent, but the most he could manage was an incoherent grunt.

'Oh, you silly herder! It means they can be saved! And look, he gave me back a whispering pearl! I know what the pearls are now! They're... Are you even listening to me?' Basax continued to blink stupidly at the girl's glowing forehead. 'What *is* the matter with you?' she demanded impatiently, realising the herder wasn't interested at all in what she was telling him but seemed fixated with something above her brow.

'Blue have something… here,' said Basax pointing to his own forehead.

'Oh, for goodness' sake!' said Blue rubbing her forehead to wipe off whatever it was he was obsessing about. 'Here I am talking about saving the fallen Eledh and all of humanity and all you are concerned with is a smudge of dirt on my face! There. All gone. Now instead of just gawping at me are you getting us out of this hole or are you planning on us staying down here all day?'

In spite of the point of light on Blue's forehead burning just as brightly as before, the herder decided to say nothing more of the matter and, with an athletic spring, lifted Blue and himself clean out of the pit.

'Basax try waking you,' he said once he'd made sure Blue could stand by herself. 'Basax thought you dead!'

'I wasn't dead,' said Blue clapping her hands like a girl at a summer fete. 'I was restoring the bridge. I did it, Basax! I reconnected the tree to the Earth's energy! The moment the connection was made I could feel the tree coming back to life again.'

'It look same to Basax,' noted the herder looking around unimpressed.

'Don't look with your eyes. *Feel* the change.' Again, the herder looked around and had to admit the cold and depressing atmosphere did seem to be lifting. 'And why did it call you "Basajaun"?' she added.

'It Basax's name… at least it was Basax's name before father drove Basax out of home.'

'Your father drove you from your home! Why?'

'Herder tradition. Young males always driven from home when they reach age of eight years. Must earn right to use full name or stay away forever.'

'Eight years old! That's barbaric! It's amazing any of you survive.'

'Many don't,' said Basax distantly.

'What about what he called me? "Amagalda" or something like that. What does it mean?'

'He call you "Ama Galdua". It means "Lost Mother". Legend very old. Name very sacred to Jentilak.' As Basax said the word "Jentilak", Blue noticed he paused to spit on the ground. 'Anyway, you say tree now saved. It still look dead to Basax.' Blue looked at the fallen tree and wondered if perhaps the herder was right. The tree still lay like a colossal stone monolith with no sign of life anywhere.' Basax began sniffing the air.

'Strange smell,' he said.

'Bad smell?' enquired Blue more soberly, remembering the herders who she still wasn't completely convinced had given up the chase.

'Not bad. Strange,' he said and began to follow its scent back along the length of the huge trunk. After a short distance he came to a stop. 'Smell come from up there,' he said and without another word began to climb.

'Where are you going?' she shouted after him.

'To find smell!' Blue tried to keep sight of the herder as he scaled higher up the side of the tree, but he was climbing so fast and so quickly that she soon lost sight of him. Peering up into the mists Blue wondered what he thought he was looking for? After waiting for what seemed an inconsiderately long time, Blue spotted the herder clambering back down out of the mists.

'Did you find anythi—" but before Blue could finish her sentence, Basax had swept her off the ground and was scaling powerfully back up the trunk with Blue clinging to his neck for dear life. When they were near the top Basax stopped and planted Blue down onto the damp, stony surface of the ancient bark. The mists at this point were thin and Blue could feel the light of the morning sun already beginning to warm the upper side of the tree. 'Smell from here,' Basax said.

Blue looked all around her but could see nothing but soft sunlight filtering through the ghostlike wisps of mist.

'Where?' she asked in confusion.

'Look at tree,' he said grinning from ear to ear. Blue peered down at the damp surface wondering what it was she was supposed to be looking at.

'A flower!' she gasped. There, sprouting shyly from a crack in the stone bark, were two bright green leaves and a small white flower with a pinkish blush at its centre. From the flower a light and delicate perfume wafted into the desert air.

'Come,' said the herder lifting Blue onto his back once she had got over the surprise and delight of discovering the flower. 'Basax show you something else.' Instead of climbing back down the way they had come up, the herder continued up and over the top of the trunk and started descending the other side. As they dropped beneath the layers of mist, the views beyond opened out.

'Look,' Basax said pausing his descent. Blue turned and looked out across the arid wilderness stretching away before them. It appeared much the same as the other side, just more of the same bleak and inhospitable desert. 'Look there!' insisted Basax redirecting her gaze further to the east. Blue looked again and this time recognised an unmistakable dark-green shimmer running just below the horizon. It was the unmistakeable silhouette of trees — *living* trees.

CHAPTER 10

Out of all those who survived the march across that desert inferno, Kai suffered the least. In fact, it was fair to say that Kai barely suffered at all. Most of the time he felt as if he walked in a dream—a dream spun by the hauntingly beautiful songs of the Uati. Whenever the slave drivers would begin cracking their whips in anger the Uati would sing, and the whipping would stop. If Kai's shackles began to rub and bite into his skin, the Uati would sing and the chafing, as if by miracle, would no longer hurt. If his arms ever grew too tired from carrying the cage, the Uati would sing and his arms would somehow feel less tired and the cage strangely easier to lift. And all the while the Uati sang Kai would listen… and learn the songs.

'Ukha?' Kai felt a small hand tugging his own. 'Ukha?' It was a small, brown-skinned child. The girl looked painfully thin. 'Ukha?' She kept repeating looking at Kai imploringly with her large eyes. Kai tried to pull his hand away, but the girl clung on to him desperately. 'Nuba!' The child nodded as if knowing what Kai wanted and slipped something cold and hard into his hand. 'Nuba!' It was a small golden figurine of a lion.

'I don't know what you want?' Kai said helplessly trying to disentangle his hand from the child's persistent grip. Seeing Kai didn't want the figurine, the girl plunged her hand into a bag tied to her waist and pulled out more of the figurines. 'Nuba!' she said again offering Kai the entire handful. The figurines were similar to the animal figurines children played with from Kai's own city, but instead of being made from bone or wood, these were made of solid gold.

'Here, I don't want them,' Kai said trying to hand them back. 'These are very valuable. I'm sure your parents wouldn't want you to give them away.'

Seeing Kai also refuse her more generous offer the small girl began to well up with tears.

'Ahatu! Ahatu!' she cried and disappeared into what Kai presumed was the open doorway of her home.

'Wait!' Kai called after her. 'I'm sorry!' but the girl had gone. The child's house, as with everything else Kai could see around him, appeared large and luxurious. Attached to the house Kai could see a spacious courtyard fringed by a beautiful portico. In the centre of the courtyard was a tree, but the tree, like the rest of the trees Kai could see lining the street, looked dead. At the end of the avenue, a golden citadel sprawled across the horizon, its domed rooftops gleaming almost as brightly as the desert sun shining down upon them, yet for all the city's opulence and grandeur, Kai couldn't help wondering where all the people had gone. Most of the houses along the long avenue seemed eerily deserted, the only remaining inhabitants he could see were crowding around a large, ornate fountain from which a dirty trickle of water was leaking much too slowly to fill any of the pots or water containers being shoved beneath it.

Kai felt another tug on his hand. The child had returned with what Kai assumed was her older sister. The sister, though beautiful like the younger girl, was also thin and hungry looking and was struggling to carry a bundle that was clearly too heavy for her as she hurried to keep up. Upon reaching Kai, the sister hung on to Kai's arm as if afraid he might leave.

'Ukha!' she said with the same pleading tone as the younger girl. Kai paused wishing he knew what they wanted from him. Seeing him pause, the older sister's eyes brightened. 'Nuba!' she said nodding at Kai hopefully and spilled the contents of her bundle at his feet. From out of the cloth jewellery, bowls, plates, cups and ornaments of every kind showered onto the neatly cut paving of the street. Every piece, from the largest plate to the smallest ring, was made from solid gold.

'Get up!' Kai felt the sharp crack of a whip across his shoulders. 'Get up! We're moving out.' He wiped his watery eyes and looked around in a half daze to see the slaves frantically struggling to their feet. Already thick clouds of dust were drifting across the arid landscape as the army thundered on ahead.

'W... Wait!' shouted Kai as the collar around his neck began to drag him forward.

'Shut up!' said the rider, rounding on Kai angrily, 'Or do you want to get us both executed?'

'Wait! We're here! The golden city. It's here. I know it!' The horseman raised his whip and seemed ready to strike Kai again, but the mention of gold stayed his arm long enough for Kai to continue. 'The city of Amon Pur, it's right here. We're walking over it. I've just seen it. It's right here under our very feet!' Had anyone else uttered such insane nonsense, they would have been flogged on the spot, but Kai's witch blood was well known amongst the Furud warriors and the guard knew Rasalas was desperate for any news that might help quiet the growing mumblings of discontent that were festering amongst the army's hot, tired and thirsty ranks. With the thought of a golden reward on his mind, the horseman charged off towards the front of the column to give the information to Lord Rasalas.

It wasn't long before two riders were seen galloping back towards the rear of the column.

'Release him,' one of the riders said upon reaching Kai. 'We've to bring him before the commander.' Kai noticed the entire army had halted their march and were beginning to set up camp. The second rider removed the chain from Kai's neck and replaced it with a rope tied to his saddle. 'Magor says he's not to forget the pet,' the first rider added gesturing at the Uati's cage. Kai gently picked the cage up and, remembering to feign a slight limp, followed the riders through a sea of half-erected tents which billowed and flapped in the desert wind like flocks of migrating birds.

When they arrived at the front of the column, Rasalas received his former servant with an impatient glare.

'This had better not be sun-talk Lybesstre, or you both shall learn the price of wasting my time!'

'Lord Rasalas, at least let him describe what he has seen, and I will be able to tell you if it is merely the product of the hot sun or whether there is more to what he says. We must be getting close to the city by now.'

'Well?' said Rasalas returning his attention to Kai. 'Are we?'

'I believe we are, my Lord.'

'And what makes you think so? I see nothing. Where are the ruins? Surely something must remain?'

'They are right beneath our feet. In a vision, I saw myself walking up a wide avenue leading to a golden citadel. A child spoke to me, but I did not understand her tongue.'

Rasalas snorted disdainfully.

'This still sounds like sun-talk.'

'What did the child say?' asked Lybesstre listening to Kai attentively.

'She kept tugging on my hand and repeated the word "Ukha" to me. She then tried to give me something: a handful of gold figurines. I heard her say the word "Nuba". Later another girl appeared, her sister, I think. The sister poured even more gold at my feet. She repeated the same words.'

'These are the words of an ancient language,' said Lybesstre. 'They would most likely have been spoken by the people of the golden city. I believe "Ukha" was the word used for both bread and life. "Nuba" is an ancient word for gold. A princely sum it appears these children were offering you for mere bread. Lord Rasalas, that tongue has not been spoken in these lands for four thousand years. There is no way Kai could have known it. The vision had to be real.'

Rasalas' eyes sparkled.

'And you are sure this is the same city your vision showed you in Tor Morona?'

'I believe it is.'

'Then, if what you say is true, you might find my displeasure at you lessening. In what direction was the citadel?'

'The avenue I saw appeared to follow the same direction we are headed in. I cannot say how deep it is buried, but if we dig down, I am sure we will find remains of the stones used to pave the street. This road leads to the citadel. At least those were my impressions.'

'Get the shovels!' Rasalas roared eagerly. 'It's time to dig!'

It took two days of hard digging before the faint outlines of ruins began to emerge from the dust and dirt. Rasalas and Magor paced back and forth screaming threats every time any man, whether slave or soldier, dared slow his pace or stop for a rest. On the fourth day, a cry of triumph went up as the unmistakeable burnish of yellow metal emerged from the dust. From that moment on, all eyes burned with a rabid lust for gold. Even the miners, having heard the exultant commander swear to send every man, whether they be warrior or slave, home with his own share of the gold, found themselves swept up with the excitement and threw themselves into the digging with a vengeance. Soon there was no end to the golden finds: bowls, buckles, rings, pins, bracelets, plates, cups, coins... At times it was as if every shovelful brought up a golden treasure and the shouts of glee rang out into the night. Kai was not so lucky. Not until the sixth day of digging, just as a huge roar marked the discovery of Amon Pur's citadel, did Kai uncover his first and only golden find. As he scraped away at the dust, the bones of a small hand emerged out of the sand. It appeared to be clutched around a golden object like pieces of broken eggshell around a tiny yolk. Kai bent down and gently moved the fingers to one side. In the hand was indeed an object... it was the small figurine of a golden lion.

No one really noticed or cared when Kai slipped the small lion into the folds of his shirt and replaced it with what little food he had left from his daily ration. No one even noticed or cared when he began mysteriously shovelling the excavated soil back into the hole he had just dug. In fact, it was only Lybesstre who noticed him sitting quietly on his own beside a small mound of dirt, his head bowed in prayer.

Kai's discovery of Amon Pur's golden city helped restore some of the warlord's faith in him, at least temporarily, so, with the entire camp feverishly digging for gold, he started to find himself free to wander where he pleased amongst the tents.

'May I enter?' he asked upon finding the tent of Lybesstre.

'You may.' Kai entered and sat down cross-legged in front of the priestess. 'I know what concerns you,' she said without looking up. 'Rasalas is losing his mind.'

'Yes! How did you know that was what I wanted to talk about?'

'I've seen you watching him. I too have noticed how frequently he slips back into his tent to admire that worthless horn he took from the temple at Tor Morona. He even talks to it. I sense something dark has attached itself to him. It will lead both he and the rest of us down a very dark path if we allow it to. He is becoming reckless beyond control. He has even started sacrificing critical supplies for gold, even though there is barely enough food and water to get us all back to the ships as it is. Once Rasalas realises his mistake, we both know what he will do to the miners to guarantee the survival of his warriors. Little do our friends realise that with every shovelful of gold they dig up, the worse are becoming their chances of ever returning to their families.'

'I noticed,' said Kai grimly. 'There are too few oryx left, but the men, miners included, are past caring. They are so drunk on the yellow metal I think they would happily follow him into the fires of Hell before they realised where he was leading them.'

'I'm afraid Hell could well be where we are headed.'

'Then we have to escape!'

'How? If we try to fight, we'll be massacred and if we try to sneak away, we'd be far too easy to track down. There are too many of us. Even if Rasalas didn't catch and kill us all, the desert surely would. No, we must be patient for now and trust an opportunity will present itself to us. We must trust in the Eledh. They would not have led us here without good reason.'

'At least he seems content,' said Kai nodding towards the Uati who was merrily gnawing on a pickled tuber.

'Indeed. His contentment fills me with hope.'

'I don't know why but I feel that way too. He watches all that goes on. I know he understands much more than he is letting on.' The Uati looked up from his meal to give them a carefree smile and returned to eating his tuber. When he had finished, he began to hum a sweet melody contentedly to himself. Kai listened to the Uati humming and grew thoughtful.

'Why is it so important I learn the Uati's songs? I still don't see the point of all this. What good is a song against warriors who live by the might of iron and steel? None of it is going to stop my father leading us all into disaster.' Lybesstre sat in silence while she gave thought to Kai's comments.

'There is a monastery not far from where I was born. The monks were kind and sheltered those of us branded as… witches. It was there that I received my early education and training as an initiate into the secret priesthoods. The monks there are keepers of the Akashai, the ancient records of the Earth. I once had the opportunity to study some of those records. In them they had two names for Aatxe. One name referred to him as the "Eledh of Power", a title you are familiar with.'

'And the other?' asked Kai.

'They called him "The Singer".'

'The Singer! What sort of a name is that?'

'There are many theories as to how the universe was created. Some say it was the result of a terrible war between the gods. Others say it was nothing more than chance, a freak accident if you like. There are a few though, especially those schooled in the ancient mysteries, who know that the universe was not created from war, or by accident... but with a song.'

'Oh, that's ridiculous! Nothing can be created from singing. There's no power in a song.'

'None? Are you so sure? Do your father's armies not sing before they go to war?'

'Okay, maybe a good song can lift a warrior's mood for a while, but no more than a warm breeze might on a cold day. Real power comes from sharpened steel and a strong arm, nothing else.'

'Kai, does not the hurricane begin as a warm breeze?'

'I suppose. But I still don't see how my learning to sing has anything to do with power, hurricanes or anything else?'

'I too received some schooling in the mysteries of the Sir-Ku, the sacred Songs of Power. I am no master like this Uati, but people say I have a fair voice. Would you like to hear me sing?'

'If you wish.'

Lybesstre smiled and closed her eyes. As she prepared herself to sing, Kai noticed she seemed to be taking great care over the positioning of her hands and body. Only once she was absolutely satisfied that they were right did the priestess take a deep breath and begin. Kai instantly recognised it as one of the songs the Uati would sing to him whenever his arms grew too tired from carrying the cage. Lybesstre indeed did have a lovely voice and in her own way sang it as beautifully as the Uati. In fact, she sang so beautifully that Kai could do little but sit spellbound watching her as she expressed every strange word and nuance of meaning with visible emotion. The fact Kai spent most of the song watching

Lybesstre's face was probably the reason he failed to notice what had occurred until the song had finished.

'Well?' Lybesstre asked waiting for his reaction.

'Yes, very pretty… gods you're floating!' he exclaimed realising that the priestess had lifted a full hand's length off the floor of the tent. The priestess smiled.

'Now are you so sure there is no power in a song?'

'But… but I don't understand. That's not possible!'

'Neither is the creation of a flower, the rising of the sun or the birth of a newborn child, yet we see and experience them nonetheless.' Kai was speechless. 'When your arms ached and the Uati sang that song for you he didn't do it to take away the tired feeling, he sang it to make the cage and himself lighter in order to ease the burden of your having to carry them both.'

'But I have practised that song many times and nothing ever happens when I sing it. Why does it not work for me?'

'Firstly, you are not singing it in the right manner. You need to be more relaxed. Secondly, you are not focussing your intent with sufficient conviction, with sufficient belief in what you are doing.'

'But what is the correct manner? I copy the way the Uati does it exactly.'

'When I sang to you what did you observe to be the most important thing about the *way* I was singing?' Kai thought deeply. He remembered seeing Lybesstre take great care over her hand and body positions.

'You took great care over the way you placed your hands and body. I'd say that was the most important thing. You must teach me the positions!' Lybesstre laughed as Kai clumsily attempted to mimic her posture.

'You noticed me doing that? I told you that I was no master. Do you ever see the Uati taking care over his hand and body positions when he sings to you?'

'Well, no, not really. He sits upright and grows still, but apart from that he does very little. In fact, I've even seen him pick his nose while singing.' As if to lend credence to Kai's comment the Uati deftly inserted the tip of an ear into one nostril and hooked out the offensive contents.

'Then there must be something else that you have missed,' continued the priestess trying not to be distracted by the Uati's unpleasant habit. Kai thought again. *What else did Lybesstre do when she sang?*

'I have no idea,' he admitted.

'You think too much. You concentrate too hard. Does the songbird think about the melody as it greets the dawn? Rarely do you look as if you are feeling what you sing. The words themselves have no meaning, at least not in any of the languages on the Earth today, but when they are expressed with true emotion, they convey great power; they unlock the heart of creation. Sadly, you have been raised by swordsmen — and swordsmen tend to make very poor singers. You have a good voice, but you are painfully self-conscious, and we must find a way for you to lose your embarrassment. The ego finds many ways to undermine what we do. Embarrassment is just one of them.'

***

By midway through the second week there was more gold than the great oryx could any longer bear; the whom were already starting to become very vocal in expressing their impatience to be moving again. The army was divided in two with one half sent to escort the gold until it was loaded onto the ships. Once there, they were to remain as protection until Rasalas' return. Even Magor was dispatched with them to ensure none might be tempted to leave until his father had accomplished all that he had set out to do.

'There are far too few oryx left,' said Kai unhappily as he watched the last of the over-laden beasts, trudge away into the dusty haze. 'There's barely enough food and water to get all of us there let alone get us all back.'

'I fear getting back will be the least of our concerns,' said Lybesstre as Rasalas rode past with a manic expression on his face.

'Get that idiot out of there!' Rasalas shrieked at a hapless oryx driver who had managed to steer the huge creature into a gully, out of which the beast was now frantically trying to climb. Rasalas climbed off his horse and leapt into the gully, whereby he threw the driver to one side and began flogging the poor beast with the driver's own whip. Clearly, he intended teaching the poor oryx how to climb out of a gully by beating it half to death. Lybesstre's expression grew more serious.

'I feel now would be a good time to try one of the songs you have learnt.'

Kai looked at the priestess as if she had gone as mad as his father.

'Kai, there are few oryx left. That oryx is carrying precious supplies of water. If Rasalas harms or kills it, which he is likely to do in the foul mood he is in, then we'll not just lose the oryx, we'll probably lose the water as well! Kai, you know the Uati's songs much better than I. Think! Is there not one that can calm both fear and fury?' Of course Kai knew exactly which song the Uati had sung whenever the slave guards had become too liberal with their whips, but the thought of actually singing it in public was as mortifying a thought as facing an army single-handed.

'Aye, sing us a song and I'll do a jig,' joked one of the youngest miners—a shaft rat Kai knew to be called Ælfweard, though most just called him Ælf.

'I can't,' he said to Lybesstre, trying to ignore the shaft rat's grinning face.

'Kai, we can't risk losing another oryx! Please at least try!'

Unable to bear watching the oryx be thrashed any more, Kai cleared his throat, and with an effort of supreme will, began to sing in a shaky voice. Incredibly, the old warlord lowered the whip and turned to see where the noise was coming from. Buoyed by his success, Kai lifted his head and began to sing more loudly.

'You!' Rasalas roared spotting his disgraced servant. Kai shut up instantly, but Rasalas was already out of the gully and marching towards him with violent intent in his eyes.

'I apologise my Lord,' Kai managed to say before a rain of fists descended upon him.

'How dare you mock me!' Rasalas bellowed as Kai raised his arms to divert the worst of the blows, though he knew to allow enough through to placate at least some of the warlord's rage—a trick Magor had taught him in a rare moment of compassion. Yet the pain of the few blows that got through his guard were nothing compared to the embarrassment Kai felt from being made to look such a fool in front of half the Furud army.

'It was never… my intention… to mock you,' Kai said between fists. 'I was… merely singing… to raise morale.'

'Raise morale! Let's see how much morale you raise with a collar around your throat! Guards! Chain him back with the slaves—and fetch that little freak again for him to carry. We'll see how musical he feels by the end of the day!' The Uati was quickly fetched, and Kai once more felt the familiar weight of the small creature's iron cage in his hands. 'If he so much as puts it down for a second I want you to strap him to that useless beast and I'll flog the pair of them together!' When Rasalas had gone Kai saw that Lybesstre was trying not to laugh.

'What's so funny?' Kai hissed. 'Look what trouble your stupid idea landed me in! I can't believe I let you convince me that would ever work.'

'But it *did* work,' said the priestess still struggling not to laugh, 'at least to a degree.'

'What do you mean it worked? I almost wound up getting flogged myself!'

'It was never my intention for you to try to calm Rasalas. You're not nearly good enough for that yet. But I did mean for you to calm the oryx, at least enough for the driver to get it out of the gully. The fact, your singing also served to redirect Rasalas' rage away from the oryx was an added bonus.'

'A bonus!' Kai was about to unleash a barrage of expletives when he noticed the oryx had, indeed, calmed down and was already allowing its driver to secure the heavy load once more to its strong back.

'As for Rasalas, perhaps your singing had more effect on his mood than you give yourself credit for. When have you ever known him to calm down from such a tantrum so quickly?' Kai looked across to see the Furud commander climb onto his horse and trot calmly back towards the front of the column. Seeing his anger subside so quickly certainly was unusual. In fact, Kai had to admit he had rarely, if ever, seen Rasalas get over such a tantrum without some poor beast or someone paying the price for it first.

'Mind you,' added the priestess, 'there are many improvements yet to be made. You are still far too tense in your upper body, and your singing still lacks the necessary passion.'

'I seen driftwood sing wi' more passion than thee,' said Ælf enjoying the opportunity, as always, to wind someone up. 'I'll teach thee a song wi' a bit o' passion in it.' As Ælf launched into a sea ditty about a lusty sailor's wife Lybesstre leant closer.

'Perhaps a little practice with your spirited friend over there is not such a bad idea after all. A few sailor's ballads might just be the answer to curing your bashfulness.'

By the end of a long and very hot day, Kai knew that he was still a long way off from mastering the songs of the Uati, but he had to admit he was at least starting to become master of the sea shanty.

It was a strange thing to be singing songs about the sea in the middle of a desert. Yet somehow the songs lifted Kai and the miners' spirits and transformed the endless leagues of monotonous burning sand and mirages into a romantic world of exotic sea creatures, wild oceans and even wilder women. Even some of the Furud warriors joined in, mingling their surprisingly good voices with the strong voices of the miners. The only one not to join in was the little Uati, who instead pinned his cheerful face to the bars of his cage and listened to their robust tales of life at sea with fascination. Up to that point Kai had not had much cause to get to know the miners, who always seemed grim and unwelcoming, but ever since he had joined the ranks of their desert choir their natural suspicion lifted and soon Kai was welcomed as one of their own.

'How come you all know so many songs about the sea?' Kai asked one day, 'I thought you were miners.'

'Aye,' said Ælf, 'miners we be, but we're also men of Stod and I bet thee'll not find a man among us who hadn't a grandfather or great uncle who at one time didn't work quayside or be skipper of a sailing barge or two. Our ancestors were all sea-faring folk. The ocean's in our blood and e'er shall it be.'

Of all the miners Ælf was by far the most talkative and agreeable and he always seemed to have a witty tale, song or comment for every situation. How he managed to always remain so cheerful was a mystery, but he and the other miners were grateful for his uplifting presence in the face of such relentless hardship. Kai found it impossible not to like the young shaft rat and it wasn't long before the two thought well enough of each other to consider themselves good friends.

'Sometimes Ælf I actually think you're enjoying this,' said Kai one particularly sweltering afternoon.

'What's not to like? Ælf replied with a clownish grin. 'I mean look at all this lovely sun… and they're really spoiling us with the grub.' As if to reinforce his point Ælf exaggerated to the point of absurd the pleasure of biting off a corner of hard tack. 'I mean what would I do without salty tubers and stale tack for breakfast, lunch and dinner? Living the dream, we be!'

'No, you're right,' said Kai joining in the fun, ''tis the life of a lord!'

Just then the Uati, who had been listening to Kai and Ælf's conversation closely, shifted into the position he usually adopted before singing what Kai now knew to be one of the Eledh's songs of power. Kai also knew that whenever the Uati did this he was expected to listen and learn the song as carefully and competently as he could. Ælf had also acquired a fascination for the Uati's mysterious and beautiful singing and had learned enough to know not to interrupt whenever the mysterious little creature was about to break into song. Together they waited in silent anticipation for the song to begin, but when it did Kai noted that the Uati, far from singing in his usually beautiful and melodic voice, had adopted a gruff and slightly rowdy tone and manner. He was even pumping his arm in much the same way Ælf did when singing one of his crudest of songs. Almost immediately Ælf burst out laughing. Kai looked at the shaft rat confused wondering what his friend was finding so hilarious.

'He's singing a shanty, you knucklehead!' said Ælf and roared with laughter again. Kai looked at the Uati and realised, between the Uati's fits of high-pitched giggles, he could recognise the colourful lyrics of one of Ælf's bawdiest ballads.

When Ælf's laughter had finally subsided, he noticed Kai had become quiet and pensive.

'What's up with thee?' he asked.

'Nothing really,' Kai answered. 'I was just thinking of the girl who helped me. You knew her, didn't you?'

'Oh aye. We all knew Blue, bless her. Best lass that ever lived. Sweet on her was thee?' Ælf winked and nudged Kai on the arm.

'Oh, Gods no! Nothing like that,' said Kai reddening slightly. 'It's just... I never really made any effort to get to know her. I didn't even thank her for all she did for me.'

'Thee's not alone there. There's many a thanks yet to be given to that lass that's for sure.'

Kai's comment was greeted with a unanimous grunt of approval from the miners. 'And I'll tell thee another thing,' he continued. 'Tha can quit worrying about our Blue. If there's one thing tha can be certain of, it's that where'er she be or whate'er scrape or pickle that lass has found herself in tha can be sure she'll have got herself out o' it again. A legion of angels watches o'er that one. Ain't that right fellers?' Again, the miners grunted in agreement.

For most of that afternoon Kai listened to the miners laughing and affectionately swapping tales of Blue's mischief-ridden childhood and wondered whether maybe she did have some sort of protective entity who watched over her. From what he was hearing, she certainly seemed to have been blessed with a thousand lives. It was strange, on the *Nefari* locked in that cage he had all but given up on getting off that ship alive and for weeks had barely acknowledged her presence, let alone been bothered to try to get to know her better, but ever since she had given him the healing not a moment had passed without his thinking of her. Of course, Kai tried to put it all down to a natural sense of gratitude, but deep down he knew there was something else, something strange and unfamiliar that rose up from the core of his being, quickening his pulse until his heart raced in his chest.

'Hold!' came a cry from the front and the column of men and beasts, ground to a halt.

'What is it? It be a bit early for a picnic,' said Ælf in mock irritation at the interruption to their march.

'They must have found something,' said Kai collapsing with the rest of the miners gratefully onto the desert floor.

'Me poor skin,' Gyd groaned trying not to touch the angry patches of sunburnt skin on his arms and feet. 'How come thee ne'er gets burnt? Tha looks like tha's got the skin of a princess.'

'I don't know,' said Kai who had also wondered why the sun no longer seemed to bother him, for as a child his skin had always burnt as readily as anyone else's.

'Aye, Kai's got the skin of a princess and tha's got the brawn,' said Ælf nudging the younger shaft rat.

'How about thee shuts up before I show thee what brawn I got!' came the irate reply. Ælf was just about to launch into a song purely for Gyd's benefit when a cry travelled back along the column for Kai and the miners to be brought to the front.

'What's up now?' the young servant groaned.

'P'raps they be wanting us to make the sandwiches?'

When Kai and the miners reached the front of the column, they could see instantly the reason for their being summoned. Great scars cut across the monotonous desert plain like the sunken ribs on a carcass.

'Do you recognise this land, Kai?' asked Rasalas. Kai wished he didn't, but he knew the horrors of that nightmarish vision would be forever engraved on his mind.

'I do,' he said.

'And the gorge in which you saw the openings to the caves of the Horim, would you recognise that too?'

'Unless the earth has swallowed it whole then, yes, I would recognise the gorge instantly. It is unmistakable.'

'Can you lead us to it?'

'I believe so, but… but what if any of those monstrous creatures are still alive?'

'Stop your whimpering! The bones of the Horim await us, nothing more — and even if there were, my warriors would quickly give you a demonstration of the mettle you are so evidently lacking. Now lead on!' Kai bowed his head in surrender, though the more he looked at the unforgiving landscape awaiting them the more his heart filled with misgivings.

'What monstrous creatures exactly was thee referring to?' whispered Ælf once he and Kai were alone at the head of the column. 'Surely thee doesn't think anything still lives down here. Not even lichens grow on the rocks.'

'There's probably nothing,' Kai replied with little conviction. 'Just promise me you will take care.' Ælf looked about to make light of his friend's warning but he could see Kai was being deadly serious.

'Aye. We'll be careful,' he promised.

***

The descent into the ravine was both a dismal and difficult affair for it seemed with every few feet the rising walls of rock seemed to squeeze what sunlight was left in that place like a stone fist crushing a rose. Used to dark places, the miners instinctively raised a hand to the shoulder of the man walking next to them, catching and supporting each other as they stumbled along, but for all the experience those men of Stod had garnered during their years toiling underground, none were prepared for the sudden, yawning abyss that opened up before them.

'Hold!' yelled Kai grabbing hold of Ælf who was whistling so merrily away to himself he almost stepped straight off the edge.

'Pfeww!' Ælf whistled straining eagerly to see to the bottom. 'That be some drop!'

'How are they planning on getting us down there?' asked Gyd peering nervously over the edge.

'Unload the ropes!' cried Rasalas.

'I guess that answers thy question,' said Ælf. 'I just hope Kai thy fears are unfounded for once we are down there, we be as good as rats trapped in a cage.' Kai said nothing but exchanged a worried glance with Lybesstre.

When the mammoth task of lowering the men and equipment had been completed, Rasalas ordered the slaves and soldiers to be split into groups and soon the impenetrable gloom of the gorge floor was filled with the sputtering light from the flames of hundreds of torches.

'What are we looking for?' asked Kai.

'Anything unusual,' said Ælf scouring the rock with his torch.

'What like?'

'Sunken areas of the floor, stained patches of earth, large cave openings in the cliff wall overflowing with priceless treasures… that sort of thing.'

'Very funny.'

'Tha never knows. Maybe we'll get lucky and not have to dig at all.'

'I'm not sure I'd call finding the Horim's caves lucky.'

The remainder of the day, though for all they could see it might as well have been night, was spent painstakingly working their way along the seemingly endless length of the gorge. Not a crack nor crevice was left unexamined and unexplored. Every discoloured section of rock, every dip, every unusual feature had to be checked and tunnelled into but search and dig as they might, not one warrior or miner found any sign whatsoever of the Horim's ancient lairs. In fact, it was not until Rasalas was on the verge of breaking out the whips to see if that might speed matters up, when a cry went up from the farthest end of the gorge.

'That sounds like Gyd,' said Kai hurrying with Ælf in the direction of the shaft rat's voice. When the pair arrived, they found a group of startled faces already gathered around a collapsed section of the gorge wall. Mirroring the stunned expressions of those around them, the pair quickly realised what Gyd had found. In the flickering light, peering out of the partly cleared rubble, was the broken horn and eye socket of a massive skull.

'See!' cried Rasalas arriving exultantly behind them. 'Did I not say we would find nothing of the Horim but bones! Clear the rubble and dig it out. I want to see what this thing looked like.' Immediately shovels were brought, and the head and shoulder of a gargantuan skeleton began to emerge.

'Look!' said Ælf as he cleared the rubble away from a drooping curled tusk that was thicker than his waist. 'It has a gold tooth!'

'Let me see!' said Rasalas shoving Ælf to one side. Sure enough, in the creature's jaw there appeared to be a slightly misshapen but distinctly golden tooth. 'That's no tooth,' said Rasalas snatching a pickaxe from out of one of the miner's hands. The old warlord jammed the pick into the side of the tooth and wrenched the gold away. As he did so, a clatter of bones fell to the ground. 'I thought so,' he said. 'It's not a tooth—it's a breastplate. This must have been one of the soldiers of the lost legion. Judging by the state of this Horim perhaps Amon Pur's final battle was not as one-sided as the legend suggests?'

'Perhaps my Lord you are right, and the creature was mortally wounded by the spears of Amon Pur's men,' said Lybesstre, 'but I suggest a more likely factor in the Horim's demise would be the mountain of rubble under which it lies. I suspect the creature deliberately caused the gorge wall to collapse upon itself.'

'Nonsense priestess! Why would it sacrifice its own life?'

'To conceal the openings to the caves.'

Rasalas paused and turned to look at the bones and gorge wall with renewed interest.

'You think there could be an opening right here?'

'Just look at the way the neck and shoulder lie. Where is the rest? The majority of the skeleton must either be missing, or it continues into the wall of the gorge itself. If we tunnel through the ribcage, I feel we may find the rest of the skeleton and the Horim's caverns beyond.'

'An amusing theory, witch,' he said throwing a shovel at Kai's feet. 'Here. Put her theory to the test. Some honest digging might put some steel back into that woman's heart of yours. Take the shaft rats to help you. I assume they know how to empty a bucket. The rest of you stop standing around gawping and get to work! There's plenty more shovel work to be done today. I want no rock left unturned!'

Kai certainly was no slouch when it came to handling a pick and shovel, having dug more than his fair share of camp latrines, but witnessing the speed and efficiency with which the two shaft rats cut and cleared the rock beneath that prehistoric skeleton, he soon realised he was more a hindrance than help so reconciled himself to carting the debris out of the tunnel with Lybesstre.

'How big is this thing?' asked Ælf taking a moment to catch his breath only once they had dug through most of the ribcage and stood in the lower belly of the creature. 'That must be near twenty yards this thing measures already!'

'Look. Here's its last dinner,' said Gyd kicking a small skull free of the hard earth. Lybesstre paused from clearing the debris and looked at the skull with a strangely sad expression on her face.

'Please don't kick it,' she said quietly.

'Why?'

'Because we are not in the Horim's stomach.'

'Where are we then?'

'We are in her womb.'

'Oh,' said Gyd with a guilty expression as he realised the small skull was a small but almost perfect replica of the giant skull that lay outside. The only difference between the two was the smaller one had short stumps in place of the long, curling tusks of its gigantic parent.

'So, this be a lass,' said Ælf. 'Poor ol' girl were pregnant. No wonder she were so upset.'

'Well, I think we should turn back,' said Gyd who had already had enough of digging. 'There's no sign of any cave here.'

'Wait,' said Ælf pushing past him. 'The rock looks loose here. Thee had best stand well back.' As Kai quickly checked that their Furud guards weren't looking—the both of whom had taken to throwing dice just beyond the dusty entrance, Ælf hacked into a point just past the hip bone then leapt backwards as a small avalanche of rocks thundered into the tunnel. When the dust had cleared, it was obvious the tunnel air had changed.

'Here, pass us a flame,' said Ælf and scrambled through the hole which had appeared in the tunnel ceiling. Moments later the shaft rat's grinning face re-emerged. 'Well? Are ye coming?'

Apart from two huge thigh and shin bones which protruded from the cavern wall and stretched across the rocky floor like felled trees, there was nothing particularly remarkable or large about the cavern they now found themselves in, though the walls did have an unnatural quality to them, as if they had been scooped out of the rock by giant hands rather than naturally worn by water over time.

'Is this it?' said Gyd unimpressed. Ælf said nothing but stood waiting for them with an infuriating grin still stretched across his face. As Kai looked around the empty space and then back at Ælf he realised that there was something definitely suspicious about his friend's grin; in particular there was something extremely odd in the way the shaft rat was holding his torch close to the ground near to the left-side wall of the cave.

'He's found another opening!' Kai exclaimed realising that the torch's flame was being pulled downwards. 'Look at the flame, the air's drawing it towards the floor!' Seeing his game had been foiled, Ælf graciously stepped aside to reveal a narrow opening in the floor which descended at an angle into the earth.

'How deep do you think it is?' asked Kai as the others clustered around.

'There's only one way to find out,' said Ælf and turned to look at Gyd.

'Tha's got to be kidding. Thee'll not get me down there!'

'Oh, come on Gyd. Thee is the only one small enough to fit down there without a squeeze. Just think of all that gold thee'll be going home with. The sooner we find these caverns the sooner tha can go back a rich man.' Kai didn't have the heart to tell either of them that Rasalas' promise to send every miner home with a share of the gold was as empty as the waterskins upon their backs.

'Oh, go on, give us a bloody shovel then,' said Gyd with a sour look. Ælf fetched a shovel and patted the young shaft rat on the back.

'Good on thee kiddo,' he said as Gyd dropped into the hole.

'Go carefully,' warned Kai looking back at the huge leg bones behind them with growing unease. Lybesstre caught his worried gaze and quietly muttered a prayer.

'What can thee see?' called Ælf after Gyd's torch had almost disappeared from view.

'Not much,' the shaft rat called back. 'It goes pretty deep. I think thee's right though, it looks like it opens out into another cavern or something.'

'Can thee see it clearly yet?' Ælf asked once the sound of Gyd's scrambling had grown faint.

'Aye,' came the distant reply. 'But there's a pillar o' rock blocking the way. I'll see if I can cut my way through it.'

As the dull sound of Gyd's shovel striking the blockage carried back up the tunnel a horrible feeling arose in Kai's stomach.

'Gyd stop!' Kai shouted but the dull blows of the shovel continued. 'Gyd stop hitting it! You need to get back here now!'

'What's thee fussing so much for?' said Ælf. 'Leave him be. The lad knows what he's doing.'

'No, he doesn't!' said Kai, 'because that's no pillar he's hacking!'

'What is it then?

'It's a finger!' Kai's pronouncement would have been greeted with much laughter if it hadn't been followed by a terrified Gyd scrambling out from the hole and a quaking shudder which travelled upwards through the floor of the cavern and almost threw the four of them to the ground. As the shudder ended, a cloud of dust shot from the vent followed by a deep and unsettling rumble.

'Run!' cried Kai. Needing no further persuasion, the four ran out of the tunnel into the peppered torchlight of the gorge. Already the rumbling had grown to deafening proportions until the very chasm walls shook and dust and debris began to fall all around.

'Back to the ropes!' yelled Kai to any within earshot. ''The Horim live!'

For a moment all eyes stared back at Kai uncomprehendingly, but when a thunderous roar split the air both warriors and miners alike turned and ran. A deep, echoing boom and a violent shaking of the earth followed at their heels.

'To arms!' a furious voice could be heard above the din. A sword flashed in the dim light and a Furud warrior fell to the ground. From the midst of the retreating men, Rasalas loomed threateningly. 'Stand your ground!' he screamed. 'I'll slay every filthy coward among you if I have to!' Seeing the warlord so resolute, the Furud warriors quickly recovered their wits and formed a bristling wall of shields and spears across the breadth of the chasm floor. 'Now we'll see how easy these Horim are to kill,' he said with a devilish grin. Seizing the spear of the fallen warrior, Kai hurried to rejoin the rest of the miners as they sought refuge against the chasm wall.

'What do we do now?' asked Ælf, noticing they were trapped between a wall of Furud spears and the huge skull which shook ominously on the opposite side of the gorge.

'There is only one option left to us,' said Lybesstre joining them. 'The moment the Horim emerges we must try to re-enter the caves.'

'Re-enter them! We'll all be killed!'

'It's the only choice we have. If we stay out here, we will be slaughtered by the Horim for sure.'

'What if we stay and help them kill this thing?' suggested Kai.

'Remember your vision, Kai. You've seen what fury is about to be unleashed upon the shields of the Furud. Even if twenty legions were to stand against them the outcome would remain the same. Those that follow Rasalas are as doomed as those who followed Amon Pur four thousand years ago. We *must* try to re-enter the caves.' As Kai desperately tried to think of anything to say which might sway the suicidal logic of the witch priestess the deafening booms fell silent.

'Well, that wasn't so bad,' said Ælf trying unconvincingly to hide the tremor in his voice.

'Silence!' hissed Lybesstre. 'Watch for where the Horim emerges. We will make for the same place. Do *not* move until I do. Is that understood?'

The miners nodded with a gritty determination. As they waited the only sound to be heard in the chasm was the crackle of Furud torch flames and the pounding of men's hearts.

Even before the great cloud of dust exploded into the chasm, Kai felt a blast of air knock him off his feet and tear the wind out of his lungs as if he had been punched in the ribs. With ears ringing and with grit and dust stinging his eyes, Kai scrambled to his feet just in time to catch a glimpse of a towering, terrifying silhouette lumber towards the flickering wall of torches. A silence followed before thunder merged with the screams of men and the sickening crunch of armour and bone. Lybesstre jumped to her feet.

'Now!' she yelled. 'Make for the caves!' Kai leapt up behind her and began to pull the horrified miners to their feet.

'Run!' he hollered, propelling them after the priestess who was speeding across the chasm floor like a gazelle. With the last of the miners away, Kai turned to steal one last glance towards the monstrous beast and froze. Seeing people crushed and battered beyond recognition, he could do nothing but stare horror-struck at the mangled and bloody heaps of flesh, metal and bone. Yet, that sight, as horrifying and gut-churning as it was, was nothing compared to the sight of the terrifying colossus which turned to look down at him; to glare down at the last warrior standing between itself and the fleeing human locusts it had come to destroy. Shreds of flesh, armour and clothing hung from its blood-drenched tusks whilst its boulder of a fist crushed a dripping, gory mess that Kai could only guess had once been men. Protruding from the knuckles of its other fist a long, straight talon held aloft five limp corpses, each skewered along its length like pigs on a spit. In the untamed fury of the Horim's gaze Kai could see nothing but an awful and inescapable doom.

It was either an act of incredible courage or downright stupidity that caused Kai to step out into the middle of the gorge and bar the way to that enraged behemoth. Whether he believed he could last seconds or minutes, Kai only knew that with his last breath he would do whatever he could to buy the priestess and his friends as much time to get away as possible. At first it seemed his bravery, or stupidity, had paid off as the monster hesitated, perhaps intrigued by the gnat-like creature barring its path. However, the Horim's curiosity soon waned and brushing off the few spears that had managed to stick into its stone-like hide as if they were pine needles, it began wading slowly through the piles of corpses towards Kai, pausing every now and then to deal with any life or limb unfortunate enough to betray the faintest twitch or tremor. Still Kai clung to the shaft of his spear, refusing to accept the utter uselessness of his weapon and the complete futility of his gesture of defiance. With the earth quaking beneath his feet, Kai raised his spear-arm and readied to throw with all his might.

'That will only enrage it further,' said a voice from behind. Kai turned to see Lybesstre standing calmly behind him, her eyes fixed on the approaching monster.

'What else do you suggest?' Kai asked knowing it was pointless ordering the priestess back to the caves. It was too late now even if she had wanted to escape.

'I suggest you use what you have learnt from the Uati, not what you have learnt from the Furud.'

'You want me to sing to that thing! Look at it. That is no oryx!'

'You cannot defeat it with weapons, Kai. The Sir-Ku are your only chance of calming its rage and curing its madness.'

The very thought of singing at that moment seemed so absurd that if he hadn't been so scared Kai might have burst out laughing.

'If I am to die, priestess then at least let me die a warrior, not a choirboy.'

'The warrior in you dreams of a glorious death, but will you buy your glory with the graves of your friends? Such glory burns in the blink of an eye and leaves nothing but grief in its ashes.'

Reluctant to heed the priestess' words, Kai once again primed his spear-arm ready to throw but just as he was readying himself to hurl his spear, a fiery sensation coursed up his spine and the vision of a charging bull momentarily replaced the terrifying sight of the approaching Horim.

'Trust the Aatxe, Kai,' he heard the priestess saying. 'He only shows you what you already know to be true. The fury which approaches is nothing more than a mirror for your own fear. Let it go.' Kai let out a deep sigh and let the spear clatter to the ground. He knew the priestess spoke true. He was all that stood between the Horim and his friends and if an entire legion couldn't harm the creature, what hope did he have? He had to at least try the Sir-Ku.

'Good,' said Lybesstre. 'Calm your breathing and try to see the creature as it used to be, not how it appears now. I will support you as best I can.' Kai closed his eyes and taking a deep breath that he was convinced would be his last, lifted his head... and began to sing.

It was some time before Kai began to wonder why he and Lybesstre, whose beautiful voice still soared and fell in perfect cadence with his own, were both still alive. He knew he wanted to look, but daren't risk it, so afraid was he that his voice might falter the moment he set eyes upon the fearsome monster again. So, with eyes closed, Kai continued to let his voice rise and weave itself into that sonorous spell which floated and echoed up and along the chasm walls.

'You can stop singing and open your eyes if you like.'

Kai had been so lost in the song he hadn't even realised Lybesstre had long since fallen quiet. He opened his eyes. At first, he feared the gargantuan monstrosity had returned to the caves to pursue the miners, but then he saw it sitting with its back leant against the wall of the gorge, its large, dark eyes looking longingly towards the forgotten skies above.

'The madness has passed,' said Lybesstre. 'The Horim is at peace now.'

'How can you be so sure?' said Kai sneaking a look in the direction of his discarded spear.

'Leave your spear where it is—unless you wish to enrage it again.' With difficulty Kai resisted the temptation to arm himself again. 'Watch,' said the priestess, and, picking her way through the bodies of the Furud, approached the Horim until she was near enough to place a hand on one of its massive, dirt-encrusted feet. The creature looked down and let out a soft, almost welcoming noise as if reassuring the witch priestess that she was in no danger. 'See,' said Lybesstre with an encouraging smile. 'It no longer sees us as a threat.'

'Okay, you've made your point. Now if you don't mind, I'd be a lot happier if you'd stop tickling the damned thing so we can get out of here!' Lybesstre laughed and gave the creature's foot a friendly pat before returning to Kai.

'Come,' she said leading Kai away by the arm. 'Our friends are waiting for us in the caves.'

CHAPTER 11

'What on Earth have you done to your hair?' said Blue failing to suppress a giggle.

Basax sat up and blinked confused. Somehow the herder's great mane of hair had twisted and woven itself into two thick braids which stuck out from the sides of his head like the pigtails of a schoolgirl.

'What so funny?' the big herder asked scowling at Blue, but his fierce countenance made such a ridiculous contrast with his hairstyle that Blue couldn't help herself and let escape a burst of giggles.

'You have pigtails!' Basax lifted his hands to the sides of his head and discovered the braids.

'What you done to hair!' he said, furious with Blue.

'I swear I haven't done anything,' assured the girl trying desperately to control her mirth. 'You must have slept funnily.'

Basax, still convinced Blue had played a lousy trick on him, began furiously tugging and pulling at the braids to free his hair, but they appeared to have been woven so deftly and so tightly that it took him almost ten minutes to undo just one of them. Spitting every foul curse available in the herder's own tongue, Basax finally moved on to the second pigtail, but as he did, from out of the thick hair at the back of his neck, two feather-like flames zipped across to the mess of unravelled hair and, in the blink of an eye, restored the braid to its former glory without the herder even noticing. As if this wasn't enough humiliation, one of the flames flitted down to the ground and plucked a desert flower of the same vibrant lilac colour as its own petal-like wings and placed it in the pigtail just above the herder's ear. Without a word the two tiny beings then darted back into their hiding place.

'What the matter?' said Basax noticing Blue's startled expression.

'I think you have, errm… guests.'

'What you mean?'

'Well, you know those flickering lights I've been seeing in the trees and scrub ever since Ankura—the ones that you keep telling me must be the "espiritua" of the rocks, trees and flowers?'

'Ahuh,' said Basax wondering where the conversation was leading.

'Well two of them seem to have taken up residence in your... hair.' At first Blue could see Basax was convinced she was teasing him, but when he discovered the newly restored pigtail which, only seconds earlier, he'd unravelled, a look of fright crossed his face.

'Where?' he demanded with an expression that combined extreme panic with intense revulsion. Blue hesitated, afraid of what he might do to himself, then pointed to the back of his head. In a blur of hands, Basax set about attempting to dislodge the small intruders, even resorting to violently whacking his head with his large hands. At first it seemed to be working as the two flame-like beings whizzed around his hands and head like disturbed bees around a rather ugly flower, but the moment Basax paused for breath they simply darted back to their hiding place as if nothing had happened. Not to be outdone Basax launched a second, even more furious attack on his head, this time ruffling his hair so hard that he sent a cloud of hair flying into the air like a moulting dog scratching madly at fleas, but again the unwanted lodgers flitted effortlessly out of the way and merrily returned to their hairy haven the second he paused for breath.

'Have they gone?' Basax asked with more of a pleading than expectant air. Blue shook her head apologetically. This time Basax leapt up and charged through the trees like a maddened pit hog and headed towards the small, half-dried-up wadi near to where they had set up their temporary camp. Upon reaching the wadi he let out a roar of defiance and threw himself headfirst into the dirty waters. Blue couldn't believe how long the herder could hold his breath and even started to wonder whether, in his fury, he might have knocked himself silly on a rock at the bottom. To her relief, and great amusement, the sodden head and smug expression of the herder broke the surface just as Blue was about to take off her sandals and wade in after him.

'You have four pigtails now,' said Blue amidst another burst of giggles. Sure enough, now added to the two pigtails on either side of his head were two more, each sticking out at strange angles from the top of his head. Incensed, Basax let out an even louder roar and launched an assault of such magnitude and duration on the two small beings and his own head that Blue found that she had to leave him to it and return to the camp for fear her sides would split from laughing so much.

It was almost dark by the time Basax finally gave up the battle and climbed out of the muddy soup he had created. Filthy, shivering and looking like he had just been dealt the worst and most humiliating defeat of his life, Basax slunk back into camp like a dog who'd been chastised by its master. Around his head was an array of beautifully plaited braids upon which the two, rather pretty flame-like beings sat as proudly as if they had tamed the Kraken itself.

'Here,' said Blue comfortingly fashioning some twine from the wiry grasses which grew in profusion around the bases of the short, stocky trees. 'If you let me tie them at the back, I think they might actually suit you.'

Basax was so tired and fed up he couldn't even bring himself to utter so much as a grunt in protest and slumped to the ground whilst Blue tied the braids into a rather elegant style at the back of his head. Both the flame-like spirits darted out to admire what Blue had done then returned to their place of honour on top of the herder's head.

'Well, at least they seem to like it.' she said again trying not to laugh. Basax muttered a final, defiant curse under his breath before rolling onto his side in a state of total and unmitigated exhaustion.

The next day, once Basax had finally managed to sleep off the effects of his marathon battle, Blue could hardly recognise him. Not only during the night had the two spirits replaced Blue's crude hair tie with a delicately woven yarn ingeniously spun from a golden flax-like plant they had found nearby, which they had somehow threaded through Basax's already beautifully braided hair, but they had also cleaned him up so that his skin and hair gleamed as if it had been groomed with the finest lotions and oils. He even smelt wonderful as if the two beings had fashioned a desert perfume and applied it to the less nasally flattering parts of his body. In fact, there was so little herderish about the already unherderish herder that Blue couldn't believe she was looking at a herder at all.

'Why you look so... well, so stately. Like... like a prince!'

'I look stupid,' said Basax.

'No, you definitely look better. A *lot* better. I'd even go so far to say you were handsome—well, for a herder, at least.'

'Basax not handsome. Basax not stately. Basax not prince. Basax big fool with two stinking glowing *labezomorro* in hair.'

'Well, I think they're cute—and they obviously care about you. They must know you helped save them at Ankura. Perhaps this is their way of paying you back?'

'If they want to thank Basax they can go back to stupid tree and turn into a stupid fruit and leave Basax alone!'

'I'm not sure they'd agree with that idea. They don't look like they're ready to leave just yet. I think the best plan is that the three of you just try getting along for a while.'

'I think best plan is Basax shave hair off, then we see what they do!'

'Oh, don't be so drastic. Honestly it looks really nice. You really do look quite princely.'

Curious to have a look, but not wanting to appear in front of Blue in any way interested in his appearance, Basax made a pretence of going over to the wadi for a drink. After discreetly admiring his reflection for a lot longer than he had probably intended, Basax caught Blue watching him with a furtive smile on her face.

'Thirsty,' he reaffirmed and pretended to drink more of the unappetisingly mucky water thanks to his antics of the night before.

'Well sorry to interrupt your… err, drink, but where exactly are we headed next?'

'We head for mountains,' he replied still unable to tear his gaze away from his handsome reflection.

'What mountains? I can't see any.'

'No, not see. But Basax smell them.'

CHAPTER 12

'Where *are* we?' marvelled Kai as he stepped out of the rough, hand-hewn tunnels of the Horim into a surreal expanse of natural underground caverns which stretched upwards and away from him for as far as the flames of their torches would allow them to see. The walls of the caverns glimmered and shone as if every inch of their honey-coloured surface had been smoothed and polished like the marble of a king's palace. Across the floor, intricate and delicate crystalline formations appeared to bloom like flowers, giving the cavern more the appearance of an unearthly garden than a cave.

'I believe we are entering the sacred chambers of Amari,' said Lybesstre, her voice filled with reverence and wonder.

'Who is Amari?' asked Kai as he continued to look up and around in amazement.

'There is little I can tell you other than she is one of the oldest and most mysterious of the Eledh. I believe she was once worshipped as a deity from one corner of this continent to the other, but little remains of that religion now.'

'I've seen some caves in my time, but I'd never imagined I'd see such a one as this,' said Ælf in awe as he gently ran a hand along the underside of one of the large crystalline flowers. 'Makes thee wonder how a land so ugly above can be so lovely beneath? Reminds me of me Great Auntie Alverdine, bless her. Now there was an ugly bird if e'er there was one. Had teeth bigger than a drayman's donkey. I remember on me fifth birthday she bent down to give us a kiss. Still got the scar!'

'Someone shut him up *please*,' pleaded Gyd.

'Anyway, what are we looking for exactly?' continued Ælf. 'These here crystals must each be worth a king's ransom.'

'No!' said Lybesstre sternly. 'No one must damage or remove anything! The walls, the rocks, the crystals… everything you can see and touch is sacred. If any feel like taking home a souvenir, no matter how

small, then I suggest you remember what we all just witnessed outside.'
Ælf quickly let something discreetly fall from his hand and began whistling.

'Perhaps it would be safer if they waited with the oryx?' suggested Kai, glaring at the shaft rat.

'That is not such a bad idea. Now it is safe I think the fewer of us desecrating this sacred place the better.'

'*Safe!*' exclaimed Ælf. 'Isn't thee forgetting what waits for us outside?'

'Worry yourself not Ælf. Thanks to Kai, the Horim is at peace now.'

'Kai killed it!'

'Err, well… no, not exactly. I erm… oh never mind.' Kai had hoped the subject wouldn't be broached.

'Kai used the Sir-Ku to calm its fury,' explained the priestess.

'*He sang to the wee beastie!*'

'Yes.'

'Then he's a braver lad than I! But how can tha be sure that thing isn't going to make jelly of us the second we step back outside?'

'The Horim will not bother any of you so long as you do nothing aggressive or stupid to provoke it.'

'What if there be more o' them down here?' asked Gyd who had started to look at every Horim-sized shadow in the distance with unease.

'It is possible, but even if there were, so long as we keep our numbers small and our voices soft, I doubt we will be perceived as a threat like the Furud army were. I am sure it was their aggressive intent and nature that provoked the Horim's furious reaction. If they had arrived as pilgrims and not pillagers then they might well have been spared.'

'I pray you are right,' said Kai starting to wish he could return to the oryx with the rest of the miners.

Once the miners had safely returned to the oryx, Kai, Lybesstre and Ælf, who for reasons known only to the priestess had been invited to accompany them, resumed their journey through the caverns alone, though, for Kai at least, the constant recollection of what else might be occupying those vast chambers caused the journey to drag interminably.

'So why did thee ask me to come along?' asked Ælf cheerily after about an hour of walking and subjecting the priestess and Kai to an endless stream of idle chatter and bawdy tales.

'Ælf please forgive me,' replied Lybesstre laughing, 'but your ability to make light of any situation is a gift I felt we could not afford to leave behind.'

'So, is thee saying the only reason tha's brought me along is because I clown around so much?'

'Well, in a sense, yes. But don't undervalue yourself so easily. It is a rare and precious gift to be able to lift the spirits of others in times of distress, a most precious gift indeed.'

'That's all right then. That's the first time me sense of humour has won any fans. Nice to be appreciated. Does thee want to hear again about that time a giant clam took a fancy to me Great Uncle Tobias?' Kai groaned.

'Just give him something to eat. That'll shut him up. In fact, I'd not say no to some food myself. I'm famished.'

'I have a little water left Kai, but I only brought food for Ælf and myself.'

'What? Why've you brought no food for me?'

'You need to fast.'

'Fast!'

'That's right. A fast will help purify and prepare you for what lies ahead.' If it weren't for the respect Kai had for the priestess, he would probably have thrown something at her.

'Well, there's a light ahead, if that be of any help?' said Ælf interrupting as he pointed to a faint glow in the distance.

'It must be sunlight!' said Kai unable to disguise his relief. 'Maybe it's a way out?'

'It's not sunlight,' said the priestess. 'We are far too deep underground. This is something else.' Lybesstre gestured for them to stop talking and closed her eyes. 'I sense we are drawing close. We must be careful.' She reached out a hand as if pushing against something tangible but after a few moments trying, appeared to give up and opened her eyes. 'Kai, I need your help. I can see no further. Your sight is stronger than mine. Tell me what you sense.' Kai doubted his abilities came even close to those of a witch priestess, let alone one as powerful as Lybesstre was reputed to be, and yet, almost the second he closed his eyes, he felt the hairs at the back of his neck and arms rising as if a powerful energy were emanating from the crystals and rock around them.

'You feel it too, don't you?' Lybesstre whispered. Kai nodded. 'Good. The fasting is already sharpening your senses. Tell me what else you sense.'

'I'm not sure. It's so hard to express in words.'

'Please try.'

'It's like an energy. No, wait, more like… a presence. I sense it suffering though. It carries a terrible pain.'

'What sort of pain?'

'It's like a pressure growing within. It's like… labour pains. It can barely contain them. I feel the pain has been building over thousands of years.'

'Why does it not release the pressure?'

'I don't know. I think it has been waiting for something. Preparing for something… or someone.'

'Preparing for who?'

'Preparing for… for me!' Kai opened his eyes in surprise.

'Close your eyes, Kai. Do not lose your focus. The presence you feel is Amari. There is more she needs you to see.'

Kai closed his eyes. This time an awful feeling overwhelmed him, as if millions of people were screaming noiselessly as they gasped helplessly for air. The horror and realism of the vision dropped Kai to his knees, and he found himself gasping for air himself.

'Steady yourself Kai,' said Lybesstre placing a hand behind his heart. 'You are panicking. Remember it is just a vision. The suffering and fear you are experiencing is not your own. Let it go.'

Kai forced himself to relax and did his best to allow the terrible emotions and fear brought up by the vision to pass. Soon he found he could drag short breaths into his lungs, but no more, for the intensity of what he had witnessed still remained very much with him.

'What did she show you?' asked the priestess seeing Kai slowly start to regain his composure.

'Millions dying!' he gasped.

'How?'

'They… they were drowning!'

When Kai had recovered from the awful experience, he turned to Lybesstre.

'What *was* that?' he asked with a look of horror in his eyes. 'Why did she show me *that*?' Lybesstre sighed.

'At one time, many thousands of years ago, Amari would have been worshipped at temples and shrines across this continent, but now all that remains are ruins and faded myths. The only few written references to her in the ancient texts all suggest one thing.'

'What thing is that?'

'That it was she who caused the great floodwaters to cover the Earth and end the Age of Innocence. It was this terrible tragedy that you sensed.'

'But why did she want *me* to see it? Is she trying to terrify me?'

'I don't know. Her reasons are her own. She will reveal them to you Kai when she is ready.'

'But if it was she who murdered all those people, then what are we doing down here? Surely it is not safe for us here? We've already seen what one Horim can do. What if this Amari is even worse? What if she is one of those you spoke about—one of the Eledh who fell prey to the darkness?'

'If she is one of the Fallen then we have failed anyway and have nothing more to lose. But you are right; I see now that it is not safe for the three of us to remain.'

Kai sighed in relief. At last, the priestess was starting to talk sense.

She went on, 'It is for this reason that you must continue this journey alone Kai.'

'I… *what*?'

'You must continue alone. The vision was clear. There is too great a risk if Ælfweard and I come with you. You are the one chosen for this task, Kai, not we. We will return and wait with the oryx.'

'But I don't even know where I am going!'

'The way will be revealed Kai, but to you alone. Amari will reveal it to none other than yourself.'

'What if you're wrong? What if that was just a warning telling me to get lost?'

'Then we are all doomed anyway.'

The burden of what Lybesstre was expecting of him and the price of his failure weighed upon Kai terribly, but the thought of having to face whatever awaited him without the priestess and his friend by his side suddenly made Kai feel very downhearted.

'Don't give in to fear and disillusionment so soon, Kai,' said Lybesstre seeing his dismay. 'You are never truly alone. The Eledh will never abandon you.'

'Still, I think I'd rather run into a whole herd of Horim than have to face this Amari by myself.'

'Thee'll be fine,' said Ælf trying to add a brave word for his friend. 'Thee'll be in and out o' there faster than a fisherwife's tongue.'

After an emotional farewell Kai could only watch in dismay as his friends made their way back through the caverns. Periodically Ælf looked back and said something inaudible to Lybesstre with a pleading look on his face, but the priestess kept shaking her head until, with a resigned wave from the young shaft rat, the pair disappeared from view.

Only once Kai was absolutely certain his friends weren't coming back did he turn to face his path again. It felt strange going on without them. In fact, he hadn't felt this vulnerable and alone since being dumped as a child in the servants' compound all those years ago. Those early years had been more than any child could bear. His only comfort had been a shadowy hand slipped into his at night and held there in the darkness until he fell asleep. It was some time before he found out the hand had belonged to Rasalas. Why the Furud commander had cared at all for a witchblood child of such low birth, a thing of great shame for the lineage obsessed Furud, Kai had never really figured out, but he knew that without the warlord's silent protection he would never have survived the violent world of his early Furud upbringing. Whatever his reasons, once Kai was old enough to enter into the warlord's service and demonstrate just how useless a servant he made, the hand that had once been his only source of comfort became a regular source of stinging rebuke.

The soft light Ælf had spotted ahead was easily visible now and a faint sound of water too could be heard trickling musically from somewhere ahead. Feeling his thirst almost as much as his hunger, Kai picked up the pace until he was looking down upon layered tiers of pools all filled with a water that seemed imbued with a soft luminescence that made the pools shine like pale sapphires. The stone too was nothing like the honey-coloured stone of previous caverns he'd passed through but had a rose-grey tint which sparkled like frost around the pools' edges. Elated by his find, Kai quickly set his waterskin and clothes aside and plunged feet-first into the nearest pool. As the cold water hit his hot, clammy skin he let out a whoop of happiness. He couldn't even remember the last time he'd been able to take a bath. Kai lay back and let the water support the aching muscles of his tired body. He could feel the worries lifting from him like a breeze lifting the feathery seeds from milkweed. He closed his eyes and allowed a sigh to escape his lips. As he lay there, strange desert scenes kept forming and fading in his mind, their stark, inhospitable landscapes haunted by the warlike visages of wandering nomads. Sometimes a town would appear, its dwindling population riddled with disease and hunger. From the shade of their crumbling walls, sand-encrusted eyes, too dry for tears to flow, stared at him from behind torn and weathered veils. From blistered lips, a hum of prayers rose and faded beneath an angry sun. Deep below the desert floor, Kai could feel a terrible pressure building. Slowly, steadily, a mighty tremor began to rise upwards, gathering strength until it shook the Earth with such force that it levelled the walls of the towns as if they were made of sand. For a moment a stillness settled on the dust and devastation, and then, with a groan, the ground split asunder and a deluge of water erupted and spewed forth, hissing and roaring across the baking sands, sweeping all in its deadly wake…

Kai grabbed at the edge of the pool. His torso burned and shook as if with fever. Tears were streaming down his face. Grabbing his clothes, he quickly climbed out and got dressed. Whether dream or another vision, what he had witnessed had been far too real for comfort. He just wished he could find this Amari quickly and get his ordeal over and done with.

Sliding and slipping from one pool to the next, Kai began to make his way down to a long lagoon into which the other pools seemed to feed. He could see the lagoon stretched from one end of the cavern to the other and offered no way around it. The sides too were high, but he thought he could see a low shelf on the far side where he might be able to pull himself out. He would just have to swim across and try.

Seeing no point in wasting any more time, Kai took a couple of deep breaths and launched himself with a running jump into the lagoon, but the moment he hit the water he realised he had made a terrible mistake. The lagoon was not a lagoon at all. It was an underground river—a river with a dangerously fast current! Turning around immediately, Kai tried swimming back to the side, but the current was too strong and threatened to drag him under any second. In a panic he began thrashing his arms and legs, but the water kept dragging him back, toying with him like a cat with a mouse. Spluttering like a drowned rat, Kai just managed to catch hold of the edge and heave himself out. He shuddered. That was much too close for comfort. Now how was he ever going to get across? Perhaps the nightmare visions of the deluge had, indeed, been a direct warning from Amari herself, a warning for him to turn back or face drowning himself.

Kai sat staring glumly into the water. There was no point trying to go on. The current was far too strong for him to cross. His thoughts drifted gloomily to all those Furud fathers, brothers and sons who had died because he had led them to this hostile, isolated place—and all for what? Kai stood up and kicked at a stone in frustration then watched it land in the middle of the river with a satisfying plop. Almost immediately the sound was followed by a second plop as a stone similar in size landed in the same place as the first. Kai looked around to see who, or what, had thrown it and found himself staring in disbelief at the affectionate grin and small brown face of the Uati.

'What are *you* doing here?' Kai exclaimed. The Uati hopped down and skipped over to the edge of the water looking as carefree and content as ever. 'Oh, I wouldn't do that,' Kai said, seeing the small creature looking like it was on the verge of diving in. 'The current is much too...' It was too late. With a skip and a hop, the Uati dived into the silent surge of water and was immediately swept away like a twig in a torrent. Kai ran along the bank trying desperately to keep sight of the small creature's flailing arms, but the powerful current kept dragging it under. Just when Kai had given up ever seeing it again, the Uati's arm shot upwards and caught hold of the slenderest of protrusions jutting out from the cavern wall. There, inches from death, the poor thing could only cling to the rock and watch Kai helplessly with its imploring, beady eyes.

'Hang on!' Kai spluttered as he flung himself bodily into the torrent. 'I'm coming!' Gagging and choking, Kai fought to keep his head above the water, but the closer he got to where the Uati was clinging on, the stronger became the water's downward pull. Cursing his unbelievable stupidity, the last Kai remembered before the surge of water dragged him under the rocks and down into the cold, cavernous depths of the earth below was a small, brown face... looking decidedly pleased with itself.

CHAPTER 13

'What beautiful trees,' remarked Blue running a hand over the silky silver bark of one of the tall trees lining the mountain path. 'It's a shame so many of them appear to be dying.'

'They called burgha trees,' said Basax. 'Good trees. Make good ziropa.'

'Ziropa?' Basax nodded and walked over to the trunk of one of the healthier looking trees. Spying something halfway up, he shimmied up the trunk like a cat and returned to place a small lump of the substance in Blue's hand.

'Taste,' he instructed.

Blue looked down at a ball of semi-hard sap which gleamed jewel-like in the morning light.

'It's beautiful. Seems a shame to spoil it.'

'Taste!' insisted Basax.

Blue lifted it to her mouth and took a small bite.

'Mmm. It's better than honey!'

'See. Good trees. Use for many things. Make good fire.'

Suddenly, Basax yelped in pain and angrily swatted at his head. The two espiritua buzzed around his big hands and ears with equally angry expressions on their tiny faces. One of them darted past his flapping hand and gave his ear a painful nip. Basax yelped again. 'Okay! Okay! Basax sorry. Trees not good for fire. Just good for ziropa.'

The two espiritua seemed to accept his apology and, folding back their wings, settled once more on the short spines protruding from his still beautifully braided hair. Blue always found it hard to contain her mirth whenever she saw the big herder interact with the tiny tree spirits. It didn't matter what he did, they always seemed to get the upper hand. She even had a sneaky suspicion that ever since their titanic struggle at the fringes of the desert, Basax had actually started to grow fond of their company, though Blue was sure much of his softening towards them was to do with his growing rather fond of his new appearance. In fact, she'd even go so far as to say he was growing rather *too* fond. Basax's excuses for delaying their journey whenever they happened upon any puddle of water large enough to reflect his handsome features back to him was certainly starting to become a far too recurrent and tiresome habit.

'So where are we headed?' she asked after Basax returned from his fifth visit that morning to the small pool he'd found at the base of a craggy overhang of rock. 'Wouldn't it have been better to have stayed on that other path? I mean, if I didn't know any better, I'd say this was little more than an animal trail. Why are we following it?'

'Basax follow noise.'

'What noise?' said Blue wondering what the herder was talking about. All she could hear was the mountain wind whining down the rocky valley behind them.

'Music noise.'

'You can hear music!'

'Been hearing music for three days. Make Basax hungry.'

'Why would hearing music make you hungry?'

'Where music, people. Where people, food.'

'Oh. I hadn't thought of that. People you say? People with food?' Blue could almost smell the delicious meals being pulled out of hot ovens. 'Gods! Why am I always so hungry in this place? Come on then, let's go find this music of yours. I'm sick of starving!' Before Basax could even lift Blue onto his back, she had already grabbed a fistful of his hair and pulled herself up. The espiritua too were sensing the excitement and kicked their heels into the crown of Basax's head as if they were riding a racehorse.

'Ow!' yelped the herder. 'Stop tugging so hard!'

'Oh, hurry up you big baboon. The sooner we get going, the sooner we can eat some real food instead of all that squirrel muck you keep digging up!' Just to add insult to injury, Blue leant down and gave his backside a rude slap. 'Go, Thunder Horse!' she shouted. Basax tried to look offended and even thought about staging a sit-down protest until Blue and her tiny accomplices at the very least apologised for their ill-mannered behaviour, but his hungry stomach was having none of it, so, with a martyr-like air, Basax submitted to the hoots and slaps of his passengers and set off through the forest until they were travelling at such a speed the trees rushed past in a blur of silver.

It was nearly two hours before the herder's relentless charge came to an abrupt halt.

'Gods!' exclaimed Blue as they nearly flew straight off the edge of the mountain. 'Where's the path gone?'

'Don't know,' said the herder just as confused as Blue.

'But it can't just disappear into thin air.' Basax nodded in agreement. 'So what do we do now?' Basax shook his head in frustration and scoured the side of the mountain for a sign or clue that could tell him why the trail had led them straight to a precipice. Seeing nothing, Basax cocked his head and listened.

'Music come from that way,' he said pointing to the impassable cliff face which curved away to their right and dropped straight down for at least half a mile.

'How are we supposed to get around that? Do you think you could climb it?'

Basax studied the mountainside for a way around, but the smooth surface of the rock appeared to offer nothing whatsoever to grip on to, not even for the catlike climbing skills of the herder.

'Too dangerous.'

'Too dangerous? I thought you could climb anything.'

'Almost anything, but not this with you on back. Someone smoothed rock on purpose.'

At first Blue thought the herder was just talking nonsense, but when she studied the rock surface more carefully, she could see brighter patches that looked as if someone had chipped away or ground down anything that might have offered anything close to a handhold.

'Why would someone do that?'

'To protect path.'

'But they haven't just protected the path, they've obliterated it! Now how will we ever reach the music?' A chittering noise drew Blue's attention to the two espiritua who had hopped down from Basax's head and were pointing across to a small protrusion some twelve metres or so from where they stood.

'What is that? Is that a branch?' Basax peered at the spot with interest. Suddenly a broad, toothy smile broke out on his face.

'Not branch, plank of wood!'

'A plank! You mean the path continues around the cliff?' Basax nodded, looking as if he had just won a prize.

'Well, I don't know why you are getting so excited. We're hardly going to fly across, are we?' As if to prove Blue wrong, the two espiritua stretched out their delicate wings and flitted out across the gap to land neatly onto the visible part of the plank.

'Bravo,' said Blue, 'but perhaps you two pickle brains hadn't noticed we don't have wings. Or maybe you think Basax is just going to hop across?'

Blue's words stuck in her throat for the herder was already sailing through the air to land with a creaking thud just past the two espiritua, both of whom immediately scurried up his legs to their favourite spot at the crown of his head.

'What the hell do you think you're doing?' she demanded. 'Get back here before you fall and kill yourself!'

Blue thought Basax was going to jump back, but instead he bounced up and down on the plank a few times as if testing its strength. Only once he was happy it could support his weight did he spring back to Blue's side as if he had skipped across little more than a puddle.

'That was quite possibly the stupidest thing I have ever seen!' said Blue. 'And what were you thinking jumping up and down on it?'

'Needed to see if plank strong enough.'

'Strong enough for what?'

'To take weight of Basax and Blue.'

'*And* Blue! Well, you can get that idea out of your head for a start! If you think I'm letting you—' Blue finished her sentence with a loud scream as she found herself head-down, hurtling through the air.

'Uck!' she said gagging on a mouthful of herder chest hair. It was probably a good thing for the hairy mouthful served to muffle a second scream as Blue suddenly found herself staring straight down at the half-mile drop below her. If it were not for the fact that the prospect of a good meal and warm bed weren't so irresistibly tempting to one who had slept rough and not eaten anything half decent in over three months —

in fact much longer if Blue included old Eofor's atrocious cooking — she would probably have continued to crouch clinging in terror to that section of rope for the rest of the afternoon. However, as Blue's imagination began to conjure up all manner of sumptuous and mouth-watering delights, she realised that she could in fact hear eerily beautiful music playing out across the sunlit expanse of Blue sky and white cloud stretching out beside her. Again, tantalising thoughts of home comforts and a full belly of warm food filled her mind and Blue soon found herself edging unsteadily along the walkway.

'Slow down you oversized ninny-goat!' she called after Basax as he loped ahead.

'Basax already going slow!' replied the herder slowing his pace even more so she could keep up. 'Hurry up. Music getting louder!'

Much to her relief, Blue's painfully slow crawl along the wooden walkway finally came to an end at a chimney-like crevice in the side of the cliff. Wedged into the rock, wooden rungs had been set at intervals to make the climb easier, but they had been spaced so far apart that Blue still had to call on Basax for help to make it to the top.

'What a useless ladder! What sort of idiot makes a ladder with rungs so far apart?'

'Huh?' said Basax bounding up like a panther. 'Ladder seem good to me?'

'Oh, forget it,' said Blue suspecting there was probably something significant about the rungs being spaced so far apart but was too hungry and irritable to be bothered to work out what that might be.

At the top of the chimney, the trail followed a natural ledge which cut into the side of the mountain, often threading its way through improbable niches hidden in the rock face, but never so hidden that Basax's incredible nose couldn't sniff them out. Inside each niche, wooden statues and figurines of weird and wonderful-looking creatures had been placed on every shelf or surface that could support one. Around them small, colourful parcels wrapped in leathery leaves had been left as offerings.

'What are they?' asked Blue curiously as she eyed one particularly odd statue that had feathers for ears and polished, orb-like stones for eyes.

'Don't touch,' said Basax anxiously. 'Statues trouble.'

'Well, someone must love them,' said Blue observing how there wasn't a statue amongst them that hadn't at least one offering placed at its base.

'Or fear them,' said Basax mistrustfully shoving one of the bundles out of the way with his foot. As his claw caught the leaf-like wrapping, the package split open allowing the blackened remains of flowers, grains, seeds and what looked like a piece of honeycomb to spill out. Visibly upset by the herder's carelessness, the two espiritua flitted down and began anxiously restoring the contents to the package.

'What's got them so agitated?'

'Heads are too small.'

'Stop being so mean. Wait, look!'

On a shelf from where the bundle had fallen a small wooden figurine, almost identical in size and appearance to the two espiritua, sat amidst a cosy heap of offerings. It even had the same delicate petal wings and pretty features as Basax's two mischievous passengers.

'Huh?'

'Look, here on the ledge' said Blue moving one of the bundles aside so Basax could see.

'The little statue. It's just like them! No wonder they're upset. The bundle you kicked must have been an offering for a tree spirit. See, I told you the statues weren't bad.'

'Statues doorways to spirit worlds. The one who left gifts know how to open them. Always bad to open doors that are better left shut.' Despite Basax's misgivings, Blue couldn't help but smile as the big herder bent down to help his two miniature companions return the repaired bundle to its rightful place at the base of the little statue. Only a week earlier just to see a spirit of any kind would have sent the herder into a fit of terror, yet, here he was interacting with the two tree spirits as if it had been the most natural thing in the world.

'You'll be tying garlands in your hair and dancing naked in the moonlight next,' teased Blue.

'Shut up,' grunted the herder. 'Don't give them ideas.' It was already too late. The two espiritua clearly thought Blue's suggestion of garlands a wonderful idea and were already harvesting colourful sprigs of mountain flowers from the verges along the trail. 'Now look what you done!' whined Basax and before he could be subjected to any more humiliating beauty therapy the herder charged off up the trail at a sprint. Seeing their quarry disappearing, the two tree spirits quickly finished off their garlands and with animated squeaks and giggles set off in hot pursuit.

'Wait!' shouted Blue seeing her chance for a lift disappearing up the mountain. 'What about my piggyback?'

'Grow wings!' Basax shouted back angrily.

***

The final part of the trail took Blue and a very sulky herder with an unusually floral hairstyle across a sharp ridge connecting two plateaus which dropped down into a series of steep wooded valleys on the other side. The greyness that for so long had hung in the skies above Ankura had now completely lifted and a gorgeous pink and lilac sunset lingered on the horizon.

'Oh my!' Blue said pausing to admire the sky. 'Basax you really ought to slow down and see this.' Unfortunately, the herder was far more intent on sulking and stormed on ahead until his flower-filled coiffure had disappeared completely over the next hill. 'Basax this is ridiculous! What a fuss over a few flowers!'

Fortunately, Blue found Basax quite quickly, but not in the manner she intended. 'What are you doing down there?' she demanded tripping over the herder as he hunched down in the middle of the trail.

'Shhh!' said Basax waving her to get down and continued to crouch catlike while staring intensely down towards a glade of burgha trees below.

'You had me worried!' she whispered crouching down beside him. The herder ignored her and continued to watch the glade in silence. Blue scoured the glade to see what it was he was finding so enthralling. Granted the grove was very unusual, with the outer trees having woven their silver branches and roots into one another to form a labyrinthine tangle around the outer edge, but other than that, there was nothing particularly special to see.

'What *are* you looking at?' she asked irritably. The herder lifted a finger to his mouth and continued to watch the heart of the glade with an intensity Blue had not seen him do before. Knowing Basax's eyesight to be much sharper than her own Blue looked again, but all she could see was a bird with pretty blue plumage drilling with its beak into the leafless branch of a dead tree. Suddenly the wind caught the branches and a haunting symphony of delicate notes rose up into the evening sky.

'So that's what's been causing the music! The branches of that tree! They must be hollow. But... oh no! That means there isn't any village and there isn't any food! Damn it you stupid herder, all this time you've had us chasing a dead tree!' Just then a movement under the trees caught Blue's eye and she realised it wasn't the glade, the bird or the dead tree that had caught the herder's interest, but two figures who were moving silently beneath its branches. Judging from the flowing hair and graceful physique of the taller of the figures, Blue could tell it was a female, but there was something about the evident strength and suppleness in her movement that made Blue find watching her so utterly compelling. She was unlike any woman Blue had ever seen. The second figure, though childlike in size, was also far more agile and athletic than any child Blue had ever seen and leapt, somersaulted and ran beside the female like an acrobat. 'Who are they? They're amazing!'

'Trouble,' said Basax and crept closer.

'Wait! She... she's like you!' Blue gasped as the female turned so they could catch a glimpse of her face. 'She's a herder!'

'She not like me!' said Basax, appalled at the very suggestion.

In spite of the herder's protestations to the contrary Blue couldn't believe what she was seeing. She'd never seen a female herder before, but there was no denying that what she was looking at belonged to the same, or at least very similar, species as Basax. Only this species was more like the creature Basax had turned into *after* the whispering pearl had triggered his extraordinary transformation than the hunched and hideous creature she remembered from the *Nefari*. Tall, graceful and undeniably beautiful, Blue wondered how on earth the male offspring of such creatures could ever become so repulsive and wicked.

'But she's gorgeous! You never told me herder females could be so...'

'She not gorgeous and she *not* a herder!' Basax insisted as the female placed a leaf-bound parcel identical to those they had seen around the statuettes onto each of two earthen mounds. When she had done this, she removed a strangely curved wooden case with a wide end from her back and would have left this too had not the child noticed what she was doing and run over to stop her. At first, a tug of war ensued as the female herder refused to let the child take it, but as the child's distress grew, she gave up, allowing the child to snatch the case from her hands and run back with it through the glade. The female dropped down beside the mound and ran her hands disconsolately through the soil.

'What is she then if she's not a herder?'

'She... a Jentilak!' This last word Basax almost had to spit out.

'Jentilak? Where have I've heard that bef...?' Blue let the question drop as she realised the female herder had stood up and was staring straight into the thicket where both she and Basax were crouched down.

'How can she see us?' whispered Blue.

'Kaixo!' the female called out, clearly able to see them in spite of the thick undergrowth into which they were both trying to shrink. Deciding there was no point any longer in trying to hide, Basax stood up awkwardly and pulled Blue to her feet beside him.

'Kaixo,' the herder grunted in reply as courteously as an ill-mannered herder was able. The female nodded and waited, clearly expecting them to walk down the hill to join her.

'What's a Jentilak?' Blue whispered as they approached with caution.

'Trouble,' said Basax using what seemed to be fast becoming his favourite answer to her questions. The word "Jentilak" was familiar to Blue, so familiar in fact she could almost picture where she had heard it.

'Of course!' Blue suddenly blurted out. 'I remember now! "Jentilak!" We heard the names at Ankura! You were "Basajaun" and I was the "Ama Galdua"!' Basax turned to his young companion and replied by unleashing a string of foul language in the herder tongue. Blue was used to such outbursts by the herder, but the female Jentilak stared at them both in shock.

'Atzerri!' she said backing away. *'Utzitakoetako Ama Galdua!'* The female Jentilak cast one last long and penetrating look at Blue and turned to race back through the glade.

'What's the matter? What did I say? What did I do?'

'Why you open big stupid mouth?' growled Basax. Blue could see the herder was furious.

'But I only thought—'

'Now she know Basax Atzerri!'

'So? What's the big deal?'

'Jentilak hate Atzerri. They kill Atzerri if they find them!'

'Well, Mr "I'm so perfect" with my oh so perfect hair and teeth, maybe if you hadn't sworn at me so much like a dumb herder she might not have freaked out. I only mentioned the names we heard at Ankura. What's so wrong with that?'

Basax placed a hand to his broad brow and shook his head.

'"Ama Galdua" is sacred name. To even say name is big blasphemy. Now we in big trouble. Soon they come back with warriors.'

'Well, if they're coming back to kill us then what are we still doing here? Let's run!'

'We in Jentilak lands now. Jentilak as good as Atzerri at tracking enemy—and Jentilak *not* scared of espiritua. Maybe if Basax fight well they leave Blue alone.'

'You're going to fight them for *me*? Oh Basax, please don't! Let's run away. At least we can get a head start!' As if to destroy any hope of escaping Blue might still have been clinging to, the ominous sounds of an angry horde could be heard approaching fast.

'What if we surrender?' pleaded Blue with one last attempt to save the creature who had gone from being her most hated and feared enemy to her dearest friend. 'They might even learn to like you? I mean anything is possible.'

Basax only shook his head and extended his deadly claws. Already Blue could hear the mob had reached the glade. Hearing them drawing close, Basax growled and dropped into a fighting stance.

'I'm sorry Basax,' she said tearfully. 'I never meant for this to happen. Oh, this is terrible!'

Basax stopped growling and for a brief moment looked at Blue with a tenderness she didn't even know the herder was capable of.

'No need for sorry. Basax proud to die for Blue.'

'But I don't want you to die! Why are you doing this?'

'Because Blue save Basax.'

'I didn't save you. You saved me!'

'No. Blue save Basax. Blue save Basax soul.'

Through her tears, Blue watched as Basax rushed to meet the charge of dark shapes which tore out of the undergrowth, but they were too many and he was quickly overwhelmed in a mass of bodies. Blue was sure he could have easily gutted five or six of them with one sweep of his powerful arms, but for some reason he didn't even appear to be trying to defend himself, even retracting his great claws at the last moment to allow the screaming horde to knock him off his feet onto his back.

'Why don't you fight back?' Blue shouted as she wiped the tears away. 'Why don't you defend yourself?' Done with their prey, the swarm of warriors stepped away from Basax's corpse and turned to face Blue. They were much shorter than Blue had expected. In fact, most of them were even shorter than Blue herself and stood grinning at her as if killing Basax had been the best bit of fun they'd had in ages. Behind them Basax's corpse sat up and looked at Blue with a sheepish expression on his supposed-to-be-dead face.

'Adur! Adur!' called out the short Jentilak warriors with one voice. It was then that Blue realised why the warriors were so small. They weren't warriors at all. They were Jentilak children. They were children who had not come to kill them. They had come to greet them.

CHAPTER 14

'Do not open your eyes.'

In a panic, Kai tried opening them anyway, but it was as if unseen hands held them shut.

'Where am I? Did I drown? Am I dead?'

'You are safe... for now.'

'Why can't I open my eyes? Am I blind?'

'Many are the blind who think they can see. But no, you are not blind. Your eyes remain closed for there are those here who could not bear to see the disgust and fear in them should you look upon me. As Kugarra suffers and its land and waters fall sick so must I share in its affliction and suffering. My appearance would... disturb you.' The female voice was soft and pleasant but it had a strange resonant quality to it that filled Kai as much with curiosity as with fear.

'Who are you?'

'You know who I am.'

'Amari? Are you Amari?'

'I am she, the one you call Amari,' said the voice, 'though I have many names besides the one you have chosen to use—as do you, witchblood.'

'I do? What names?'

'Questions for which it is not the time for answers. First there is much I must tell you for I cannot stay with you for much longer. Their souls pray for an end to the suffering... and soon, I fear, their prayers will be answered.'

'Whose souls? What prayers?'

'You have heard their call, the children of the desert. They once looked to me for healing and guidance, but no more. Now they heed only the call of darkness; they hear only the voice of the Fallen.'

'The Fallen? Who are they?'

'They are the servants of darkness. The bringers of destruction. For centuries, the Fallen have been using their pawns to take over the temples and holy places and turn them into cesspits of violence and vice—and now they would destroy the last true temple of Kugarra, the Temple of E-Apsu. This they hunt relentlessly and all who serve it. The Fallen know that if this is destroyed the human race will be powerless to hold back the strongest and darkest of their number, the child of the lost sun, the great worm Sugaar. Should Sugaar break free so too will the waters of the deep rise in its wake and burst forth onto the land; waters meant to heal, waters meant to nourish and bring life back to the desert and the dying races who dwell here. If the temple dies then so too dies Kugarra's last hope as the deluge brought forth will be of such unstoppable and destructive power that the mountains will be toppled and all the races of Kugarra will be cast into the abyss.'

'What is this great worm, this Sugaar? I have never heard speak of it before.'

'What the chained one is and how it came to be here is not yet for you to know. The burden of such knowledge at this time will be too great for you. Only once the Ama Galdua is fully awakened can possession be taken of such ancient memory. Only she has the strength to stop it.'

'Then where is this "Ama Galdua" person? Help me find her and let's be rid of this monster.'

'You already have found her. Now all that is needed is for her to find herself. But she will need your protection, Kai. Only you can keep the hordes of darkness at bay, but it will come at a cost.'

'I have no idea who you are talking about or what you mean. Anyway, what help can I be, to such as one as that? I am nothing but a dirty witchblood. The son of a slave whore. None of what you say makes sense.'

'Is that what he told you? And yet it is because of your "dirty witch blood" the Aatxe has shown such interest in you? Your mother was no slave whore, Kai. It was she who began your instruction in the Sir-ku.'

'She taught me the Sir-ku! That makes no sense!'

'How else did you think you could have learnt the songs in such a short time? It would take the greatest student a lifetime to learn a fraction of what you have mastered in a matter of weeks.'

'But I have no memory of her. How is that even possible?'

'When you were in her womb, she would sing the songs to you. But we will speak no more on this matter now. You have much yet to accomplish and we can ill afford distractions.'

'Distractions! Why should I believe any of this? For all I know you might be one of these Fallen yourself.'

'You already know I speak the truth, for much of what I describe you too have seen. You have seen the paths of the future stretching out like the branches of a tree. You have seen the shaking of the Earth and the floodwaters which follow. You have seen the devastation they bring.'

'Yes. I have seen all that and more, but I have not seen a way to stop it happening.'

'Restore the temple and humanity's strength before it is too late. Deliver the children of the desert and bring life back to the land that has been sucked dry by the leeches that feed upon it. Do this and your vision of the future will change.'

'But how can I restore any of this? I am no preacher nor am I any king with an army at my beck and call.'

'No, you are *much* more. All you must do is embrace your power. But you must also resist the many deceits that will be laid before you. The darkness is desperate to reclaim its lost son. Many times will it try to lead you astray and draw you into violence and fear. It knows a path lies before you that runs red with blood. If you succumb to temptation the darkness will make sure you walk this path. It senses your coming and will do all it can to reclaim you.'

'What do you mean "*re*claim" me?'

'Many are the lives you have spent on the Earth, Kai. Your climb out of darkness to where you are now has been long and hard. But of this I can say no more for as I have said the burden of too much knowledge at this time will be too great for you. For now, it is best you forget these things.'

'Then at least tell me how I may find this temple?'

'Where the desert turns to mountain and the last of the great forests lies, there you will find the road to Sippara, the Bird City. There is one living there who still knows of the temple's whereabouts. However, if he is to help you, you will need to earn his trust. Only when you have shown him you are worthy will the temple's last steward reveal himself to you.'

'Who is he?'

'He is one of the last of a dynasty who have stayed loyal to the temple since before the coming of Amon Pur. His name is U-an. Be discreet when you look for him for the Fallen would give much to learn of his whereabouts. For centuries they have hunted him and the last of his kind. Make no mention of him or the temple to any but those you know you can trust. Many, not just the Fallen, hold his kind in great fear and would happily betray him.'

'Exactly what "kind" is he?'

'That you must also discover for yourself.'

'But how will he know me? We have never met.'

'I will give you three gifts. The first gift is a shell. If you wear this gift above your shirt when you arrive at the city, U-an will know it comes from me.' Kai felt something placed around his neck. 'The shell will also help you gain access to Sippara. It is tradition for all pilgrims travelling the road to Sippara to wear a shell about their necks. Already the pawns of the Fallen have a firm foothold in the Holy City and none may enter or leave without their knowing. It is vital the priesthoods see you as a wealthy pilgrim come to leave a tithe to their gods and not one of the many poor and infirm who gather at the gates, barred from entering by those who proclaim their poverty and sickness the deserved mark and punishment for their wickedness. Only those pilgrims who can afford the extortionate prices charged by the priests and charlatan healers are deemed worthy of gaining access to the Holy City.'

'But how will I gain entry into Sippara? I have no wealth of my own?'

'Have faith Kai and a way will be found.'

'Then what is the second gift? I hope it holds more value than a shell.'

'The second of my gifts to you are the waters the shell contains. These waters are drawn from the most sacred of my pools. They are the same I gave to the Horim when they first sought refuge within my caves. It is these waters that have sustained them with life for four thousand years. Use them whenever you feel you most have need. And now I must leave you. I have brought you as close to your destination as I am able. You will always have my love.'

'Wait,' he called out as the powerful presence drifted away, 'I still don't know what the third gift is!'

'You will,' said the voice fading into silence. With Amari's departure, Kai felt whatever power had held his eyes shut weaken and die. Greatly relieved, he opened them and looked around at the murky world surrounding him. He immediately wished he hadn't.

He was still under water.

CHAPTER 15

In the soft evening light, amidst a throng of tugging hands and beaming faces, Blue and Basax found themselves being bustled into an exotic landscape where bizarre formations of rock rose up amongst the trees like obelisks from a forgotten age. At first Blue thought they had been led into the overgrown remains of a vast and ancient temple complex, but it was only when Blue began to notice inquisitive faces peering out from the many round openings that peppered the obelisks that she realised the great monoliths of stone were not solid at all but were the dwelling places of the Jentilak themselves.

'Is this their village? Wow! Isn't it incredible?' Basax didn't reply but looked about him like a rabbit about to bolt its hole. 'Will you relax,' said Blue worried the herder was about to do something foolish. 'They seem very friendly.'

'Seem not same as being,' he replied suspiciously.

Arriving at a large rust-coloured stone obelisk near the heart of the village, the Jentilak children clustered excitedly around Blue and Basax like they were heroes returning from war whilst two of their number dashed merrily inside. After a short wait the two reappeared accompanied by the very same female who had run from them in the glade and a far less welcoming looking group of Jentilak warriors. In the midst of the warriors walked a tall and proud male elder, who studied the new arrivals with an unfavourable air. The elder, by the lines on his face, had to have been at least eighty years old, yet his straight back and strong build suggested the magnificently carved staff he bore was more a sign of office than something he depended on for walking.

'*Ongi Etorri,*' the elderly Jentilak said to Basax and Blue respectively. 'My name is Otzak. My niece tells me I must welcome you to our village.'

Figuring the elder was of some standing amongst the community, Blue returned his rather lukewarm welcome with a curtsy whilst Basax merely shrugged to acknowledge his greeting then looked about him as if he wished he could disappear.

'Please pardon the misguided enthusiasm of our children,' the Jentilak elder continued. 'You must understand it is not often that my niece proclaims the "Ama Galdua" has returned.' The hint of irony in the elder's voice was not lost on Blue nor the young female by his side, who muttered something then stamped her foot angrily.

'Very well Nekane, I will ask her, then perhaps you will allow me to return to my duties.' The elder turned once more to Blue. 'My niece insists I ask you to remove the hair covering your forehead. She seems to think it might somehow convince me that you are, indeed, who she believes you to be.' Hearing his comments caught Blue by complete surprise for she herself had only recently discovered the point of light left there from the Eledh's kiss and had taken to fastening her hair across her brow to hide it. Nevertheless, seeing the burning look of expectation on the faces of all gathered there, Blue reached up to untie her hair and allowed it to fall naturally about her shoulders. Around her the air filled with gasps.

'Well, well!' said the Jentilak elder staring in amazement at the gold-and-emerald point of light in the centre of Blue's brow. 'It looks like there is something in what my niece says after all. Please forgive me and let me be the first to welcome you both as our honoured guests.' Blue knew that whoever it was that they thought she might be was nonsense, but she was also very aware of the precariousness of their situation, particularly for Basax who looked convinced he was about to get lynched from the nearest tree, so she bit her tongue and let Otzak continue uninterrupted. 'But let us hear no more talk of such matters until you have both eaten and rested. My niece says your friend has suffered much and is in need of sustenance and much rest.'

'She did?'

'That and much more. My niece, as you may have gathered, is our Albokalari, though her disregard for her gift and the needs of her people is a source of… concern I'll admit.'

'Albokalari?' said Blue, clueless what he was talking about.

'Ah, of course, you are unfamiliar with our ways. My apologies. The Albokalari see not the flesh like you or I.'

. 'Do they not?' asked Blue, her curiosity growing, 'What do they see then?'

'The flame of the soul.' Basax growled as he realised the young female was staring straight at him… or rather into him.

'Nekane!' snapped the Jentilak elder knocking his staff sharply on the ground to get her attention. 'Sometimes her gift leads her to forget her manners.' The elder turned to the crowd. *'Soko, alboka!'* he called. From their midst the boy they had seen somersaulting in the glade came running up and held out the oddly shaped wooden case he'd been so desperate to stop Nekane from leaving behind. The female Jentilak at first refused to take it, but when her uncle thumped the staff sternly into the ground, she bowed her head and accepted the boy's offering.

'Before my brother died, all expected his son to inherit the gifts of the Albokalari, but fate, it seems, had already chosen his daughter to become his successor. I hope you will understand then why it saddens me to see how my niece lets grief blind her to her duty. Perhaps,' said the elder turning to Nekane, 'you might at least do me the honour of welcoming our guests into your home?'

Blue could see the words of her uncle stung the female Jentilak, but she bowed her head in obedience, nevertheless. Otzak turned back to Blue and Basax. 'Perhaps we may speak more of this once our good friend here has fully recovered from his ordeal? It must have been terrible.'

'His ordeal?'

'Being held captive for so long by the Atzerri. My niece informed us all about it.'

'She did?' Blue looked at Nekane in confusion. The young female kept her eyes averted as if trying not to give them away. 'Yes it… it was terrible,' said Blue wondering why the Jentilak had chosen to lie on their behalf. Basax gave Blue the look of a condemned man who had just had the noose removed from about his neck.

'Please do not feel you need to speak of such horrors now,' said Otzak. 'I can see it has scarred our noble friend deeply and we must do all we can to bring our beloved Jentilak back to his old self.' Blue cringed at the irony of the old Jentilak wanting to bring Basax back to his old self. If only he had known what a monster Basax's "old self" had really been.

The way to Nekane's home turned out to be much more of a trek than either Blue or Basax had expected. The home itself was not in the Jentilak village at all but sat at the end of a lonely trail in an isolated spot high up the valley side. Unlike the much grander obelisk dwellings down below, the angular lump of rock from which the home had been made sat overlooking the picturesque valley like a grumpy and unwelcome stranger. The interior, though not nearly as poky and cramped as Blue had feared, was, nonetheless, a rather sorry looking place as if no one had bothered to care for it for some time.

'Do you live here alone?' Blue asked trying her hardest not to sound impolite. Nekane nodded. 'I imagine it gets quite lonely being so far from the village.'

'It can do,' said Nekane quietly, 'but I have the iratxoak to keep me company and Soko, my cousin, visits whenever he can.' Blue had no idea what the iratxoak she had referred to were but wondered if they had anything to do with the patter of tiny feet and hushed chatter of small voices she could sometimes hear as they passed from room to room.

'Please, your rooms are this way,' Nekane said. 'I will bring you something to eat shortly.'

Basax and Blue's rooms were towards the upper levels of the rock dwelling and, like the stairs they had climbed, preserved much of the flowing character of whatever ancient forces of nature had originally hollowed the rock. Nevertheless, as with the rest of the home, there was a weariness and sadness that lingered about the place and reminded Blue very much of the home she had left behind all those miles away in the fishing village of Stod.

'Tell me,' asked Blue when she and Nekane were alone, 'why did you tell your uncle Basax had been held captive by the Atzerri?'

'How else was I to explain his vulgar way of behaving and speaking? The moment I heard him speak I could tell he wasn't a true Jentilak, though his appearance, I must admit, is very… striking.' Blue noticed the two espiritua were listening keenly to their conversation from the doorway.

'You think so?' said Blue remembering the almighty furore that ensued every time the espiritua attempted to rearrange the herder's hair. 'I still don't understand though. If you knew he was an Atzerri then why did you help us?'

'Because I can see your iratxoak trust him.' Nekane nodded to the two espiritua still peeking inquisitively at the Jentilak from around the corner of the entrance. 'Iratxoak make excellent judges of character.'

'The tree spirits! So that's what "iratxoak" means. You'll have to excuse them, they're not normally this shy.'

'They are shy because they know I can see them. They are not used to being seen.'

'But I can see them easily enough. Basax can see them too. Isn't that the same for everybody?'

'Your Atzerri friend sees them because they choose to let him see them. But with you it is different. The light on your brow tells me your eyes have been forever opened to their world. Never again will they be hidden from you.'

'Your uncle said you also see differently from others. He said something about you being able to see our souls? It must be wonderful to see such a thing,' said Blue.

'Sometimes it is. I can see the subtler energies that radiate from all living things. This includes the fire of the soul... but I also see the darkness they carry within.'

'Still, why does your uncle say you are reluctant to be the Albokalari? I would love to have such a... gift.' Nekane lowered her eyes.

'I loved my father and brother dearly and grew up always believing my father's alboka would be inherited by my brother. In times past it has always been the male descendants who inherited the sacred gifts of the Albokalari. Besides, my brother would have made a much better Albokalari than I. He had a brave and noble heart. It does not feel right for me to take his place, especially knowing how they...' Nekane's voice trailed off and angry tears came to her eyes.

'What is an Albokalari?' Blue asked hoping the question might help take the Jentilak's mind off such evidently painful recollections. 'Would you tell me?' Nekane wiped her eyes.

'I can tell you the tale my ancestors have always passed down from one generation to the next if you like?'

'Please,' said Blue. 'I'd like that. I've not had any company other than that fleabag next door for weeks.' Nekane laughed and sat down on the bed beside Blue. Taking a wooden cup, she poured some milk into it from a jug and handed it to her.

'Try to drink some of this.'

'I'm not really a fan of goat's milk,' said Blue eyeing the cup dubiously.

'It is not goat's milk. It is made from the seed of a flower and sweetened by the sap of the burgha trees that grow around the glade where my brother and father are buried. It will help you rest and heal. Your energy is much depleted from your ordeals and travels.' Blue took a sip from the cup. The taste of the milky liquid was heavenly, floral and sweet with a woodspice fragrance that made Blue feel like she had drunk from the cup of a woodland goddess. Quickly, as Nekane had promised, the liquid began to warm Blue's insides and a deliciously pleasant feeling spread from her stomach to the rest of her body and limbs making the soft bed look incredibly appealing.

'Lie down if you like,' said Nekane seeing Blue looking longingly at the bed. 'I will talk as you rest.' Nekane waited until Blue was comfortable then began telling her story.

'Traditionally, the Albokalaris were little more than bards and musicians, earning their keep by playing from village to village. They had a poor reputation amongst the Jentilak, especially amongst the females, for too easily did they grow bored with a domestic life, always making excuses to leave their families behind and return to the mountains and wild places they loved so much. It is said it was their children who became the first Atzerri, growing up to be angry and rebellious without a father's love to guide them. Then one day, many years ago during one of the first of the great droughts to curse these lands, a young bard called Launedda returned home to his family to discover his wandering soul had levied a heavy price for his absence, for no welcome did he find but the grave of his youngest child placed in the ground at the edge of his wife's village.

"How dare you come back to us now!" cried his wife upon seeing him standing heartbroken before the grave. "How many more of your children must I bury before your heart desires to do that which a father's duty demands? Be gone with you for too many grow hungry here to feed a mouth as selfish as yours. This land is dying and so are we, but not before we see the back of you, you scoundrel!"

Shamed by her words, Launedda agreed to leave, but silently made a solemn vow to return once he had found a land where water and food were plentiful; a land where his family and people could live and prosper without fear of hunger.

'After months of wandering in vain and finding nothing but growing desert, Launedda was overcome by exhaustion and despair and lay down to rest beneath a great rock that stood black and stark against the wide desert sky. There, under the burning sun, he prayed with his heart and soul for an angel to come and guide him to a place where his family and people could survive. Yet it wasn't a winged angel that came to him, but a horned devil whose skin gleamed red like fire.

"I know a secret place," said the devil with a cunning grin, "a place where the land is green and the rivers flow all year long. I will promise to take you there if you will do me a small favour first."

"What is it you ask of me?" the bard replied, knowing nothing good ever came from the promises of devils.

"An eagle nests high on this rock. This eagle was sent to torment me. All I ask are the feathers of her tail. Bring these to me and I will see to it your prayers are answered and your people saved. But should you fail in your task I will exact a terrible price."

"What price is that?"

"I will take your eyes." Launedda knew this was, indeed, a terrible price, but so desperate was he that agree he did, and soon was climbing strongly and swiftly, as any Jentilak could, up the great rock until he was but inches from that majestic bird.

"What reason have you to bother me here?" spoke the eagle whose feathers were keener than the sharpest blade and shone like the lightning that strikes from the sky.

"I come for the feathers of your tail," said the bard with surprise, for such a bird he never had seen. "Give them to me, I beg you, so my family and people can live, for dirt and dust is soon all they will have to eat."

"If feathers you want then feathers you shall have, for I see you have an honest soul. Yet first a small favour of you I must ask. Below lives a devil who wishes me dead. Bring me the horns from his head and the feathers are yours." So climb back down did Launedda and presented the eagle's price to the devil.

"So the eagle thinks she can outwit me and rid me of my powers," laughed the devil with flickering tongue. "Then take her my horns for she forgets I can still climb without them!" Then removing his horns, he handed them to Launedda with a wicked grin.

'Once more that young Jentilak climbed the rock and presented the horns to the eagle. "I thank you for these," said the eagle, "and you have earned your reward. But know this, if, you take the devil the feathers of my tail you will save your own family but condemn mine to death, for without them I cannot fly and fetch food for my young," and so saying did the eagle move to one side to reveal a brood of chicks beneath her. Moved to tears, the young bard knew he had failed for no true Jentilak could ever willingly take lives so innocent and precious.

"I cannot take your feathers," he said. "It would be a sin most grave if I did."

"True goodness deserves its reward nonetheless," said the eagle and taking the bard's own flute from his back, attached the devil's horns to the end. "When the devil has exacted his revenge upon you and all seems lost, then must you remember this gift I give you. Then is the moment you must play this flute."

'With a heavy heart, the bard climbed back down and faced the devil and all its fury and spite.

"Betrayed!" it shrieked upon seeing Launedda had returned empty-handed. "Then blind you shall be!" and with a vicious claw, it tore out the eyes of the poor bard. Sightless and afraid, the bard recalled the words of the eagle and, taking the horned flute from his back, placed it to his lips and began to play. But it was no ordinary music he made, but a flaming tempest that drove the devil back under the rock and down to the land of shadows below. With the devil gone, the bard stopped playing and found to his joy his sight had been restored, but not as before but with eyes that made all living things shine with a divine light.

"There is one more thing I would give to you," said the eagle, gliding down beside him. "Follow me and I will lead you to this secret place the devil promised you, a place where the rain still falls and the trees ever grow green and thick."

And true to its word, the eagle led Launedda to a valley where the rivers ever ran clear and the harshest of summers seemed unable to scorch. And there, to that valley we today call "Lekuona", Launedda led his family and people and here in that valley their descendants have remained to this very day.'

'That's a lovely tale,' said Blue, 'and are you one of those descendants?'

'I am, as are all who live in the Valley of Lekuona.'

'So this is Lekuona. What does the name mean?'

'It means simply "the good place".'

'Well, it certainly is a good place!' said Blue laughing. 'And is that which you carry on your back the flute from the story?'

'It is, or so we are told, though we no longer call it a flute, but an alboka. I can show it to you if you like?' Blue nodded enthusiastically. Nekane took the curved wooden case off her back and from it removed the strangest of musical instruments. The central part, a double chamber with five holes on one side and three on the other, was crafted from a richly burnished wood whose polished grain flowed like an auburn river. At one end a mouthpiece had been carved to resemble the head and beak of a magnificent eagle whilst at the other the alboka spiralled out into two hollow horns that, indeed, looked as though they had come from a creature straight out of the pages of a legend.

'What an amazing instrument,' said Blue fascinated by the beautifully crafted object. 'Does the wood of your alboka come from the wood of that dead tree in the centre of the glade we saw?'

'You have a good eye for the wood did indeed come from an Al-Arzi tree much like the one you saw in the glade, though that tree is one of the last of its kind for there are said to be very few Al-Arzi left living today.'

'Its wood must be very valuable then.'

'Indeed, it is valuable.'

'Maybe you should cut the tree down, I mean before that bird spoils it any more?'

'And once we cut it down what happens to the bird and the nest it has built in a hollow of one of its branches?'

'But if you cut it down you could save the wood and use it to make more instruments like your alboka.'

'That bird when it sings has a song more beautiful than can be played on any alboka. Would you take that away from the forest?'

'Well... no.' Blue felt ashamed she had even suggested the idea.

'Don't be ashamed,' said the Jentilak smiling. 'Your suggestion was honest even if it was a little misguided. Tell me, do you play an instrument?' Blue shook her head.

'No but the man who used to look after me knew how to play a flute, though his looked a lot simpler than your alboka to play. When I was younger, he used to play it to me at bedtime. I remember I could never get to sleep at night unless he played the same tune over and over to me. Silly really.'

'Not at all silly. What was his name?'

'His name was Eofor. Though everyone called him "Old Eofor". I think they called him that even when he was quite young. It was probably from all the time he used to spend out at sea. You know, he had one of those sailor's faces that looked like it had been pickled in salt and left out in the sun to dry too long. He loved his boat. He loved it so much I think he would have lived in it if he didn't have to come home to look after me. He played the flute really well—at least until the Speris banned music from the village and confiscated all the instruments. After that he just got drunk all the time. I had to learn to sleep without it. I still miss it though.'

It was strange. Blue had barely thought of her childhood home or of Old Eofor much at all since the herders had kidnapped her and taken her aboard the *Nefari* but talking to Nekane like this made her suddenly miss her old childhood companion very much.

'Try to relax. You might want to close your eyes. I'll play for you a while.'

Blue lay back on the soft sheets and did as the Jentilak asked. When she was comfortable, Nekane lifted the alboka to her lips and began to play.

'That's Old Eofor's tune!' said Blue, stunned upon realising the Jentilak was playing the very same melody Old Eofor used to play to her at bedtime. 'How could you know it?' Nekane smiled at Blue's shocked expression but continued playing without answer. Blue considered pressing the Jentilak to reveal her secret, but the deep mellow tones of the alboka and the skill with which the melody was being played quickly filled Blue's heart with so much tender emotion that she found herself turning away from the Jentilak to hide her tears. Lost in half-forgotten memories of a time when she and Old Eofor had actually been happy in their small cottage by the sea, Blue hardly noticed when the Jentilak began to weave a strange new melody into the old familiar tune.

At first Blue disregarded the warm, wave-like sensations which travelled from the soles of her feet to the crown of her head as nothing more than the effect of the milk she had drunk. The fact the waves rose in perfect accompaniment to Nekane's flute playing she shrugged off as merely a coincidence. However, when Nekane began holding each quivering note for longer and the sensations became much stronger, as if the waves were shifting the energies of her body, Blue began to suspect something more was going on. Sometimes, when Nekane's breath would quiver in an unusual way, tiny shocks and spasms would pass through her body, ending only when the melody moved on. At one time, when the waves of energy from the music seemed to pass through her heart, Blue felt a flood of shadows rise out of it like phantoms from a tomb. Another time, as the music seemed to reach her throat, Blue realised she had begun to murmur to herself in a language she had never even heard before. While this was going on, Blue could feel the brow of her forehead and back of her skull becoming hotter and hotter, so hot, in fact, that sweat began to pour down her face and neck.

'Stop!' she yelled out as her skull felt as if it would burst into flame. Nekane ignored her and continued to play. 'Stop!' she pleaded trying to sit up. This time the Jentilak stopped and quietly returned the alboka to its case. Blue sat up and turned on the Jentilak accusingly. 'What do you think you're doi—?' Blue's words failed her for Nekane no longer sat beside her. In her place a bright and flowing figure of colour, energy and light sat looking back at Blue with eyes of fire. 'You're one of them!' Blue gasped. 'One of the Eledh!' The figure laughed.

'The Eledh? I assume you mean the Aingeru? No, I am still Nekane, a humble Jentilak.'

'But you are all light and flame. What has happened to you?'

'Nothing has happened to me, but much has happened to you. You no longer see me with your physical eyes but are seeing me with your full vision awakened. Now you see me as I see you. I knew from the moment I saw you there was something very special about you, but when I saw the kiss of the divine burning upon your brow, I knew the eye of the soul was being readied to be fully opened. All it needed was a little... nudge.'

'So the legend was true! The horns of the alboka really *were* taken from that devil!'

'The legend is very old. Whether every detail of it is true I cannot honestly say, but certainly when I play the alboka I find my gifts come to me more readily. I must leave you to rest properly now,' said the Jentilak standing up. 'Make yourself at home as best you can. I will make sure no one disturbs you. My uncle expects me to perform my duties as the Albokalari and I have dishonoured him enough already. I must go and attend to your friend and help him recover his strength.'

'He hardly needs help with that. He's stronger than ten oxen put together.'

'Still, I am sure he might like to hear me play also.'

'I wouldn't get your hopes up about that either. I suspect he's as ignorant as a pig when it comes to music... or anything else for that matter.'

'Then we must educate him—especially if we are to keep the elders from finding out he is an Atzerri.'

'Well, good luck with that,' said Blue. 'You can always try, though don't be too offended when his snoring drowns out your best efforts. Perhaps you should start with educating his eating habits... oh and, of course, there's the problem with his swearing. You should have heard him the other day, it was enough to make the toenails of a pit hog curl.'

The Jentilak smiled but said nothing in reply. 'Nekane,' said Blue as the Jentilak made to leave.

'Yes?'

'I'm sorry about you losing your family. Maybe you will tell me some time what happened to them, if it is not too painful?' Nekane nodded, but even though Blue could see no tears, she could sense them building inside the Jentilak like a cloud crossing the sun. 'But only when you're ready,' Blue added quickly. The beautiful Jentilak smiled again and nodded.

'Sleep well,' Nekane said gently and left.

CHAPTER 16

Once Kai's prolonged and slightly overdramatic fit of hysteria that he was about to drown finally came to an end — and it began to dawn on him that in fact he wasn't going to die — a strange liberating feeling began to rise within him.

'I can't drown!' he declared exultantly and watched a trail of bubbles rise towards a pinprick of light far above. That must be the way out, he decided, though judging by the murkiness of the water, it was pretty obvious he was no longer in the waters of Amari's sacred caverns. Keen to be back on dry land, Kai kicked his legs and began to swim towards the light. Soon it became apparent he was swimming up a natural rocky shaft the which was rapidly getting narrower. The shaft ended at a murky cleft through which the light filtered. The cleft was barely as wide as himself, but with a bit of effort and a few scrapes, Kai squeezed through and out into what appeared to be a pool of slimy water. From what he could make out from his unusual vantage point two metres below the surface, was that the scum covered pool in which he found himself seemed to be in continual motion and infuriating popping and slapping noises travelled through the water from the surface like barbed arrows through his skull. Unable to bear the slime and noise any longer, Kai swam up through the last couple of metres and poked his head above the surface. Immediately a flash of yellow burst above him and landed on his face with a stinging, wet crack. The crack was instantly followed by a loud scream. A little dazed Kai tore the soggy linen off his face and looked up at the startled face of a dark-skinned woman over whose shoulder a round-faced baby stared out from a papoose fashioned from a colourful stretch of patchwork cloth tied about the woman's back and midriff.

"Boo!" said Kai trying to lighten the mood. He instantly regretted it. Almost leaping out of its papoose in fright, the baby started bawling at the top of its lungs. In seconds a ring of agitated women had crowded protectively around the mother and her child, but when they realised a male had infiltrated an area traditionally reserved exclusively for Kugarran females, the women covered their faces and began shouting and wagging their fingers at Kai angrily. Apologising profusely, Kai scrambled out and, tripping over piles of washing, fled the building into a hot and dusty street outside.

When Kai felt he had put a safe distance between himself and the angry washerwomen, he ducked into a shadowy alleyway behind a large beehive-shaped building made from mud and straw and took stock of his surroundings. Apart from the commotion his unwelcome appearance in the laundry had made, he appeared to be in a sleepy market town at the fringes of the desert. The market itself, whether due to the time of day or to the lack of goods on display, was largely quiet, the only voluble noise coming from a bony and flea-bitten herd of goats who bleated pitifully to be released from their hot and waterless pen. Unmoved by their suffering, their drover slept nearby beneath the shade of one of only two bennu trees in the square. Nearest to Kai, three men armed with cruel looking blades seemed to be arguing with a trader over the price of a dog-sized cocoon. The cocoon hung from the straining cross-pole of the merchant's threadbare tent and every now and then would have a fit of wriggling so violent that Kai expected at any moment to see the entire flimsy structure collapse to the ground. Clearly the armed men weren't interested in agreeing to a fair price and seemed more intent on teasing the merchant over the door-sized gap in his two front teeth than making a purchase. Desperate to appease them, the trader offered a basket of what looked like some sort of flatbread along with a small jar of honey as a gesture of goodwill, but the offer merely provoked a chorus of sarcastic laughter and the bullying continued.

Suddenly a voice at Kai's side drew his attention away from the trader's plight.

'Eresu, akalum. Isu se'im eresu? Isu nadanu eresu?' Kai looked down to his side to see a young girl with her open palms outstretched towards him. The child was so similar to the one that had appeared to him in the desert that Kai had to pinch himself for fear he had slipped back into another vision of the past. In spite of the pinches the girl remained to repeat her request, but after studying Kai from head to foot

and seeing how damp and dishevelled his own clothing was, concluded he must be worse off than herself and reached into the folds of her scruffy, knee-length dress to produce one of the same flatbreads Kai had seen the merchant try to offer the three, armed men.

'Ilu talalu su,' she said as if administering a blessing and, tearing the bread into two halves, handed a piece to Kai.

'Wait,' said Kai visibly touched that one so young and so poor could show him such kindness. The girl paused at the mouth of the alleyway, clearly curious to know what Kai was fumbling for in the folds of his shirt. 'Still got it!' said Kai relieved and handed the girl the small gold lion he'd found in the desert. 'This should buy you plenty of bread.' On seeing the gold glinting in the palm of her hand the girl's eyes widened and her mouth fell open.

'Ilu talalu su! Ilu talalu su!' the girl repeated over and over, kissing Kai's hands.

'You're welcome,' Kai said a little embarrassed by her reaction. With a final blessing and kiss, the girl ran over to the market stall and began pointing enthusiastically at a host of items the merchant had on display. At first the armed men seemed to find the girl's impudent interruption of their cruel banter amusing, but when she produced the gold and succeeded in drawing the merchant's attention entirely away from them, their mood darkened considerably.

'Edin na zu!' said the stockiest of the three and struck a mean blow to the girl's hand in which she clutched the lion. The lion spun out of her grip and landed in the dirt beside her. Crying out in alarm and pain, the girl tried to retrieve Kai's gift but the man grabbed her by the hair and, laughing, placed the heel of his sandal over the figurine.

'Hey!' shouted Kai, smouldering with anger. 'Let her go!'

For a moment the three men faltered uncertainly as their gaze tried to penetrate the shadows of the alleyway, but when nothing but the soggy and boyish looking Kai appeared still wearing the same threadbare clothing in which he had crossed the desert, their confidence and smirks returned.

'Barra!' shouted the stocky man as he gestured dismissively for Kai to get lost before he got hurt. Normally Kai would have happily obliged and walked away from such a one-sided confrontation but a voice in his

head, like a song, seemed to flood his chest with fire, compelling him to step forward until he found himself just inches from the man's face.

'Let her go!' Kai spoke with a tone of ice matched only by his gaze. He could only hope the man understood what he was saying, but he suspected the glassy look in the man's eyes was not so much from a lack of understanding, but from an afternoon misspent drinking in the local taverns. Sure enough, the bullying smirk quickly returned and, with a contemptuous snort, the man shoved Kai so hard the young Furud tumbled back into the shadows from where he had emerged. The very sight of Kai tumbling head over heels back into the alley led to a chorus of guffaws from the other two that only stopped when Kai dragged himself back to his feet and marched back into the sunlight to confront the bullies once more.

'Barra!' repeated the bully, though this time with genuine menace in his voice, and again moved to shove Kai backwards. With an almost hypnotic calmness, Kai caught the man's hand and, with what appeared to be little more than the gentlest of tugs, caused the arm to fall limply to the man's side. The man, his smirk fading quickly, looked down at the limb hanging lifelessly beside his body and wondered why it wouldn't respond. At first a dull sensation seemed to return to the arm, then an expression of acute pain shot across his features.

'Kashshaptu!' the man screamed and looked to his friends for help. At first the other two men blinked in confusion as they tried to work out what had just occurred, but soon the predicament and very real pain of their companion became undeniable and, drawing their blades, together lunged at Kai.

As gently as he could Kai pushed the girl out of harm's way and then, in the same fluid motion, evaded the whirling blades coming at him whilst sending the second man slamming painfully into the third. Meanwhile the first had recovered his wits enough to draw his own knife with his other hand and with it made a clumsy swipe at Kai's face. The blade whistled through the air but met with nothing as Kai had already slipped out of its path. The other two men gathered themselves for a second attack but before they could even raise their blades Kai had stepped inside and slapped the knives out of their hands with no more difficulty than had they been toy swords in the hands of children.

Realising they were being severely humiliated in front of the small crowd that was gathering to watch, they turned on Kai with hatred, taking turns to swing angrily at the impudent youngster's face and torso with whatever they could lay their hands on. Again, Kai easily weaved, ducked and skipped out of the way of their best efforts and before a single blow had come even close to connecting, he sent all three tumbling heavily to the floor. With the breath ripped from their lungs, the three men only just managed to stand, but it was clear none of them were in any state or mood to continue. Done with being made to look such idiots in front of the gathered crowd, the three men staggered back down the street, each one looking back at Kai with bewildered expressions matched only by Kai's own, who was as confounded as they as to how he had just utterly humiliated three fighting men without earning so much as a bruise in return.

'You're a rare one,' said the merchant fashioning a bundle containing all that the young girl had asked for and more besides, 'You show the heart of a warrior, but you move like a dancer.'

'A dancer!' said Kai offended. 'I was raised by the fighting Furud! I am no dancer!'

'I did not mean it as an insult,' said the merchant as he attached the bundle to the girl's back and accepted the gold lion from her outstretched hand, 'but whether warrior or dancer, you invite big trouble for yourself. The Dayan Sami is a dangerous enemy to make.'

'They were so drunk I doubt they'll even remember what I look like.'

'It is not drink that fuels their malice. It is a flower—a flower the Dayan Sami gives to all his followers. His Kalibi will do anything to get them. They are like dogs constantly begging for scraps from their master and it is to this master they now run.'

'Who is he, this Dayan Sami?'

The merchant looked around uneasily in case any of the other market traders might be listening then began speaking in a low tone.

'His real name is Lasanan, the only surviving grandson of the Great King Sul, a king great in title, but little else.'

'Why? What did he do?'

214

'Like so many of his ancestors before him he blamed the droughts and famine that plagued these lands on the idleness of the people, constantly rebuking and punishing them until he had all but driven them to despair. Then one day, after the droughts had so eaten away at his wealth that even his generals abandoned him, the people decided they'd had enough.'

'What did they do?'

'They yoked the king and his family to a plough and worked them to death like cattle. Lasanan was the only one who survived, though it might have been better for him if he had died for all they did to him. Eventually I believe he escaped, fleeing Kugarra for dear life.'

'So what's he doing back here?'

'He came back. Ten years ago, he reappeared and, in a great show of public humility, placed a yoke about his neck, swearing never to remove it until all who had suffered under his grandfather's rule could find it in their hearts to forgive what had been done to them. Many did forgive, and to these he gave a gift; a flower he claimed he had received from a living god. The flower, he promised, would banish hunger and help all who took it forget all their troubles and woes. Many accepted his gift gratefully for the years without rain had been hard and long, but once they had consumed it they quickly fell into his trap for it was not forgiveness Lasanan sought, but revenge. Forgetting about family and home, all they soon cared for were the flowers, doing anything for Lasanan to get more. Naming himself the Dayan Sami, the Judge of Heaven, Lasanan began to carve out for himself a new kingdom, a kingdom run by his Kalibi dogs. Since taking over these lands he has done terrible things, but most people are too afraid or too weak to resist. It is best you do not stay in this town long. The Kalibi will soon tell their master how you humiliated them.'

'Don't worry, I don't plan on staying long. But it would help if I knew which way I must travel. I must find a way to a holy city. It is called Sippara, the bird city. Do you know how to get there?' The merchant scowled as Kai mentioned the name.

'Holy city!' said the merchant spitting in disgust. 'Sippara is no holy city. I travelled there once with my father. He was very ill at the time and believed Sippara's great healers and holy men could help him. When we

215

got there, we found hundreds of sick and dying begging for help at the gates to the city, but none were being allowed in and no one came out to help them. Nowadays only the wealthy are granted access to the healers. Even before the Dayan Sami started to work his influence into Sippara your "holy city" was rotten to the core. My father is still buried at the roadside a hundred yards from those gates.'

'I am sorry for your loss. But I still need to find it. There is something very important that I must do. There is one who lives there that I must find.'

'Even if I told you the way, Sippara will not be easy to reach. It lies on the far side of these mountains, and once you clear the mountains and forests you still have to cross the Plains of Sisu. The road is not easy and it is evident you will need a guide who speaks your northern tongue. Maybe we can make a deal?'

'Well, I have no more gold if that is what you were thinking.'

'I will be honest with you stranger, times have not been kind to me recently and I cannot afford to take you to Sippara for nothing, but any fool can see you are carrying no more gold. If you will forgive my being so blunt, you look like an escaped slave. Perhaps you were taken from a wealthy family who would be grateful for your return?'

'I have no family,' said Kai, 'at least none that I know of.'

'A shame,' said the merchant. 'It was a just an idea. Perhaps that thing you carry about your neck might be worth something? Maybe I could get a good price for it in the markets of Wardum.' Kai lifted Amari's gift out of his shirt so that the merchant could see it was nothing more than a shell strung from a chord.

'Ah, so you are a pilgrim. Well, even pilgrims who cannot pay the price of entry into the city remain outside.'

The merchant's words made Kai realise how rash he had been to give away the gold lion so easily. Now he had nothing with which to bribe the guards and gain entry into Sippara.

'I'm afraid I have nothing more to give them.'

The merchant looked at Kai's fallen face.

'Maybe Hamsum can think of a way to help you. There is good money to be made in the markets on the road to Sippara, but they are dangerous; full of bandits and Kalibi thieves. If I were to go there, I would need protection and it is clear you know how to do that. Who knows, maybe your young northern smile might bring me a change in fortune. How about we work together? I guide you to Sippara and pay for your entry into the city and you protect me and help me sell my goods on the way. Besides, it has been a long time since I visited the grave of my father. A return is long overdue. What do you say my friend? '

'I'm not sure if I will be much good at protection. I'm not really one for fighting.'

'You could have fooled me!' said the merchant still amazed at the fighting skills Kai had just displayed. 'My offer stands.'

'How long do you think it will take us to sell your goods? I cannot delay my journey for long.'

'That will depend on how lucky your face is.'

'And once we sell the goods, you'll take me straight to Sippara?'

'Hamsum promises,' said the merchant beaming contentedly.

'*And* pay for me to get inside?'

'Hamsum swears on the grave of his father he will guide you to Sippara *and* pay for you to get inside—*if* we sell all of my goods.'

'Then we have a deal,' said Kai, finding no reason to doubt the merchant's sincerity.

'Excellent!' said the merchant and, whistling merrily through the gap in his teeth, lifted a gourd from his belt and poured a brown liquid into a small bone cup attached to the gourd's neck. 'Here. To our partnership!' Kai accepted the cup and dutifully downed the contents.

'What is that!' Kai choked, almost gagging the foul liquid back up again.

'You do not like kash?' asked the merchant incredulously. 'I make it myself from the finest gina'abul in all the desert!' Kai could see his evident lack of enthusiasm for the merchant's liquor was in danger of sabotaging their relations before they had even begun, so, with a supreme effort, forced the grimace off his face and managed a watery smile.

'No... I didn't mean that. I was surprised at how... rich the, erm, kash tastes. I've never tried one so... rich.'

'Ahh,' said the merchant reassured. 'I can tell you and I will become good friends. I have a treat for you. Wait here. I will bring you the finest gina'abul in all the desert!' Kai waited apprehensively as the merchant dashed off, wondering what on earth the mystery "gina'abul" ingredient might actually be. After a while a cry further up the street announced the merchant's return. At first Kai thought his new friend was being pursued by a bow-legged rhinoceros, but he quickly realised it was no rhinoceros, but a huge, scaly lizard which the merchant was leading on a leash towards him.

'This,' said the merchant proudly presenting the lizard before Kai, 'is Uzzaga!' Kai stood speechless as the lizard, almost as large as a juvenile pit hog, flopped onto the hot ground and began sniffing through the piles of dung for anything tasty to eat.

'This is your… gina abul?'

'She makes the best kash in all the desert! I feed her nothing but the finest herbs!'

'Err, forgive my ignorance, but how exactly does she make the kash?'

'How? When she pass water of course. She does not go often, but when she does, she makes the finest kash in all the desert; very strong, with good scents.'

By the time Kai had finished retching up the last of the kash as discreetly as he could behind a wall, the merchant was already packed and ready to leave. The tent and some of his goods were strapped securely to the strong back of his beloved liquor-piddling lizard and the rest he had made into two neat packs, one for both he and Kai each to carry.

'We must leave quick before those Kalibi cowards find courage to tell their masters what you did to them.'

After a nervous passage through the gate, Kai and Hamsum were soon making swift progress along a rough dirt track towards a jagged line of black mountains which stretched across the horizon like the bony spines of a herder's neck.

'We call the mountains Kur-Babba. Kur not only means mountain, but also holy—Babba means silver.'

'Why silver? Is there much to be found here?'

'Not the metal silver, but the trees that once covered these mountains. It was these that gave the mountains their name.'

'Really? So what happened to the trees?'

'Some still grow in the higher places. But with the passing of each year the desert grows wider and the mountain forests smaller and what the desert doesn't kill, the Dayan Sami burns to ash so he can grow more of his flowers. It will not be long before there is nothing here but desert and our bones to show a great people once lived here.'

CHAPTER 17

Blue stretched like an overfed cat and rolled over. The sun was already high in the sky and shone through the broad opening to bathe her legs and feet in a luxurious, golden warmth. As always, her breakfast had been laid out for her, a sumptuous harvest plucked from the abundant forest gardens of the Jentilak; gardens which shone like emeralds against the mountainside and filled the air with an exotic elixir of scents that drew Blue every morning after breakfast like a flower draws a butterfly. For hours Blue would lose herself amongst the verdant foliage and bright flowers or would sit watching the silver-blue flashes of fish leaping up the giggling rapids of the only river she had seen since leaving the It-Eru delta. Often, as she sat there contemplating the beautiful spectacle of nature before her, Nekane would join her and teach Blue the ways of the Jentilak, leading her on a fascinating journey into the very heart of the forest. On days such as these, Nekane might bring Blue a seed or herb and help her to understand its mystery and wonder.

'Look at this seed,' she would say placing a tiny burgha seed in Blue's hand. 'Some say the ways of the Jentilak are steeped in wisdom, yet our wisdom comes not from the study of scriptures or books, for all the libraries of Kugarra could not contain a fraction of the information held in this tiny seed. Already this seed knows when to break free from its shell and shake off the darkness that surrounds it; it knows to lay roots deep and strong before reaching for the sun, catching and storing its bountiful rays to send forth its fragrant blossom, and from this blossom bring into this world the greatest joy and gift life has to offer; its fruit, its offspring. Know then it is only from observing the natural world of the Creator that true knowledge and wisdom are gathered.'

It was from lessons like this that Blue began to learn not just the role and significance of every insect and wild creature, every flower, herb and tree, but also the ways of the Albokalari, learning from Nekane how to use her abilities to sense the presence of giant elk or mountain lions deep in the forest and then draw them close, often so close she could touch their great antlers or soft fur without any fear of being attacked. Blue also saw how the spirits and energy of the plants and animals of the forest responded to the energy and touch of those around them, shrinking and darkening if one should pass through in an ugly mood or glowing as if with pleasure for any who walked beneath their boughs with a light and joyful heart. The only skill Blue struggled to master was playing the alboka. No matter how hard she tried to imitate Nekane's moving and beautiful melodies, the poor girl only succeeded in making the ancient instrument sound like a pit hog passing wind. Yet, under Nekane's infinitely patient gaze, Blue persevered until finally the melodies that began to issue from beneath her fingers not only resembled music but could one moment dance like the skip of a young buck racing across the forest floor only to soften and sigh like the wind passing peacefully through the trees. Basax, of course, was far too busy stuffing his face to show interest in either her musical accomplishments or take much notice of the beauty and lushness of his surroundings—though his bashfulness around the doe-eyed Jentilak suggested to Blue he had at least taken notice of one beautiful thing that land of forest and mountain had to offer. He even allowed Blue to talk him into impressing Nekane by trying his hand at a spot of gardening; pulling up the dead weeds and roots from around the house, removing rocks and boulders from the soil and carrying armfuls of flowers, shrubs and young saplings up from the forest so that Blue and he could replant the tatty old garden. When Nekane returned one late afternoon and saw the little eden they had created for her, she was so thrilled that she forgot her Jentilak reserve and planted a kiss so big on Basax's lips that the herder's face flushed redder than the sackful of bennu he had just eaten. Spurred on by the kiss to even greater domestic heroics, Basax set to transforming not just the garden, which he extended to almost three times its original size, but also Nekane's home, gutting, cleaning and fixing every table, chair, and door; scrubbing every sill, wall, floorboard and stair, until the whole house gleamed like new. This rather odd behaviour, at least odd as far as Blue was concerned, won Basax such admiring and adoring looks from Nekane that Blue frequently found herself making embarrassed excuses to go outside and leave the pair to coo and fawn over each other alone. It also earned them ever more frequent visits from Otzak and other senior members of the community, who would walk around the house and garden inspecting the changes with favourable grunts and sniffs as if overseeing some sort of prenuptial courting ritual. As for Basax's over-fondness for Jentilak gastronomy, neither did he do his relationship any harm with their Jentilak hosts, who seemed to see it as their moral and divine duty to fatten Nekane's guest and potential suitor as much as they were able, sending Soko up from the village each day with a basket almost as big as himself laden with edible delights from every corner of the valley.

'You're getting fat,' said Blue interrupting Basax's third breakfast that morning. 'And so are they,' she added looking at the growing troupe of woodland spirits who had taken to loitering around Basax's room like a marooned band of pirates.

'Jentilak like Basax fat,' he said tipping a wrinkle-faced hedgerow spirit off his plate so he could cram more food into his mouth. 'Anyway, so are you.'

'Me! I am not fat…! Am I?' Blue quickly looked down to check her waist and thighs. She certainly hadn't piled on the pounds like the herder, though, thanks to weeks of rest and Jentilak hospitality, neither could she say she was any longer the scrawny urchin who Basax had snatched from the floor of Algar's kitchen. The lean, wiry limbs and skinny frame of the young shaft rat had clearly begun to fill out. Even Blue's usually scruffy hair seemed to have benefitted from her improved diet and now hung in lustrous gold and copper swirls down her back.

'Good job you not fat when Basax see you on *Nefari* or Basax have gobbled you down in three big bites. Yum! Yum! Yum!'

'Not funny!' she said whacking the herder across the head, the act of which was greeted by a ripple of disapproving squeaks throughout the room.

'Ow,' said Basax rumbling with laughter.

'Well, if you'd been as fat as *you* are now you wouldn't have been able to drag that big rear of yours out of its hammock to catch me!'

'Oh no!' said Basax making a point of springing his "big rear" out of his chair as nimbly as ever and made as if to sink his teeth into the plump flesh of Blue's legs. Blue screamed and turned to escape the exaggerated flailing of the herder's claws, only to collide straight into Nekane coming in through the doorway.

'Oh, sorry Nekane,' said Blue helping the beautiful Jentilak back to her feet. Nor had the Jentilak's attractiveness that morning appeared to have been wasted on the herder, who no sooner than see her entering his room, tucked in his bulging belly and blushed redder than a tomato. 'Are you okay?' Blue asked, sensing an unusual gravity about the Jentilak's face. Nekane shook her head and looked on the verge of tears.

'Do you have a moment?'

'Of course,' said Blue. 'What's the matter?'

'I need to speak to you about something. Something important.'

'Okay. Do you want to sit down?' Nekane shook her head.

'What is it you want to speak about?

'I need to tell you what happened to my father and brother.'

'Oh... Um. Okay. I'm listening.' Nekane clutched her hands together as if to give herself strength, then began to speak.

'Two years ago, a stranger came to us, a travelling priest. He spoke little but we managed to learn from him that he had come from lands far to the north. At first there was panic amongst the Jentilak who feared our homelands had been discovered, but we checked his trail and found him to have been travelling alone. Some wanted to kill him, fearing he would lead others to us, but my uncle and the elders of the village argued against this, saying we should honour the ways of the Jentilak and strive to learn all that we could from him, to learn all that we could about his race for none of us had ever seen his like before. He seemed unconcerned that he would live as our prisoner and quietly spent his days under lock and key or under the direct supervision of our warriors. After a while, his cooperation and quiet nature earned him greater trust and persuaded my uncle and the other elders that he should be allowed to take short walks around the village and surrounding forests. I believe the elders hoped the trust and freedom might awaken something inside of him, a warmth and sympathy perhaps for our ways and customs, but my father was not happy with this for he suspected something was not right with him.'

'Why?'

'Because my father was unable to see into the priest's soul.'

'But I thought he was the Albokalari?'

'He was, but it was as if the priest knew of some black art to be able to block his sight and hide his intentions from us. One evening the priest had still not returned from one of his walks so my father, concerned he was up to some mischief, set off with my brother to track his whereabouts. Three days later they were both found dead near the northern border.'

'That's terrible! What happened to them?'

'They had been torn to pieces and...' Nekane paused as she mustered the strength to speak the words, '... their flesh eaten almost to the bone.' Blue looked at Nekane in horror. 'The elders put it down to a tragic accident.'

'How could such an end be seen as an accident?'

'Because they were found dead at the base of the Sugatz Rock, a rock Albokalaris have visited and climbed for centuries. On the day my father died we found signs a violent storm had passed through that way. The elders think my father and brother were honouring this tradition when the storm struck and caused them to fall.'

'What about the bodies of your father and brother? You said their flesh had been eaten.'

'The elders believe scavengers found the bodies and stripped them of their flesh, but they should know no animal, no matter how wild nor hungry, would ever dishonour the corpse of an Albokalari in such a way.'

'Then you doubt this is what truly happened?'

'I do not doubt, I *know*! You see the rock is the very same as that discovered by our forefather, Launedda. It was here he inherited his powers.'

'The devil's rock!' said Blue slightly alarmed. Nekane nodded.

'Just before my father died, I overheard him talking to my brother about the rock's energy. He said he felt it was turning dark. I've never heard him sound so worried. He spoke of terrible portents; of storms and sightings of a serpent seen near the rock—a serpent red as flame. He was convinced the priest had something to do with it all. I believe my father and brother went to the rock to find out just what it was the priest was up to and paid for it with their lives.'

'But why are you telling me this now?'

'Because this morning the priest returned.'

'He's returned! Then you must speak with your uncle and the elders! They must confront him immediately and find out what he knows.'

'They already have. They confronted the priest as soon as he arrived, but he is a sly one. Already they seem convinced he had nothing to do with my father and brother's deaths. He says little, but when he does choose to speak, his voice can turn as cold as the hoarfrost that clings to the upper banks of the river in winter. When this happens, his words have a way of unsettling you, of shaking your convictions and filling your mind with doubt. Yet I do *not* believe him. That is why I have come to seek your help, Blue. I need to find out more. Like with my father, the priest seems able to stop me from seeing into his soul. It is as if he places a wall of shadow around himself so that I cannot tell whether he is lying or not. I need to know where the priest was on the day my father and brother died. I need to know the truth!'

'Then we'll send Basax to deal with him. He'll get the truth out of him in no time.' Beside them the herder grunted his agreement.

'Thank you, but an open confrontation might only drive him deeper into his shell, and if we scare him too much he might leave before we can learn anything. Soko has been following the priest all morning. He says he is already acting strangely, as if he were trying to garner provisions for a journey. I don't think it is his intention to stay with us for long.'

'Where do you think he is planning on going?'

'To the Sugatz Rock. To the place where my father and brother died. I think the priest has returned to finish what he started two years ago.'

'Then what do you want me to do?'

'You are the Ama Galdua. Your abilities far exceed those of an Albokalari. I need to know if you can do what my father and I could not. I need you to look into his soul and tell me what you see.'

'I can try. Where is he now?'

'The last Soko told me was that the priest was making his way down towards the river. The river will be busy at this time of morning for the Jentilak like to bathe before breakfast.'

'Perfect. I'll go down and bathe with them. I'll be able to watch him from the water.'

'Thank you, Blue,' said Nekane.' I'd hoped you would agree. Soko already knows to expect you. He promised me he'd keep an eye out for you in case you show up. I cannot risk going with you. I'm certain the priest knows of my suspicions and is wary of my presence.'

'What if he tries to leave? Do you want me to follow him?'

'No. Stay where there are crowds. We do not know how dangerous he is yet. If the priest tries to leave anywhere, send Soko to fetch us straight away. Basax and I will track his movements together.'

'And stay with crowd,' insisted the big herder, not at all comfortable with the idea of Blue going alone.

'I will,' Blue promised. I'm only going to take a quick look.'

CHAPTER 18

By the time Kai and Hamsum had reached their third market, Kai was seriously considering abandoning his friend and trying to reach Sippara alone. It wasn't that Hamsum's goods were in any way inferior to any of the other goods on display, it was just that Hamsum made a dreadful salesman and seemed incapable of starting any negotiation without insisting every potential customer sample a draught of his disgusting kash liquor. As Kai knew from experience, one taste was enough to send anyone running. As for Hamsum's warning that the markets on the way to Sippara were dangerous places, Kai quickly discovered that most of the danger came from Hamsum's own customers who, having sampled Hamsum's lizard elixir, frequently expressed a heartfelt desire to wrap the gourd of kash about the merchant's own head. Hamsum, however, remained blissfully ignorant of how unpopular his favourite tipple was making him and continued to sell his goods at a snail's pace whilst Kai did his utmost to calm and soothe the hostile reactions of his less-than-impressed customers.

'Hamsum, we have to talk.'

'What is it my friend? You are worried I see. Don't be. Today is going to be a good day, you'll see. Hamsum has a fresh batch of kash today. Today we will sell many goods and make a lot of money.'

'Hamsum, tell me honestly, when was the last time you had a good day?'

'The last time! Well, it was... now let me think, when was it?'

'Was it the last time you ran out of kash?'

'Ran out of kash? Well, actually, I think it was. Very strange day. Why do you ask?' Kai gave a deep sigh. He knew what he was going to say was going to upset his new friend, but if he didn't, he knew they would never reach Sippara.'

'How do I say this? Your drink, the kash... well, it's putting people off buying your goods.'

'What are you talking about? My people have traded goods like this for hundreds of years.'

'And are your people famous for trading goods?'

'Of course not. My people are gina'abul shepherds. We know nothing about trading. I am the first of my people to make a life from this.' Hamsum stood up proud and tall as he spoke.

'Hamsum, your kash... it's not working. Your customers, they don't... like it. It stops them wanting to buy anything from you. In fact, it makes a lot of them want to hurt you... some quite badly.'

'Hurt me! Don't be stupid. Everybody loves kash!'

'You remember that last man you nearly sold an entire case of honey to. He came back saying you tried to poison him. I even had to stop him from setting fire to your tent.' Hamsum opened his gourd and took a sniff of the contents.

'I cannot understand. It has good scents. With every sniff I can smell the desert flowers rising up like a spring meadow.' Hamsum closed his eyes and inhaled the aroma deeply.

'I'm not sure everyone else has such an educated nose as yours, Hamsum. There may well be subtle undertones of desert flowers, but it's the overtones of lizard pee that causes such offence. Trust me, Hamsum, that stuff makes your eyes burn. You're going to find few people around here who won't be upset at having to drink it. We have to try a new way of selling your goods.' Hamsum looked around at the piles of unsold goods and his countenance fell. Even his prize cocoon had scuppered Hamsum's one and only financial coup d'état by hatching mid-sale into the biggest moth Kai had ever seen and taking off into the desert sky.

'What do you suggest?' said the crestfallen merchant. 'You expect me to sing and dance?'

'Well, maybe not dance, but if you agree to just one day without giving anyone kash, maybe I have a song or two that could help you sell your stock.'

'A song? You are going to sing to sell? You are crazy!'

'Just give me one chance.'

Hamsum fell quiet for a while, fiddling with the stopper on his beloved gourd whilst he contemplated his unsold stock.

'Okay,' he said finally, 'You sing for one day and if sales are still bad, we go back to kash.'

'Agreed.'

'Good! Then let's drink to seal the agreement! Uzzaga!'

***

By the close of day, not only had Hamsum sold, replenished and resold his stock four times over, but a crowd the size of a small army had gathered in the market square to listen to Kai sing.

'I think it's time we left,' said Hamsum, spying a group of armed men trying to push their way through the crowd. 'That is the local Kalibi.' Kai nodded and started to pack the tent.

'Leave it,' said the merchant. 'We'll buy a new one.'

By the time the Kalibi had forced their way through the tightly packed crowd, Kai, Hamsum and the lizard had already left the square and were hurrying up a dusty mountain trail lined with trees whose drought-ravaged bark, indeed, glistened like silver just as Hamsum had described.

'My friend. You are a *dingir*!" said Hamsum, once they were out of view of the town.

'Dingir?'

'One sent from the gods. A blessing. An angel! By nightfall we arrive in Wardum, the last big town before Sippara. There, my friend, we will feast like kings!'

CHAPTER 19

When Blue reached the banks of the river, the idyllic scenes that unfolded before her almost caused her to forget the very reason she had been asked to go down there. Jentilak, young and old, laughed in the warm sunlight as they leapt from rocks or wallowed with a joyful abandon in the cool, lazy waters. The air above was a constant whir of wings as white-throated mud swallows snatched at fat mayflies, often inches above their heads. On the grassy banks, lime-green crickets trilled or scattered beneath the tottering steps of giggling infants as they gripped shiny river pebbles like treasures to their small chests. Blue sat down at the river's edge and dipped her feet into the water. She couldn't see the priest, or Soko for that matter, but she was sure they would appear sooner or later. Half an hour passed by. No sign of either one of them. Small fish had even started to nibble around her feet and toes. She pulled them out and rested them on a warm rock to let them dry in the sun. More time passed. Nothing.

Bored with waiting, Blue got up and decided she ought to try further downstream. There were still sections of the river where the water slowed and deepened enough for bathing. There were also plenty of Jentilak around so she didn't feel unduly worried that she was having to take herself ever farther away from the village. And yet, with each new bend of the river, the numbers of bathers thinned until nothing but a broad and empty section of water stretched out before her. Blue knew where she was; it was a spot rarely visited by the Jentilak for the bearded catfish in that part of the river not only were said to be large enough to swallow a pig whole, but it was also a popular place for herds of ramhorns who frequently came down off the mountains to drink, churning the banks of the river with their sharp hooves into a muddy bog. Fortunately, on this occasion there were no ramhorns... but neither was there any sign of Soko or the priest. They must have returned to the village by some other route.

Deciding she really ought to head back, Blue suddenly felt the energy of the trees on the opposite bank withdraw sharply like a child touching a scalding pan. Immediately she realised something very un-Jentilak was lurking close to the water, but not close enough to allow itself to be seen. She closed her eyes, concentrating hard until she was able to sense a shadowy figure standing a few metres away from the water's edge. If only she could be certain, it was the priest.

'Hello,' Blue called out assuming the figure must be able to see her. The figure kept silent then began to move away. She shivered. She could sense it leaving a mucky wake behind like a ship passing through silt-clogged waters. It was then she could have sworn she heard a voice calling to her from the forest—a voice not unlike that of Soko.

'Soko? Is that you?' The forest remained quiet. 'Damn it Soko! Where are you?'

Now she was in a real predicament. Did she risk leaving the river to follow the sound or did she ignore it and head back to safety? But what if it really was Soko and he needed her help? Again, a voice cried out from the forest and again Blue could have sworn it was Soko calling her name. That decided it. Blue searched along the bank and found a point where it seemed shallow enough to wade across, then, trying not to think of what might be gliding past her feet, crossed carefully to the other side. Once at the far bank, Blue pulled herself out and paused to listen. The forest remained deathly quiet.

'Blue!' This time she could hear Soko's voice ringing out loud and clear.

'I'm coming!' she cried and ran into the forest.

CHAPTER 20

Wardum, to say the least, was a disappointment. Rather than nestle upon the side of a mountain like many of the small mountain villages they had visited, the entire town appeared to be sliding off it like an old drunkard slipping off his barstool. The town at least did possess a few grand buildings that suggested a slightly more illustrious past, but these were in such dire need of renovation that they served more to highlight how far the town had fallen than add any touches of nostalgic charm to the whole shabby affair. As for Hamsum's idea of feasting like kings, Kai discovered to his great disappointment that its finest inn — and there appeared to be an unnaturally large number of those — was nothing more than a smoky drinking hole full of sweating bodies intent on drowning their sorrows in the local dida; a strong, ruby-coloured ale which tasted no better than the vat of overcooked and tasteless stew which bubbled over a miserable fire in the centre of the room. Nevertheless, Kai made the best of it and tried his hardest to keep pace with his kash-drinking friend, who devoured every last thing the skinny serving boys brought him, with a gusto of one who believed themselves to be dining in the finest kitchen in all the land. At first Kai had to admit the dida left him feeling light and marginally happy, but by the time a sloppy and unidentifiable desert arrived, the which tasted even worse than the stew, Kai began to wish he'd never set foot in the place at all.

'What's the matter?' said Hamsum spotting how his guest's enthusiasm for their celebration was starting to flag.

'Isn't there any water to drink? This stuff makes you feel like a horse is kicking you in the saddle bags.' Hamsum looked at his young friend swaying precariously in his chair and chuckled.

'This is Wardum,' he said raising his hands as if that answered everything. 'Did I not say you would be better drinking kash with me? The beer is not what it used to be.'

'What about that green juice the barwoman keeps drinking?' Kai pointed to a jug filled with an appetisingly fresh-looking fruit juice.

'Durma juice! You want durma juice?'

'Durma juice? Yes, juice sounds nice. I think I'll have a jug of that please.'

'But that is a woman's drink!'

'I don't care. Durma juice it is! That's what I want.' Hamsum looked at his Furud companion uncertain whether he was joking or not, but when Kai made a show of emptying his recently refilled mug of dida back into its jug and slamming his empty cup on to the table, the merchant was left with little recourse but to send a bemused serving boy to the cellar to fetch what Kai had asked for.

Soon a slender-necked carafe filled to the brim with the green juice, together with a thimble-sized glass, were duly placed in front of Kai's expectant gaze.

'I won't be needing that?' said Kai knocking the tiny glass to one side and, grasping the neck of the carafe in his fist, began decanting the contents into his eager mouth.

'Go slow my friend!' warned Hamsum noticing how fast the carafe's contents was disappearing down his young friend's throat. Kai ignored the warning, so desperate was he to be rid of the taste of dida and to shift the lump of stew that had lodged itself in his gut like a wad of clay.

It was only when Kai had drained the last drop and had placed the empty carafe back on the table, that he realised he had made three glaringly stupid mistakes. His first mistake was not having remembered, especially at the moment Hamsum had told him durma juice was a drink for women, that at least half of the drunkards they had seen shambling along Wardum's streets had, in fact, been women. His second mistake was to assume that the very small glass the serving boy had brought with the carafe was perhaps because they had run out of tankards. He now realised, to his shame, that the glass was actually in perfect proportion to the intoxicating potency of the "juice" placed before him. Kai's third, and perhaps most glaring mistake of all, was when he stubbornly continued to drain the contents of the carafe even after the vast majority of the inn's highly inebriated patrons had begun to applaud each and every heroic gulp. Of course once the carafe was back on the table and the "horse" that had previously been kicking him in his privates moved up to his head, he realised what an utter fool he had been.

'I really don't f-feeel sho good,' he slurred as his elbow slipped off the table. 'I think I should go out for shome air.'

'Ha ha my friend!' responded Hamsum delighted that Kai was at last starting to get into the party spirit. 'So strong and yet a little dur juice beats you like a girl. Hurry back for soon we must begin the dancing!'

Outside Kai stumbled and slumped against the trunk of an old, bowed tree. Through its thin foliage, a crescent moon winked mockingly at him from behind the peak of the mountain.

'And you can jussht sshod offf,' he said aiming a rather impressive kick in the moon's direction, the momentum of which caused him to do a half flip and land flat on his back. From this new position Kai briefly contemplated whether a brisk walk, or perhaps brisk crawl, might help clear his head, but after struggling to get up and then managing twice to lose the steep path — the second time rolling twenty feet down the side of the mountain — it was clear he was probably best just staying where he lay.

'A little shleep, that'sh all I need,' he said and belched so loudly a flock of birds abandoned their roost and flew off into the night's sky. Kai rested his head against a pillow-sized rock and allowed his eyes to fall shut. The night was warm and the wind gentle. Just a little nap, he decided, and then he'd rejoin Hamsum for a dance or two…

CHAPTER 21

It didn't take long before Blue began to regret her decision to follow the sound of Soko's voice away from the river and into the forest. It was as if the moment she reached a point where she thought she'd heard him calling to her the voice appeared to come from an entirely different place. Not only that, like the elusive and at times dangerous trail that had led her and Basax into the lands of the Jentilak, the trail the young boy's voice was leading her along was in many ways just as difficult and treacherous to follow and was making catching up with him near impossible. The trail also showed Blue just how fragile a hold the Jentilak had on the life of the forest, for once she passed beyond the northern ridge overlooking the Lekuona valley, the trees quickly began to display signs the forest was losing its fight against the encroaching desert heat as resin seeped from their cracked bark like blood leaking from a wound.

It was just getting to the point that Blue was really starting to suspect something unnatural was going on when the forest abruptly ended at the top of a cliff and a tall, black rock loomed into view. The rock itself was an impressive structure, rising one hundred and fifty metres straight out of a flat and arid desert plain which stretched from the base of the cliffs all the way to the horizon. Yet it wasn't the imposing size or unusual, black colour of the rock that caused Blue to stop in her tracks, but that she was sure she had seen it before somewhere, as though from a dream... or nightmare. There was also an overwhelming sensation that the rock did not belong there; like a nail hammered through flesh. Suddenly a footfall behind her caused her to spin around.

'Soko!' she cried seeing the welcome sight of Nekane's nephew smiling back at her. 'Thank the gods! I was starting to think I was losing my mind. What are you doing all the way out here? Nekane is going to throttle us both when she catches us! She told me not to leave the river. She'll think we've been kidnapped or something!' Soko walked past

Blue without reply and waved for her to follow him down towards the base of the black rock. Blue would have insisted on them returning straight away, but the young Jentilak seemed determined she should follow.

'This had better be important!' she shouted as she scrambled down after him.

Once at the base of the rock Blue found herself wanting to sit down. Her limbs felt very heavy, though it wasn't the sort of heaviness gained from fatigue, but a leaden, dead feeling that she really did not like at all.

'Perhaps we should leave?' she suggested struggling even to lift her head to speak. Soko offered no reply but began mumbling something under his breath. Around them a strong wind began to pick up, swirling about the rock, causing clouds of dust and sand to spin and dance. High above, the shadow of a huge eagle had begun circling the rock, its wings beating to the rhythms of the wind as if the blustery weather were somehow of its own doing.

'Speak up Soko. I can't hear you above this wind.' Soko ignored her request and continued mumbling inaudibly to himself. All around the wind continued to gather strength until it raged like a gale at sea.

'What's happening?' said Blue having to raise her voice just to be heard. 'I've never seen the weather turn so fast. Soko, come shelter under the rock with me. This doesn't look good at all.' The young Jentilak didn't respond, instead raising his arms towards the eagle as if defying it to do its worst. Growing concerned and slightly annoyed with his incomprehensible behaviour, Blue was about to scold him for being so reckless when a movement down to her right silenced her instantly. Forcing its way out through the earth near the base of the rock slithered a monstrous serpent, its skin gleaming red as fire. From two wounds at the top of its skull, blood dripped onto the ground, each drop scorching the rocky surface where it landed as if its blood were hot like burning oil. Suppressing a scream of fear, Blue tried to move out of the serpent's way but the creature moved too fast, wrapping its thick coils about her body to pin her arms and legs.

'Soko get away from here!' Blue gasped as the serpent's hot tongue flickered across her face but, far from running away, the young Jentilak moved even closer.

'Go Soko, please!' The Jentilak ignored her and stepped closer still. He was so close now Blue could see the green of his eyes, or were they turning black? His skin too seemed to be changing, growing paler whilst in place of his simple Jentilak garments, dark robes now covered his elongating frame.

'You!' she said spying the flicker of white flames where his robe parted below the neck. 'But I saw you drown!' The Speris smiled and began to mutter again under his breath. Far below, deep beneath the earth, Blue sensed something stirring, like the juddering scrape of immense coils unwinding. From the foot of the rock where the serpent had appeared, winged creatures so black they appeared like shadows also began emerging, rising into the turbulent air, their piercing shrieks cutting through the air like knives.

'Leave her alone!' Blue cried realising the winged terrors were rising up to attack the great bird. Fighting back with beak and claw, the eagle managed to cast dozens of them to the ground, but for every one that fell, two more rose to take its place until so many had taken hold of its wings that the eagle came tumbling out of the sky to hit the ground with a sickening thud. Silently Blue prayed the bird might yet recover and take flight once more, but dark hands were even reaching out of the earth, pinning the eagle to the floor by their sheer force of numbers. Walking over, the Speris leant down and began whispering foul incantations over the great bird's struggling body. Meanwhile the serpent watched all with an insidious smile.

'Let it go,' Blue pleaded as tears of pity rolled down her cheek. One tear fell upon the serpent's hot scales. So small and insignificant a thing it seemed, yet the serpent reared up as though bitten and sent Blue spinning from its coils like a bobbin from a loom. Without thinking, Blue leapt up and sent a burst of pearlescent flame towards the eagle, the flames scattering both Speris and shadows alike.

'Fly away!' she screamed, 'Fly away from this place!' Finding its wings free, the eagle lifted itself onto unsteady legs and launched itself with a loud cry once more into the air.

Screaming with anger, the Speris motioned for the dark terrors to renew the chase but this time lightning crackled all around, driving the creatures back beneath the rock to whatever hell they had risen from.

Enraged, the serpent arched its neck as it turned towards Blue and, like an arrow shot from a bow, sank its long fangs into the soft flesh of her thigh. Blue screamed, but not from the pain of the bite, terrible though that was, but from the burning of the devil's venom, which she could feel filling her veins like fire. As the fire spread throughout her body, nightmarish figures and forms seemed to dance around her, making Blue wonder if they were real or the product of a venom-induced madness. About her neck Blue could feel the serpent's coils tighten as it began to pull her down under the rock, dragging her into the depths of a bottomless, black abyss.

CHAPTER 22

When Kai awoke the only thing on his mind, other than the cold stone of a strange floor pressing against his hot cheek, was the lingering question of how a nest of angry hornets had managed to supplant his brain. It was bad enough that Kai had regained consciousness to find his hands bound and himself behind bars *again*, but to find himself imprisoned with the headache from hell was an added joy he would have happily forsaken. As for Kai's prison companions, he didn't think he had ever seen such a sorry looking bunch of drunken degenerates in all his life, all of whom shared the blame for filling the prison atmosphere with the unflattering stench of unwashed clothes and stale dida—the latter being possibly the last smell on earth Kai wanted filling his nostrils. In spite of Kai's own alcohol-induced torment, he could just about think straight enough to know that the tell-tale looks of fear on the faces of the more sober of the prisoners meant they were all in serious bother. He also knew from the sounds of cheering and chanting that carried down the long flight of stairs leading from the prison, that the fate which awaited them was going to be a very public affair.

Kai had to clear his head—and clear it fast. He looked around to see if there was any chance his captors might have left something to eat or drink, but apart from a stained bucket, the contents of which he preferred not to examine, the cell was bare. Ominously, Kai knew from the way Furud commanders often treated captured enemy soldiers that starving them of food and water was common practice. It made them more docile before execution. Kai rubbed his eyes and shook his head to try to clear it, but all he managed to do was to dislodge the shell from his shirt and make his thumping headache even worse. Groaning, Kai fingered the shell and wondered if it still contained any water. Even if it did, the shell was so small it would barely hold enough to moisten his tongue, which felt drier than a Speris' smile. Still, he resolved, anything was better than nothing so, tilting the shell to his mouth, he invoked the waters and waited without much hope. At first, as expected, nothing happened, but just as Kai was considering snapping the cord from his neck and hurling the shell into a corner, a drop of water landed on his hand and ran down his wrist. Quickly, afraid the shell's tiny reservoir would drain before he had even tasted a drop, Kai put the shell to his lips and allowed the trickle of water to run onto his parched tongue. Surprisingly, Kai soon found he had a mouthful of water so crisp and so cool that he could almost have imagined it had been drawn straight from the deepest of Amari's sacred pools. Gulping the shell's offering straight down, Kai continued to press the shell to his lips in case there remained any last traces of moisture. His mouth filled again. He could hardly have imagined such a small shell could ever have held so much, yet when Kai found himself not only having to gulp down a third mouthful, but a fourth and then a fifth, he understood there was far more to Amari's gift than he had realised.

'Do Furud fathers not teach their sons to share?' enquired a voice from the adjacent cell. Astonished his Furud origins were so obvious, Kai looked over to see an elderly gentleman sat straight-backed on his prison stool dressed in clothing as clean and neat as the carefully trimmed beard upon his chin.

'It's just water,' said Kai assuming the old man thought it might be some sort of liquor.

'You talk as if I were a drunkard,' replied the old man, with an amused twinkle in his eye.

'I'm sorry,' said Kai realising the man was probably just thirsty. 'Here,' he said passing the old man the shell. The old man accepted the shell and without taking his twinkling eyes off Kai, took a long and thirsty draught before returning the shell to Kai. 'Do you know why I've been brought here?' Kai asked hoping the man might be able to shed some light on their situation.

'You are here for the same reason we all are; to play our part in a circus.'

'A circus?'

'A circus of death. Our death.' As the old man spoke the excited roar of hundreds of voices from above them suggested the "circus" had already started.

'Why us?'

'Look around. What do you see?'

'I see drunks and criminals. Maybe a murderer or two. Why?'

'Drunks they might be, but to the Dayan Sami that is not a crime but a virtue. Oh, believe you me they will all be presented to the crowds as murderers and thieves so it looks as though order is being kept in Wardum's city streets, but really their only crime is to fall behind with debts owed to the Dayan Sami's lenders.'

'Forgive me for saying so, why are *you* in here with us? You hardly strike me as one short of a few coin. In fact, to look at you I would never have believed you even came from this town. Your dress and speech are too...'

'Refined?' the old man offered with a sad smile. 'A stranger in my own home have I become 'tis true. The people of Wardum were not always like this. Most you see filling the streets and taverns are recent arrivals, come only to Wardum because they know the liquor is cheap and the entertainment as sick as their bloodthirsty hearts. When I was a child Wardum was very different from the town you see today. The Wardum I grew up in was known far and wide as a place of great learning. Its academies and libraries rivalled even the very finest in Sippara. Now, as you have seen, the scholars are gone, the academies and libraries turned into brothels and taverns and the few good people who managed to survive the Sami's purges have either fled or are in hiding.'

'Were you a scholar then? Is that why they brought you here?' The old man straightened up to his full height and surprised Kai with how tall he was.

'My name is Entar, Senior Scribe and last surviving member of the High Academy of Edubba. According to the Kalibi, my crimes are many, but as far as I am concerned, I am to be executed here today for being a troublemaker and a traitor; an accusation of which I must admit I am rather proud.'

'Why a troublemaker and traitor?'

'Perhaps the sparkle of hope shone too bright in my students' eyes. Perhaps their cry for freedom rang too loud. The Dayan Sami feared what he saw in them and devoted his Kalibi to finding the one responsible for putting such foolish and dangerous ideas into their heads. It wasn't long before they began arresting my students and trying to force them into betraying their teacher.'

'And is that what happened? Did your students betray you?'

'No. None betrayed me. They suffered the beatings and their imprisonment in silence.'

'If none betrayed you then how did the Kalibi catch you?'

'I betrayed myself. What teacher could go on hiding knowing he had become the cause of his students' suffering. Maybe I should never have interfered. Maybe I should have got out of this town when I had the chance… or stayed and drowned my senses and sorrows in the Dayan Sami's poisons just like the rest of them.'

'You mean the flowers?'

'Ah, yes, the flowers. But the Sami's flowers are not the only poison he has used to gain control over us. When he first arrived in Wardum he struggled at first to gain any real influence over the people. We were far too learned to take serious notice of his preachings, eloquent though he was I grant you, and his toxic little flower held little attraction to those whose thirst was for knowledge and wisdom, not escape. Yet he had another weapon at his disposal.'

'Like what?'

'Like gold! What better paves the way for great sins to follow than that cold, hard deceiver? The Dayan Sami knew the academies were struggling to survive so reinvented himself as a great patron and benefactor of the intellect and of the arts, investing huge sums of gold in Wardum's institutions and academies under the pretence he was only trying to save them, to preserve what, in his words, was our greatest treasure. Of course once the academies began to fall under his golden spell he set about making changes, first replacing our oldest and wisest scholars with greedy and ambitious buffoons who had not the sense to see the trap he was leading them into, and secondly, clearing our libraries of any scroll worth the ink it had been written with. Of course he told everyone at the time he was sending them away to be restored, but just like the old scholars, the scrolls never returned. With the wisest of us out of the way, it wasn't long before the influence of the academies began to wane and he was able to turn his attention back to the population at large. He knew the people of Wardum had been wary of taking his flower, but he could also see a few of us were developing a growing weakness for drink, a fondness for anything brewed or fermented. I suppose it was only natural considering how empty our lives and how poor the water drawn from the wells was becoming, water so stale and brackish it was making the people who drank it ill. Soon dida and durma could be found in every tavern, in every home. As the harvests continued to fail and the wells dried up, all the Dayan Sami had to do was make sure the dida and durma kept flowing, even lowering their price when the cost of everything else began to rise—just so long as we kept going back for more. For most people it was already too late before they discovered he had been lacing both drinks with an extract derived from his flower. And now we are all going to pay for our indolence by becoming clowns in his circus.'

'Well, this Dayan Sami might find inside this clown beats the heart of a bull!'

'Those are bold words my friend. I only wished there were more warrior spirits like yours.'

'Trust me you don't want more spirits like this one.'

Before the old scholar could enquire as to what Kai was talking about, Kalibi guards poured into the room and began manhandling the prisoners out of their cells. Soon Kai found himself being thrust up a long flight of stairs and out into a wall of noise and light. When the noise and commotion abated, Kai realised he and the prisoners were penned into an enclosure on one side of a large rectangular arena, though its appearance reminded him more of the Furud courtrooms he'd seen Lord Rasalas sometimes preside over back home. Along one wall a giant mural attempted to recreate the story of the city's foundation and history, whilst opposite a long viewing gallery strained from the weight of hundreds of baying spectators. Facing the prisoners, a second, much smaller gallery with a pink chiffon curtain drawn across it overlooked a lectern or pulpit which lay on the floor in two pieces as if a great axe had cleft it in two. It was pretty evident to Kai the building had been built to serve a far higher purpose than the one it was serving at present; a purpose made ominously clear by the dark red streaks smeared across its mosaic floor.

'Was this some sort of law court?' he asked as Entar arrived beside him.

'Not quite,' replied the scholar with a look of pride mixed with regret. 'This was once the famed Hall of Oratory. It was in this very hall the legendary debate between Aeschilius the Abstinent and Gezthud the Gambler took place; a debate that lasted almost forty years!'

'Really? Who won?'

'Neither. They argued for so long both forgot what the debate had been about in the first place. In the end the contest had to be declared void.'

'Sounds like most of my Furud history lessons. What about you? Did you ever debate here?'

'Debate, teach, study, eat, sleep… I spent thirty-five years of my life here. This was my place of work and my home.'

From behind the chiffon curtain the outline of a man was spotted arriving and the excitement in the auditorium grew. As the figure settled into his seat, Kai noticed a second, darker figure appear, behind him. Unlike the first, who seemed restless to the point of distraction, the second figure remained as still as a statue. Although the curtain made it impossible to see much more than a silhouette, Kai couldn't shake the feeling the figure was looking straight at him.

'Who's the loon?' said Kai referring to the restless character who, in the space of a minute, had gone from sitting quietly in his chair to standing on it, snipping his fingers at invisible strings above his head.

'That would be the Dayan Sami himself.'

'What's up with him? He seems very… unsettled.'

'Too many flowers,' said Entar who'd obviously witnessed the ruler's erratic behaviour before. 'Recently he's been getting much worse though. He knows his days in power are numbered.'

'Why are they numbered?'

'His flowers are losing their potency. They require a rare ingredient to be mixed with the soil they are grown in. Without it the flowers are as much good to him as a salad garnish.'

'What's the ingredient?'

'It is a well-guarded secret, though some believe it only to be found in a mine far to the north. Whatever the ingredient is, the Dayan Sami has been desperate to find a new supply. I hear his stocks of it are starting to run dangerously low. Sadly, they will not run out in time to save us my friend.' As Kai wondered if the mine he referred to, could possibly be the same as that which Blue had destroyed, the Dayan Sami flapped down from his chair and twirled about like a dying swan. Still crouched in a dying pose, he slipped a thin, almost feminine hand through the chiffon fabric and silenced the crowd with a mere raising of his finger. To see such a large and restless crowd silenced with so simple a gesture was disturbing enough, but when the wildly fluctuating tones and dramatic pauses of the usurper's voice began to send the audience into rapturous outbursts of applause and cheering, Kai realised it was not just the Dayan Sami who had lost his mind, but half the population of Wardum.

The speech ended and like the hush preceding the opening scene of a much-anticipated play, the audience waited for the curtains to be drawn. Ever so slowly, undoubtedly to build the excitement to volcanic proportions, the curtains were slid open to reveal not two people as Kai had expected, but just one; a man who stared back at the audience with eyes like saucers. Hanging from the man's long, thin frame was a flowery robe that looked like something stolen from a concubine's wardrobe, whilst around his neck the yoke, symbol of the Dayan Sami's penitence, of which Kai had heard so much about, was still on display for all to see, but this yoke was nothing like those Kai had seen clamped around the sweating necks of farmyard oxen, for it had been decorated across its beam with inlay of gold, silver and ivory. Even the metal pins and bow of the yoke had been cushioned with padded silk so that no part of it might rub or chafe any part of the Dayan Sami's oiled skin.

'That was a clever trick,' said Kai as the eruption of noise died down enough for him to be heard.

'Trick?'

'Well, where did the other one go? The one who was standing behind the Dayan Sami's chair?'

'Interesting,' said Entar sounding intrigued. 'You are not the first to mention seeing an "other" standing behind the Sami. Those that claim to have seen him call him the Shadow Man, though we scholars suspect he is more deception than devil.'

'Probably just a stunt to get our attention,' agreed Kai, though the manner in which the dark figure had so dramatically disappeared left him doubting his own words. Hearing the noise of the crowd diminish, the saucer-eyed ruler reached into a wide porcelain bowl by his side and carefully lifted out an exotic looking flower with petals that tapered to a point like ghostly fingers. This he caressed sensually across his sharp nostrils before placing the flower into a velvet lined box which he threw into the sea of outstretched arms beside him. Teasing the crowd like this, the Dayan Sami dangled a second box before the crowd until feverish chants of *"Sami shurpu telalu!"* filled the air. Only when the chants were at the right pitch of hysteria did he launch the flower into the crowd then sat down so the main event could begin. Taking this as their signal, the arena doors were opened and a colourful pageant of musicians, jugglers, dancers and acrobats played, danced and tumbled their way out onto the arena floor. Behind these a second but very different procession followed; a procession of slaves carrying the weapons and instruments of torture to be used that evening. In their centre strode a figure so broad, tall and strong Kai feared at first that he must be a herder, until the figure removed his hood to reveal scarred but distinctly human features. The man was dressed in a knee-length linen robe and, like the Dayan Sami above, also bore a yoke about his neck, but his yoke was much more like those Kai was accustomed to seeing around the farms of his homeland, its only embellishment being the pits and scratches earned from a hard life of toil in the field.

'Who's the other one with the yoke? I thought only the Dayan Sami wore one?'

'That is Haelm, the Dayan Sami's favourite and chief executioner. The yoke he wears is a token of his master's gratitude; a reward the Sami likes to bestow upon all his favourites. The "Mitutu" we call them. They are the most devoted and loyal of all his followers. They are also the deadliest. It will be Haelm who begins the night's entertainment—a delightful twist on an old tradition that allows a condemned man to die fighting for their honour and freedom. We can expect such an invitation from Haelm shortly.'

From the gallery the Dayan Sami plucked another flower from the bowl and this time cast it not into the audience but at Haelm's feet. Kneeling down, the executioner picked it up and touched it to his lips like a lover kissing a rose. Once he had inhaled enough of its heady perfume, he began rubbing the soft petals of the flower into the skin of his face, arms and chest. When nothing was left, the heavy yoke was removed from around his neck and a long and vicious looking scythe placed in his hands. This he lifted above his head and, with the weapon raised as if in supplication, bowed before the Dayan Sami to receive his blessing. In mocking contrast a small, rusty dagger was thrown to the floor in front of the prisoners' pen.

'That doesn't seem very fair,' said Kai wryly as the procession of executioners and performers withdrew to leave Haelm alone with the prisoners.

'Remember this is not a competition,' said Entar sombrely. 'It is an execution.'

'Gana!' cried the Dayan Sami with a gesture that signified the show should begin. As the enclosure gate was opened to release the prisoners Haelm leapt to his feet and began whirling the scythe about his head and body like an entertainer at a king's feast. From the incredible speed and dexterity with which he was handling the weapon, Kai could see he had been expertly trained. Meanwhile, to the even greater delight of the audience, two of the more drunken prisoners had begun to put on a performance of their own, squabbling over the rusty dagger like hungry dogs over a bone.

'Unless you want to die quickly, leave the dagger be,' said Entar in Kai's ear. 'It is how you accept Haelm's invitation.' Noticing the two drunkards fighting, Haelm suddenly ran across and, lifting the scythe above his head, brought it down in a single, graceful arc that sliced clean through both prisoners' necks as if they were no more than sheathes of wheat. The headless corpses toppled to the floor and lay in a pool of blood which spread out from their severed necks like crimson halos. Picking the heads up by their hair, the executioner flaunted his trophies in front of the crowd as though he were an actor seeking an encore. The crowd screamed their approval.

'And so, it ends,' said Entar stepping through the remaining terrified prisoners to stand purposefully over the dagger so that Haelm could clearly see his intent. Seeing his invitation accepted so boldly Haelm smiled and, dropping the heads to the floor, turned to face the old man, but when Entar failed to pick up the dagger, Haelm looked up to the Dayan Sami's box as if unsure of what to do.

'Gana!' screamed the Dayan eager for more blood to be shed. Inspired by the scholar's bravery, Kai too pushed past the prisoners and followed Entar out into the arena, this time very deliberately picking up the dagger, and placing himself squarely in front of the old man, so all could see clearly he intended to fight in the old scholar's stead. Seeing this faceoff between prisoner and executioner the audience hushed with excitement.

'Ah,' said Entar with a degree of admiration in his voice, 'bull-hearted you are indeed my young friend!' Kai said nothing in reply but readied himself for the executioner's onslaught.

It took a few moments for the crowd to realise not everything was following the usual pattern of events. Firstly, when Haelm's broad swing of his scythe caused him to miss so badly he ended facing in completely the wrong direction, many in the audience thought this some adaptation to the executioner's usual style of showmanship and generously laughed and applauded their favourite entertainer. Yet, when a second, third and then a fourth attack missed as badly as the first, a few boos began mingling with the applause. It was the fifth swing, though, that plunged the room into an uncomfortable and pervasive silence, and not because of any wild miss on Haelm's part for this time the executioner found his mark with perfect accuracy, but because the steel blade, far from remove Kai's head from his shoulders, wrapped about the prisoner's neck as if it had been made of lambskin. It was then that an unexpected and unnerving sound could be heard cutting through the silence like a shaft of sunlight. All eyes turned to Kai. The prisoner was singing! Haelm let go the now completely misshapen weapon and stepped back in fear. He looked up helplessly towards the Dayan Sami but the half-crazed ruler had already retreated behind one of his curtains. Slowly the silence began to be replaced with a quiet and steady chant which rose and echoed off the arena ceiling and walls, growing in volume until it reached a deafening pitch.

'What are they chanting?' asked Kai as Entar approached cautiously, staring at his young protector in astonishment. 'Are they calling for our release?'

'Sadly not,' the old scholar replied dolefully. 'They are chanting *"Kashshaptu"*. I'm afraid it means "Witch".'

It was evident from the speed with which Kai and Entar were suddenly ushered out of the arena and into the back of a prison wagon that the Dayan Sami had been as unnerved by Kai's performance as the rest of the arena audience.

'Where are they taking us?' asked Kai as the wagon rolled out of Wardum and onto a bumpy road that seemed to follow a thin brushstroke of stars dividing the night's sky above them.

'We are on the road to Nan Garu. It is a high place about three hours ride from here where the sun can be seen rising over the Valley of Kas.'

'That doesn't sound so bad. Perhaps we are to be released after all?'

'Sadly not. I'm afraid Nan Garu is the traditional place where witches are thrown to their deaths.'

'Oh. That's not so good then.'

For two long hours, the wagon rumbled on, jarring every limb and bone with each rut and stone the wheels encountered, but at least a soft ochre line of light drew Kai's eyes out across long valleys of flowering juniper, sage and wild cotton. Among these, broad strips of flowerbeds lay, their fleshy buds clenched into small fists that shook in the morning breeze. From the ridge above them a lean vixen barked, calling her pups to follow her home. The air was warm and filled with scents and stories of the desert.

'Well, I can't think of a nicer place to die,' said Kai reluctantly admiring the view. 'It's certainly better than that blood-soaked arena.'

'Don't be taken in by the beauty you see,' said Entar. 'Those are the Dayan Sami's flowers. '

'Still, you have to admit they are very pretty.'

'They are now, but they are grown in a poisoned soil. Next year these valleys will begin to die. Soon nothing will grow here. You will see this as we approach Nan Garu. The Valley of Kas was once a land of great fertility and beauty. Most of our fruit, herbs and grain came from there. Now it bears nothing but the tread of ghosts.'

For the remainder of their journey, Kai sat in silence, wondering if it was really possible for a place so vibrant with life and beauty to die so suddenly, but just as they reached the great jawbone of rock known as

Nan Garu, ugly stretches of dry, blackened soil filled the landscape, whipping about in the wind to sting both eyes and mouth, leaving Kai with a bitter, caustic taste on the tongue.

'Soon every valley will look like this one,' Entar explained with an acidic tone. 'Once the Sami's flowers are harvested, nothing more can grow.' Kai would have responded but the heavy wagon was already rumbling to a stop. With a grating squeal of hinges, the carriage doors were flung open and their Kalibi escort wasted no time in pulling their prisoners out and were soon shoving the pair towards the jawbone archway and what looked like a very long drop below it.

'Well, my friend,' said the scholar with a resigned look on his face, 'unless you have learnt to sprout wings as well as bend steel, I guess this time it really is goodbye.'

'We'll see about that,' said Kai and before Entar could add another word tore himself free of his Kalibi escort, took five great strides, and hurled himself off the edge.

CHAPTER 23

A dirty rain began to fall from the vault of darkness above. Lifting a head like a mountain, Sugaar craned its neck back as far as its chains would allow and swallowed the rain in one gulp.

'Worthless creatures,' it said with a voice that made the earth quake beneath Blue's feet. 'Why do you waste your time on them?' The monstrous worm turned to look down at the rebellious speck with disgust. 'Can't you see their souls are filth? They must be devoured, every last one.' Blue knew the creature was insane. Most days, when it wasn't waiting to feed on the rain of damned souls from above, it did nothing but gnaw and gnash at its chains until molten metal and blood poured to the floor of the abyss. But there were other moments, glimpses of sanity when its terrible rage and hunger calmed and it began to speak with an alluringly dangerous lucidity. 'Look at them!' it said sniffing the nest of carcasses upon which it lay. 'They were given everything. A paradise was laid at their feet and they trampled it into a hell. Give them a butterfly and they will tear its wings off and wear them as earrings.'

'Is that what happened to you?' said Blue looking at the long, jagged scars running down the creature's back. 'Were those once wings?' The creature looked down in surprise at hearing the speck speak. Usually, its mere presence was enough to drive most souls into apoplectic fits of terror, yet even after three days, the ocean-eyed girl was still coolly defiant.

'Who are you to pity me imp? Tell me *"Ama Galdua",* what other titles did they flatter you with? "Queen of the pixies"?' The great creature laughed with a sound like thunder.

'They can change. I've seen it. I can help them. Maybe I can help you too.'

'Oh, I see. You think you're a little saviour, do you? I like saviours. I've always liked saviours. I might have even sent one or two up there myself.' Sugaar paused to lick its enormous lips and smiled wickedly.

'It's their followers you see. The *saved* always taste so much better than the damned.' Blue knew the creature was deliberately stirring up fears within her and fought to control them, but its words had a way of creeping under the skin like a thorn. 'You think you've saved him don't you? You think you've tamed the Atzerri; that you've turned the lion into a kitten. Let's see how tamed he really is.'

Like a window opening in Blue's mind, she could suddenly see Basax pacing back and forth beside her as if she were standing in the room with him. Though the room was dark Blue could see the herder's eyes had a disturbed, even frightened look, yet the focus of his concern seemed not on her nor on the colossal beast towering above them all, for the herder gave no hint that he could see either one of them. Instead, his attention seemed consumed by a figure that lay quietly in a bed beside him; a figure that lay so still Blue had to wonder whether the person was asleep or dead.

The creature's voice dropped to a low soothing hiss almost like it was singing a lullaby to a baby. 'Do you remember the tassste?' For a moment Blue thought Sugaar was directing the question to her, but then she realised with a shudder that a long, blood-red serpent was snaking out from its mouth and sliding its way into Basax's body. 'You do don't you?' the creature continued, delighting in the unsettling effect its words were having. 'You remember it all; the ecstasy of ripping, of shredding, the tearing of limbs, the sweet blood dripping from your chin… the taste of warm flesshh!'

'Stop it!' Blue shouted. 'Leave him alone!' Blue could see Basax was trying to fight the temptations rising inside of him but the great worm's voice was too compelling and the herder's mouth began to salivate like a dog anxious to be fed.

'Oh, it's not *him* you should worry about,' whispered the beast to Blue with teasing softness. 'It's the one in the bed you should worry about the most. *Go on*,' it goaded the herder, again adopting a singing tone, 'take a peek under the covers. Just a little look. No one will know.'

As Basax eased back the covers, the full dreadfulness of what the beast was doing became sickeningly clear. There, lying in the bed, her lips pale and breath weak as if near death, lay Blue herself.

'What a tasty morsel she looks. So tender. So helpless. What was it you said? You would have gobbled her up in three big bites. "Yum. Yum. Yum!"

CHAPTER 24

Never in all his life had Kai made such a leap of faith as his great leap into the unknown at Nan Garu. It was with great relief then that he found his ability to levitate had dramatically improved since he had failed so miserably to emulate Lybesstre's floating feat in her tent near the ruins of Amon' Pur's golden city. Of course with every success came new challenges and he now found that, although hovering in the air proved relatively easy, getting back to land required an altogether different skill. Perhaps with hindsight he ought not to have taken quite so spectacular a leap off the edge, but at least it had had the desired effect of sending their terrified Kalibi escort running back to the safety of Wardum before their "witch" prisoners could turn them all into toads.

'Would you like me to fetch you a branch to pull you back in?' asked Entar who had been studying Kai's flapping and flailing of arms and legs with fascination for at least half an hour. 'Or maybe a broomstick?'

'Very funny!' said Kai and plummeted twenty feet straight down before recovering the song in time to stop his falling any farther.

'Ah I see. It is the song that gives you the power to rise into the air! Fascinating! Well, I'll not be able to reach you with a branch now,' the old man concluded. 'Try not to fly off anywhere and I'll see if I can find some rope.'

Once a rope had been found and Kai was pulled back to the safety of the arch, it wasn't the white bearded scholar who greeted him at the other end of the rope, but Hamsum with a gap-toothed smile as big as a house.

'Hamsum!' said Kai thrilled to see his friend. 'You found us!'

'Of course. And Hamsum would have found you sooner if I could have got this big *"duggae"* to move faster.' Uzzaga grunted as Hamsum shoved her with his foot, then got back to the business of seeking out an itch at the back of her neck.

'How did you know where they were taking us?'

'A barrel of dida and plenty of kug never fails to get a Kalibi dog barking.'

'How much kug exactly?' asked Kai who was already familiar with the Kugarran word for gold.

'Enough.'

'How much is enough?'

'All of it.'

'ALL OF IT! But that means we're ruined! How will we get into Sippara now?' For one who had just sacrificed the small fortune they had both worked so hard to make, Hamsum still seemed annoyingly cheerful.

'Stop worrying. I made a little investment first. I am not stupid.'

'An investment in what?'

'In you.'

'*Me?*'

'Of course. No one ever accepts Haelm's challenge and lives. I knew I'd get excellent odds.'

'You gambled on me not dying! What if I had?'

'You forget I saw what you did in the marketplace. I knew you'd find a way to survive, though I never expected you to do it quite like *that!*''

'I did what I had to. Anyway, how much did you make?'

'A little. Well maybe a little more than a little.'

'How much is a little more than a little, Hamsum?' Unable to hold back his delight any longer the merchant boomed with merriment.

'We're rich! I spotted Eridu traders in the audience. When they're drunk, they gamble more than a Pyskan prince on his wedding day. And guess what… they love kash! I made more money in one evening than I could make in a lifetime! Did I not say you were sent by the gods! Now I'll take you to Sippara—but first we buy horses.'

'Horses?'

'You said you were in a hurry. Why walk to Sippara when you can afford a horse?'

CHAPTER 25

The windpump, with its five blades missing like the teeth of an old sailor's snarl, stood at the entrance to the horse merchants' yard and gave as much a sense of welcome as the empty stables behind it. From these nothing but the constant "chee chee" noises of Kugarran mountain quail could be heard punctuating the stillness. The quail, with their dainty crests and bobbing tails, were the same hardy type favoured by many farmers in the region, bred for their dark meat and their ability to lay disproportionately large eggs for a bird so small in size, but these had the appearance of renegades rather than residents, opportunely nesting in any hayrack or feeding trough they could find. Of course, the fact the hayracks and feeding troughs were full of marauding quails instead of fresh hay did not bode well for their plan to purchase horses. In fact, no sight nor sound of anything remotely horse-like was forthcoming from any quarter.

'I thought you said these were the only horse traders for a hundred miles?' demanded Kai impatiently. 'Where are the horses?'

'I'm not sure,' said Hamsum. 'But just look at these eggs!' The merchant reached into a feeding trough and began robbing a nest of its ivory horde, the which he happily deposited into a sack as though he were a child finding chestnuts. 'How do they get such a big egg out of so tiny a hole?' To further his scientific inquiry Hamsum caught hold of the nearest quail and subjected the poor bird to the indignity of being tipped upside down and having its tail feathers blown away from its fluffy privates so he could gauge the size of its anus. He then took another egg and cracked it open to examine the yolk. 'Remarkable!' he said replacing the bird back on its now empty nest. 'Look at the yolk. It's red!'

'Would you leave the eggs alone and go find out where these traders of yours are hiding their damned horses!'

'Okay, okay. I'm going! You won't be complaining later when Hamsum makes you his special 'hallachamama' omelette.'

'I will if it has kash in it!' Entar nodded in Kai's support having already been treated to a dose of the merchant's lizard liquor from hell during their first meeting at Nan Garu.

'Ill-bred barbarians,' said Hamsum and marched off in search of horses. After a short wait Hamsum returned with a perplexed look upon his face.

'They've gone,' he said and scratched his head. Uzzaga huffed beside him and scratched her own head in a like manner.

'What, the horses or the traders?'

'The horses *and* the traders.'

'Where have they gone?'

'I have no idea. The stable doors are all broken from the inside as if the horses had kicked their way out. I think they've all escaped.'

'Escaped!' exclaimed Entar. 'Let me take a look.' The old scholar hurried across the corral and entered the first of the stables only to find it exactly as Hamsum had described, with the door splintered and broken as if the horse it had contained had vented every ounce of its strength kicking its way to freedom. Visibly perturbed by what he found, Entar proceeded to investigate each and every stable and door until, with a satisfied grunt, he bent down and picked up a green object, which he began cleaning carefully with his hand.

'What have you found there?' asked Kai walking across to get a closer look.

'It is a jade eye,' the old man replied, 'a charm often kept by traders to bring fortune and ward off evil. Charms like these do not come cheap, especially ones as big as this. To find one so carelessly cast aside suggests to me its owner was in more than just a hurry to be gone from here.'

'As were the horses,' said Kai noting how some of the doors were smashed beyond recognition. 'I've never heard of a breed with the strength to kick itself free of its own stable though.'

'It was not just strength that gave these horses the power to break out of their stables,' said Entar sombrely.

'What else was it then?'

'It was fear.'

'What could possibly cause such fear that a horse kicks down its own stable door?'

'Of that I am not yet sure.'

'Not all have escaped!' declared Hamsum relieved to see what, indeed, looked to be a horse left abandoned in an area of heavy shade at the back of the stables, 'I believe you will find that is a fine mare waiting for a new owner!'

'Bring me a rope and see if you can find a saddle,' said Kai determined at least one horse should go with them to Sippara.

Having come from an island nation more inclined to surprise its enemy from the sea than ride openly to war on the back of a horse, Kai might have been forgiven for not knowing a thoroughbred from any one of the mixed breeds so commonly used by mainland farmers. But despite his lack of equestrian expertise, even the lowest Furud foot soldier could have told Kai the mare he was looking at was neither a thoroughbred nor was it a common farm horse. The horse he was looking at was unmistakably and unquestionably... dead. When he was younger Kai remembered seeing dead warhorses left forgotten by the wayside and knew in that regard this dead horse was no exception: the exposed bones of the ribs; the bleached teeth loosely gripped in a half-decayed jaw; the pearly glaze of one eye and absence of the other; the parchment-dry skin curling back from muscles eaten almost to the bone. Everything was as should be and could be expected for a horse that was, indeed, dead. Everything that is if it weren't for one glaringly obvious problem: this dead horse was still standing.

Had the bitterest of biles not risen to his throat and the blood seemed to drain from his veins, Kai might have reconsidered his calling a horse that was evidently still standing as "dead" when the term "undead" was undoubtedly a far more apt description for so ghastly and unnatural a horror as this.

'Do you need some help?' offered Hamsum seeing Kai not only had made no progress in roping the mare but had managed to drop both rope and saddle without appearing to notice or care. 'I said do you need some help?' the merchant repeated hearing no reply. Again Kai appeared not to hear the question.

'Entar, am I talking too quietly or has he gone deaf?' Entar, too, seemed unnaturally quiet. 'Hello? *Hello!* Is anybody listening to Hamsum?'

Both Kai and Entar could hear Hamsum's voice, but the merchant's words became lost as a noise like a dry stone being dragged across a rusted blade began to rise from the undead horse's throat.

'Ninkasi save us!' said Hamsum finally realising why his friends had fallen so deathly still. The horse turned its hideous head to fix Kai with its pearly eye. 'Aye Ama!' cried Hamsum. 'Why does it look at you like that? Run!' Kai probably would have run if that aberrant vision of death had not reared up in front of him then galloped straight through the paddock fence like a wind passing through branches.

'Entar, what was that thing?' said Hamsum still horror-struck long after it had departed. The old scholar fell quiet as though searching out a memory then, in a voice barely above a whisper, began to speak;

"No bit nor bridle must e'er restrain,
The mares of Minasul's domain.
No whip may cut nor halter break
Those mares that roam by Apsu's lake"

'Apsu's lake!' said Kai recognising the name of Amari's secret temple immediately. 'Are you saying that... *thing* came from a lake called Apsu?'

'There *was* a lake, at least once upon a time. Its waters were said to lap against Sippara's very walls. But there is no trace of any lake there today, nor has there been any trace for more than a thousand years.'

'But if there was a lake called Apsu, then maybe there is a street called Apsu too. It could lead us right to the temple!'

'I don't want to dampen your enthusiasm,' said Entar, 'but as far as I recall there are at least fifteen streets with Apsu in the name and twice as many temples.'

'And a bridge,' added Hamsum, his voice still trembling from what he had just witnessed. 'I've heard there used to be a pie shop with the name too.'

'Yes, but it's a start! I'd rather have thirty names than none.'

'Thirty-two,' said Hamsum. 'Unless of course they've closed the pie shop down. Wouldn't surprise me if they had. Pies tasted worse than a tanner's apron.'

'Kai is right though,' said Entar. 'It certainly is a start. We scholars often consider street names as our maps of history.'

'See! Then let's get going! We have to find these streets.'

'And the pie shop?'

'No Hamsum, not the damned pie shop!'

CHAPTER 26

It was with such speed that the streak of lightning shot out of the firmament towards Blue that neither she nor Sugaar had time to react before it exploded into the girl's chest in a burst of talons and flaming feathers, but when the pain of the impact and the intense heat had passed it was no longer the mountainous terror that slavered over her... but Basax.

'Basax don't!' she cried seeing the herder's fevered stare and drooling mouth. 'It's me, Blue!' The sound of the girl's voice was enough to lift the herder, if just for a moment, out of the madness that had seized him, but with it came the full crushing realisation of what he had been on the verge of doing. 'It's okay now Basax!' Blue reassured him, 'You're okay now. It's over.' Basax wished it was over but a sickening hunger remained.

'What's happened?' cried Nekane running into the room with the real Soko close behind. 'Is she awake?' Spinning around, Basax gave the Jentilak a look like a murderer caught with dagger in hand. 'Basax what's wrong?' Too horrified at himself to reply, the herder stumbled backwards and with eyes that pleaded with them both to stay away, fled the room.

'Basax! Come back!' Blue cried, but the herder was already gone.

The following days of Basax's absence were unbearably hard for Blue. No effort or reassurance of the Apkallu or Jentilak that they were doing all they could to find him did anything to console her. Nor could the company of scores of woodland spirits do much to ease her misery, who gathered around her bed and pressed their tearful faces into the soft curls of her hair as much for their own comfort as for hers.

'Here drink this,' said Nekane passing Blue a cup of fragrant burgha milk. Blue nodded and dutifully sipped some of the liquid before handing the half-empty cup back to Nekane. Even the deliciously woodspiced milk could not lift her mood.

'I have some news,' Nekane said sitting down beside her.

'You've found Basax!' Blue was so excited she tried to jump out of the bed but the pain in her chest was too great and she fell back onto her pillow.

'We have, but please do not try to sit up yet,' said the Jentilak softly. 'Your body is still very weak from your… experience.' A memory of flaming talons as they exploded into her chest flashed into Blue's mind.

'Why did the bird attack me? I thought it was meant to be a friend of the Jentilak's.'

'It did not attack you Blue. It gave itself to you. It sacrificed itself so that you could live.'

'It sacrificed itself? But why?'

'You are the Ama Galdua. Any of us would do the same given the opportunity.' Talk of her being the Ama Galdua bothered Blue at the best of times, but never so much now that news of Basax had arrived.

'I don't want to talk about that now. I just want to see Basax. Where is he?'

'He is with Soko right now. But you cannot see him,' said Nekane with a serious expression. 'Not yet anyway. He's not… ready.'

'Ready!' said Blue kicking off her bed covers indignantly. 'For what?'

'He did not exactly come back of his own accord. A scouting party found him sniffing around a bear kill early this morning. They had to capture him, Blue.'

'You captured him! Like an animal! But why?'

'Please understand Blue, Basax is not yet… himself. He is still very dangerous. A battle rages not just within his soul, but *for* his soul. He will need time.' Blue's face fell.

'Can he be saved?'

'Not here. It is my uncle's wish he be taken to a great temple. It is a temple that has remained hidden for many centuries, but there are whisperings in the forest its power is soon to be reawakened. We must take Basax there and consult with the steward of the temple. The steward will know what to do. You too could do with the temple's healing yourself. You came closer to death than you think.'

'I don't care about me. I just want to help my friend. Where is this temple?'

'It is in a city named Sippara, the Bird City. The journey is long and hard so we leave at first light.'

CHAPTER 27

Kai sipped his tea and looked out from his balcony across the incense and smoke-filled haze of the temple city of Sippara. Already the funeral pyres were being lit and a clamorous stream of pilgrims jostled alongside flotillas of servants bearing the litters of their dead or dying masters come in the hope of finding a miracle cure or for their loved ones to be cremated by the Ensi, the only caste of priests permitted to light the crematorial fires. The city's high priests were an inconspicuous bunch, preferring to marshal the business of lesser priesthoods and fleece the pilgrims and tourists of their money from behind closed doors. Of course, Hamsum's now bottomless purse had not only bought them entry into the city, a relief considering the unhealthy mass of cutthroats, thieves, beggars and refugees that seemed to have taken up permanent residence outside the city gates, but it had also permitted them the luxury of hiring rooms in the most desirable quarter of the city, an area that provided Kai with the perfect vantage point from which he could observe the shady comings and goings of the secular population and be able to contemplate at his leisure the many possible locations of the Temple of E-Apsu. Kai had been in many strange cities but he had never seen one built in such a confusing and chaotic manner, with endless chains of islands cut off from one another by an incomprehensibly complex network of ditches. He could only assume the islands and their arrangement once held some religious significance, but the ditches themselves seemed to serve no greater purpose than as glorified dumping grounds into which all manner of religious paraphernalia and every other type of refuse one could expect from a large city teeming with visitors with too much money and too little sense was thrown. Even dead bodies regularly wound up at the bottom of the ditch, unceremoniously discarded by outraged families whose love for their dearly departed suddenly evaporated upon discovering the exorbitant fees charged by the Ensi. The only thing preventing the city from turning into a haven for infestations of vermin and plague was an army of lepers who, after most of the city's inhabitants had gone to bed, would be allowed into the ditches to scavenge through the refuse until the first light of morning when, like rats escaping into a sewer, they would vanish back into their holes as quickly as they had appeared. Kai often wondered what the lepers could possibly want with so much rubbish. His home city had always had its fair share of beggars and scavengers, but he had never seen such efficient and thorough foragers before. In fact, the lepers were so efficient at what they did that by morning there would be nothing left in the ditches at all. Even the abandoned bodies were gathered up and carted out to wherever their colony was hidden.

'How many temples do you think there are?' asked Kai as Entar and a rather bleary-eyed Hamsum emerged from their chambers to join him.

'It's hard to say. There are so many different denominations and cults. Then you have to distinguish between the higher temples and the lower. Of the higher I'd say there must be at least a hundred, maybe more.'

'And the lower ones?'

'Well, again, it's so hard to say. You've seen some of them, they can be as small as a broom cupboard. Of those maybe ten times that number at least. Why?'

'Because we've been traipsing across this city for almost a week now and yet we've only covered a fraction of it. We're getting nowhere. None of the Apsu names have led to anything at all and we still haven't heard or seen anything of this U-an fellow. We could be here for months and still have found nothing.'

'What do you suggest? You know we can't exactly just barge in and ask where he is.'

'I don't think we have to. There's something we're missing. Something we're not seeing.' Across the city the bird-like cries of the Migir slaves rose from the city's minarets to announce the first wave of ceremonial processions. Soon the garish and grandiose costumes of the priests would appear at the top of temple steps across the city and the daily rounds of extortion would begin.

'You know I don't think I've seen a bird since we got here. Why is Sippara named "The Bird City"? Is it because of the cry of the Migir?'

'Not at all. The priesthoods only began bringing Migir slaves here three hundred years ago. The name "Sippara" is much older. Turn over your cup.' Kai drained his tea and turned the cup over to see a crude emblem of a long-legged bird pressed into the clay.

'It looks like a water bird.'

'That is well observed. It is a water bird—or at least it was. A type of egret, I think. That is the true source of Sippara's name. The archives of Sippara's history talk much of the city's migrations of water birds.'

'Water? Wait a minute, that's it!' Entar and Hamsum stared at Kai blankly. 'Don't you see? Water! The ditches! They're not ditches at all. They're canals!' The blank stares continued. 'Look, just meet me by the bridge tonight at sundown and I'll show you. I'll show you exactly how we're going to find the temple of E-Apsu.'

CHAPTER 28

'So what are we supposed to be looking at?' asked Hamsum looking less than impressed at having to sacrifice his nightly sojourns to the District of the Karkid, the district of Sippara's notorious temple prostitutes.

'The ditch.'

'Watch the ditch? That's it! That's your bright idea! You think the temple of E-Apsu is in a refuse ditch?'

'Just watch the ditch and stop complaining. Trust me. I know what I'm doing.' Hamsum threw his hands in the air and turned to Entar hoping the elderly scholar would talk some sense into Kai's muddled young brain, but the scholar seemed as fascinated by the ditch as Kai. Seeing he was outnumbered by idiots, Hamsum undid the gourd from his belt, and taking a large gulp of kash, moodily joined in with their night vigil. As usual the floor of the ditch was covered in the day's detritus and it wasn't long before the first of the lepers appeared to begin clearing it away.

'I don't see anything special,' said Hamsum after a tedious half hour of watching lepers scurrying back and forth with armfuls of dirty and broken junk.

'Just look at what they're doing.'

'I am. They are collecting rubbish, same as they did last night. Same as they do every night. I could be in the arms of a priestess with breasts the size of a man's head. But no, you think I prefer to watch lepers scavenging in a filthy ditch. I hate you.'

'No. You've got it all wrong. They're not just collecting it, they're clearing it! Don't you see?'

'No.'

'It's not the rubbish they care about—it's the ditches!'

'Why would anyone care about ditches?'

'Because they are *sacred* ditches! The lepers are the ones Amari spoke to me about. The ones who the Fallen have been hunting for so long.' Kai laughed at his own ingenuity. 'Yet here they have been all this time, right under their noses!'

'I think you are a very silly boy,' said Hamsum. 'They are lepers and they live off scavenging rubbish. Nothing more. No priest in Sippara would let lepers anywhere near a sacred temple.'

'Why do you think they cover their bodies with bandages and their faces with those veils?'

'To hide their sickness of course!'

'Wrong. They wear them to look like they have the disease, but really it is to hide their true identities from the priests. Look at how they move. Do you see any signs of weakness or discomfort?' Hamsum studied the lepers hard for a while then pointed at one of them.

'There!' he said pointing triumphantly towards a leper who was struggling to drag a particularly heavy door along the floor. Kai sighed. He could see Hamsum was not going to believe a word he said unless he could offer him more convincing proof. Even Entar was looking sceptical.

'Watch. I'll show you.' Kai scrambled over the wall at the end of the bridge and dropped the ten feet or so into the ditch. 'Here let me help you,' he said offering the startled leper a hand. The leper shook his head and waved the exuberant youth away, but the young Furud was not to be deterred. 'Really, it's no problem,' he said and took hold of the other end of the door. 'I'll help you carry this back to your...' Kai's friendly demeanour and physical closeness was clearly too much for the leper who dropped his end of the door and, with a cry, ran off in the other direction. 'Wait!' said Kai chasing after him. 'I just want to help!'

Although Kai would have been the first to admit he had never exactly built a reputation as a fighter amongst the war-loving Furud hordes he had grown up amongst, he did, however, command a certain respect when it came to a foot race, even at times matching the blistering pace of Rasalas' supremely athletic son, Magor. Yet the manner and ease with which the leper was pulling away from him as they tore through the ditches and backstreets of Sippara made Kai start to wonder if the wound Magor had inflicted upon him at Tor Morona hadn't permanently robbed him of the one and only thing the Furud warriors did not constantly ridicule him for. Finally, watching his nimble-footed adversary disappear around one corner too many, Kai was forced to pull up and give up the chase or risk collapsing from exhaustion.

'What's so funny?' Kai demanded upon seeing Hamsum's amused expression awaiting him as he rejoined his friends on the bridge.

'That went well,' said the merchant suppressing a laugh. 'Maybe you forgot to wash this morning?'

'Very funny,' said Kai aware how foolish he must have appeared. 'It's no problem. I'll just find another. They can't all be as quick as him.'

By the third day chasing lepers was by far becoming Kai's least favourite sport—and Hamsum's favourite. It didn't really matter which leper he chased, the night always seemed to end as badly as the first.

'Here comes our heroic young champion,' said Hamsum laughing as yet another leper successfully foiled Kai's attempts to unmask him.

'Shut up,' said Kai thoroughly fed up with having become the butt of all of Hamsum's jokes.

'Watch how he moves, with the stealth and speed of a panther...'

'Shut up.'

'...the grace of a gazelle.'

'Shut up!'

'...the heart of a lion.'

'SHUT UP!'

'More wine?' asked Entar, offering to refill Hamsum's glass from the hamper the merchant had brought for their evening's entertainment.

'I've told you they are *not* lepers! There's no way a real leper could run that fast.'

'Unless you are just very slow?' suggested Hamsum enjoying himself immensely. Kai looked ready to explode.

'I AM NOT SLOW!'

'Forgive me for asking,' said Entar intervening before Kai threw the merchant off the bridge. 'Just what exactly are you trying to achieve by all this?'

'Isn't it obvious?'

'No. Not really.'

'I'm trying to prove to you two donkeys that they are not lepers!'

'Then why don't we just go in the daytime to where they live and ask them, instead of all this charging around at night frightening them half to death?'

'Don't you think if I knew where they lived then maybe I would?!'

'Well, it's not that hard to work out.'

'It's not? Well, go on then,' said Kai forcibly calming himself down.

'Go on with what?'

'WORK IT OUT!'

'As you wish,' said the scholar struggling to hide his smile. 'Well, for a start their colony has to be quite near or they would never be able to carry all that rubbish with them, but equally it must also have to be outside of the city as there is no way the Ensi priesthoods would allow lepers permanent residence inside the city walls. I would also expect it to be in an area well away from pilgrims as there is no chance the Ensi would risk the lepers scaring off their best customers.'

'Okay. So where do you think they live then?'

'It's easy. Their colony must be somewhere inside the slums of Ma-Addir.'

'And you are sure of that?'

'Absolutely.' Kai felt like screaming.

'So I've just spent three days charging around like a complete ass when you could have told me this three days ago!'

'If you had explained what you were doing, I would probably have told you sooner—though maybe not too soon. It was, after all, rather entertaining to watch.' Entar and Hamsum burst into laughter.

'Laugh all you like. As soon as it gets light, you're both coming with me. We're going to Ma-Addir the three of us together.'

CHAPTER 29

Thanks to Hamsum's restocked hamper and Kai's upbeat mood now he was certain he was on the verge of solving the mystery of the temple's location, the trek across the city was an enjoyable and light-hearted affair and all three arrived at Sippara's western gate in good spirits, but once they had passed beyond the city walls and descended into the lawless squalor of Sippara's forgotten and dark underbelly, their good humour faded and the smiles fell from their long faces.

'I'm getting tired of this,' said Kai as another door rattled shut in their faces. 'And why do they keep making that ridiculous sign on their foreheads? We're only asking for directions?'

'It is a sign of protection,' said Entar.

'Protection? 'What do they think we're going to do, eat them?'

'They make the sign not to protect themselves from us, but from the impure ones whose homes we seek.'

'They could at least point us in the right direction.'

'They are afraid. They have been taught to see disease as a punishment and curse. They are afraid if they assist us the evil spirits afflicting the diseased ones could return to take vengeance on their own families.'

'What if we showed them some gold?' offered Hamsum. 'I bet they'll soon start blabbing once they've seen a gold piece or two.'

'I wouldn't advise tha…' began Entar but it was too late for Hamsum had already pulled two shiny gold coins from his belt and was chinking them together like the finger cymbals the temple dancers used to lure wealthy men into their bed chambers. In seconds, dozens of unsavoury looking characters had spilled out of every hut, hovel and hole and descended upon the three men like crows onto corn.

'My hamper!' wailed Hamsum as his picnic basket was whipped out of his hands and disappeared down an alleyway. 'My gold!' he cried as his purse disappeared down another.

'Forget them,' said Kai doing his best to keep himself and the other two men moving forward for he knew a wrong word or action could easily turn their situation very ugly indeed. 'Let them take what they want.'

'My kash!' Letting the hamper and his purse go was hard enough for the poor merchant, but seeing his beloved gourd yanked from his belt by the hands of a dirty old beggar was simply too much. *'Mas-Anse! Nam-mash-tu!'* shouted the merchant angrily and let a fist fly into the face of the thief.

Kai knew shouting insults at such a desperate and determined mob was probably not the brightest of ideas but bloodying the nose of a poor old man in broad daylight was the surest and stupidest way to get them all killed.

'Hamsum! Have you lost your mind?' shouted Kai having to protect himself as kicks and fists started to pour in on them.

'They can try to take my life,' shouted Hamsum furiously, 'but Ninkasi help them if they think they can have my kash!'

'They'll be having both if we don't get away from here soon you kash-muddled lunatic!'

'There *is* no way out of here!' shouted Entar holding up his long arms to shield himself. Kai looked around and saw that the old scholar was right. Every alleyway and door were heaving with angry faces. Suddenly a cry lifted above the chaos to send the mob scattering in every direction.

'Why are they running?' wondered Hamsum.

'I think here comes your answer,' said Entar as out from the clouds of dust a ghostly procession of eight veiled figures emerged.

'The lepers!' exclaimed Kai recognising the bandages and clothing instantly. Silently the procession glided past then disappeared into an alley so narrow it looked almost as if they had melted into the wall.

'Quick, let's follow before they escape,' said Kai quickly herding Hamsum and Entar into the alley before the opportunity to follow was lost, yet the high-speed chase Kai feared might break out the moment the lepers realised they were being followed not only failed to transpire, but far from attempt to run away, the lepers seemed to slow their pace even more turning their pursuit into a marathon of endurance.

'Can't they speed up a bit?' moaned Hamsum after nearly an hour's walking at a snail's pace.

'I'll admit I didn't expect this,' said Kai almost wishing the lepers would start running away.

'I think our ordeal may be close to an end,' said Entar with a degree of relief as the procession slowly fed into a long street which narrowed at one end like the neck of a wine bottle. Here, a giant cork of rubbish as large and imposing as the keep of a castle had effectively turned the street into an impassable dead end.

'This leads nowhere,' said Hamsum stating the obvious.

'Or does it?' said Entar pointing to the base of the pile. 'See, a door.'

'Are you sure that's a door?' said Kai fearing they might be walking into a trap. 'It looks more like a funeral bier to me.'

'You are right,' replied Entar, 'and yet you are also wrong.' Sure enough, one of the lepers produced a large key and fitted it into a small keyhole cut halfway up the right side of the bier. Once unlocked, the whole thing was swung open to reveal a man-sized rat hole worming its way through the centre of the heap.

'Should we follow?' asked Hamsum eyeing the tunnel dubiously as one by one the lepers disappeared inside.

'Unless you plan on facing a mob who just watched you punch an old man in the face then, yes, I would suggest we do.'

'Ay, Ninkasi protect me!' said Hamsum covering his mouth with his sleeve before following Kai and Entar into the tunnel.

The journey through the mountain of rubbish was a strange experience for Kai and his two friends for it seemed as though they were travelling back through a thousand years of Sipparan history, with unfashionably dour temple furniture and even dourer saints being gradually displaced by a much older generation of relics; relics brash and vibrant with colour and swarming with heathen gods which seemed to scream at them from the walls and ceiling of the passage as they beat upon their savage drums. Yet there was nothing savage or heathen about the quiet, meandering lane that greeted them when they reached the other side. With its pretty houses, each fronted by an immaculate veranda and balcony from which flowers and vegetables of every size, colour and variety cascaded to the ground, anyone entering there might be forgiven for thinking they had passed into some sort of enchanted oasis and certainly not a leper colony situated in the heart of Kugarra's biggest slum.

'What a wonderful place!' said Kai, astounded.

'Thank you,' said a leper who had hung back from the rest of the group and now limped purposefully towards them. 'We are proud of our home. Take a closer look if you like. Everything you see was once unwanted and thrown out by someone—a bit like ourselves.' While the leper chuckled at his own joke Kai stepped closer to one of the houses until he could see the house's gable had been created entirely from discarded prayer tablets that had been carved and fastened together to form a remarkably intricate lattice effect. The rest of the house was much the same, having been constructed entirely from items recovered from the ditches, all of which had been ingeniously reworked and fashioned so that the house looked more like the home of an eccentric lord than a beggar.

'I am sorry there are not more of us come to greet you,' continued the leper. 'Normally we are more welcoming of visitors, so rare is it that anyone comes to see us these days.'

'See,' said Hamsum quietly in Kai's ear. 'You have made them so scared of you that they now hide.'

'Don't be ridiculous,' said Kai. 'If they are hiding for any reason, it is because they know their secret is out. Just watch.' Kai stepped forward and began to address the lepers in what he deemed as polite a tone as befitted the occasion.

'Forgive us for intruding upon your privacy, but I know...' Kai paused to lend drama to the moment, '... the secret of your true identities.'

Other than a muffled snigger from Hamsum, Kai had to admit being disappointed by the underwhelming reaction from the lepers. Kai persisted. 'I know you only pretend to be lepers; that you use people's fear of your disease to keep strangers at bay. I also know U-an, Steward of the temple of E-Apsu hides amongst your numbers, but, fear not, for I come at the bidding of the Eledh to help restore your great temple.' Kai was certain this last pronouncement would cause a bigger stir yet the lepers betrayed not so much as a ripple of emotion. When he was sure

Kai had finished saying all he wanted, the leper who had addressed them turned to mutter something in Kugarran to one of his companions.

'What is he saying?' Kai asked Entar.

'He has asked his companion to remove their veil for you.'

'Fantastic!' said Kai with a look of triumph. 'Get ready for a surprise.' With some difficulty the second leper lifted bandaged hands to the corner of the veil and pulled it away. From behind the veil a face appeared. It was the face of a woman, yet a woman so ravaged by disease that all three gasped in shock. Kai felt sick with shame. The first leper nodded and the woman replaced her veil to hide her face once more.

'Now are you so eager to unmask us?' said the leper more sternly. Kai was mortified.

'I... I am so sorry!' he said bowing his head with genuine remorse. 'Please tell me if there is anything I can do to make up for the... offence.' The leper stood looking at the young Furud as if gauging the sincerity of his offer.

'Well, maybe there is something you could do. We have started clearing an unused area of wasteland at the southern edge of Ma-Addir, where the city meets the Plains of Sisu. It is backbreaking work so we could certainly use three extra pairs of hands to help us. In fact, we are headed there now.' Kai nodded only too pleased to be given an opportunity to redeem himself. Hamsum, however, was looking much less enthused with the idea.

'What if I catch the disease?' he whispered to Kai with stricken look. 'I am still young and looking for wife.'

'Really?' said Kai. 'I didn't know the brothels of Karkid had also started to offer wives.'

'That's not fair!' protested the merchant.

'Besides,' Kai continued, 'Entar says it's almost impossible to catch leprosy from another human.'

'*Almost* impossible, but still possible!'

'Gentlemen,' said Entar intruding upon their conversation, 'I believe our friends are wishing to depart.' Hamsum and Kai fell silent as they realised the group of lepers were stood waiting politely for the two to finish their conversation.

The walk to the southern edge of Ma-Addir was a sobering experience for the three friends, for not one of them had ever seen such heart-breaking poverty as that which they witnessed passing through those impoverished streets. But far more disturbing was the aversion and fear they witnessed directed at their diseased companions, who had only to appear at the end of a street for the street to empty, with people dashing into their houses, frantically making signs of protection on their brows as they slammed their doors.

'Are they always this afraid of you?' asked Kai.

'People have always been afraid. But recently their fear has grown much worse.'

'Why recently? What has changed?'

'There have been many reported disturbances and... disappearances. At first, we heard of horses being driven mad by something unseen. People tried blaming it on a sickness but then children from the slums and city orphanages started to go missing too. We now fear it could be the work of a predator coming out from the desert.'

The mention of mad horses brought a shiver to Kai, as he remembered the broken stable doors and the ghastly undead mare they had seen at the horse traders. 'You know something of this?' asked the leper noticing Kai's unease.

'I might know something. We tried buying horses on our way here, but the trade post had been abandoned. The horses had all gone. All except one.'

'Was it lame?'

'No, it was not lame. The horse was most certainly dead, and yet this dead horse still... walked.'

'*A Mare of Minasul*!' The other lepers gasped at mention of the name.

'So you've heard of them too? Could these be your predator?'

'To hear such horrors have taken to wandering so far from their desert tombs is a worry indeed but I have never heard of Minasul's mares preying on the living?'

'Has anyone spoken to the City Watch about all this?'

'Both the City Watch and the priesthoods were informed. They seemed curious about horses going mad, but as far as they were concerned regarding the missing orphans, the fewer slum children there are begging on the streets the better and so nothing has been done. Come, if the devil's mares are rising from their tombs then we can afford to tarry no longer.'

With images of undead mares and missing children consuming their thoughts, the three men followed the lepers out through Ma-Addir until they arrived at the edge of the city's outskirts. Here, as expected, another mountain of rubbish lay, though this one lay heaped against the base of a small hill beyond which an empty plain of dust and scrub stretched to the horizon.

'I'm guessing they want help shifting this,' said Kai hoping the hard work might take his mind off more depressing thoughts involving undead horses and missing people.

'But there is so much!' said Hamsum looking at the heap in dismay. 'It will take days to clear!'

'Then we had better get started.'

***

In spite of three extra pairs of hands and the added help of Uzzaga, who grumbled almost as much as her owner, Hamsum's prediction was not far wrong for even after a week's solid labour the mountain of rubbish was still not fully cleared away, some of which, judging by the look of it, must have been lying there for the better part of a century. Yet just as Kai was starting to feel their generous act of penitence was being taken more than just a little for granted by their quiet hosts, unusual shapes and hollows began to emerge beneath their feet, quickly followed by fan-shaped terraces which spread out across the hillside like the tail feathers of some exotic bird. Finally, as the last pieces of rubbish were cleared away, a milk-white entrance rose from the hillside like the petal of a flower.

'Is that a tomb?' asked Hamsum as scores of lepers, each laden with buckets of cold water and brushes for scrubbing, disappeared inside.

'I wonder,' said Kai trying to contain his excitement. 'What if it's a temple?'

'Strange place to keep a temple if you ask me,' said Hamsum dubiously.

'Not if you don't want anyone to find it. Who would think to look here, beneath a rubbish dump beside a slum?'

'I think it's just a system for catching rainwater.'

'Rainwater! When does it ever rain here?'

'Not often—which is probably why they never bothered to clear it.'

'Instead of arguing, why don't we just go take a look?' suggested the scholar in ever-pragmatic fashion.

'Agreed,' said Kai hurrying to reach the entrance first. 'See,' he said upon his arrival. 'They've even taken their sandals off. Now why do that if this was just for collecting rain?'

'Makes perfect sense to me,' said Hamsum arriving close behind. 'My mother would always make us take our shoes off before entering the milking room. She was forever catching my brother Sebu with his sandals on. It's why his ears grew so big from all the times she pulled them.' As Hamsum was reminiscing over his brother's ears two tall figures appeared at the entrance and silently bid the three friends to follow them inside.

'Are they the lepers?' asked Hamsum in a low voice, for although both wore veils, the familiar bandages and rags of the lepers had been replaced by soft white robes that whispered like leaves as they moved.

'I believe so,' said Kai struggling to contain his excitement.

Once inside, it soon became clear there was much more going on than just cleaning, for everywhere they looked there seemed to be white robed figures lighting candles and incense or sprinkling perfumed water on the floors and walls as if preparing for an impending ceremony. The main focus of their attention, though, seemed to be upon a large chamber dominated in its centre by a wide, empty pool at the bottom of which a great sinkhole, perhaps caused by some great calamity in the pool's past, dropped for as far as the eye could see.

'Shouldn't that thing have a fence or something around it?' said Hamsum stumbling backwards. Seeing the merchant lose his footing, one of the robed figures put out a hand to help steady him.

'That does not look like leprosy,' whispered Entar in Kai's ear. Kai looked at the leper's hand and noticed the skin had a faint, scaly sheen much like the skin of a fish.

'Nor to me,' he replied. The leper, noticing Kai and Entar's gaze, quickly retracted the hand. 'Who are you?' demanded Kai in a voice loud enough for all to hear. Upon Kai's question, a hush filled the chamber. The leper paused as if deciding how best to answer then with one hand pulled back his veil to reveal a strong, streamlined face covered in silvery scales like those on the backs of his hands. His eyes too were unlike any human's, large with silvery irises and sapphire blue pupils that gleamed with an inner light, much like the water of Amari's caverns.

'My name is U-an, Steward and protector of the Temple of E-Apsu. I am he who you seek.'

'I knew it!' said Kai as much elated as shocked by the steward's appearance.

'B... but the woman,' stammered Hamsum still struggling to comprehend what he was seeing, 'we saw her face!'

'Indeed, you did,' said U-an with an air of sadness. 'The woman's name is Ashishak. Many times, has she helped allay the suspicions of the wolves who come sniffing at our door, though often do I wish she could have found us sooner, before the disease had taken so grievous a toll upon her once beautiful face.'

'Who are you though?' asked Kai desperate to learn more. 'Your... kind I mean.'

'Our *kind*? Why we are the Apkallu. Many eons ago we came forth from the waters to be a friend to mankind. It was we who helped you find many of the Earth's sacred places and create your temples of healing.'

'You came from the waters to live in a desert!' said Hamsum disbelievingly. To help dispel any doubts Hamsum might have had the Apkallu lifted his hand and extended his fingers. The fingers were long and flat and when closed the hand resembled more the flipper of an aquatic creature than a hand.

'What about Sippara?' asked Kai. 'Was the temple city also designed by the Apkallu?'

'Much of the layout was designed by us, but the temples were built by the priesthoods. No Apkallu would enclose a temple of the divine within a dead shell of stone.'

'Then where are we now. Is this not the Temple of E-Apsu?' U-an laughed.

'No, it most certainly is not! This is the House of E-kur, a sanctuary and one of the many sources for the great temple.'

'I'm not sure I understand you,' said Kai, confused. 'If this is not the temple then where is it?'

'Why, it is here… and it is there.' U-an made a sweeping gesture that Kai interpreted as encompassing not just where they were standing, but also the sleeping city of Sippara as well as the vast dusty plain that spread out beyond it.

'Well, he's lost me completely,' said Hamsum, scratching his chin in bewilderment. Entar simply smiled.

'Do any of you know what Ma-Addir means?' U-an asked.

'It comes from the ancient Kugarran word for "ferryboat",' said Entar.

'Indeed, it does!' said U-an, nodding respectfully to the scholar. 'From here people were once able to travel by boat out across the vastness of the sacred E-Apsu. The city of Sippara grew up along the edge of the great lake to benefit from its life-giving waters and healing energy.'

'The Temple of E-Apsu was the lake itself?' said Kai incredulously.

'The greatest and holiest of all lakes!'

'Then how does Amari think I am to restore *all that*?'

'Tell me about the shell you wear about your neck.'

'The shell? It was a gift.'

'A gift from holy Amari herself, was it not?'

'It was.'

'And did she awaken in you the power to call forth its waters?'

'Well… I guess she must have, if power is what you want to call it, but I wouldn't get excited about it, the waters only trickle out when I call them. I'd struggle to make a puddle with it let alone a lake.'

'Show me please.'

'Very well,' said Kai and lifting the shell to his mouth quietly began invoking the sacred waters.

'Speak the words louder please,' requested U-an.

'As you wish,' said Kai and did as the Apkallu asked, speaking the invocation out loud, though, as expected, nothing more than a trickle of water began to flow from the shell's mouth. 'See, nothing to get excited about.'

'You might want to stand back,' warned U-an with some gravity. Through the soles of their feet all could feel a soft rumbling building. Suddenly a gasp burst from the sinkhole followed by an explosion of water that began filling the pool and surging down the channel to the outside.

'Did *I* really just do that?' asked Kai incredulously as he and the others jumped back from the pool's edge.

'Indeed, you did,' said U-an delightedly, 'and much more of the same must you do before this night is over. A lake does not get filled from just one source, especially one as vast as E-Apsu. Many more of Amari's springs must you awaken before the dawn breaks.'

***

All that evening and through the night, as the Apkallu and Kai's friends celebrated, U-an led Kai to many secret places, not just around the House of E-kur, but across Ma-Addir and the city of Sippara itself, until the sounds of flowing water could be heard from every temple, street corner and square as the air filled with a freshness and smell like summer rains.

'What now?' asked the young Furud as a slender moon gave way to a robust dawn. 'Is there anything else we need to do?'

'Indeed, there is. Now we replant the gardens!'

CHAPTER 30

By the time it took for the pools below the House of E-kur and the city's
canals and waterways to fill, few had escaped being recruited into U-an's
green crusade. Even Hamsum had been dragged out of his kash-stinking
pit only to witness with bleary eyes a bucket and spade being shoved into
his hands. Many of the poor and humble inhabitants of Ma-Addir, seeing
the miraculous events taking place on their doorstep, soon overcame their
fears and joined in with growing zeal, digging over any hard earth they
could find, sometimes using nothing more than their bare hands to break
up the dry crust of the street until the whole area looked like it had been
blessed with the finest tilled soil. Yet none gave themselves to the project
as much as the Apkallu, whose energy and skill was an inspiration to all
as they dashed about the sanctuary terraces and streets of the slums with
rapturous cries, directing and praying over each and every seed and nut,
every bulb and root that was laid in the ground, until not just the House
of E-kur and the hill above it, but the whole of Ma-Addir was bathed in
a sea of tiny green shoots that seemed to defy every law of nature,
sprouting from the earth the moment E-Apsu's sacred waters touched
them.

In the desert, a growing glint of silver spreading out beyond the city
walls told Kai the great lake was already starting to form, yet the euphoric
reaction Kai had hoped would materialise, particularly from those inside
the city, most certainly did not. In fact, far from flocking to Ma-Addir
and the sanctuary to see what was happening, many of the inhabitants
from the city's wealthier districts began to abandon Sippara altogether,
heading out past the lake into the desert.

'Where are they all going? Why are they leaving?'

'Someone is drawing them away,' said U-an. 'Even the priests have
abandoned the city and have led many out to the desert. They are saying
the devil lives in the waters; that to drink from them means certain death.'

'Who is saying this? How can anyone believe such lies?'

'The city is full of rumours. Some say it is a wild man of the desert who is drawing them; a man who speaks with a demon tongue and gathers all who would listen to him like an army.'

'Has anyone been out there yet? To see if the rumours are true?'

'We dare not go for we have heard he has already turned the people against the lepers and people of Ma-Addir as if he knows it was us who brought this "calamity" upon them.'

'Then let me go. I'll soon find out if we have anything to worry about.'

'Not yet, Kai. Let the rumours calm down. In a week or two, once they see nothing bad has happened, they will return of their own accord. They will soon tire of the desert heat and these lies. Besides, there is something we need your help with first.'

'What is it?'

'Visitors arrived last night. They brought two patients with them. The first refuses to eat and resists any attempt to heal him. It seems he wishes to be left to die. The other, a young woman, seems in good health but is very distressed by her companion's condition. She also seems uncomfortable entrusting him into the care of anyone but herself. We wondered, as she speaks with the northern tongue, whether you might be better able to convince her we mean no harm, at least so she lets us assess what is wrong with her companion. I must warn you though, she has quite a temper.'

'I can try,' said Kai.

Kai followed U-an into the complex and heard a commotion long before he reached the room where the patients were being tended to.

'Get her away!' said a voice that had more growl than grammar in it.

'Tell him he can threaten all he likes but I'm not going anywhere.'

'Please,' a third voice said that Kai took to be one of the Apkallu, 'it is unwise for you to remain here with him while he is in this... condition. You really should leave.'

'I've told you I'm not going anywhere. Let him eat me, then we'll see how stupid he feels afterwards!' Kai could only see the young woman from an angle but already he could tell her beauty was as striking as her stubborn resolve.

'Please. We cannot calm him while you remain. Your presence only aggravates his… illness.' One of the Apkallu tried to lead her out by the arm but she tore it from him.

'Touch me again fish face and you'll get a slap in the gills!'

'It's okay,' said Kai recognising the voice and temper even if the beautiful creature before him resembled nothing like the excrement-covered girl he remembered from the *Nefari*. 'You can leave her with me.'

'And who the hell do you think you…' As Kai's beaming smile appeared in the doorway the young woman let out a shriek and threw herself into his arms. Kai didn't know why, but in that moment, he couldn't think of anything but the wonderful scent of flowers and cedar lifting from the soft copper and golden swirls of flowing hair pressing into his chest. 'Oh Kai, I don't know what to do!' Blue lifted her face to Kai's. He could see she had been crying. 'I've tried everything. It's awful. It's like he's gone back to his horrible old self and nothing I do makes any difference.' Only then did Kai shift his focus to the patient and the five huge strangers who were trying without much success to calm him down.

'Herders!' he gasped, stepping in front of Blue as if ready to protect her.

'Oh, there's no need to fear them,' said Blue reassuringly. 'They're here to help. Anyway, they're not really herders, they're Jentilak.'

'They're what?'

'They're Jentilak. They're what the herders used to be before they became the Atzerri. Although I suppose Basax is a Jentilak too now — of sorts — only he's back to behaving like a herder again. Oh, I don't know, it's all so confusing.'

'*That* is Basax!' Kai could scarce believe the handsome, flowery-haired creature being restrained on the bed was the same ugly monster everyone had so feared on the *Nefari*.

'Of course it's Basax, you numpty. Haven't you been listening?'

'It's just he looks so different… as do you. And what's that glowing thing on your forehead? Are you ill too?'

'No, I am not ill!' snapped Blue recovering some of her fire. 'That was a gift—a kiss from one of the Eledh!'

'A kiss! Ah, okay. I'm sorry. I didn't mean to offend you.' Blue tried to remain cross but seeing Kai's familiar face again she couldn't help but break out into a smile.

'Oh, Kai I'm so glad you're here!' she said again throwing her arms around Kai's waist.

'I'm glad to see you too Blue,' said Kai still keeping an eye on her dangerous looking companions. 'Come,' he said disentangling himself from her embrace to place her warm palm in his. 'Leave the Apkallu and your Jentilak friends alone with Basax. Let them care for him a while. If anyone can find out how to help him, the Apkallu can. I promise you can trust them with him Blue.'

'Are you sure they know what they're doing?'

'I'm sure. Come on. Let me show you around. Let me show you all that we've done here and you can tell me everything that's happened to you. I've been desperate for news of you.'

'As I of you!'

CHAPTER 31

The lazy, sun-drenched days that Kai spent with Blue as she waited for news of Basax's recovery were undoubtedly the happiest he had ever known. Slowly, Blue's mistrust of the Apkallu faded and the sadness that had clung to her every expression was replaced by a contented glow that grew brighter with each and every day spent in the company of her young Furud companion. With the departure of many of Sippara's wealthy pilgrims, especially its ruling classes of overbearing and overfed priests, the city seemed to rise from the replenished waterways like a dirty old sinner reborn as a saint. It was as if the flowing waters and bubbling springs brought not just a freshness to the air but seemed to revive the tired façades and dusty streets, imbuing them with a subtle beauty and gentle grace long since forgotten. Inevitably, the city quickly became the favourite playground of the young pair, who seemed to find around almost every corner a new and fascinating world of undiscovered curiosity and bewitching enchantment. But when a seventh and then an eighth day passed and still no news came of a cure for Basax's malady, Blue couldn't help but begin to worry again.

'This is taking too long!' she said, pacing up and down whilst Kai aimlessly dabbled his fingers in the water of a fountain.

'You know they say fish have returned to the great lake,' Kai said resting his chin on one hand as he watched the shining droplets run down his fingers and hang from his nails like tiny crystal balls. 'I wonder how that could happen so quickly. Do you think Entar knows?'

'I should never have left him,' continued Blue in spite of Kai's rather absent reply. I haven't been to see him for days.'

'An egret too was spotted flying low over the water somewhere near the eastern shore of the lake.'

'What? Kai can you please listen to me! This is important!'

'Um. I am.'

'So what am I talking about?'

'Err, fish?'

'No!'

'Egrets?'

'NO! I've been talking about Basax. He should be getting better by now.'

'Oh, that. They're just letting him rest. Don't forget herders can sleep for days.'

'Well not this herder!' Blue hitched her dress up over her ankles and set off at a march up the hill towards the sanctuary.

'Where are you going?'

'I'm going to see how well he sleeps with a bucket of cold water poured over his head!'

Back at the sanctuary, an almighty commotion was already underway with Jentilak and Apkallu seeming to be running in all directions.

'What's going on?' demanded Blue, finding Otzak in a deep conversation with U-an. Hearing Blue's voice, the pair swapped troubled glances before Otzak turned to answer her.

'It's Basax,' he said with an apologetic look. 'He has disappeared.'

'Disappeared! When did he disappear?'

'We're not sure. The slightest intrusion was making him agitated and angry. He could even smell us approaching so we thought it best to leave him in peace for a while.'

'And just how long is a while?'

'Perhaps as much as three days.'

'Three days! I knew I should never have left him. At least tell me you have some idea where he has gone?'

'We have an idea,' said Otzak. 'Nekane picked up his trail near the great lake. She thinks he may be headed to the wild man's encampment.'

'Why would he want to go there?'

'We fear he could be... hungry.'

'Hungry? Haven't you been feeding him? Oh!' Blue's face paled. 'You're not suggesting he's gone there looking for... meat!' Blue could hardly say the word the idea so appalled her.

'His condition has been making him crave human flesh like... an Atzerri.' The old Jentilak hung his head in shame.

'I don't believe it!' Blue said going cold at the thought. 'I *won't* believe it! If Nekane were here she'd tell you the same. He is no more capable of eating someone as you or I!'

'I don't believe he truly wants to hurt anyone either Blue,' Otzak replied with as apologetic a look as the hard old Jentilak could manage, 'but the shadow that drives his hunger is powerful indeed.'

'Then I'll just have to go to this desert camp and bring him back.'

'That might not be so easy. You do not exactly... blend in.'

Blue unwound a sash about her waist and wove it fashionably about her head in a style worn by many of the wealthier women of the city so both her coppery fair hair and the point of light on her forehead were completely hidden.

'See. All I need is a little oil to darken my skin and you have yourself a fine Kugarran lady.'

'You still speak no Kugarran. What would you do if you were challenged by the Kalibi?'

'I would answer, *"Peta babkama luruba anaku?"* or of course I could say, *"Ati me peta babka".*'

'You speak like a Kugarran!' exclaimed Otzak amazed to hear Blue speaking the language so convincingly. 'Who taught you to speak the desert tongue so fluently?'

'Urakgha taught me.'

'Urakgha!' Both Otzak and U-an looked at Blue in astonishment.

'She teaches me things. Many things. It happens at night mostly when I close my eyes to sleep. She whispers things to me. At first, I was afraid and tried to shut the voice out, but then I realised who it was. Now I can't hear her enough. She tells me such fascinating things.'

'To hear the spirit of the storm bird guides you gives an old Jentilak great hope, but you must know Blue there is more to worry about at this camp than just the Kalibi.'

'Why? What else is there?'

'It is not so much what is there,' interrupted U-an, 'but *where* the camp has been placed.'

'Where is this camp then?'

'The camp lies deep in the Plains of Sisu. It is in a hot and waterless place most unsuited for the numbers that have been led there. Yet what concerns us most is it has been placed within sight of ruins we Apkallu have long avoided.'

'Why have you avoided them?'

'Because they were once the stables of an ancient king. A king whose name you have already heard. The king's name was Minasul.'

'If this is true,' said Kai sternly, 'then a journey to this encampment has been put off for far too long.'

'Indeed Kai, but you must also know that with each passing day more reports come back of similar horrors being seen walking abroad.'

'I understand. We'll be careful.'

CHAPTER 32

'Penny for your thoughts?' said Blue desperate for a bit of conversation, if only to break the monotony of their journey along the ever-expanding lake shore. All Kai had done since they had left was to ride in silence whilst fiddling distractedly with something he carried in a small leather purse tied around his neck.

'I was just thinking about what you said back there, how Urakgha speaks to you at night. Aatxe talks to me too.'

'Really? What does he say?'

'Well, he doesn't talk so much. Rather, he sings. Last night, though, was different.'

'Why? What happened?'

'He sang something I'd never heard before.'

'Really? Why don't you sing it to me?'

'I'd rather not.'

'I promise I won't boo.'

'It's not that. It's just that this song is… different to the others.'

'What's wrong with that? I like different.'

'Not this kind of different. To be honest it scares me. I mean really scares me.'

'It scares you!' said Blue laughing. 'I didn't realise your singing was that bad.'

Kai didn't laugh.

'This is not a joke,' he said solemnly. 'If I sing it I fear something terrible will happen.'

'Well, okay, if you insist, Mr Moody Pants. At least, if you're not going to sing, you can tell me what that thing is you keep fiddling with around your neck.'

'This?' said Kai lifting the object out of the purse so Blue could see. 'It's a gold lion. It's just something I found in the desert. I thought

Hamsum had sold it, but he must have been keeping it for me. He gave it to me before we parted.'

'That was kind of him. I can see it means a lot to you.'

'Yes, I suppose it does,' said Kai returning the lion to the purse and carefully tying the string. 'But the reason he gave it to me wasn't so I kept it for myself.'

'Why did he give it to you then?'

'So I could give it to someone he knows I really... care about.'

'Really?' said Blue with a look of mock surprise. 'I'm not sure you're Basax's type.'

'Wh... *what?*'

Blue guffawed at his horrified reaction.

'Oh, go on, give it here then and give us a kiss!' said Blue puckering up in a ridiculous fashion with her hand held out to receive the lion.

'Well, if you're going to be like that, I won't give it to you at all.'

This time Blue's face registered genuine surprise which quickly turned to embarrassment.

'Oh, so it was meant for *me!*'

'Of course it was. Who did you think it was for? Oh here. Just take it will you.'

Still taken aback Blue accepted the gold figurine and lifted it out of the bag as though lifting out the most precious pearl necklace. Once she had inspected every detail of its tiny body, she returned the lion to the leather pouch and carefully hung it around her neck.

'Thank you,' she said quietly as she dropped her eyes. 'I'm not really accustomed to men giving me expensive gifts. Normally they just hand me their chamber pots.' Kai laughed as he remembered how he and Blue had first met.

'I'm just glad you like it,' said Kai, relieved that the embarrassing ordeal was over.

'Look!' said Blue suddenly noticing a large bird gliding across the water with plumes as pure as freshly fallen snow. 'That must be the egret you heard them talking about. Gosh, what a beautiful bird! The only birds we ever get back home are cliff crakes. You find them nesting among all the cottage rooftops. Make an awful racket. In summer you can hardly sleep for all their noise.'

'They sound like the korax that nest along the battlements. Rasalas used to hate them. He once caught Magor trying to feed them so made him set fire to all the nests. It was springtime so many had eggs and young in them. It was horrible. Magor was only ten at the time. I think it still gives him nightmares. It didn't even get rid of them. Just made the next generation of korax even more aggressive than before. The following year you couldn't get more than ten yards along the top of the walls without them attacking you.'

'No wonder Magor is so messed up. Our cliff crakes can be quite aggressive too. The last person to catch a fish in the harbour got mobbed by them. Took his fish and half the scalp of his head.'

'Ouch,' said Kai with a wince. 'Have they always done that?'

'Not always. It started after the boats stopped bringing the catches in. Poor things were just hungry I guess.'

'I wonder if any of the fish in the lake are big enough for the egret to eat yet?'

'I'm sure they will be. Did you see how fast the plants sprouted up in Ma Addir after we watered them? There's something magical about these waters. Ooh look at all the dragonflies!' she said, pointing to the pink shimmer of translucent wings taking off from the water's edge.

'Still,' said Kai once the dancing bursts of pink had settled once more on the young reeds sprouting along the lake shore, 'I think it's amazing how any fish get into the lake in the first place. I mean we're miles from any other water.'

'They get carried here by water birds.'

'Carried here by birds! That's just stupid.'

'It's not stupid! Nekane told me fish eggs stick to a bird's feet when it wades through the mud of another river or lake, then when the bird flies off to find a new place the eggs get washed off and hatch into their new home. Isn't that interesting? Just think, one minute you could be a doomed little egg stuck in a dying, dried-up pond and the next thing you've hatched into a big, beautiful lake like this one. She says that's how the Eledh see most of us—little eggs stuck in a mud of our own making.'

'She should be a teacher like Entar. I could imagine him coming out with a comment like that.'

'She is a teacher—a wonderful one. Since coming to Kugarra I've been spoilt for teachers; first Lybesstre, then Nekane and now Urakgha. The only schooling I ever got back home was from old Eofor—and most of that was to do with how to tie bowlines or skeining limpets and mussels for bait.'

'Well, I can't say the Furud are big on education either. The last thing the army wants are warriors with the wits to think for themselves. Lord Rasalas had to smuggle in a foreign tutor to school Magor and myself.'

'For Magor and *yourself.* Now why would a warlord pay for a servant boy to be educated?'

'I don't know. I never really gave it much thought.'

'Come on Kai, work it out. Why do you think Rasalas kept you so close all these years? You even admitted to me you made an awful servant.'

'To be honest I don't have a clue. Why? What's your point?'

'My point is… well I'm only saying what a lot of people suspect so don't get upset, but I'll bet anything Rasalas was your father.'

'My father!'

'Of course. You even look like him.'

'Nonsense,' said Kai struggling to even contemplate the idea. 'If that were true why lie about it for so many years?'

'I guess he had his secrets. It's a shame you can no longer ask him.'

'It certainly is,' said Kai glowering.

'You see, now you're angry. I wish I'd never said anything.'

'So do I,' said Kai and fell into a moody silence that endured not only for the remainder of the day but through most of the next as well.

***

Late into the third day of their journey, they were able to pick up a trail of refugees that led over a small ridge and down into a hot and wide depression of land that had served to trap so much heat of the afternoon sun that soon they felt as if they were walking through a blacksmith's forge. Across the smouldering sands, a vast migration of reptiles and insects seemed to be taking place, swarming across the desert floor like

293

routed soldiers fleeing a battlefield. The mules too would go no further, snorting and gnashing their teeth as they backed up in fear to the point that both Kai and Blue had to quickly jump off and let them go for fear of being thrown or kicked.

'Well, there goes our ride home,' said Blue watching the mules gallop back towards the lake. 'What's got them so upset? The insects?'

'Maybe. Or they just want to get out of this heat like the rest of us.'

'I don't think so,' said Blue. 'See down there. Since when does a dune mantis run beside a sand skipper? The sand skipper is its natural prey yet they are so close to each other they are almost touching. Something is definitely not right here.'

Kai might have shown interest in Blue's possible insect amnesty if he hadn't noticed three faint plumes of smoke snaking up into the cloudless expanse about a mile ahead.

'Looks like we'll soon find out,' said Kai pointing to the smoke. 'That has to be the encampment.'

CHAPTER 33

The wild man's encampment sat upon an island of rock which rose from the sand like a scab on scalded skin. On top of the island, it was as if the entire population from inside the city had simply got up and followed each other onto that sizzling slab of stone like crayfish crawling onto a skillet. The only thing going for the side of the encampment Blue and Kai had arrived at was the miserly amount of shade being offered by the few fissures in the ground wide enough for people to fit into, but these were already overflowing with sweating Ensi priests who acted as if it was their god-given right to monopolise what little shade there was, regardless of how much more others in the camp might have needed it. The only other shade they could see came from a dark and imposing silhouette which dominated the horizon about a quarter of a mile further to the east. Here shade seemed to be in plentiful supply but, for some reason, none of the priests or island population seemed to have the slightest interest in going anywhere near it. The silhouette could only belong to one thing: the ruined stables of King Minasul.

'This doesn't make any sense to me,' said Kai, noticing the large numbers of fresh Kalibi recruits, their eyes inflamed with a new and unsettling look that reminded Kai more of a religious fervour than the hazy intoxication of the Dayan Sami's flowers. 'From what I can see I'd say it was pretty obvious someone is trying to raise an army here, but if that is the case, why gather together so many young, old and infirm? Look at them all. They're everywhere. Any soldier could tell you, they'd just slow an army down.'

'The children could be the ones that went missing from Ma-Addir.'

'There's too many to be just from Ma-Addir. It's as if he's emptied every orphanage for a hundred miles from here.'

'Perhaps he thinks he's rescued them. What if this wild man is not as bad as we think?'

'I don't think so. See how they huddle together as if seeking each other's warmth. No one could be cold in this heat.'

'No, you're right. They're not cold. They're frightened. Even the priests seem scared. But of what?'

'They must have heard the rumours about the mares,' said Kai.

'I know very little about them. Do you know much of their story?'

'Only what Entar told me before we left. Apparently, the wild mares that roamed these lands were born not from the union of a stallion and mare, but straight from the lake itself. It was understood in those days that so long as the mares were allowed to roam free by the lake's shores these lands would stay rich and fertile. The king, however, in his royal wisdom, one day declared that anything that lived within the borders of his kingdom belonged to him and so had the horses rounded up and herded into new, luxurious stables he had built solely for them. It was there they were to be broken-in and turned into the pride of his imperial cavalry. When the people heard what he had done, entire villages and towns marched on the stables to beg the king to release the mares or bring a terrible curse upon all of their heads.'

'I'm guessing he didn't listen.'

'Not only did he not listen, he had his soldiers beat them from the stable gates. What Minasul did not expect was that the mares could no more endure captivity than a flower can endure without sun and so one by one they began to sicken and die. For Minasul that was the start of the end for as they died so too did the great lake and land around it until both lake and land were as dry and barren as the rest of the Kugarran desert.'

'Why didn't he let the mares go? Surely he could have seen what was happening?'

'They didn't call him "Minasul the Mad" for nothing. It seems he somehow convinced himself all he needed to do was to substitute what he'd stolen with something equally innocent and pure.'

'And what was that?'

'The blood of children. I don't know how many he brought out here to be slaughtered but I'm told it was a lot.'

'That's vile,' said Blue understandably disgusted by what she had heard.

'It is. And I intend to find out what is driving the mares once more from their tombs.'

'How will you do that?'

'By going inside that ruin. If anywhere holds the key to all this it's inside there.'

'And that's your big plan?'

'What's wrong with that?'

'Well, you could try adding "*we*" into that sentence for a start. What if Basax is in there? Mind you, I can't imagine what would possess him to go to such a place. He's terrified of ghosts and from what you've told me that place must be crawling with them.'

'Look!' said Kai suddenly pointing excitedly down at markings in the dust running along the edge of the encampment.

'Footprints!' exclaimed Blue 'Those belong to a herder! It must be Basax!'

'But who do those other tracks belong to?' said Kai noticing a set of much smaller feet running alongside the first.

'They look like they belong to a child,' said Blue. 'Maybe one tried to escape?'

'Well, the child didn't get very far,' said Kai noticing how the tracks suddenly vanished as the herder's converged above them. 'Poor thing.'

'Poor thing!' said Blue turning on him angrily. 'What are you implying?'

'What does the wolf do when a calf gets separated from the herd?'

'Basax is not a wolf!'

'Well, whatever he is, I'm taking a quick look. I want to see where these tracks lead.'

'You can look all you like but you won't change my opinion!'

'I won't be long,' said Kai, carefully following the tracks out across the baking sands.

Kai could only have been following the tracks for a couple of minutes when a cry was raised to Blue's right.

'Oh mercy!' said Blue as three dark shapes thundered out from a small outcrop of rocks and headed straight towards Kai. Spotting the three approaching Kai doubled back as quickly as he could but the shapes were already bearing down on the young Furud at an almost impossible speed. Finding himself suddenly surrounded, Kai exploded into motion, ducking and weaving so fast and furiously not even ten men would have been able to lay so much as a finger on him. But these weren't men. These were herders.

CHAPTER 34

Witnessing herders eating was as sorry and stomach churning a sight as anything Kai had ever witnessed. Lips smacking, bones crunching, loud belching and fatty crimson juices running from chins. One herder even swallowed a foot down so fast he succeeded in choking part of it, toenails and all, back up into another herder's face. The victim, instead of reproaching his neighbour's disgusting feeding habits, acted as if his luck was in and wolfed down the bile-covered chunk of meat, gristle and bone down before the offending herder had even realised, he had lost out.

'That was mine!' accused the herder who had spewed out the chunk of foot.

'You spat it out Ler. Me thoughts you didn't want it.'

'You lyin pig!' As the first herder lunged at the second, a frightful row broke out. With each flail of claws and flash of teeth more herders were dragged into the fray, until all bar one was embroiled in a deafening mêlée that shook the very stones of the ruins around them. Kai had thought himself familiar with all the herders of the *Nefari*, but the one who remained calmly eating its food was quite different, not just from those of Caronte's ship, but from any herder he had ever seen. Instead of the bald head and wiry hair that grew across the back and shoulders, this one had a shaggy mane that grew right over the crown of its head. Although it was resting on its haunches much like the other herders had been doing, Kai could see it carried less weight on its body than they. Of course his immediate fears were that it was Basax, though a much leaner Basax than the one he remembered seeing being restrained by the Jentilak in the sanctuary at Ma Addir.

'Enough!' snapped the strange herder. 'Leave us!' Incredibly, the brawling herders quieted down almost immediately and left without complaint. Kai knew that under normal circumstances only the very strongest and most self-assured of herders would ever dare speak to the others in that way, but this herder did not look to have half the strength of even the smallest of their ugly band. With its back to Kai, the remaining herder tore the last of the meat off the bone and chewed slowly.

'You're not hungry,' it said with a mouth full of meat and gristle. Kai figured the comment was more of a statement than a question so remained silent. 'Shame,' it said slurping. 'This is good.'

The herder finished its mouthful, stretched and scratched, then plodded over to curtains which had been hung to partition off a dim space at the back of the room. Mumbling disjointed nonsense to itself, the herder passed through to the other side and seemed to confer with a shadowy figure who leant close to it as if whispering instructions into the herder's ear. Kai knew exactly where he had seen such a shadowy figure before. It was the same he had seen whispering into the ear of the Dayan Sami at Wardum.

'Who are you?' Kai demanded.

'Who am I?' it muttered, though the question seemed more directed at itself than at Kai. Kai watched with an ominous presentiment as the curtains were pulled apart and the herder removed a heavy animal hide from its head and shoulders. In its hands, it carried a glistening black horn with a jewelled hilt. The horn's tip dripped with blood.

'Do you really not know me?' it said, moving into the dim light of a flickering torch. 'Do you not know your father?'

CHAPTER 35

'Curses!' said Blue kicking a tent pole so hard that the tent collapsed. She flopped miserably down beside the fallen folds of canvas and cupped her head in her hands.

'Not having a good day are we my dear?' croaked an old lady in a peasant's shawl pulled across her face, no doubt to protect her from the merciless sun. Blue was feeling so dejected that she didn't even register the old lady had spoken to her in the northern tongue. 'Perhaps a little more discretion would be wise?' The old woman drew Blue's attention to a Kalibi guard who stood nearby watching over the sweating crowds like a menacing sentinel. 'Particularly considering the predicament you and your reckless young friend have found yourselves in.' This time the old lady's disconcerting familiarity with her and Kai's situation brought Blue rapidly back to her senses.

'Who are you?' Blue demanded, more angry than upset that her and Kai's plans seemed to be going from bad to worse.

'One who has been praying for your safe return for weeks.' The old lady moved her shawl aside so Blue could catch a glimpse of her face.

'Lybesstre!' she cried and would have thrown her arms around the priestess if the guard hadn't been standing so close.

'Oh Lybesstre, I've been praying for you too! However, did you know it was me?'

'Well for starters, Sipparan ladies don't go around swearing like Stod shaft rats.' Lybesstre lowered her voice. 'Come, it's time we left here.'

'Where are we going?'

'To the ruins of course.'

'B-but the herders and the guards! And what about Kai? We can't leave him here! We have to help him!'

'That is exactly why we must get to the ruins. And don't worry about the herders and guards. We witches have ways to get about without being noticed—as you may recall.'

Blue did recall. The number of times she had slipped about the decks of the *Nefari* unnoticed had seemed almost miraculous, but this was the first time she had heard the priestess make any sort of admission she had been the one behind it all.

'Oh, and I also set fire to the Kalibi guard's tents,' the priestess added as a smoky uproar erupted somewhere near the centre of the encampment.

Taking advantage of the chaos that ensued, Blue followed the priestess out across the desert wastes, yet it wasn't long before her attention became inexorably drawn away from the commotion they had left behind and towards the towering walls of Minasul's stables looming ahead, which seemed to rise from their dark foundations like the hunched wings of a feeding vulture.

'I can't believe they were once stables,' said Blue struggling to take in the sheer scale of what lay before them. 'It looks more like a fortress.'

'Indeed,' said Lybesstre. 'Quite something isn't it? To think a man would build all that for a herd of horses he hadn't even caught yet... unless of course there was another purpose for its construction?'

'What other purpose could there be?' asked Blue.

'That we will have to see for ourselves.'

Blue said nothing more but with a growing feeling of unease let Lybesstre lead her across the final stretch of desert until they arrived at a long and pitted ramp of stone and dust which lolled out from the ruin's cavernous entrance like a thirsty tongue. Lining either side of the ramp statues of wild horses reared and kicked at the air, though most were so eroded by time and desert winds they more closely resembled nebulous phantoms than horses.

'What is that smell?' said Blue as they mounted the ramp. 'The air is almost sweet. Wait a minute!' she said like a bloodhound catching a scent. 'I know exactly what that is!'

Blue stormed past a bemused Lybesstre and entered the ruins. As she emerged on the other side, she found herself in a vast space that separated the outer wall from a second inner wall even more imposing than the first. In this space, an oasis had somehow burst to life with bennu trees being by far the lords of that leafy domain, some even poking their bushy crowns out through the domed rooftops of crumbling stable blocks which seemed to line the entire circumference of the outer wall. As the crowns shook in the warm breeze, puffs of pollen floated into the air, coating everything they touched, whether wood, stone or skin, in a golden patina that lent such an otherworldly quality to the already bizarre spectacle that Blue wondered if she might be dreaming.

'There he is!' Blue announced ducking under the leathery leaves of a nearby tree to kick the mass of pollen-coated fur snoring beneath it. 'Wake up you menace!' she shouted provoking not one, but two sleepy faces to lift yawning from their slumber. Blue might have smacked the herder's pollen covered cheeks to encourage him to wake up faster if she hadn't realised the second sleepy face belonged to a child who, far from looking like she was in any danger from the herder, lay snuggled protectively against the herder's round and quite evidently very full belly. 'Just what exactly do you think you are doing here?'

'Hullo Blue,' the herder said blearily.

'Enough of "hullos"! I asked you a question!' Basax looked around as if briefly trying to gauge exactly where "here" was, then, seeing the bennu trees all around, gave Blue a watery smile.

'Um Basax was hungry,' he said as if that explained everything. 'Fish face food yucky.'

'And the child?' said Blue stabbing a finger at the herder's belly. 'Is she on the menu as well?' Basax scowled in disgust at the very suggestion.

'Basax find child in desert so bring child here, where child safe!'

'You think these stables are safe! You do know this place is crawling with espiritua, or even worse, don't you?'

At mention of the espiritua, Basax looked across at the hollow openings of the stable blocks and shivered.

'That *why* Basax come here,' he said quietly as if fearful of disturbing the dead.

'You knew there were herders here didn't you Basax? You knew they would be too afraid to come here, that's why you brought the child here.' Hearing this from the priestess Blue's angry demeanour softened.

'Is that who has been snatching children from the orphanages and streets of Ma-Addir?' Blue asked. Basax growled in affirmation. 'Oh, you great daft lump,' she snivelled throwing her arms about the herder's big neck. 'What were you thinking? Have you forgotten we just crossed half a desert together to escape those monsters? What if they had caught you? Have you thought about that?'

'Herders not catch Basax,' the herder declared proudly. 'Basax too fast!'

'I think you're confusing fat with fast,' said Blue looking less than impressed at his big belly.

'I'm more concerned with why herders are helping this wild man snatch children off the streets?' said Lybesstre.

'What do you suspect?'

'Look behind you. Tell me what you see?' Blue turned to see nothing but the immense second wall barring her view. Other than the wall's pyramid shaped battlements and a few broken flights of steps, there was little else worth remarking on.

'Am I missing something?' she asked.

'You most certainly are,' said Lybesstre. 'Perhaps you should look again.' Blue did as Lybesstre asked and scrutinised the wall carefully.

'Of course!' she said suddenly realising the significance of seeing stairs on *their* side of the wall. 'The stairs are on the wrong side. The wall is back to front!'

'On the contrary, the wall has been built exactly as it was intended.'

'What intention could that be? I don't know much about war but even I can tell it's no good for defence whatsoever.'

'What if it was never meant for defence, but for containment?'

'Containment! How did you work that out? Just look at all the stables. Anyone can see the mares were kept on *this* side of the wall!'

'What if it wasn't the mares the wall was meant to contain? Do you see the larger stones placed at the bottom of the wall? It might surprise you to know, these pre-date the rest of the wall by at least ten thousand years.'

'Ten thousand years! So Minasul simply reinforced what was already here then built the stables around it. Why was the original wall built then? What were they hoping to contain?'

'Come,' said Lybesstre, leading Blue to the only flight of stairs that still looked intact. 'Step carefully. You need to see this.' After the dizzy heights Blue had experienced crossing into the lands of the Jentilak, the climb to the top of the wall was nothing for her and she quickly skipped past the priestess to be the first to step out onto the battlements.

'Oh!' gasped Blue the moment she reached the top and for an instant looked as though she might topple backwards.

'Steady Blue!' said Lybesstre catching Blue as she teetered near the edge.

'I... I'm okay,' she said gripping onto one of the wall's pyramid-shaped embrasures.

'Do you understand now?' the priestess asked pointing to a black chunk of rock rising at least thirty metres straight up from the heart of the ruins. Though the chunk was not as impressive as the towering rock of the Albokalaris, the moment Blue saw it, the same awful sensation she had felt when first she set eyes upon the Sugatz Rock came flooding back to her. It was that same awful sensation of a nail being driven into flesh.

'From the looks of you, Blue, I'd say you had seen its like before?'

'I have,' Blue replied wishing she hadn't. 'It was on the borders of Lekuona. It was there that I encountered the Black Worm, Sugaar.'

Lybesstre nodded and lowered her gaze.

'Both are shards of the black sun. It is the reason the wild man is gathering so many here in the desert.'

'His army?' said Blue.

'This is not an army.'

'If this is not an army then what is it?'

'It is a sacrifice.'

Blue gasped in horror.

'It is no coincidence so many are being gathered near the place where Minasul built his stables,' continued the priestess. 'This wild man intends to replicate the mad king's deeds. Those people have been lured to this place believing a saviour will come to rescue them from the "devil waters", but the saviour they await is the devil himself.'

'Then what do we do?' asked Blue.

'We must rescue the children. We must rescue them all. Without their innocent blood, the sacrifice cannot take place.'

'And just how do we do that? There must be hundreds of children there.'

'Two hundred and seventy-three at the last count,' said Lybesstre. 'And there will be even more in a day's time when the remaining herders return.'

'Well at least we've one less to rescue,' said Blue gesturing towards the child still snuggled into Basax's belly below.'

'Yes. You are right. Two hundred and seventy-two thanks to Basax… and he must help us rescue many more before this night is over.'

'Surely you can't be expecting Basax to rescue them all? The herders will tear him to pieces!'

'I don't expect him to rescue them all which is why I have arranged for some help. But even that won't be enough to deter the herders. That's where you come in, Blue.'

'Me! What do you think I can do?'

'Tell me Blue,' said the priestess, 'during your time with the Jentilak, did you manage to learn any of their ways?'

'A few. Their Albokalari, Nekane, was given the task of my education by her uncle, Otzak.'

'Was she now? Then perhaps this Nekane taught you a way to attract the wild creatures of this land?'

'She did. In fact, I became rather good at it. I still don't see how that can help us here though. There is barely a living creature within ten miles of this place. We even watched the insects trying to escape.'

'Then I suggest we turn our focus away from the living.'

'I'm not sure I follow you. Do you want me to attract a living creature or not?'

'Not exactly.'

'Then what?'

'More of an… undead one.'

'You want me to attract one of the mares!'

'Not one. I want you to attract the entire herd.'

CHAPTER 36

So Blue had been right. Rasalas was his father. But *why?* Why all the lies? Why had he been so ashamed? He could at least have spared Kai the indignity of having the herders tie him up like some baby in swaddling then leaving him there to die. Kai couldn't fail to see the bitter irony. And yet, for one brief, almost tender moment, Rasalas had walked over to where he lay and placed a hand in his just like he had all those years ago. Kai even thought he might draw his sword and cut the cord that bound him. But he didn't. Instead, bloodied horn in hand, he simply turned his back, donned his armour... and left. Left as he'd lived. The shadow man.

In the corner, a high-ranking Ensi priest sat watching the last two herders feeding with a cold look of contempt in his eyes.

'The Ensi deem eating like a gluttonous pig the epitome of sin,' he said, popping a sweetmeat into his mouth. With just one claw, one of the herders fetched another hunk of meat out of the barrel.

'Shame the Ensi taste as bad as thems company,' it replied tearing a chunk off with its teeth, 'or Garoa might fancy meat a bit fresher than this old gristle.' The priest seemed to know when to back off and remained watching the herders with disgust.

'Will you hurry up!' he said impatiently. 'If we don't finish this soon, *we'll* be the sacrifices!'

Garoa growled. 'Just remember, after he drownded Garoa gets his head.'

'And Ler his feet,' added the second herder.

'And *Sugaar* his soul,' reminded the priest, 'or perhaps you have decided you serve a different master now?'

Just then, a second priest entered the room, though this one wore robes of a very different style and kept his hood raised so Kai could not quite see his face. Even though the newcomer entered without saying a word, all could feel his arrival as if ice water had been poured down their spines. Kai didn't need to see the priest's face. The cold gleam of white flames flickering around the neckline was more than enough to know his death sentence was written. Seeing the Speris enter, the herders suddenly recalled their task and hauled Kai out of the building like farmers dragging swine to slaughter. Outside the evening air hung so thick with mists that Kai could see little more than the sweat gleaming off the herders' ugly, bald heads.

'Quickly!' hissed the Ensi priest, as the farther away from the encampment they travelled, the more the herders' pace slowed until, reaching the shoreline of the lake, the herders pace slowed to a complete stop.

'What's the matter?' snapped the priest impatiently.

'Somefing out here,' said Ler, casting frightened glances to either side.

'Somefing nasty,' said Garoa, mirroring Ler's unease as if convinced something might leap out at them any second.

'The only thing that's *nasty* out here is you two. Now get a move on and drown him!'

Sniffing the air, the herders would have doubled back to the encampment had the Speris not teased open his robes to reveal the black sun burning upon his chest. Deciding the immediate menace of the Speris was more frightening than any imagined terrors the approaching night might hold, the herders resumed their murderous task, tiptoeing nervously out into the lake's shallow waters until they hit a bank of mist so thick even their razor-sharp senses could not penetrate through it.

'Now what!' shouted the priest as Ler lifted his big nostrils and began sniffing the air.

'Can't see,' said Ler. 'Mist's too fik.'

'Bit like you then, Ler,' said Garoa.

'Say that to me face,' said Ler extending his claws as a warning.

'All right then,' said Garoa as the pair squared up to each other. 'Bit like you then Ler,' he repeated but instead of directing the comment to Ler's face, Garoa bent down and directed the words to the herder's backside.

'That's enough!' intervened the Ensi priest before another fight broke out. 'Night is closing in. We still have much to do. Now hurry up!'

Despite their desire to quarrel, a hiss from the Speris was all it took for the pair to cool their boiling tempers and return to their task, wading out into the lake until the waters rose above their waists. Once there, Kai suddenly felt himself lifted into the air and violently plunged into the shock of cold below.

'Him dead yet?' asked Ler lifting Kai's head out of the water after what seemed like more than enough time to drown him. Kai almost felt embarrassed as he inadvertently allowed a cough to escape from his throat.

'Nope,' said Garoa. 'Dunk him under again.'

Once more Kai felt himself shoved bodily under the surface and held there, this time for a considerably longer period.

'There, him dead now,' declared Garoa as Ler pulled Kai out for a second time.

'You sure?' said Ler. 'Can hear hims still breavin.'

'It's you Ler,' said Garoa reproachfully. 'You doins it all wrong.'

'How is me doins it wrong?' said Ler. 'Unless him can breave out his bleedin backside!'

'What's taking so long?' called out the Ensi priest.

'Ler finks him can breave out his backside,' replied Garoa.

'Me did not say that!' said Ler.

'Did too!' said Garoa.

As the herders began to squabble, Kai noticed a distinct and disturbing sound drifting through the mists towards them. It was a sound he knew only too well... a sound like rusted blades scraping across dry stone. At first the herders seemed too caught up in their bickering to notice, but when sinister silhouettes began forming along the fringes of the shore, the pair fell silent and began to take note of what was happening.

'Behor mamuak!' exclaimed Garoa as dozens of pale eyes, like a hellish constellation, stared in morbid fascination at them. Suddenly, a scream rang out followed by a flare of golden light that lit up the shoreline like a small sun.

'Korri egizue!' yelled Garoa as the pair decided they had seen more than enough and fled in one direction leaving Kai to try to work out how to crawl beneath four feet of water with his hands and legs tied. Of course he failed miserably and ended up shuffling along the lake bed like a sea slug until he was so disorientated he didn't know whether he was heading back to shore or out into deep water. Completely lost and by now probably at the bottom of the deepest part of the lake, Kai suddenly felt his wrists and ankles seized from both sides before being propelled backwards through the water. Wriggling and kicking, Kai did his best to break free of whatever held him but its grip remained firm.

'Please stop kicking us,' a voice said as two scaly, silver heads appeared above the water's surface. 'We're trying to swim you back to shore.' Kai instantly recognised the voice of U-an.

'U-an, don't swim me back to shore!' Kai spluttered. 'There's terrible danger there!'

'Don't be afraid,' interrupted U-an reassuringly. 'We know what awaits us. You need not be afraid.'

Curious to know why the Apkallu were saying he need not be afraid, Kai reluctantly allowed himself to be swum back to the shoreline. Once the waters were shallow enough to stand, he let himself be cut free of his sodden bonds and cautiously approached an eerie light burning a short distance inland. When he arrived, to his utter disbelief, he discovered none other than Blue who knelt crouching over what appeared to be the Speris lying in a state of abject misery. Encircling her, a nightmarish ring of mares stood, yet these mares, rather than appear as a threat to the girl and a small band of Jentilak warriors beside her, all faced outwards as though forming a ring of protection about them all.

'About time you found him!' exclaimed Blue, overjoyed to see Kai returned safely to her. 'Let him through!' she commanded. Obediently the ring of mares parted to allow a speechless Kai to enter. Once he was safely inside, the protective circle re-formed around them and Blue was able to redirect her attentions back to the Speris, unleashing a glorious burst of flame from her hands into the steadily brightening sun on the Speris' chest. The Speris shrieked and writhed as if his entire body were being dipped in acid. Beside her, the two herders, Garoa and Ler, lay curled in a ball, clutching their guts like babies with colic. Watching over them stood a very unsympathetic looking Basax who glared at the pair as if daring either one to raise so much as a finger in protest.

'Basax, let the Jentilak take those two now,' said Blue. 'They'll not be causing any more trouble.' Basax grunted and stepped aside so that the waiting Jentilak could carry the groaning herders out into the dim evening light. Meanwhile Blue returned her attention to the Speris to make sure he was still breathing, despite his efforts to the contrary.

'Help meeee!' he pleaded, looking at Kai as if the young Furud might offer some sort of reprieve.

'Oh, so you *do* speak,' said Blue, clearly growing tired of the Speris' histrionics. 'Well, there's no point begging Kai to save you. You're only suffering because you can now feel all the pain you've caused. I suggest you get used to it.'

'No more. Pleeassse!' Ignoring his plea, Blue unleashed a wondrous display of light and multihued flame which engulfed the Speris and drowned out his shrieks with a deafening noise. Finally, the flames died away to reveal that the Speris had fallen silent and, like the herders before him, had curled himself into a tight ball.

'Okay. That's him done as well,' she said. 'Basax you can take him too now. It's time we left before the Kalibi and herders recover from their panic and realise what we've stolen.'

'What exactly *have* we stolen?' asked Kai still struggling to understand what was going on.

'Their sacrifice of course.'

'I thought *I* was their sacrifice?'

'You and a few hundred more,' said Blue. 'I'll explain everything on the way back to the ruins.'

As they headed back across the desert, Kai listened with a growing feeling of unease to all Blue had to tell him until the ominous outline of the ruins loomed ahead. Kai had only seen the ruined stables from afar but now he was drawing closer to them, their scale and foreboding presence was like nothing he'd ever witnessed nor experienced. Of course still being surrounded by Blue's unearthly escort of ghastly mares didn't exactly help his nerves. It was with a sense of great relief then when Blue finally gave the command for the mares to depart, each one dissolving into the evening mists like nebulous phantoms. However, as the group neared the great gatehouse, Kai spied something lurking beneath its jagged towers that caused him to wish the mares had

311

remained. There, half-hidden in the shadows, at least a hundred and fifty Furud warriors stood in wait, the glint of their hard eyes visible beneath their lion helmets.

'An ambush!' shouted Kai.

Hearing Kai's voice, one of the warriors broke rank, and came running straight at him. The young Furud had no time to question why he was being singled out for attack but knew if he was quick, he might have a chance of dispossessing the warrior of his spear before it could be brought into play against him. Waiting until the warrior was almost upon him, Kai seized his attacker's arm, and with a roll of his hips, threw the man to the ground.

'What's up with thee?' the warrior grunted as Kai got ready to rip the spear off his back. 'I thought thee'd have been pleased to see me?'

'Ælfweard!' Kai helped the shaft rat to his feet and found himself caught in a hug that would have cut the breath from a bear.

'Steady on,' said Kai surprised by his friend's strength. He could see Ælf had grown by at least another inch and had managed to pack even more muscle onto his already brawny young torso. 'What are you doing dressed like that?'

'It's that priestess o' thine. She's had us training night and day. Not let up for a second. Nearly killed us she has.'

'Lybesstre! What does she know of training warriors?'

'Oh, she's not been doing the training herself. It's been him o'er there that's done most of it. We pulled him from the dead in the Horim's gorge. Once Lybesstre had patched him up and got him back on his feet again, she's had him at our throats ever since. Right tough feller he is.' Kai looked across and recognised the warrior Ælf was referring to immediately. His name was Mitra, one of the veteran warriors of the Anausha. A member of the fighting elite of the Furud army.

'You're not kidding,' said Kai. 'That's the man Rasalas had train me and Magor. I'm not sure he likes me very much. I wasn't exactly his most enthusiastic student.'

'I'm not sure he likes anybody. But, he's pretty handy like. Only got the better of him a couple of times.'

'You got the better of Mitra!' Kai didn't believe a word of it. 'It takes years to master a Furud sword. How could you have beaten him?'

'Oh, I didn't use a sword. I beat him with this.' Ælf removed the spear from across his back and handed it to Kai.

'What's this?' said Kai realising Ælf had handed him a spear without a point. Where's the spearhead?'

'Lybesstre had us remove them—said she didn't want any serious injury. Should've seen the look on Mitra's face. Soon won him over though. That lass could charm a crab out o' its shell if she had a mind to. Don't worry though, it's all part of the plan.'

'Don't worry! Please tell me you're joking. When the Kalibi realise what we've done they will descend upon these ruins like a storm. We can't honestly be planning on defending ourselves with miners carrying sticks!'

'Ahem,' interrupted Ælf. 'Elite Warriors of Stod thee means.'

'Yes, that is exactly what I intend for us to do,' said Lybesstre, appearing from the ruins accompanied by a large contingent of tough-looking men and sleeker looking Apkallu from Ma Addir. Both were similarly armed with wooden staffs like the miners.

'What kind of plan is this?' Kai asked in disbelief. 'We'll all be slaughtered.'

'A slaughter is precisely what it will avoid. It's the one thing our enemy wants and it's the one thing we must not give them.'

'But a slaughter is what you *are* giving them! *Our* slaughter!'

'Not if our enemy's weapons and armour are useless.'

'And just how do you intend on achieving that?'

'Oh, just a little idea I got after talking to a man making his way back from Wardum. A very interesting tale he told me about a witch prisoner who couldn't be killed.'

'Wait a minute! I know what you're thinking. You heard how I used the Sir-ku to soften the metal of Haelm's scythe. Well, I hate to disappoint you priestess but these ruins are over a quarter of a mile wide and probably just as deep. Our enemy's attack could come from opposite sides at once. Maybe you hadn't noticed but I don't have lungs the size of a whale.'

'No, you don't—but they do.' Kai followed Lybesstre's finger to the top of the gatehouse tower. Poking its long neck out of one of the narrow windows was the unmistakeable outline of a Migir slave.

'The Migir! When did they get here?'

'We rescued them with the children. There are more of them occupying the tower at the northern end of the ruins.'

'Fine, but just who do you think is going to teach them? The Sir-ku are a nightmare to learn. That song alone took weeks of practice!'

'Yes, the Sir-ku require a very special set of skills to learn them, but if there is one thing the Migir were born to do — though I'll admit they're not much use for much else — is to sing.'

'Oh, this is absurd!' said Kai, growing annoyed. 'Why am I wasting my time listening to this?'

'Ælfweard, I see Kai needs some convincing. Would you go up the tower and sing one of your ballads to the Migir you find there, please?'

'Aye, if thee likes. Any particular one caught tha fancy?'

'No. Any will do.'

'It'll be my pleasure,' said Ælf, running off towards the gate tower.

Within five minutes of the shaft rat being gone, the clear, rich sound of Migir slaves singing one of Ælf's favourite shanties began to spread across the desert:

"Oh, the finest gal I ever met was lusty Serafina,
But the very next day as we sailed away, I wished I'd never seen her
For she left me skint, me clothes was gone, and so was Serafina,
She'd stole me crown, she'd sunk me down, that dirty she-hyena!"

'Maybe I should have insisted on something a little more tasteful,' mused the priestess.

Kai had to admit he was impressed. Not only had the Migir slaves been able to learn Ælf's rude sea shanty word-perfectly after just one hearing, but had even managed to capture Ælf's broad northern accent as if the slaves had spent their whole lives growing up in the village of Stod.

'I just hope this works,' Kai said still doubting it would be enough to hold back the fury soon to be unleashed against them.

'It has to work,' said Lybesstre, 'because if it doesn't every creature and every Kugarran from here to the Sea of Ab will be slain.'

'So what do we do?'

'We place the miners and Jentilak along the battlements. If we can convince the Kalibi a Furud garrison is stationed here it will at least hold off their attack long enough for the Apkallu to shore up our defences. It might just buy us the time we need.'

'Time to do what?'

'To defeat the Black Worm.'

Just then a cry rang out from high up on the battlements.

'What is it?' asked Kai seeing someone waving to them from the top of the ornate parapets.

'It's one of our lookouts. He's signalling that Nekane has returned. She's been keeping an eye on an approaching army since you left.'

'Then we must hurry to speak to her,' said Lybesstre, leading a group of anxious faces to the nearest gate.

'What news have you of our enemy?' she demanded the moment Nekane and Basax had disentangled themselves from each other's embrace.

'Our enemy has reached Ninurta's Well,' she replied. 'They must have been marching night and day to get there so fast.'

'Ninurta's well!' exclaimed U-an. 'So soon! How many were they?'

'Ten thousand at least. Most of the army is made up of Kalibi and savage men recruited from the nomadic tribes of the desert, but there were others with them, robed Speris monks and strange warriors I have never seen before. They numbered nearly two thousand men.'

'You saw Speris! And the warriors with them, can you describe how they were dressed?'

'The warriors wore armour of dark steel, the plates overlapping like scales, and their helmets were... like his!' All turned to see the female Jentilak was pointing directly at Ælf's lion helmet.

'Magor! Rasalas must have got word to him somehow,' said Lybesstre with a worried look. 'Then we must hurry.'

'But surely our defences aren't even close to being ready!' said Kai.

'They are as ready as they need to be,' said Lybesstre. 'As for you, Kai, the best you can do now is focus on the Migir. Teach them a song that will take the teeth out of our enemy's bite. That is our best chance. Remember, our only hope is to prevent the bloodbath they so desire. Only this can stop Sugaar breaking free of its chains.'

'I pray you're right, priestess,' said Kai looking up at the gate towers dubiously.

'As do we all,' said Lybesstre.

CHAPTER 37

'Dug kisi!' Blue looked down to recognise the face of the child Basax had first rescued from the edges of the encampment. *'Dug kisi!'* the child said again, this time jumping up and down with her knees pinned together.

'Do you need to go to the... um cinder box?' Blue made a discreet gesture hoping the child would understand. The child nodded and continued hopping from one leg to the other. 'I'm kind of busy. Can't someone else take you?' The child looked at her imploringly. 'Oh, go on then, I'll come with you. I'm just taking this little one to do a... well you know what,' she called out, but Lybesstre and the assembled group were huddled around the light of a fire far too engrossed in drawing out their battle plans to pay her and the child any attention.

With Blue successfully in tow, the little girl skipped confidently through the moonlight and headed towards the immense inner wall. 'My, you are a shy one,' said Blue as the child failed to stop when they arrived but continued searching along the wall for a spot away from prying eyes. 'Okay that's far enough,' she said as they reached a large bennu tree with roots that grew straight out of the wall's foundations. 'I'll wait here until you have finished.' As the child disappeared between the roots, Blue tried not to think about what might also be watching from the darkness.

'Have we finished yet?' she asked after waiting for what seemed an interminably long time. The girl gave no reply nor made a sound. 'I think you've had long enough,' she said stealing a peek to check her progress but instead of finding a child crouching between the roots, all she could see was a tunnel running straight under the wall.

'Why you little menace! Where have you gone?' Blue's question was answered by a giggle and the sound of scuffling. 'Right, I'll just have to come and get you!' Crawling on all fours, Blue squeezed her way inside but failed to gain any ground on the sounds of giggling which seemed to match her for pace no matter how fast she tried to crawl. The child's mischievous behaviour was upsetting enough but when Blue became aware of the eerie whisper of not one, but many children's voices ahead of her, she started to grow afraid for their safety.

'Come back please!' she pleaded trying to use the whispering pearl to cast light ahead of her but the tunnel just kept spiralling downwards. *What is this place?* she wondered with a growing presentiment as the passage not only widened to the point where she could stand up but started to open out into a cavernous vastness that even the light of the whispering pearl could not penetrate to its end. Suddenly a flash of red drew her eye to the flicker of a serpent's tail disappearing as if into the floor ahead.

'No!' she said as her fear turned to anger. 'You're not taking her!' Blue began running to where she thought she had seen the serpent vanish but her chase ended as abruptly as it had started when a yawning chasm opened out beneath her.

Get ready, said a voice in her mind.

'They've taken that little girl!' Blue cried upon hearing Urakgha's voice. 'What should I do? I can't get down there!'

'You can.'

'But how?'

'You fly.'

Blue might have been tempted to suspect Urakgha of talking deluded nonsense if it weren't for the arcs of white fire that were beginning to fan out behind her from her shoulder blades like huge wings. Blue could feel the point of light on her forehead blazing with such brilliance the very air around her began to smoulder and glow from the energies being unleashed. One arc of fire struck the earth beneath her, instantly turning rock to ash, causing the very ground beneath her to disintegrate and drop away. Yet into this abyss Blue did not fall, but arching her back and stretching wide wings of blinding light, she rose briefly into the air and then, into the void... she dived.

CHAPTER 38

Along the walls, the thin line of defenders stood silent as tombstones, their indomitable gazes locked onto the hordes gathering in the cool of the morning desert before them. At first the enemy's numbers looked underwhelming but over the course of the day, reinforcements kept arriving from the west, swelling their ranks until the ruins literally shook from the tread of their feet.

'There are so many!' said Kai. 'There must be thousands!'

'I know,' said Lybesstre as a huge drum beat in the distance. 'Get prepared. They are readying for the attack.'

As the priestess spoke, a blood-curdling roar filled the air and waves of attackers began pouring across the landscape, shrieking their fealty to their devil god, like demented banshees.

'May the gods have mercy,' Kai prayed as the first flurry of arrows whizzed past his ears like angry wasps. Nodding to Lybesstre, Kai waited for the briefest of lulls then gave the signal to the nearest gate tower for the Migir to begin. Across the ruins the sound of singing began to rise and spread, filling the air with the haunting beauty of the Sir-ku.

'Is it working?' asked Ælf wondering if it was safe yet to show his face above the parapets. While he spoke another volley of arrows was unleashed, clattering against the wooden shields of the defenders like drums. One arrow struck the miner next to him fully on the chest. The miner went down on one knee then quickly stood up again and laughed.

'Aye it works!' the miner cried exultantly picking the arrow up for all to see. The head of the arrow had not made so much as a scratch on his leather breastplate but had ended up so bent and out of shape its tip pointed back towards its feathery tail.

'Now let's pray it works on swords and axes,' said Kai.

***

The battle for the ruins raged on far longer than Kai or anyone had hoped. For four straight hours, the defenders held firm, fighting toe to toe with the enemy, using the immense strength of the Jentilak and the speed and guile of the Apkallu to offset, at least for a while, the huge advantage in numbers the enemy held over them. The bold men of Stod and Ma Addir, proud to stand in such company, did little to shame themselves, fighting back-to-back in defence of one another, yielding not so much as an inch of ground against all the malice and hatred the Kalibi could throw at them, yet still the enemy kept coming like waves crashing against the shore.

'Why haven't they given up yet?' said Ælf covered from head to foot in sweat and bruises. 'They must know by now their weapons are useless.'

'It is the fear of retribution that drives them on,' said Kai. 'Look towards the encampment. Can you not see the pyres already burning for their fallen? Those men were not slain by our hand but by herders who harry and kill all those whose courage fails them and turn their back on the fight.'

'Shame the Uati never taught thee a song that might soften their claws.'

'It is a shame, for the herders will continue to drive these Kugarran forces ever against us until our enemy has found a weakness in our defence.'

'Kai! Ælf!' shouted a desperate voice from the courtyard below.

'Why it's young Gyd,' said Ælf waving down at the young shaft rat. 'What's up with thee?'

'We've trouble!' the shaft rat shouted back.

'Oh no!' said Ælf with a look of great consternation, 'Tha's not used the last o' the paper in the latrines again?'

'Ælf this is not a time for jokes!' scowled Kai.

'What's the problem, Gyd?'

'It's the Migir! Listen!' Both Kai and Ælf strained to hear above the sounds of fighting along the ramparts and heard the Sir-ku being sung perfectly from the southern tower, but from the northern tower a strange, discordant noise seemed to jar rudely against the beautiful harmonies coming from the other.

'That doesn't sound right,' said Ælf, trying to work out what it was they were hearing until a momentary lull in the fighting allowed the words of a familiar song to reach their ears;

"Oh, the finest gal I ever met was lusty Serafina…".

'Too right it doesn't sound right!' said Kai with a murderous look at his friend. 'It's your idiotic sea shanty!'

'Oops!' said the shaft rat.

'We've tried getting them to sing the other song,' continued Gyd, 'but they just pull a face and carry on. We're struggling to hold the wall. At this rate, the northern wall will be overrun within the hour.'

'Look there,' said Ælf with a rare expression of genuine concern as he pointed to a line of figures in dark robes peeling off from the back of the enemy's ranks. 'Do they look familiar to thee?'

'The Speris! Quick, we have to get to the southern wall. There's only one reason they would choose this moment to get involved. They must know our defences have failed!'

When Kai and Ælfweard arrived at the northern wall, Lybesstre was already there with an ashen expression. Beside her stood Otzak and U-an looking equally worried. Only metres from them Basax was leaping from rampart to rampart, swiping attackers off the wall ten at a time with his huge arms.

'So what now?' asked Kai seeing the enemy ranks amassing below. 'Should I try teaching the Migir the song again?'

'It's too late for that,' said Lybesstre. 'They are readying themselves for an assault. We have to find a way to stop them. We have to buy more time.'

'More time for what?'

'We *must* buy more time for Blue.'

'For Blue. Why? Talking of which where is that girl? I haven't seen her for hours!'

'Blue is exactly where she is meant to be.'

'And where is that?'

'She is in the lair of the Black Worm.'

CHAPTER 39

So fired up and focussed had Blue been on her impending confrontation with Sugaar that when she arrived in its lair like an avenging angel, only to find the beast worryingly and frustratingly absent, she almost completely failed to notice the pale boy crouched trembling amongst the great nest of carcasses upon which the mountainous terror was supposed to be chained.

'I'm sorry,' said Blue, realising her fiery arrival must have appeared terrifying to the boy. 'There's nothing to be afraid of. I'm not here to hurt you. I hunt much larger prey than you, but I see it's already too late.' The boy refrained from responding and continued to gnaw at the ends of his thin fingers and cracked nails, which were as black and dirty as his face. What struck Blue was how similar the boy looked to the hungry foundling orphans she and Old Eofor had used to see begging at the gates of the old workhouses in Port Stroenshal. It wasn't just the boy's short-cropped hair that was the same, but even the coarse grey tweed of his torn waistcoat and knee-length breeches were identical to the workhouse uniform worn by those ill-fated wretches, whose sad faces sometimes even moved old Eofor to pity them enough to share what little lunch he and Blue had brought with them for their journey.

'Don't do that,' said Blue noticing the boy had bitten one of his fingers so hard he had drawn blood. 'You're hurting yourself.' Blue reached across and carefully moved the hand away from his mouth and started to gently wipe both blood and dirt from his fingers. She was worried her cleaning his fingers might be hurting the boy, so sore did they look, but the boy did nothing but stare at the leather pouch dangling from her neck.

'What's in there?' the boy asked, his large eyes looking at the pouch inquisitively.

'In this?' said Blue. 'Not much really. Just a gift from someone dear to me. It was once a piece from a game, I think. Would you like to see it?' The boy's eyes shone.

'Yes! I would like that very much!' Blue undid the cord and lifted the tiny golden lion Kai had given her so the boy could see.

'A lion!' the boy said and jumping excitedly down the heap, he began rummaging under a corpse. After a frantic bout of searching, the boy pulled out a larger pouch and ran back to Blue's side.

'Here!' he said tipping out the contents of his own pouch at Blue's feet to reveal a collection of golden animal figurines so similar to the one Blue held that they could only have come from the same set.

'Here's a bull, and an eagle, and there's your lion of course... and ooh and here's a little winged child! Shall we play? Pleeeease!'

The boy's suggestion was so unexpected and felt so out of place in that dismal realm that Blue did not know how to answer.

'Well... I... really have something very important I must do first.' The boy looked away as if to hide his disappointment and returned to gnawing at his fingers. 'Maybe we could play later,' she added trying to lift the boy's mood to where it had been just a moment before. 'How about first you tell me your name?'

'You want to know my name?' The boy gave Blue a strange look as if at a loss how to answer such a simple question.

'Yes. You do remember, don't you? What did they call you?'

'My name... is Mabon. My name is Bray, my name is Skoks, my name is Barkana, my name is Cloti, my name is Perk, my name is Nummun...'

'Stop! Stop!' pleaded Blue, for as the names began to spill from the boy's mouth, she heard not just the names but felt with each one an entire lifetime of a lost child pass by her; a life filled with poverty, with woe, with neglect, with abuse. 'Who... *what* are you?' she demanded still reeling from the trauma of what she had just experienced. The boy didn't answer but looked up at the grey firmament hanging like a dead man's curse above their heads.

'We do not have long,' he said with a voice heavy with sadness. 'I feel it approaching.'

'Feel what approaching?' said Blue with trepidation.

'The rain.'

Before Blue could respond, a sudden flicker of red sliding amongst the carcasses caught her eye.

'Get behind me!' she warned, realising they were no longer alone. 'The Black Worm sends its devils to greet us!' Slithering out from under the mountain of carcasses, not one, but hundreds and then thousands of serpents began to emerge.

'I'll burn every last one of you if I have to!' she shouted as lightning and gold flames crackled about her fingers.

'Don't hurt them!' pleaded the boy.

'Don't hurt them! Are you serious? Those things are evil! They come straight from Sugaar's black heart. If that big worm is too frightened to show itself then at least I can leave it a message it will never forget!'

'Are they not hurt enough already?' The boy reached a hand and tugged on Blue's arm. 'If you hurt them, I won't be able to help you any longer.'

'Help me? When have you helped me?'

'Many times have I helped you.'

'Like when?'

'On the ship. It was I who awoke you.' Blue was so taken aback by his comment that it took her a moment to collect her wits enough to reply.

'That was *you*?' she said incredulously. The boy nodded.

'I am always the one to awaken you.' Blue struggled to take in what she was hearing, but now the boy mentioned it, his face and eyes were certainly very like the ones she remembered fading to nothing as she had struggled to awaken from her drugged sleep on the *Nefari*.

'Well, if you like helping me so much, right now would be a good moment to do so.'

'I could call them to me if you like?' he suggested. 'I know their names. It calms them when I call to them with their names. '

'Call them then,' Blue said, her eyes turning to steel, 'but if they so much as hiss at me, I'll turn them to toast.' The boy nodded and looked down at the fiery red mass slithering up the mountain towards them. Stepping towards the edge of the nest he raised his arms.

'Come little birds,' he called. 'Come my pearls. Come Bray. Come Skoks. Come Barkana. Come Cloti…'

CHAPTER 40

'I know how to stop this,' said Kai as a screaming mass of men attempted and failed for a second time to breach the northern gate. Behind them the Mitutu wielded their great scythes in feverous anticipation while to the rear black-eyed Speris muttered profane incantations.

'How?' asked Lybesstre as a twinkle of hope returned to her eyes.

'Aatxe's final song. I dreaded this moment but I now know it is the only way.'

'What song is this? What does it do?'

'Just get Basax and whatever Jentilak we can spare and have them meet me at the gate. I'll need Mitra as well. I'm sure the Furud commanders would be interested in learning what he has to say about the Horim's gorge.'

As Basax, Mitra and a handful of Jentilak listened to Kai's plan, neither one could believe what he was telling them, but the fluttering of Furud banners arriving at the back of the gathering army was enough to convince all three that the tide of the battle was about to turn dangerously in their enemy's favour. Already a tenebrous gloom had begun to enshroud the ruins, no doubt an effect of the Speris' sorcerous mutterings, and they knew the final attack was imminent. Far to the back of the attackers, the sounds of Rasalas and Magor's voices roaring orders could be heard rising above the stomp of feet and the clash of armour.

'You had all better step back,' said Kai warning the others. Basax inclined his head and moved back slowly whilst Mitra and the Jentilak nodded but gave the young Furud a look as if to suggest they were just as worried about Kai himself as the impenetrable wall of Furud steel and Mitutu muscle they were about to throw themselves against. 'What about them, are they ready?' Kai asked, looking straight at Basax. As if knowing exactly who it was Kai was referring to, at least twenty small heads popped out from the herder's great mane of hair and looked at Kai with expressions that seemed as determined as they were small.

'They ready,' said Basax nonchalantly stretching the muscles of his big arms and shoulders.

Once Kai felt the others had given him enough room, the young Furud began to sing softly to himself. At first, nothing seemed to be happening other than an occasional whisp of hot vapour that would escape from his mouth like a ghost. Gradually though, all could hear and feel the song growing in strength and power, resonating from Kai's expanding chest like a great horn announcing a hunt. Suddenly Kai threw his head back in agony as thick horns began sprouting from his skull. Dropping to all fours, Kai could only paw at the ground as the fingers of his hands and feet clenched together, hardening into four great hooves that gouged deep channels into the earth. His body shook, growing in size and strength as the skin covering the rippling muscles of his heaving chest stretched and darkened until his massive torso gleamed sleek and black. Finally, with his breath steaming from flaming nostrils, the terrifying vision of Aatxe stood before them. Lifting its flared snout to the skies, the bull let out an almighty bellow then, dropping his magnificent horns almost to the floor, charged straight at the gate, shattering it into a million pieces as he thundered straight through and into the midst of the enemy amassed on the other side. Using his great head and horns, Kai began ploughing a path straight through the unprepared first ranks of warriors, casting men aside like leaves swept from a path. Keeping as close as they could, Basax and the others did their best to protect the bull from the rear, but so few remained standing in Kai's wake that their hardest task lay in simply trying to keep up. Seeing the terrifying beast laying waste to all who dared stand in its way, the Mitutu, muttering dark curses, leapt into the bull's path, their scythes flashing bright and deadly in the evening light. Yet for all their skill and steel, it was as though no weapon could touch nor harm so much as a hair of the bull's gleaming black hide, for whenever their weapons came anywhere close a tiny hand or flash of light would knock the blade away before the huge horns came crashing back down, sending attackers flying on all sides.

'To me!' roared Rasalas as an impenetrable wall of Furud formed a human shield between their commander and the terrifying vision coming towards them, but even they were not enough to slow Kai's thunderous charge, for with a final deafening bellow, the bull smashed through the last barriers of men and metal, shattering swords, spears and shields as though made of glass. With the wall breached, Rasalas could only stare in abject horror as Kai came crashing through, thundering to a stop with the tip of his great horn a whisker from the warlord's throat.

'Back off,' warned Mitra as the Furud closed in around them.

'Do as he says!' ordered Rasalas, a look of terror in his eyes as the bull towered over him, its fiery breath scorching the whiskers of his face. After the warriors had stepped back, the bull's form began to shift and blur until all could see it was none other than Kai standing breathless before them. Quickly, before Rasalas or any of the Furud could react, Basax took Kai's place and seized the warlord by his throat, looking around fiercely as if daring any to move so much as an inch in their direction.

'Sorcery!' choked Rasalas through gritted teeth. 'See, the boy is steeped to his neck in it!'

'So this is how you betray us,' said Magor pushing through the encircling ranks of warriors, a gleaming sword in hand.

'There is no betrayal, Magor,' replied Kai. 'Look at your commander. Look at his eyes. He no longer hears anything but the call of darkness.'

'Lies!' screamed Rasalas in spite of the threat of Basax's strong fingers around his throat. 'Lies! Seize this half-bred slave bastard!' In response, Magor raised his sword, moving the point of the blade close to Kai's chest, but Kai sensed already there was a reluctance to his action.

'It's all right Mitra,' said Kai as the veteran looked ready to intervene, 'there is to be no more killing here today.'

'You saw what he is!' screamed Rasalas. 'The boy has traded his soul with a devil!'

'The only one who has traded their soul with a devil is *you* father; a devil that consumes you. Your words have become poison.' Kai then turned to Magor. 'This unholy alliance with the Kalibi is all a lie. You already know this, Magor. The devil that possesses our father's soul would gladly watch us all die and still think it too few. Tell him, Mitra. Tell him what happened in the Horim's gorge. Tell him how their commander led us all into that gorge knowing he was leading us to our deaths.'

The veteran nodded. 'That is what happened,' he said grimly. 'That is what he did. He sacrificed our men to feed a monster.'

'S-silence him!' spat Rasalas. 'Silence the blasphemous little snake!'

'Enough,' Magor said letting his sword hand fall.

'What are you doing?' screamed Rasalas as though possessed. 'Finish him! Finish that witch's bastard!'

'I said *enough*!' Magor turned on his father, his eyes smouldering with anger. 'Enough of this madness. Enough of these lies! I know who Kai really is! I've always known!'

'Silence!' screamed Rasalas but Kai could see tears were rolling down the warlord's cheeks. Magor ignored him and turned to Kai.

'Your mother was no slave, Kai. It was *my* mother who was born a slave.'

'Then... who was my mother?' asked Kai, shocked that Magor knew so much.

'She was a sacred daughter of Ratha. She was one of the Bija Kai. One the Thirteen. He had to lay waste to half a nation just so he could steal you from her.'

Kai and all who stood listening gasped.

Rasalas dropped his head and let out a laugh laced with bitterness. 'So you think you know the truth?' he said. 'You think you know everything? You know nothing. I didn't murder the Rathans. I spared them!' Rasalas gripped his hands before his chest as though the recollection suddenly caused him physical pain. 'I spared them from what he was to become if he had remained there! She was born of the sun... and yet, do you know under which sun she was born? I'll wager you don't!' This time Rasalas began to roar with laughter as if party to a hilarious private joke but his laughter was short-lived for it soon dissolved into a fit of uncontrolled weeping.

'What is he talking about?' said Kai, appalled at his father's words and behaviour.

'Don't listen to him,' said Magor coldly. 'Anyone can see he is no longer in possession of his own mind. Lock him in chains! Our commander is in no state to lead this army any longer.'

For a moment the Furud hesitated but seeing the whites of Rasalas' eyes, realised their commander had completely lost his wits and began to do as Magor asked.

'We'll bring him back with us,' Magor said once Rasalas was stripped of his armour and properly bound and chained. 'He should think himself lucky I don't throw him in the same hold he thought fit to put you in. When we return, he will have to answer for everything he has done.'

'Magor, would it not be wiser to leave him here? It is not just a madness that has hold of his senses, but a devil more dangerous than you can imagine. There is a sanctuary near here where he could be taken. Those that protect the sanctuary have knowledge of such matters. They might be able to free him of that which has taken possession of his soul.'

'This is a Furud matter, Kai, and it will be a Furud justice our father faces. We will at least grant him that honour.'

Kai could only watch as the crazed old warrior was dragged away, his smouldering gaze following the departing army like a ravenous lion whose kill has been snatched from its jaws.

Magor waited until he was the last to leave then turned to speak to Kai alone. 'Forgive me… brother,' he said with a look filled with remorse.

Kai nodded but could find no words with which to answer.

'I'll leave you a ship,' Magor added, then, hardening his expression, departed without saying another word.

CHAPTER 41

That evening, the celebrations across the city were tinged with a sadness that all could feel like the moon's shadow passing across the face of the sun. At first, all had rejoiced to hear the form of a huge bird with wings that shone like the dawn star had been seen gliding across the still waters of the lake, but the rejoicing did not last, for although there were those that knew the bird's sighting meant Blue had survived her encounter with Sugaar, instead of joining their celebration she chose to withdraw and be by herself, speaking to no one about her experiences.

'What's the matter with her?' asked Kai who felt the girl's sadness more than anyone. 'Did she fail us? Is that why she avoids us? Is everything lost?'

Lybesstre looked down across the descending terraces of starlit pools before answering.

'I think if she had failed, the Black Worm would have made its presence felt long before now, yet the evening remains calm and the song of the nightcallers can still be heard by the shores of the lake. If something were amiss, they would have long fallen silent. Why don't you go down and sit with her? If you wait quietly by her side, she might be willing to share that which troubles her when she feels ready.'

'I will!' said Kai, relieved that there was maybe something he could do to help. 'I'll go down to her right now.'

Threading his way between the pools, Kai took little time in reaching Blue sitting by the lake's edge, her chin rested on her hands as she gazed at endless ribbons of silver washing against the moonlit shore. As quietly as he could, Kai sat next to her, but not so close as to intrude upon the girl's thoughts. He could feel a sadness weighing upon her. Sensing his presence Blue leant into the warmth of his body and rested her head on his shoulder.

'What happened, Blue?' Kai asked finally as a light rain began to fall. Blue let a sigh escape from her lips.

'Kai I've done something... unforgiveable,' she confessed.

'What could be so unforgiveable? We're all still alive aren't we? There's no sign of the Black Worm.'

'Yes, but for how long? I failed. I failed you all!'

'How did you fail? You're here, aren't you? You did defeat it... didn't you?'

'I defeated nothing! I had the chance to destroy it forever. I could have burnt Sugaar into ash... but I couldn't bring myself to do it.'

'What did you do then?' Blue remained quiet a moment.

'Kai, I used my power to burn through its chains. Kai, I set it free!'

For a while Kai was too stunned to speak.

'What were you thinking, Blue?' he said as calmly as he could, once he had got over the shock.

'I didn't understand what the Black Worm was. I shot down there like a fiery assassin ready to destroy whatever I found, but I didn't find a terrifying monster like the first time I was taken to its lair. I found the spirit of a boy. I found a child, Kai!'

'Are you saying Sugaar is the spirit of a child?'

'Yes... and no. Perhaps at the beginning he was just one child; a child who came here only to be judged and branded as sinful, as worthless; a child who came to experience love but found nothing but brutality and fear. And now he is not one child but thousands upon thousands of them. I watched the boy call to them. I watched them merge into one before my eyes. I saw them become the beast I went there to destroy! When the boy called their names, I could feel all that those children had endured whilst they had been alive. I could understand their pain and their anger, their desire to right the wrongs that had been done them. They came here so innocent, so pure, so full of love and hope for the future; a hope and a future that we keep destroying! It was we who turned them into devils! *We* created the monster we all fear so much! We have so failed them, Kai. How could I hurt them any more than they have been hurt already?'

Kai kept silent and watched the silver ripples lapping around the edges of his sandals.

'You couldn't, Blue,' he said finally. 'And maybe what you did was the right thing after all. Maybe that's the reason we are all still alive, because finally someone acted with compassion, and not with judgement and fear; someone finally took responsibility for the mess this world is in instead of always passing the burden and blame on to others, on to those too innocent or too poor and wretched to know any different. If there is anything I've learnt over these last few months it's that there is real, tangible power in love and only heartbreak and ruin in fear.'

'But it is not over yet, Kai. I wish I could say it was, but there is so much hurt yet to be healed, not just with Sugaar and the souls of those poor children, but across the entire face of this sorry Earth and I don't know if we have the strength to carry it out.'

'Then I guess we'll just have to find out if we do have the strength.'

'Will you come with me? Will you help me?'

'I'll help you. Wherever you go, I'll follow. But there is something I have to do first, Blue. Something I have to do alone.'

'What?'

'There are things my... brother told me. Things I never knew; things about my homeland, about my mother and about myself. I have to try to find her, Blue. I have to know the truth. Give me a couple of months and then I'll come and join you.'

Kai watched Blue cast her eyes down and felt another shadow of sadness pass over her.

'I promise Blue. As soon as I return, we will start a life... together.'

Out in the lake, the waters began to stir and an unearthly light began to form beneath the surface.

'What's that?' said Kai jumping up and pulling Blue away from the water's edge. 'Is it the Black Worm? Has it come for us after all?'

Blue peered across the waters then let out a cry of joy.

'I know what it is!' she cried elated. 'Look! See there! Remember how you told me the Mares of Minasul were born straight from the waters of the lake. It's a foal!' Sure enough, climbing out of the water, a newborn foal emerged and made its way on shaky legs to the sandy beach of the lake's shore.

'You know, we really should be getting back to the celebrations,' Kai said after they had sat a while watching the foal getting stronger with almost every step it took. 'Hamsum is desperate for us to meet with his temple dancer. He's convinced he's in love with her. He's even given up drinking kash.'

'Thank the gods,' said Blue. 'If he can do that then maybe there *is* hope for us all.'

'Maybe,' said Kai laughing. 'Maybe.'

Behind them, the noises of the sleepless city could be heard drifting far across the waters, filling the air with music and laughter and the sounds of celebration.

EPILOGUE

Blue wiped the condensation from the attic window and peered out across the cottage rooftops. Nothing much had changed, only the collapsed chimneys of the abandoned mine on the other side of the cove and the gentle greens of the spring gardens growing around them told her that life had improved for the residents of Stod. Behind her, a light tap at the door, let her know her breakfast had arrived.

'Thank you, Guigen,' she said as the Speris cleric brought in her morning tray and placed it on the soft bed. So far the bed was the only luxury Blue had afforded herself. Of course, after they discovered Kai's brother had not only left them a ship in the It-Eru Delta, but also a hold filled with gold, she and the miners of Stod could quite easily have bought themselves each a palace to live in, but all seemed quite content to leave things pretty much the way they were.

'What is it, Guigen?' she asked realising the Speris was still loitering at the door.

'Forgive me, Mistress Blue, but I regret to inform you they are fighting again.'

'Oh, for goodness' sake! All right, I'll be down in a minute.'

Blue looked out again as a raucous family of cliff crakes landed on the adjacent roof. The dirty brown and white streaks running down the old tiles reminded her that she had promised the neighbour she would make a flight above the cottages to see if she could scare them away. Well, it would have to wait. She had more immediate business to attend to.

Marching down the narrow staircase, Blue already could feel the bangs and wallops from below shaking the walls of the house.

'Right!' she said bursting into the kitchen. 'I've had it with you two! Who started it this time?'

The two herders picked themselves off the floor and pointed at each other. In their big paws, the offending apples, now mashed beyond recognition, dripped sweet juices onto the stone flags of the kitchen floor.

'Ler! Garoa! How many times have I told you to share!'

The herders looked down at the ground ashamed. 'Sorry Mistress Blue,' they mumbled.

'I'm telling you now, if you two haven't cleaned this mess up and learnt to get on by the time I get back I'll have the pair of you careening yawls for the rest of the week!'

Blue gave the herders a stern look to make sure they knew she meant it this time then, motioning angrily for Guigen to follow her, slammed the kitchen door on their way out.

When the pair reached the harbour, the tide had turned and the booms and crashes of the waves during the night had softened to a soothing wombing and whisper. Around the headland, they could hear the insistent yelps of newborn mirounga pups demanding milk from dozing mothers. Behind them, the night lanterns placed in the cottage windows to guide the fishing yawls back to shore had almost burnt dry, their tiny flames clinging to the last fumes of oil until all the ships had made it safely home. In the air, the strong odour of chub and fish oil told Blue a large catch must already have arrived. Leading the way, Blue crossed the quay and headed up the winding path to the top of the cliffs.

'Where are we going, mistress?' asked Guigen who was yet to receive an explanation for why Blue had wanted him to accompany her.

'There is something very important we must do today.'

'And what might that be?' the Speris asked intrigued.

'You will see,' said Blue enigmatically and continued up the path. As the pair reached the top the Speris noticed that the forlorn figure of the grey girl waited a little distance from the cliff path as if expecting them to arrive.

'You know, it was only when the Eledh at Ankura kissed my brow that I realised who the grey girl really was,' said Blue, stepping off the path to kneel down near to where the girl stood. 'I'd always assumed she was just another sad and sorry soul who had drowned along this stretch of coast.'

336

'Then who is she?' enquired the Speris looking softly from the grey phantom back to Blue.

'Look carefully. Can you see that faint sheen of light stretching out behind her back?'

'Now that you mention it, yes. It is like… wings.'

'They are wings! She was the guardian of a great tree that once overlooked the bay, a tree very much like the one at Ankura. She is one of the Eledh. It was she all along who guided me to the whispering pearl… only it is not a pearl.'

'What is it then?'

Blue removed a shimmering whispering pearl from her pocket and smiled.

'It is a seed.'

'A seed!'

'Yes. That is why she has lingered for so long here at the top of the cliffs. She is not waiting for the return of a ship or a love lost at sea like so many say, but for the return of her beloved tree.'

'Then we must replant it!'

'Indeed, we must!' said Blue laughing and, using her bare hands, she dug a small hole into which she gently placed the whispering pearl. 'There,' she said replacing the loose soil. 'I've been wanting to do this for so long.' As she spoke, the grey girl smiled then turned her gaze back towards the rising sun, her diaphanous form fading beneath its rays until there was nothing to tell of her ever being there but a peaceful stillness.

'You know I wish Kai had been here to see this. 'How long has it been, Guigen? How long since he left for Ratha?'

'It must be near nine months now.'

'That long!' Blue shook her head. She couldn't believe so much time had passed since she'd last seen Kai. 'But he promised me he'd be back by now!'

'He did promise, mistress, but Ratha is vast. His people are scattered far and wide. Finding word of his mother could take some time.'

'But *this* much time! What if he forgets me? What if I end up as nothing more than a faded memory for him? Do you think he's even considered maybe I might like to be a mother too someday?'

'I'm sure he has. I'm sure that is all he thinks about.'

'Well, I tell you, he's not getting off that easy.'

'What do you intend to do?'

'Something I should have done months ago. We're leaving. We're getting out of here before I go mad.'

'Where are we going, mistress?'

'We're going after him, Guigen. We're going to Ratha. We're going to find Kai and we're going to bring him back.'

'We might not have to,' replied the Speris, his sharp eyes fixed on a point just below the horizon.

'What can you see?'

'A sail, mistress.'

Blue stared hard out to sea until she was sure she could see the faintest of canvas peaks rising and falling with the ocean swell.

'What sort of sail is that? I still can't make it out?' A rare smile lit up the Speris' usually expressionless face.

'It is a Furud sail, mistress. A Furud sail.'

End of Book 1